THE GALLERY OF DEATH

a DCI Wiggins Adventure

THE GALLERY OF DEATH

a DCI Wiggins Adventure

~ Book Two ~

IAN C. GRANT

For Ellie

Love Always ~ Dad

For Mum

Thanks just aren't enough

ISBN: 9798577338084
Imprint: Independently published

iancgrantbooks@outlook.com
www.facebook.com/iancgrantbooks

Cover design by Ian Christie using royalty-free photograph released under public domain license at Pikist.com

Contents

Chapter 1 - The Caretaker

"There are always some lunatics about. It would be a dull world without them."

Sherlock Holmes - The Red-Headed League

Jonas Crake loved warming his feet by the open fire. "You'll bloody well singe those socks before the night is through and I ain't darning them again for you, Jonas Crake," his wife would announce each evening. Jonas shrugged and wriggled his toes even more. 'Lovely,' he would think.

That night the rain lashed, and the wind blew. Lighting cracked overhead, rattling the toffee brittle glass in the windows of the Crake cottage. The chilly air whistled through the gaps in the rotten window frames of the little presbytery. "When you gonna fix 'em winders, Jonas Crake?" demanded his wife irritably.

Jonas shrugged. "No rush, Maisie. They're as good as new 'em winders," he countered, rubbing his stockinged feet together enthusiastically. "Last for years yet they will."

"You're a lazy hound and no mistake, Jonas Crake. My mother always said you was a no-good layabout. I should have listened to her and married your brother, Arthur," admonished his wife as she went to draw the curtains for the evening. "Old Reverend Brook would be beside himself if he knew just how lazy you really is."

"I keeps the grounds spick and span, don't I? Babbling Brook never said nothing abouts keeping the buildings ship-shape n'all did he now?" argued Jonas as he settled down to his evening pipe. "Besides, I need to check the Church tomorrow. I ain't been up there for over a week now. Probably full of leaves, mice and damned filthy pigeons and such like." Jonas blew down the stem of his pipe and reached for his tobacco pouch.

"Here!" exclaimed Maisie as she peered out into the gloom through the unwashed grime of the cottage's little sash windows. "I thinks you'd best get up there right now, Jonas. Something is going on in the old Church, I can see lights flashing around inside."

"Probably just the lightning playing tricks with your eyes," replied Jonas, determined that he would not be shifted from his cosy fireside on such a brutal night. "I ain't goin' nowhere tonight. It's blowing up a storm out there, Maisie, and anyways, me shoes are off for the evening now, ain't they?" He tamped the rubbed tobacco into the bowl of his pipe, offered up a match, puffed on his pipe, and wriggled his toes some more. 'These new wool socks are wondrous soft,' he thought contentedly.

"What if it's the lightning, Jonas? What if there's a fire a brewing in the Church. The whole place is nought but kindling. Old how's yer Father will have us turfed out of here sooner than you can say, Jack Robinson. Then what would we do, Jonas Crake? Then where would we be, I asks you?" enquired Maisie sternly, her hands set firmly upon her ample hips.

Jonas was resigned to the fact that the scold's tongue would eventually prise him out of his comfortable chair and away from his cosy fireside, out into the uninviting menace of the night. He reluctantly slipped on his shoes with an acquiescent look and a grunt of dissatisfaction.

The rain and wind lashed at him as soon as he stepped over the threshold. The biting rain stung his face like the pricking of ice-cold needles, and he yanked up the collar of his jacket in a forlorn attempt to fend off the relentless storm. Jonas screwed up his eyes against the rain and looked towards the distant, dark shape of the church silhouetted in the moonlight. He could see a throb of light playing against the stained-glass windows as he trudged up the tree-lined lane, leaning into the wind whilst holding his flat cap atop his head. The branches of the trees whipped back and forth like numerous cat-o'-nine-tails and the wind howled to an almost deafening degree. *'I hopes none of these trees come down,'* he thought. *'I don't care to have to chop up any of these fellows. There'll be plenty of branches to pick up tomorrow as it is without me breakin' me back.'*

As he neared the front door of the church a crack of lighting thundered overhead, hitting the spire of the Church, and illuminating the night sky for an instant. The noise was explosive, and Jonas was convinced his heart had leapt out of his mouth and just as quickly leapt right back in again. A primal surge of dread coursed through his veins. "Sweet baby Jesus!" he cursed "I nearly lost me life there!" What he had lost was his cap, which went spinning off into the darkness, closely accompanied by his nerve. Jonas clutched at the cast iron ring of the door and fumbled in his pocket for his loop of keys. The rain drove into his eyes making it difficult for him to distinguish one key from the other. His fingers searched through numerous options and eventually he identified the correct key, the largest one, more by touch than by sight. He turned the rasping key in the lock and pulled the door ajar. Jonas could feel light and warmth ebb out towards his receptive body and, encouraged, he slipped through the narrow opening and shook the rain from his dripping head and coat. "What the Hell's going on in here?" he muttered to himself under his breath, stamping his feet on the tiled floor of the porch. "Probably some young rapscallions playing doctors and nurses I'll wager."

All the while, he was aware, subconsciously, of a low, moaning canticle resounding around the fourteenth-century building, like the chanting of ghostly monks. He shook his head clear and focused his attention on the altar. What he saw there literally took his breath away and almost chased his eyes from their sockets.

A writhing mass of bodies, some partially clothed, most naked, convulsed together in what appeared to be a groaning entanglement of human carnality. Enclosing this squirming mass sat a circle of figures, sitting cross-legged, each bedecked in a scarlet, hooded gown that concealed their features. Each of these individuals chanted a steady canticle of some ancient, long discarded language. "Moratum di Omni de fastigat Som. Moratum di Omni de fastigat Som." The mantra was repeated steadily, over and over like a low echoing drumbeat.

Above this thrashing mass of humanity, floated the seemingly unsupported figure of a man, his arms outstretched in a cruciform shape, his ankles crossed as if nailed together with some invisible brad. As Jonas looked on, his mouth agape in astonishment, Luca Radasiliev levitated higher still, his head thrown back as if in the throes of orgasm. "Rejoice, rejoice my children. Drown in the baseness of the Master's depravity. Glory in his satanic majesty. Give yourself up to the Lord of Darkness and all his unholiness," roared Radasiliev, turning his oily black eyes towards the nest of intertwined human vipers writhing below him.

Jonas Crake whimpered unwittingly. Radasiliev immediately turned his inky orbs towards the stricken caretaker. Jonas felt the Russian's stare penetrate his very soul and grip forcefully around his heart. An involuntarily hot dampness spread across Jonas' groin. He ducked as quickly as he could behind the rearmost pew of the church and crouched there panting, his heart pounding like a drum, hoping beyond hope that the terrifying floating man had not noticed his presence.

The chanting continued, growing gradually louder and faster with each repetition. Jonas Crake could feel the noise infiltrate his brain, resounding around the inside of his skull. He felt himself being irresistibly drawn to peer over the pew. He tried desperately to resist but was unable to defy the temptation. His head slowly rose over the timber backrest of the pew. Terror surged like a bolt of electricity through every fibre of his being as he found himself nose to nose with the levitating man. He could feel and smell his hot, fetid breath engulfing him. It seemed to Jonas Crake that Radasiliev's head was unfeasibly larger than his own, a black-eyed snorting bull of a head.

"BOO!"

As the caretaker fell sideward, and just before he lapsed into unconsciousness, Jonas Crake saw that despite this face being less than an inch from his own, the black-eyed man's body remained where it had been, forty feet away, hovering over the throng of naked, squirming acolytes.

"Just some children up to mischief, my dear," informed Jonas Crake to his wife as he stamped into the cottage shaking himself free of the weather. He pulled the rickety door closed behind him, shutting out the wind and the mini cyclone of leaves that had danced a reel following him across the threshold.

"I hope you ain't made a state of me hall carpet, Jonas Crake," scolded Maisie from the confines of their tiny parlour, as her husband entered.

"I cannot rightly recall one way or t'other but if there is, I'll surely clean it up in the morning, Maisie," replied Jonas. "I feel a bit peculiar after being out in that storm to tell you the truth. Soaked to me very marrow and a bit light-headed and giddy. That wind would take the 'ed off Lord Nelson atop his column, make no mistake." He had made his way into the parlour and sat back down in his favourite fireside chair with a triumphant grunt. "I've seen a man make do with one good eye, even manage life's struggles with a single arm, but you ain't gonna be worth tuppence with no bonce," he chuckled as he dried his hair with his handkerchief.

"You is a lazy bleeder and no mistake, Jonas Crake," slated Maisie reciting her oft-repeated mantra. Jonas seemed not to hear her. He had closed his eyes against the dwindling light of the fire and was engulfed in a torpid blackness. Shapes and shadows danced and leapt at him through the gloom like satyrs cavorting in some impenetrable forest.

Maisie sat opposite, talking incessantly about a distant neighbour whose life was the latest into which she had inserted her inquisitive nose. "Elsie Crump is having no ends of trouble with her lazy, philandering, good for nought, lump of a husband," she preached, all the while accompanied by the incessant clicking of her bone knitting needles. "Out down the Green Dragon all hours of the day and night, spending what little money they got. Pissing it all away and running around with God only knows which piece of cheap skirt he can lay his drunken mitts on. It's disgusting I tell ya, absenlutely disgusting is what I says!" Occasionally she would lay down her knitting to look at her husband who sat immobile, chest on chin, seemingly sound asleep. "Are you listening to me, Jonas Crake?" she demanded.

Crake jerked back to reality. "Of course, dear, Charlie Crump is a no-good drunken womaniser. I knew that these last twenty years woman, ain't no news to me." Inside Jonas Crake's head, an orgy of unspeakable deeds was being acted out amongst the dark theatre of his mind. The oversized head of the floating man drifted in and out of his consciousness, sometimes laughing, oftentimes urging him towards unspeakably repellent acts.

"Don't you talks to me like that, Jonas Crake. That old mucker of yours is driving poor old Elsie up the pole, I tells ya. It's absenlutely disgusting is what it is. I wouldn't stand for no behaviour like that from you, Jonas Crake, and that's for sure." Clack, clack, clack went the needles as they worked ever more rapidly at the scarf Maisie was working on, the speed of her knitting increasing as her self-induced indignation continued to rumble and rise. "Don't you even begin to think abouts going on a jolly with that good-for-nothing, Charlie Crump. You hear me?"

"Of course not, dear," replied Jonas, adding 'I wouldn't dare,' under his breath.

Maisie threw him a look that could have pulled a nail from a fencepost. She put aside her knitting melodramatically and strode purposely to the parlour window. She peered out into the storm. "I can still sees lights coming from the Church, Jonas, are you sure you properly chased them rascals away?"

Jonas Crake opened his eyes and shook his head causing a needle-like pain to shoot from one temple to the other. He winced in agony and tightly closed one eye in a vain effort to staunch the pain.

"Don't you wince at me, Jonas Crake," pounced Maisie. "I swear if you don't like the sound of what I'm saying you can fend for yourself, you lazy old goat. My mother always said I should have married your brother. He's got a proper job he does, looking after all those poor filthy people in Spitalfields for that nice Mr Grice. Makes sure they have the money to pay their rents he does. A proper job that is. Not like you, Jonas Crake, sweeping up some old Church that nobody ever uses as it was intended, and forgetting to repair them winders." Maisie returned to her chair and her knitting. Clack, clack, clickity-clack. "Ain't you gonna put more logs on that fire?" Clack, clack, clickity-clack.

An explosion of fury erupted inside Jonas Crake's tormented head.

Detective Sergeant Jem Pyke strode purposely through the open door of Detective Chief Inspector Albert Wiggins' office scanning the piece of paper he held in his hand. "Sorry to bother you, Guv, but we've had a report of a strange one down Kent way."

Wiggins was standing at the window of his office, watching the grey-brown waters of the Thames as they rolled towards Hungerford Bridge. His hands were clasped tightly behind his back. He turned towards Pyke. "Strange? In what regard, Sergeant?"

"Well, you did say to keep an eye out for anything peculiar, anything that may have a whiff of that Russian, Luca Radasiliev, about it," responded Pyke, handing Wiggins the transcript of a telephone call received at the Yard a few minutes earlier. Wiggins took the document from Pyke and sat down at his desk. He brushed a stray trace of ash from the paper before reading. Pyke looked at the ceiling.

"Forty-year-old woman, down Kent way, name of Maisie Crake, found dead in her parlour with a knitting needle rammed so deep into each ear that they almost exited the opposite sides. On first inspection, it looks as though she may also have been strangled with a scarf she had been knitting. It was found stuffed in her mouth," explained Pyke as Wiggins carefully read the report. "Been deceased for a couple of weeks they reckon, on accounts of the decomposition present."

"Husband? Any children?" enquired Wiggins in a rising tone.

"No kiddies, Guv, and the husband has disappeared. Scarpered. Local Bobbies reckon he's good for it. Neighbours, such as there are, reckon he was as hen-pecked as a pile of seed," replied Pyke taking the seat opposite Wiggins.

"Such as they are? What do you mean, Sergeant?"

"Well, seems they live in a presbytery cottage on the grounds of a disused church near Staplehurst. Caretakers as such. Minister's name is Reverend Abercorn Brook."

"And this has just come through?"

Pyke nodded whilst fishing in his pockets for a cigar. "Just got it from Desk Sergeant Ash."

"How is Nosher Ash coping with his new position here at the Yard, incidentally?" asked Wiggins looking up momentarily from the report.

"He finds it well, Sir. Fewer drunks to handle than he was used to at Paddington, and the desk ain't ever been run so efficiently," replied Pyke reaching for the box of vestas on Wiggins' desk, making a mental note to replace them in exactly the same position. '*Guvnor is mighty particular about that sort of thing,*' he reminded himself.

Wiggins considered the report in front of him. "My initial feeling was to let the local constabulary deal with it, but I feel your intuition may be right Jem, there is the distinct scent of Luca Radasiliev about it. Why don't you and Constable Murray go and investigate first thing tomorrow?"

Pyke blew a smoke ring into the air and watched it whirl and dissipate, then blew another directly through the centre of the enlarging first. "No time like the present, Guv. I'll get me hat."

Chapter 2 - The Old Man

The old man sat in his bedchamber surrounded by relics from his past. His liver-spotted head seemed strangely out of proportion compared to his age-diminished body, a body which had once surged with strength and vitality. Only a few pale wisps remained of his once leonine mane, but ferocity still burned within his intense, intelligent eyes. He lifted a palsied hand to stroke the .577 Black Powder Express elephant gun that lay across the tiger skin rug that warmed his permanently chilled lap.

He scanned the room, each trophy and weapon bringing back vivid memories. An enormous water buffalo head was mounted over the mantelpiece of the fireplace. A trophy brought down with a single bullet that had punctured the centre of its noble skull as it had charged towards its slayer. '*The most dangerous of all the African plains creatures,*' he reminded himself with a sense of inner satisfaction. The fireplace itself was constructed from aged-yellow ivory with pilasters formed by the tusks of a bull elephant.

The even larger head of a rare white rhinoceros that looked disparagingly down over his bed, had been felled back in seventy-nine by the very same gun that now lay resting upon his knees. Heads of several antelopes, a leopard, and its cousin the black panther were all displayed around the forbidding comfort of the only room in his vast rambling house that he now occupied. And of course, his greatest prize, the mighty Bengal Tiger, the kill that had cemented his reputation as the greatest big-game hunter of his day. He had single-handedly tracked the man-eater for three days through the mangrove forests of Sundarbans. Its full pelt and head now adorned his intricately carved Keralan four-poster bed.

His mind wandered, as it often chose to do these days. The odour of gunpowder, the squeal of the kill, the bloodied, whipped back of a native bearer, the scent of sweat and fear and death. The old man clutched a red silk handkerchief to his mouth as a hoarse, rattling cough escaped his throat. He rubbed his scarred neck. It would have been apparent to any observer that at some juncture in his life this man had survived the gibbet. He looked with disdain at the black bilious sputum that now rested within his cupped handkerchief. "The doctors say the cancer is everywhere from the colon to the oesophagus," he grunted to the young man sitting opposite him. A brief, awkward silence ensued. "From my arse to my throat, in other words," he added tersely for the benefit of the younger man. "They say I'll be dead 'err summer is gone, and there's many who will rejoice at my passing no doubt. I blame the tiger meat. Take my advice boy, never be tempted to eat the flesh of Panthera Tigris, no matter how hungry you may find yourself to be. He has had the last laugh!"

"I will endeavour to remember not to do so," responded the young man as he rested his hand upon the old man's great paw-like hand.

"Away with you!" grunted the old man, pulling his hand away. "I'll have no signs of affection; do you hear me? Such is for the weak, the demented and womenfolk."

"Yes father, I apologise," replied the younger man, embarrassingly staring down at his shoes. '*Even now,*' he thought, '*he is dominant over me to a terrifying degree, as a lion is to the weakest gazelle.*'

"How fare you in your new post my boy?" asked the old man, his trembling hands involuntarily polishing the barrel of the elephant gun.

"It goes well, thank-you, father. They suspect nothing," replied the young man, buoyed at the opportunity of imparting good news to his fearsome parent. The old man nodded his satisfaction then proceeded to hack another body wracking cough.

A light knock at the door was followed by the entrance of a middle-aged nurse carrying a tray of medication. "Your medication, Colonel," announced the nurse in an optimistic, breezy voice as she sashayed into the room. The young man felt slightly aroused at the sound of her dress rubbing against her underskirts. He felt repulsed and ashamed at his reaction.

The old man grunted. "Leave it on the table and be away with you."

"My, we are in a mood today, an' no mistake," replied the nurse mockingly, casting a knowing look at the younger man. "Be sure he takes his medicine now, young Sir. Doctor's orders you know."

Once the nurse had departed, the old man swallowed the pills with the accompanying glass of water but poured the small vial of acrid smelling viscose liquid into a large, ornately painted plant pot to the side of his chair. "I take the pills but discard the morphia. It may dull the pain, but it also relieves one of one's senses, although as you can see, the Aspidistra seems to thrive upon it." Lowering his tone ever so slightly, "Now you are sure that they do not suspect you? These are clever people we deal with."

"No father, they regard me very much as one of their own," confirmed the young man proudly.

"It is good that they see you as being in a position of trust," nodded the old man, satisfied. "The old Doctor and I have many scores to settle from days long gone and I want that young mudlark dead in his boots before I am."

Chapter 3 - The Photograph

"Did your husband or either of his two work colleagues ride a bicycle to and from work, Mrs Schoon?" enquired Pyke.

"Why, what a strange question, Sergeant," answered Irene Schoon, looking up at Pyke as she poured tea from a chintz-patterned teapot into three matching bone china cups.

Wiggins and Pyke had exchanged a nervous glance as they knocked on the front door of the immaculately kept terraced house in Killick Street only fifteen minutes earlier. It was the Islington home of Mr Charlie and Irene Schoon. Irene had answered the door with a pleasant greeting and a smile, and ushered the two detectives into a spotless, albeit fussy front parlour, filled as it was with bric-a-brac, chinaware, prints, framed photographs, books and inexpensive yet pretentious furniture. The overall impression was that of an overdressed exhibit of a room.

"Sugar, gentlemen?" she asked. In her mind the importance of how her guests took their tea, far outweighed whether her husband Charlie had owned a bicycle. 'Besides, it was such a silly question,' she thought to herself.

"Two for me, one for the Guvnor," smiled Pyke. Mrs Schoon administered the sugar and sat down opposite Pyke, pointedly straightening the antimacassar on the shoulders of her chair before she did so. Irene Schoon subtly examined Pyke's battle-scarred, but handsome face. His oft-broken nose, square-set jaw and muscular neckline made her decide that this was a man of violence, an honourable man perhaps, but one who could intimidate and punish. However, she was not a woman to be daunted by looks alone.

"Nice tea," nodded Pyke appreciatively after taking an initial sip.

"Thank you, officer, Charlie was very particular about his tea. Just had to be Twinings. He could spot the difference as quick as a flash you know." Pyke nodded his appreciation as if he could tell the difference between Twinings and a cup of builder's brown from old Sid's café on the corner of Branch Road.

"Your tea, Chief Inspector?" reminded Mrs Schoon, looking towards the figure of Wiggins who was drifting around the room, studying its contents intently. He picked up a framed photograph from amongst a collection displayed on the front bay windowsill, mindful to ensure he did not disturb any of its closely grouped neighbours. He looked intently at the two figures that stared back at him, one diminutive, robust, and heavily moustachioed, the other tall, broad-shouldered and angular, a monolith of a man. "Is this not your husband with Detective Inspector Edmund Reid, Mrs Schoon?" asked a now intrigued Wiggins.

"That's correct, Mr Wiggins," answered Mrs Schoon filled with obvious pride. "Charlie was in CID, 'H' Division out of Leaman Street under Inspector Reid. Charlie always said what a great man he was," acknowledged Mrs Schoon, stirring her tea. She could see that Wiggins was a thinker. An intellectual. Well spoken, articulate, and well dressed and immaculately groomed. She imagined that he may well be a very particular individual, precise and obsessive in his habits. The two detectives looked at each other. Charlie Schoon had just risen immensely in both their opinions. Wiggins turned to their host. "Then Mr Schoon would have been involved with the Ripper case?"

"Indeed, he was Mr Wiggins. Brought it home with him n'all. Got him down in the dumps something rotten, you might say. Put a real strain on our family, it did. I cannot say as he ever got over the things he saw back then. Never talked about particulars, but I could tell it weighed heavily on his mind. He always found it difficult to get to sleep after that did Charlie. It was a dark time for everyone, but Charlie got dragged down by it all."

"Bitten by the Black Dog?" rumbled Pyke.

"That's exactly what me Charlie used to call it, Sergeant. Bitten by the Black Dog," answered Mrs Schoon, gazing into an undefined point in the middle distance as she distractedly continued stirring her tea.

Both detectives looked sympathetically at Mrs Schoon who had picked up another picture from a spotlessly polished sideboard behind her. She looked longingly at the photograph of the young man and baby girl smiling from some seaside promenade. "Brighton, most likely," she murmured to herself with a smile." Victoria were just a little nipper then," her head shaking.

"Your daughter?" observed Wiggins.

"Yes, Chief Inspector. All grown up now. University education an' all. She were always the bright one in the family." She smiled a loving smile. "Charlie would always tease her that he didn't know where she got her brains from on accounts of me being a domestic and him an 'umble copper. Proud as punch he was. Don't see much of her now." She dabbed the corners of her eyes and looked upward, blinking rapidly in an attempt to stem her tears.

"I know your husband served with distinction, Mrs Schoon," reassured Wiggins.

"If he lasted the course on the Ripper case with 'H' Division then he was some mighty copper," added Pyke affirmatively.

"He were a good man, my Charlie, and no mistake. Always provided for us as best he could, he did." She sat and looked at the ceiling as if to contain her tears within upturned eyelids. She swallowed hard, and after a moment turned her gaze back to the two police officers, forcing a fond smile. "He and Archie and Mickey used to go down the Eagle for beer and skittles every Thursday night. Now all three of them have gone. Disappeared," she lamented, drawing a lace handkerchief from her sleeve, and dabbing at her nose.

Wiggins cleared his throat. "Forgive me, Mrs Schoon, I could not help but notice that all the while you have been referring to your husband in the past tense."

"Well, they're dead ain't they?" retorted Mrs Schoon with an unexpected edge. "You don't have to be bleedin' Sherlock Holmes to figure that out, gentlemen. Charlie's habits are ... were regular as clockwork." Her voice faltered, and she brought the handkerchief back to her face and began to weep.

Pyke and Wiggins exchanged an uncomfortable look and waited for Mrs Schoon to compose herself. After a considerable pause, she lifted her head proudly, signalling that all was well. "The answer to your question is no, by the way, Mr Pyke. Neither Charlie nor his mates owned a bicycle. Why such a strange question Sergeant?"

"Well, we spotted what looked like a bicycle tyre mark on the door threshold of the Cruciform Building the night Charlie and his colleagues went missing," explained Pyke. Wiggins cast his Sergeant a look of admonishment. Pyke shrugged his shoulders in a '*what's the harm?*' gesture. Wiggins noticed that the stitching on the seam of one of the shoulders of Pyke's jacket was slightly undone. '*Hardly surprising given the bovine nature of his neckline,*' thought Wiggins to himself.

Mrs Schoon looked at her hands clasped in her lap and asked, "Why would anyone kill my Charlie and his mates, Mr Wiggins? Was something stolen from the Cruciform? Something that was worth the lives of three decent and just, old men?"

A pensive grimace played across Wiggins' face. He decided that he owed this woman some degree of explanation. "We believe that an extremely valuable item may have been removed from the secure facility where your husband works." Wiggins made sure he used the present tense when referring to her husband. "The item in question is of national importance. This is our current line of enquiry."

Mrs Schoon considered this carefully for a moment. She coughed before speaking. "Do you think that my Charlie had something to do with it? The robbery, like? Do you think him, and his mates have run off with this *valuable item* then?" She stood unsteadily and waved her finger at Wiggins. "Because, if you do, Detective Inspector, I can assure you that you are barking up the wrong bleedin' tree!" Pyke could see the woman shaking with repressed fury. "Not at all," he interjected. We reckon your Charlie and his mates defended their post valiantly and in doing so, it may have cost them their lives."

Mrs Schoon slumped back into her chair and tried stoically not to succumb to a flood of grief. Wiggins offered up her teacup which she took with a trembling hand

and an appreciative smile. She nodded her head as if silently communicating with her husband. Wiggins rose from his chair, closely followed by Pyke, who read his superior officer's signal to leave. "Thank you for your time, Mrs Schoon, we will keep you no longer. I hope this hasn't been too upsetting for you. We will of course keep you updated with any developments."

"I'm just sorry I couldn't have been of more help," she lamented, guiding them through her hallway. Mrs Schoon noticed that Wiggins had observed several cards standing on the hall consul table. "From well-wishers, Mr Wiggins. People have been so kind." Wiggins nodded in empathy, whilst attentively scanning the cards. "People generally are," he added. As he turned to exit, his eye caught a glint of light cast from the glazed front door reflecting upon a small object sitting within the array of cards. Wiggins picked up the small jade dragon and a shiver shot through his body.

And this, Mrs Schoon? Was this a gift from a well-wisher?"

"I think so, Mr Wiggins. It turned up in the post, anonymous like, a day or two after Charlie and his mates went missing. Beautiful ain't it? Aren't people kind?"
"Yes, it is beautiful, Mrs Schoon, and yes ... people can be kind."

The two detectives exchanged a knowing glance. Each had immediately recognised the calling card of the Jade Dragon, that of London's most merciless killer, the evil Chinaman, Mr King.

Chapter 4 - The Clearing

"Shouldn't you be pushing a pen in your new office Guv, after all, you are now Chief Inspector, the new Sheriff in town and pursuer of all that is unlawful and unjust?" asked Pyke in a rather mischievous manner. Wiggins looked at his colleague with a circumflexed left eyebrow. "I believe that title will go to our new Chief Superintendent, whomsoever he turns out to be. I must say, I still expect to see the Chief Superintendent MacDonald sitting in his chair when I enter that room. To tell you the truth Pyke, I'm glad that someone new will be brought in."

"Didn't fancy it yourself then, Guv?" asked Pyke, ducking below a low hanging sycamore branch. Dry leaves crunched satisfyingly beneath their shoes as they progressed through Highgate Woods, which was decorated in an early morning dew that sparkled in the emerging sun. Wiggins smirked and thought carefully before answering. He looked at the sun through a break in the trees. "MacDonald served the Force and this city with a bravery and intensity at which most of us would baulk. His job is not all the mere frippery it seems from the outside. Endless phone conversations, mountains of paperwork and meetings that take forever and seem to ultimately solve nothing. They are obviously a huge part of the job but keeping all of this together whilst fending off the politicians and allowing us to do our jobs is, I would imagine, no mean feat. Also, there is the small matter of having to bear the consequence of ultimate responsibility. Not a position I would readily welcome."

Pyke nodded, "Watch out for the muddy patch there, Guv. Wouldn't want to get those polished shoes stained with North London mud. The clay soil dries like rock it does."

Wiggins was thinking of the job he had turned down. "I would have seldom got to dig out clues or get my hands, or indeed shoes, dirtied for that matter. I fear my synapses would have withered and died if I were unable to investigate actual cases in the field. The new office would have been as a prison cell to me. You know as well as I, that this is what I am supposed to do, and I'd like to think that over the years I have indeed become rather adept at it."

"No doubting that to be fair," replied Pyke pushing another errant tree branch out of the way. "Whatever synapses may be." Wiggins smiled and breathed in the morning air with relish. The two detectives had been following Constable Bunce through Highgate Woods for almost ten minutes. The sunlight pierced through the tree branches to reveal a dappled, circular clearing approximately half the size of a rugby pitch. It had blossomed into a beautiful sunny morning and bluebells danced in the light breeze in clutches below the trees, their beauty and delicate innocence, the antithesis of what lay up ahead.

Directly in the centre of the grassy grove sat an upturned metal bucket. The bucket was surrounded by a ring of stones and rocks placed at what appeared to be regular intervals as though they were sentinels standing in a cordoned guard. Two uniformed Constables stood in the clearing conversing in what appeared to be a conspiratorial exchange. Wiggins and Pyke approached from the copse, their pace quickening now that they were free from the restricting branches and roots of their earlier journey. The two constables broke their conversation and stood to attention.

"What *is* that, Boss?" questioned Pyke to Wiggins as he pointed ahead.

Wiggins absorbed the scene. "I have absolutely no idea, Jem. We were informed, were we not, that there was a dead male found here by a passing dog walker, but to me, that object looks nothing more than the size of a small dog itself." The two men advanced sufficiently enough to make out the scene more distinctly.

"Why it's nothing more than an upside-down wash pale!" remarked Pyke incredulously, scratching his head under his perennially present brown Derby hat.

"What have we here then, Constable Milton?" asked Wiggins, of one of the attending uniforms, as he came within reach of the pair. Milton saluted but the obviously anxious young man remained tight-lipped, his head nodding and his wide eyes pointing repeatedly towards the upturned bucket as if it were some filthy secret of which he wanted no part. Wiggins' brows furrowed as he tried to comprehend the rather strange response. Normally he would have admonished the Constable for ignoring a direct question from a superior officer, but something instinctively told him to temporarily withhold any reprimand. He stared directly at Milton whose brown eyes remained fixed squarely upon the bucket whilst an uneasy look played upon the young man's face. Wiggins looked from the constable to the bucket then back again before crouching down on his haunches. His gaze remained immovably on Milton as he lifted the bucket. As he did so the young man turned his head away involuntarily from the scene. Only then did Wiggins look down to see that what had been concealed under the pale was the severed head of a man. A head so severely bruised, bloodied, and disfigured that it had been rendered unrecognisably human.

"Man Alive!" exclaimed Pyke.

"An excellent turn of phrase but a rather misplaced one given the present situation don't you think, Detective Sergeant?" countered Wiggins.

"Who on earth would decapitate someone and place the head under a bucket in the middle of the bloomin' woods?" puzzled Pyke, glancing around as if trying to prise some sense out of the surrounding woodland. Wiggins arose, stood back one pace, and surveyed the bizarre scene for several moments, scrutinising every available bit of data at his disposal. He stroked his chin then crouched back down again. He produced a magnifying glass from his overcoat and began to examine the head more closely.

The head, which sat upright upon its neck, was a bloodied, bloated mess, but it was clearly that of a male, a fact corroborated by its receding hairline which was matted with dirt and dried blood. The head was covered in contusions and swellings, and both eyes were swollen tightly closed. One eye socket bore the deep depression of an obviously fractured orbital cavity. The nose was flattened, crooked, and noticeably had been broken, as Wiggins reasoned, on more than one occasion. A deep laceration was visible on the forehead and there seemed no square inch free from discolouration or bruising. A police photographer and pathologist had now entered the dell and were making their way towards the red bullseye directly at the centre of the clearing. The pathologist struggled under the weight of his fully stocked examination case. Wiggins continued to investigate the grisly scene for a few moments further. He drew a deep breath and stroked his neatly trimmed moustache before standing upright. "I think you will find that this head is in fact still firmly attached to the owner's body."

"Guv?" questioned Pyke, taken aback.

"Rather, this unfortunate individual has been buried up to his neck, and my initial suspicions are that he has been repeatedly kicked or bludgeoned to death." Wiggins examined the ground within and outwith the circle of stones, muttering occasionally as he did so. His examination complete, he confirmed to Pyke, "A lone assailant, Jem. The murderer worked alone. The morning dew helps enormously in allowing the ground to tell its tale. Our victim was dragged to the centre of the clearing, presumably unconscious or drugged, and then buried. The hole may or may not have been pre-dug, it is impossible to tell."

Pyke surveyed the same scene as Wiggins had. He began to walk carefully around the circle of stones. "How do you know he was still alive when he was buried?" probed Pyke.

"Good question, Jem. He may have been unconscious when he was interred but he was certainly alert once the onslaught began. Observe the teeth lying randomly around," pointed Wiggins. "Clearly, they have been spat out only in a forward direction, and besides, why would someone kill a person *then* dig a hole to bury them in if not trying to conceal or dispose of the body?"

"Right enough Guv, a hell of a lotta work and effort digging a vertical hole rather than a shallow horizontal grave. Come to think of it, why in a clearing and not within the woods themselves? Seems to me this body was intended to be found. But what of this circle of stones? They appear uniformly placed and certainly not randomly distributed as if thrown. I can't see any other stones that size or colour anywhere around here." Pyke scanned the periphery of the clearing. "Any idea as to their significance?"

"Excellent reasoning, Jem," complimented Wiggins. "I wager a closer inspection and forensic blood analysis by Doctor Pascoe will confirm that the blood clearly visible on the stones matches the blood type of the victim and that they were in fact the murder weapons. I hypothesise that rather than having been beaten and kicked, this poor soul has been stoned to death! Imprints in the grass indicate that our murderer placed each stone in this circle once the deed was done."

Pyke winced at the thought of being stoned, and in such a defenceless position. A barbaric and abhorrent ending to a life. "Here comes the very man now," announced Pyke nodding his head towards the large shambling figure approaching the scene. Pyke was about to discard an extinguished match he had just used to relight the previous night's last cigar when he was met with a booming reproach from the advancing figure.

"Pocket, Sergeant Pyke! Pocket it! You know the rules!" Pyke shrugged and tusked the blackened vesta into his waistcoat pocket.

"Good morning, Doctor Pascoe," greeted Wiggins as he turned to the forensic pathologist. "We have a rather unique mystery for you to untangle."

"It's not a *good* morning for that poor fellow by the looks of it, but morning all the same Inspector ... sorry, Chief Inspector. It is indeed a rather splendid morning, and this looks a rather fascinating proposition," responded Pascoe with a worried looking face. Doctor Nelson B. Pascoe's features made him look as if he was perpetually worried. His red, bushy eyebrows were so far from his eyes that he gave the appearance of being continually alarmed. He was nearing retirement age and had worked as a police surgeon for the CID for many years before moving into the study of forensics at the turn of the century. He was a big burly man who constantly complained of his gout affliction, caused by a lifetime of inflammatory arthritis and not from his love of fine Port and sweetbreads. "Please do take your photographs before I commence," he urged the accompanying photographer who fumbled frustratedly with his tripod.

"Constable Bunce, you Milton and Robinson, do as Doctor Pascoe requires," instructed Wiggins. "Sergeant Pyke and I will return to base to type up a report and await the good doctor's scene of crime statement in due course." Pascoe threw Wiggins a nod of acknowledgement.

"Enjoy Doc!" Pyke waved his customary breezy farewell to Pascoe. "Keep yer head down, mate!"

"As always," replied Pascoe with an exaggerated smile. He knelt gingerly and turned to his work.

"The victim is a Deacon Hamilton Lancaster, aged sixty-seven years," read Pyke from the full crime scene statement and forensic autopsy reports he held. He leant casually against the door frame of DCI Wiggins' third-floor office at Scotland Yard. Wiggins himself sat behind his desk in front of the turret bow window which looked eastward up the Thames towards Hungerford Bridge. Pyke continued. "He stood five feet and eight inches and weighed nine stone two pounds. There were nineteen separate blunt force impact trauma injuries to the head and face. The head exhibited multiple cranial fractures. Says here that tremendous velocity was required to cause the injuries present. Fractures to both zygomatic bones, three fractures to the nasal bridge, fractures to the frontal process of the maxilla, the lacrimal bone, and the sphenoid of the left eye, and both temporomandibular joints were dislocated, such that his jaw was detached from the skull. The combined effect of all these injuries ultimately led to massive and fatal intracranial bleeding." Pyke drew a breath before continuing to read Wiggins the findings. "Goes on at some length about the injuries and such, but basically his boat was smashed, and his loaf was broke."

"What of the blood types?" enquired Wiggins eagerly. Pyke scanned further down the document. "Here it is Boss, states blood present on the stones and assorted debris was B-positive which matches that of the victim."

"So, it looks as though my initial suspicions were, in fact, well-founded and that the murder weapons, namely the stones, were strategically positioned at regular intervals, in a circle, after the deed was done and the victim was deceased," ruminated Wiggins. He lit a cigarette and walked over to a wall that, amongst other documents, displayed a detailed anatomical chart of the human skeletal system.

Pyke continued to scan Doctor Pascoe's autopsy report. "Doc Pascoe states here that the hands were bound at the wrist behind the victim's body using long strips of canvas. His left glenohumeral joint was dislocated, and severe bruising was evident to the left talocrural joint. There were also three fractured ribs on the left side of the thoracic cage. Blah, blah, blah ... essentially old Pascoe concludes that, in his opinion, the victim was abducted forcibly, possibly knocked unconscious resulting in him falling heavily on his left side causing dislocation of that shoulder and severe spraining of the ankle. States it is impossible to tell from the number of head injuries present as to which of them could have been the initial concussive blow, nor indeed which was the fatal one."

"I see. Anything else of import, Jem?" probed Wiggins whose gaze lingered over the anatomical illustration, focusing on the cranium through the rising smoke of his cigarette.

"Ehm ... says further down that a slip of paper was found in the right-hand pocket of Deacon Lancaster's gown, with the sentence, "*For whoever wants to save their life will lose it, but whoever loses their life for me will find it.*" The report adds that it was written in a childlike scrawl. "Sounds like the religious rantings of another Nathaniel Cripes for Heaven's sake," offered Pyke.

"Thankfully, Cripes is safely locked away in Saint Luke's Asylum, so we can dismiss that particular deviant. I suspect the childlike scrawl Pascoe talks of is a means to disguise the perpetrator's handwriting. The note was most likely written with his non-dominant hand," added Wiggins.

Pyke continued. "I did some initial investigation after I'd received the good Doc's findings late yesterday, and for the past twelve years Hamilton Lancaster has been Deacon at Saint Stephen's Church on Castlebar Hill in Ealing."

Wiggins digested this information, his brows wrinkling at possibilities. "So, we can surmise that he was transported some distance from his parish to Highgate Wood, which suggests that the particular spot chosen was selected specifically as the location for his demise. What else did you discover, Pyke?"

"Well I spent the early morning down in Ealing and the church is widely celebrated for running a home for recently widowed women left with no available means of support. The Deacon is regarded as somewhat of a saviour by these unfortunates. A literal Godsend for these women. The Deacon had been missing for forty-eight hours. Seems he was a universally liked, generous and kind. A true man of God. Nobody I spoke with had a bad word to say about the man, which makes his abduction and the gruesome nature of his murder all the more baffling. I also found that the quotation left in the Deacon's gown pocket is from the book of Matthew; sixteen, twenty-five."

"Excellent work Pyke!" acclaimed Wiggins. "So, what exactly do we *know*? Well, we know that the murderer evidently wanted the body to be found but there remain several unanswered questions. Why choose a Deacon to murder, and why this particular Deacon? Was he selected because of a personal reason; something he had done, a dispute, or a historical grudge or bad feeling perhaps? Or was he selected simply because he was a Deacon? Why choose stoning as the means of murder and why use nineteen stones and not twenty, or eighteen, or eighty for that matter? Why choose the clearing in Highgate Woods to perpetrate the killing?" Wiggins paced around the room, his mind seeking connections. "What does the quotation found on his body refer to, if anything at all? For all we know Deacon Lancaster could have written it himself, it may very well be an idea for a sermon for all we know. We need to compare it with a sample of his own handwriting to discount that possibility." Wiggins mind was racing now. "What do we know about Lancaster? I need to *know* him, to understand him. Does he have relatives, friends, or more importantly, enemies? I need to know every scrap of information regarding this unfortunate man. Someone killed him for a reason!"

"Understood, Guv," replied Pyke.

"Assemble an investigation team, Jem. Yourself, Murray, Bunce and Milton, along with Doctor Pascoe. Let us set up an incident room and arrange an afternoon briefing."

Chapter 5 - The Invalid

"Murray checked with the wives of Micky Milligan and Archie Stout and confirmed Mrs Schoon's statement that neither of them owned or had the use of a bicycle," confirmed Pyke as he sipped at a generous whisky in the flower festooned cobbled yard of the George Inn. "In fact, Murray reckons that old Mrs Milligan wasn't even too sure what a bicycle was. She seems a little, how would you say?"

"Mentally challenged?" offered Wiggins.

"Touched," I was going to say, Guv. "Anyways, we got some unwashed laundry from each of the wives and took old Darah the bloodhound down to the Cruciform building, but she drew a blank. Only got as far as the kerbside and no farther. Not like her to lose a scent, got a nose like old Harry Filch she has."

Wiggins nodded. "So, we can presume, somewhat safely, that all three night-watchmen were either murdered or rendered unconscious, and then taken to a vehicle of some description for disposal elsewhere. Although we must not for a single second discount one, or perhaps two of them, being the perpetrators themselves," mused Wiggins thoughtfully. His glass of tawny port remained untouched, much to Pyke's chagrin, eager as the Sergeant was for a second whisky.

"I can't believe for one second that an old copper, and one as dedicated as Charlie Schoon, could be guilty of a crime such as this," responded Pyke. "You only got to look at his record, Guv. It's exemplary, and anyway, that Jade Dragon can't be merely a coincidence."

"No doubt you are correct, Jem." Wiggins was admiring the Tudor façade of the old coach house, which nestled just off Borough High Street. Its first-floor galleried balcony and ancient oak beams fascinated him. He seemed to drift off subject. "Imagine the countless thousands of travellers who have rested and slaked their thirst at this establishment over the last two centuries," pondered Wiggins. "Merchants, vagabonds, the good and the great, brigands and pastors, families and lost souls."

Pyke sucked on the remnants in his glass with an exaggerated smack of his lips and placed it rather too dramatically atop the barrel table at which they stood. "Well, I ain't never known Darah to ever be wrong, and if you ask me those three unfortunate gents are long gone no matter what happened. I reckon what remains of them poor lads will be lying in some rancid lime pit down Cheapside way, I expect."

"All things considered, Jem, I fear that you are correct. That all three would simply vanish from their place of employ on the same night is simply inconceivable." Wiggins, much to Pyke's relief, eventually raised his glass towards his lips. Before drinking, however, he turned to Pyke, leant forward, and spoke in a conspiratorial whisper. "MacDonald is convinced that King is behind this and that he does indeed have the virus. But damn it, Jem, we have so far heard nothing from the evil menace, nor seen any evidence of his having taken the virus from the Cruciform Building, far less used the contagion." He slammed down his glass, still untouched back onto the barrel lid, causing some port to splash onto the ground. Pyke looked to the heavens. '*Man alive! Are you pullin' me chain, Guv? Just drink the drink!*'

Wiggins stood and clasped his hands behind his back, as was his wont, and began to stroll slowly around the enclosed cobbled courtyard, lost in thought. Pyke looked on as Wiggins drifted from one floral display to the next, admiring the colourful blooms and testing the air to catch their scent. Hanging baskets, pots and troughs tumbled with colour. Pyke lit the remnants of a cigar he had produced from the recesses of his waistcoat pocket and blew smoke up into the afternoon air. He doused the match, as he habitually did, between a spit-moistened thumb and forefinger, and pinged it high and accurately into a plant pot housing purple hyacinths. He knew from experience of Wiggins' body language that he was formulating a plan, tidying his thoughts, mental housekeeping.

Wiggins returned to the barrel table and reached for his glass. Pyke's eyes followed the movement with eager anticipation. '*Take a drink for Bleak's sake!*' "Let us recollect our thoughts, Jem," suggested Wiggins, raising his hands from his glass to stroke his neatly clipped beard. As he did so Pyke wondered at the straightness and accuracy of the shaven line of Wiggins' facial hair. The precision of the lines, the uniformity of clipping. '*He must visit Johnston's barbershop every other day,*' decided Pyke.

"So, what's the plan, Boss?" asked Pyke. "We have Luca Radasiliev still on the loose, a perplexing murder in Highgate Wood, not to mention the very real threat of a mass plague infection at the hands of that Chinese maniac, King."

"First the virus, Jem. It is our priority as it currently constitutes a more widespread threat to our populace than does Radasiliev. Murray and Bunce are making further enquiries regarding our good Deacon and they promised me their report as soon as the ink is dry." Wiggins continued, "We need to discover exactly where King is holed up and establish whether he actually has the contagion. He may in fact not have the virus and just be holding us to ransom. You find his location as a matter of urgency Pyke. Use any means at your disposal. Meanwhile, I will petition the Commissioner for a warrant to remove what Professor Abel is adamant is the pristine, and only sample of the virus in existence, from the Cruciform Building. As

Director of the facility, I would expect some resistance from him as regards our enquiries. The Cruciform is, after all, a restricted building in which highly secretive work and research are carried out. Once we secure a sample of the virus, I hope the lab coats can then test this to establish if it has been tampered with in any way. If it has, and given that we can locate King, we then crush him and retrieve the contagion."

"Now you're talking, Sir. I'll find the rat. After all, he is the biggest rodent in this God-forsaken sewer. I'll use every contact I know, the Heap, Boniface, Demerara Smith, the Boys' Brigade, every beggar, cutpurse, Molly, and thief this side of Westminster. When I find him, his rotten yellow carcass won't be worth a Scotch farthing. He will pay for what he did to old Mac and the slaying of some of our boys." Wiggins could see the anger boil within his Sergeant. "By the time I'm finished with him, London will smell a little bit sweeter."

Wiggins listened to his Sergeant, admiring his sense of justice and determination. His mind floated back to the image of Pyke single-handedly engaging the savagery of the maniac that had been the Beast, Doctor Joseph Bleak, in the depths of the bascule chambers of Tower Bridge, several weeks earlier. Pyke grasping the wrists of the cannibal's arms as Bleak tried ferociously to tear at the detective with his self-fashioned steel scalpel talons that had taken the lives of seven innocent women. Pyke repeatedly thundering his skull against that of the monster, time after time after time. Again, and again, an onslaught that had chilled and sickened Wiggins in the scale of its brutality, whilst simultaneously filling his soul with pride at the level of its bravery. He remembered his fallen colleagues, savagely slaughtered by the Beast. Men like Constable William Potts who selflessly sacrificed his own young life that Lady Constance Harkness should survive. He felt weighed down by an intolerable burden of guilt that he had been unable to prevent their deaths.

Wiggins also thought of the unimaginable ordeal suffered by his erstwhile commander. Superintendent Magnus MacDonald, at the hands of the fiendish crime lord, Mr King. How the mysterious Oriental, along with his drug-addled henchman, the monstrous Hercules Chin, had subjected MacDonald to the most horrific of tortures. He flinched as he recalled how he and his men and intervened just in time to save Mac's life as a starved rat, held within a wicker basket which had been strapped to his, had begun to gnaw its way through his abdomen. '*The pain must have been sickening,*' speculated Wiggins. He recoiled at the thought. He also recalled how King had booby-trapped Stephenson's old granary warehouse, killing several of his officers by drowning them under tons of grain released from overhead silos.

"You all right, Guv?" he heard Pyke's voice cut through the memory.

Wiggins shook his head and smiled. "Yes, yes, of course, Jem." He pulled his Hunter watch from his waistcoat pocket. "I am to call on MacDonald at his new rooms at the Demosthenes Club at two o'clock. I wish to meet the physician he has hired to take care of him, tell the fellow how much MacDonald means to us all. Would you like to accompany me?"

Pyke shook his head. "Best be getting on the trail of that Oriental Devil. My blood is up. Give the Boss my regards and tell him I'll call round Sunday after me weekly visit to Church," winked Pyke. Wiggins shook his head and took a hearty gulp of his port. "Time for another, Jem?"

"Man alive, I thought you'd never ask! I'm as dry as the Highveld in an African summer," spluttered Pyke, stifling a laugh.

The cab ride from Borough Market to Pall Mall was prompt and without incident. Wiggins, as was his habit, had made a point of taking not the first cab on offer, nor the second, but the third. A precautionary measure he had picked up from his erstwhile mentor. He always paid particular attention to the cabbie, and to the route he had selected. His habitual sense of caution had been heightened to an intensity that he felt reflected the recent rise in abnormal criminal activity within the Metropolis. King was, after all, a devious maniac whose tentacles seemed to extend to all corners of the City. His poison was everywhere. A killer, a torturer, an extortionist whose evil knew no bounds. His instinct, accompanied by the generally neutral behaviour of the driver, had not given Wiggins any undue cause for concern, and he had settled into the brief journey which lasted just long enough for him to collect his thoughts. The cab proceeded to draw up outside the Demosthenes Club. The Club revelled in a rather anonymous façade that was at odds to the extravagant splendour that lay within its white stucco walls. Wiggins thanked the driver for his efficiency of route and tipped him generously.

"Thanking you kindly, Sir," saluted the cabbie touching the peak of his cloth cap. As he did so, the cuff of the driver's leather glove rode up slightly, revealing a small but distinct jade dragon tattooed on his wrist. Wiggins caught the briefest glimpse of the tattoo and started in surprise. He and the driver exchanged a knowing glance before the twosome pulled swiftly back into a busy Pall Mall and was lost among the living river of traffic. Wiggins cursed under his breath. '*King and his emissaries of evil are everywhere. They are a poison that flows through the veins of this City.*' The thought sent a chill tremor of apprehension through his body. '*They are trailing our every move!*'

The Demosthenes Club sat just off London's most exclusive thoroughfare in the heart of the West End's gentlemen's clubland, and ranked alongside its neighbours, the Reform Club, and the Athenaeum Club, not only in the influence of its membership but also in the wealth required of its patrons to satisfy its substantial subscription fees. Although not as long-established as the grand old institutions of Boodles and Whites, its members were of an equal stratum of Society. Unlike its sister club, the nearby Diogenes, famous for its patronage by Mycroft Holmes, and its all-encompassing vow of silence, the Demosthenes, as one would expect from its name, actively encouraged open debate, and fostered vigorous oration amongst its members on the subjects and politics of the day.

Following his torture and near death at the hands of Mr King and his monstrous henchman, Hercules Chin, Magnus MacDonald, former Superintendent of Scotland Yard CID, had retired to private rooms within the club wherein he had employed a physician, Doctor Maxwell Ward, to look after him during his long months of recovery. MacDonald had been a member of the Demosthenes for several years and had enthusiastically embraced the verbose culture of the establishment. He had regularly participated in the club's weekly round table debate, more often than not, accompanied by fellow member, the now notorious Doctor Joseph Bleak, the monstrous beast that terrorised the inhabitants of London just months before.

Wiggins pressed the brass bell button mounted into the brilliant white rendering of the portico entrance. Two long rings and one short blast was his habitual calling card. As always, he used the highly polished surface of the bell surround as a makeshift mirror and straightened his collar and tie. A white-coated attendant opened the door. "Detective Chief Inspector Wiggins to see Superintendent MacDonald," announced Wiggins. The attendant nodded and ushered him across the marble threshold before silently taking Wiggins' hat and overcoat which he carefully draped over his arm.

"This way, if you please, Sir," indicated the doorman, efficiently passing the detective's garments to an ancient, although sprightly looking cloakroom attendant. Wiggins noted that, as with his earlier visits to the Demosthenes, at no time had he been asked to display a calling card of any description. '*No doubt such vulgarity is frowned upon in such an establishment,*' he rejoiced inwardly. As he was led through plushily carpeted, high ceilinged corridors, lined with intimidating portraits of distinguished members past and present, he could not help but consider that perhaps this privileged, almost isolated environment, may perfectly suit his temperament. '*What more relaxing a place to rest and think?*' he mused. The crumping sound of shoe leather on deeply piled carpet interspersed with the occasional creak of an unsecured, underlying floorboard, added to the comfortable, almost hypnotic atmosphere of the Club. A smell of polished mahogany and oiled oak interspersed with a whiff of tobacco smoke, permeated from the various lounges and reading rooms that led off on both sides of the main corridor.

He found Magnus MacDonald in his ground floor suite of rooms, being tended to by his faithful housekeeper, Millicent. MacDonald was obviously delighted to receive his visitor. "Sit doon, laddie. Thank ye for coming," he declared enthusiastically, attempting rather vainly, to push himself to a standing position on Wiggins' entrance to the room.

Magnus MacDonald was a bulldog of a man in his late fifties. Scottish by birth and granite hard in nature, he had worked his way up within the Metropolitan Police, over a thirty-year career, from beat uniform to Superintendent of Scotland Yard CID. His razor-sharp intelligence, aligned with strong leadership qualities and limitless drive, had made his career a successful one. MacDonald's man-management skills were always rewarded with the dedication of all who worked under his command. His unerring sense of justice and brutal, sometimes ferocious will, had made him the scourge of London's criminal underworld for more than a generation. He still regarded the City as his, and its denizens, his to serve and protect.

"Please do not rise, Sir," pleaded Wiggins, moving swiftly forward and putting a firm but gentle hand on MacDonald's shoulder. He could see that even this slight effort had put terrible stress upon the older man. '*Obviously, his injuries are more far-reaching than even I had imagined,*' he thought with regret.

"Mr Wiggins is correct, Sir. Don't strain yourself," added Millicent, smiling her silent appreciation to Wiggins. "Doctor Ward has insisted that he gets as much rest as possible."

"Stop yer fussing woman. I'm more than capable of standing to greet a colleague," responded MacDonald in his usual, somewhat affected, curmudgeonly manner. "Come and sit next to me, Digger, sorry, *Detective Chief Inspector!*" Wiggins laughed at the mention of his old moniker, and the two erstwhile colleagues shook hands heartily. Millicent's slightly too pointed nose sniffed the air as if catching the scent of something unpleasant as she departed the room. "I shall fetch you some tea, gentlemen."

"And perhaps, some of your wonderful Dundee cake, please, Millicent," winked MacDonald, shifting in his chair to alleviate the discomfort of his pressure sores. The housekeeper left the room. "You know Bert, I developed a taste for the King o' fruitcakes during my early twenties when I spent a few months living in Dundee." The old man seemed lost in thought for a few seconds. "It was whilst I was there that the rail bridge spanning the River Tay collapsed during an awfy storm. Back in seventy-nine, it was. Killed every single man, woman, and child on a train that wiz, unfortunately, crossing at that precise moment. That section of the bridge collapsed, and the carriages plummeted into the dark depths of the fast-flowing, unforgiving river. Seventy-five of them in all. Very few of the bodies were ever recovered. Imagine laddie, ten minutes either way and all those lives wid hae been spared.

Providence or tragedy. Life is aboot fine margins as well we know, Bert." MacDonald looked to the floor and shook his head.

'*Who knows what memories are haunting him,*' ruminated Wiggins. '*So many cases, so many deaths, so many regrets of lives almost saved.*'

MacDonald shifted position again, pulling himself back to the present and recovering his composure. "Millicent is a treasure, no doubt about it," he announced, changing the subject, "but don't let her know I said so," chuckled MacDonald mischievously. "The board of the Demosthenes have very generously relaxed their regulations regarding having women on the premises in Millicent's case. Given my injuries, and the circumstances in which they were administered...," MacDonald flinched involuntarily at the memory, "...together with my need for almost constant care, the Club elders took a rather charitable view towards my situation. Not only have they provided me with these rooms at an affordable rent, but they have also allowed me the privilege of having Millicent visit each day to see to my needs, although, even in these more enlightened times, she does still need to enter by the tradesman's entrance. Rules are rules you ken. I have also engaged a doctor at a reasonable cost to attend to my needs twice a week. A Doctor Maxwell Ward is his name. A lovely wee fella who has the most amazing bedside manner, and better still, warm hands," winked MacDonald.

'*Still, there must be a degree of humiliation for such a man in this position,*' sympathised Wiggins. "Charitable of the board members indeed, Sir, and most forward thinking. I wonder if Boodles or Whites will follow suit?" he wondered, opening his leather, brass lined cigarette case and offering it to the Scotsman.

"You refer to the prospect of women members? I hardly think that such an eventuality will occur within oor lifetimes, laddie," reflected MacDonald as he picked a double gold-banded cigarette from within the case. Wiggins leant forward and lit the Scotsman's cigarette and then, in turn, his own. The gold-banded cigarettes were made to order for Wiggins by Fribourg and Treyer's in The Haymarket. The blend was a subtle mixture of Virginia and Turkish tobaccos and Wiggins had found lately that he could no longer smoke anything else, so flavoursome did he find the mixture.

"A very pleasant smoke this," remarked MacDonald, exhaling towards the ornately plastered ceiling rose in the centre of his room whilst examining the tip of the cigarette. "There's no nicer way to die, smoking yer'sel to death," cherished the Scotsman gleefully. Wiggins considered this statement and decided against contesting MacDonald's assertion. '*Peacefully in bed, or perhaps whilst napping in one's garden with birds a twitter and the Sun warming one's face,*' he thought would be his chosen way of demise.

Millicent swiftly returned carrying a tray upon which sat a teapot, snugly covered in what Wiggins suspected was a personally hand-knitted cosy, two china cups on matching saucers, a delicate sugar bowl with silver nips and a small jug of warmed milk. This she placed carefully on a table which separated the two police officers.

"Thank you, Millicent," declared MacDonald. Wiggins nodded his appreciation. "The Cake?" enquired MacDonald with a quizzical raise of an eyebrow which accentuated the deeply lined furrows that crisscrossed his forehead like a railway intersection. He was a huge admirer of Millicent's bakery skills, particularly when she turned them towards the almond topped fruit cake for which he held such fondness.

"Presently," sniffed Millicent. "I'm not one of those octopup things. I can only carry so much at one time, Mr Mac!"

Wiggins chuckled at her mispronunciation and the tone of her reply. This was the first time he had heard this term of familiarity between the two, and he inwardly remarked on how like an old married couple they had become over the long course of their association. Millicent straightened her apron and spun on her heels, with a sniff to the ceiling and stalked off towards the adjoining scullery in a cloud of admonishment. Once gone, MacDonald admitted, "I couldna' dae withoot her."

Wiggins removed the cosy, took the lid from the teapot, and stirred the tea within, six times clockwise and six times anti-clockwise. He then replaced the lid and cosy and carefully poured each of them a cup of tea.

"So, what of the world of Scotland Yard laddie? What news do you have?" asked the Scotsman taking the proffered cup from Wiggins, who noted a tremor in MacDonald's hand.

Wiggins settled himself and began. "Radasiliev is in the wind I am afraid to inform you. The Russian appears to have disappeared into thin air, though we feel that a recent murder that we are looking into may bear the hallmarks of his involvement." He took a sip of tea and relished its taste. "We are also currently investigating a most mysterious case. That of a man buried to the neck in Highgate Wood, and seemingly having been stoned to death at the site."

MacDonald spluttered in surprise and took the teacup from his lips. "Gruesome but interesting. Tell me more."

Wiggins hesitated, weighing up the appropriateness of sharing too much detail with a man who, although up to recently, his superior officer, was now, to all intents and purposes a civilian. MacDonald sensed his hesitancy. "Dinnae worry laddie, I can assure you, I am as safe as the Old Lady of Threadneedle Street. Maybe safer."

"Of course, Sir," apologised Wiggins, momentarily ashamed at his brief misgivings as to the honesty of this bravest of men. He cleared his throat and continued. "The body was positioned with an upturned bucket placed over the head, buried upright in a copse within the woods. It was surrounded by a circle of nineteen stones which have been forensically shown to have been the weapons of murder. The brutality inflicted upon the individual was savage and sickening in its violence."

MacDonald nodded his appreciation of the gravity of the crime, his detective's mind was searching for some deep forgotten bell that was ringing distantly in his head. Just then Millicent re-entered bearing two bone china plates, each laden with a generous slab of resplendent fruit cake. "Just the one slice each now," she warned. "I have to keep some for Mr Pyke and that lovely Doctor Watson when they calls around on Sunday." Wiggins raised both eyebrows in wonder. '*Well, who would have thought it!*'

While Millicent made herself busy elsewhere, each man took a bite of the rich, moist Dundee cake. "Buried vertically you say?" asked MacDonald, brushing some errant crumbs from his waistcoat lapels.

"Yes, Sir. With a tin wash pale placed over the head," confirmed Wiggins.

"Most intriguing," mused MacDonald, washing down the last of his cake with a slug of tea. "Look to our records, Bert. Something within tells me that I have heard of such a thing, but I cannae call to mind exactly where or when."

"I shall make a note to do so," affirmed Wiggins.

"And what of the Russian?" asked MacDonald, leaning forward keenly. "Radasiliev is no doubt a madman, but one of incredible influence and power. One only needs to recall the incidents at the Russian Embassy to comprehend his powers over the minds of others. Let us not forget that he left a building full of formerly high-functioning professional diplomatic staff, a veritable asylum of crazed lunatics." MacDonald placed his teacup carefully back upon its saucer. "I have heard that he consorts with demons and rapes our women," spat the Scotsman vehemently.

"Both Pyke and I can attest to his mesmeric powers and Dante Van Hoon, who continues to assist us with investigations on occasion, is of the opinion that he is a practitioner of the dark arts, capable of summoning demons, not only from within ourselves but also from, how shall I put it … deeper realms," responded Wiggins, carefully moving a few stray crumbs from his trouser leg back onto the plate. "The recent incident I referred to earlier was down in Kent and smells more than slightly of the Russian. A man murdered his wife by ramming knitting needles into her ears. We are looking into the incident presently."

"Sounds like the work of this Russian devil, to be sure. I do not doubt that you will prevail, laddie." MacDonald paused. "And, what of yourself? I was somewhat disappointed that you refused my vacant position when it was offered," he prodded. "You were the obvious and natural choice laddie. You have every quality required of a top-ranking detective. You have acute intelligence, strong leadership qualities, you are brave, inspiring to your men and hae an inner drive that rivals even my own. You are forensic in your thinking and attention to detail and your powers of deduction, as one would expect considering your background, are well honed. You realise, no doubt, that you were my recommendation as my successor. Why then did you no accept?"

Wiggins gently placed his half-drained teacup upon its saucer and deliberated for a few seconds. He picked his words carefully. "Much as I was flattered by your recommendation, Sir, I concluded that those very strengths which you have just outlined, serve our community best from my current position. I am no administrator, nor could I endure the political shenanigans that I have seen drown you in frustration. My strengths lie in solving crime, of digging out clues, and for me to continue to do that, I need to be active in the field, leading my men. Besides, who on Earth else could possibly control Jem Pyke?"

MacDonald laughed. "You are no doubt correct aboot Pyke, a harder individual I have never met in thirty years, but still I think you underestimate your ability to manage from above. The position brings its rewards."

Wiggins hesitated before replying. "I do not doubt my ability to carry out the role as such Sir, it is more that I recognise that for now, I best serve the City from where I am. Perhaps at a future date when I can physically no longer continue the chase."

"Perhaps," agreed MacDonald, somewhat enigmatically. "But new blood had to be brought in. I am an invalid, currently bound to bed, quarters and wheelchair. Lestrade is retired to a smallholding in Kent. Abberline is seventy-five years old and enjoying what life he has left down on the coast in Bournemouth and Edmund Reid? Well, Reid could charitably be referred to as leading a life of eccentricity from his self-styled Ranch on the seafront at Herne Bay. Even Commissioner Gregson only has a couple of years' service remaining but could easily retire at any given time." The Scotsman paused for effect. "You, laddie, are the best we've got. Our hope for the future."

Wiggins shifted uncomfortably in his chair and decided to top up both teacups from the pot. MacDonald smiled benignly at Wiggins' obvious discomfort. He decided a slight change of subject was in order. "You may have heard rumours over the years that I was involved in some Government work?"

Startled, Wiggins nodded, his attention now pricked by this unsolicited comment. "I had heard some such rumour, Sir." Wiggins was intrigued. Was he finally about to hear the truth regarding the myths that surrounded the great Magnus MacDonald?

"They are true ... to a degree," confirmed the Scotsman. "You are aware, no doubt of the Secret Service Bureau?" MacDonald observed Wiggins closely.

"Indeed," answered Wiggins, now completely fascinated. He drew himself forward in his chair. MacDonald had him hooked. "A Home Security counterintelligence service set up a few years ago to protect British democracy from infiltration from foreign powers, most prominently the Germans and to a lesser degree the Irish."

"Correct, laddie. I am impressed. The first chief was William Melville, who handed the torch over to yours truly a couple of years ago. Seems they have a penchant for Directors whose surnames begin with the letter 'M'," laughed MacDonald.

"Wiggins dropped what was left of his Dundee cake onto the plate he was holding in his other hand. He was stunned. '*MacDonald, head of the SSB. This is unbelievable,*' he thought. '*He must be privy to the most sensitive intelligence and matters of national interest.*'

"Close yer mooth laddie, ye look like a Pitlochry salmon leaping the ladder," joked MacDonald. Wiggins took a long draught of now tepid tea and tried to regain his composure. MacDonald continued. "My former position not only enabled me to enjoy the comfort and safety of my current surroundings but also still affords me some privileged access to highly sensitive information. The real reason I asked you to call today was to tell you that beyond any doubt, and mark my words, laddie, *any doubt*, that bastard King has the bubonic plague virus in his possession."

"But we have checked, we have assurances," Wiggins stuttered. The authorities have assured us that the contagion remains safe within the Cruciform Building, Sir," his voice trailed off. He was no longer sure of anything.

MacDonald leaned further forward. "Believe me, whatever is locked up in that Building in Euston, it is *not* the virus. It may be pond water, heather honey, bull's piss, or a mixture of all three for all I know, but it is not the virus. King has it. I advise that you get whatever is left in the Cruciform Building to Van Hoon, he more than anyone else I know, will be able to tell you exactly what it is."

Wiggins sat back. "I have only this afternoon, laid out a plan of attack regarding this matter. Jem Pyke is currently *digging through the filth* as he likes to put it, to find a location for King, and I intend to apply for a warrant enabling a search of the Cruciform Building tomorrow."

MacDonald nodded his head, his hands raised to his upper lip, fingers touching as if in prayer. "Excellent. Let Pyke do his dirty work, although I suspect King is somewhere within the environs of Chinatown where he feels safe and protected. As for the warrant and the judge, forget them. Go to the Cruciform directly and tell them I sent you. I will make a few calls to a few people as a matter of urgency. As for tomorrow, do it today!" Wiggins nodded. How quickly he had forgotten how impressive MacDonald's clarity of thinking and appetite for action were. He shook the Scotsman's hand and thanked him. "No need, lad. Thank *you*," replied MacDonald. "Call me tomorrow."

Wiggins shouted his thanks to Millicent as he headed for the front door of MacDonald's apartment. He turned to say one more thing to the Scot but saw that he was holding his index finger to his lips. "Not another word, laddie. Pity your surname does'nae start with an 'M.' There is another vacancy I could recommend." The old Scotsman winked knowingly. Wiggins shook his head and left the Demosthenes Club in a bewildered but energised mood.

Chapter 6 - The Contagion

Wiggins arrived at the Cruciform Building having called ahead earlier in the day to arrange an appointment. He felt sure that MacDonald would already have spoken to his contacts within the Home Office to help smooth his progress as he had promised. He was greeted by a fresh-faced young attendant who radiated an eagerness to please that bordered on annoying. '*The experience of veterans like Charlie Schoon and his colleagues has obviously given way to a fresh influx of youth and enthusiasm,*' noted Wiggins, unconvinced as to whether this development constituted progress or regression. The Detective introduced himself and the young security guard ushered him through the gothic architecture of the Cruciform's entrance foyer, and thereafter, up several flights of marble-clad stairs towards the office of the Institute Director, Professor Ericson Abel. The youthful attendant knocked on the oak office door and turned a nervous smile towards Wiggins, who recognised an air of anxiety playing on the young man's freckled features. Wiggins returned the young man's smile in what he hoped was a reassuring fashion.

"Come!" came the authoritative voice from within. The young attendant entered the room and announced in a quavering voice, "Detective Chief Inspector Wiggins of Scotland Yard CID to see you, Sir."

"Thank you, Hopkins." Professor Ericson Abel was a tall, slender man of late middle age. He sported a trim goatee beard and a large waxed moustache, curled at each end in the fashion of a Persian slipper. Although his cheeks were heavily pockmarked from the scourge of acne he had endured as a young man, Wiggins could not help but admire the neatness of the man's grooming. The professor extended his hand. "Chief Inspector Wiggins, how delightful to meet you." The Director's handshake was flaccid and weak, almost as if he were afraid to touch the hand of another man.

"And you, Professor. I take it you are aware of the purpose of my visit?"

Abel indicated that they should both sit. "Yes, indeed Inspector, Mr MacDonald's influence continues to reach to the loftiest of heights. However, I must reiterate what I told your officers at the time of the incident. I can assure you that nothing has been removed from our secure laboratory. The contagion, as you and your colleagues refer to it, is safely secured within its customary chamber, under close guard and lock and key. I can guarantee you categorically of that." Abel stroked his goatee in what Wiggins regarded as a rather nervous manner.

'Perhaps he's not so sure after all,' pondered Wiggins, noting the academic's indecisive body language. "None the less, Professor, three men, all in your employ, are missing and presumed dead. We have been informed by reliable sources within the national security forces that there is robust evidence to suggest that the virus has fallen into the hands of enemies of the state."

Abel was momentarily taken aback at the confidence of Wiggins' statement and the eloquence of the detective's reply. Wiggins could see the Professor stiffen and a slight flush rise from under his highly starched collar. He decided to push the point. "May I see for myself, Professor? If only to put my inquisitive mind at rest."

"This is most irregular, Inspector," blustered Abel. Wiggins allowed a pointed silence to do his work for him. "... but I suppose, given the circumstances, I could make an exception," acquiesced the Professor before making a call to the secure basement laboratory to herald their visit. The two men proceeded to the basement, making small talk as they proceeded. Wiggins remarked on the labyrinthine nature of the Cruciform Building whilst Abel commented on how demanding modern police work must be. Despite the amicable nature of the exchange, Wiggins could sense a rising disquiet, possibly even resentment from the Professor. As they approached the steel doors to the secure laboratory, Professor Abel waved a hand of acknowledgement towards the two guards who stood watch over the door. Wiggins noted the uneasy glance that was exchanged between the two men.

"Thank you, Jones," instructed Abel as the more senior looking of the two men produced a ring of keys and proceeded to unlock the heavy steel door. Wiggins and the Institute Director strode into a large and extremely well-equipped laboratory. Floor and walls gleamed with pristinely clean, white ceramic tiles, interspersed by floor to ceiling glazed walnut presentation cabinets. Within the cabinets, Wiggins could see glass jars which contained a diverse and somewhat gruesome array of preserved anatomical samples, of both animal and human origin. Long workbenches covered with reports, test tubes and other chemical paraphernalia stretched the length of the laboratory. Each workbench sported a row of Bunsen burners. Despite it being comprehensively equipped, the room was populated by only a single, white-coated, laboratory technician who stooped studiously over a large binocular compound microscope, lost in his work. Professor Abel looked around the room, somewhat confused.

"Is there something amiss, Professor Abel?" asked Wiggins, sensing the older man's obvious bewilderment. The solitary technician, his back towards the two men, was seemingly oblivious of their presence. He continued about his work, as though he were still alone in the room. He lifted a test tube and gently shook it from side to side, nodding slightly as the contents turned from viscous grey to a dull ochre.

"Why, this laboratory should be a hive of activity, Inspector! There are normally at least a dozen technicians and researchers at work here. I simply do not understand." The Director moved towards the lone technician. "You there, my good fellow! Can you explain? Where are your colleagues?"

The lab coat remained hunched over his instruments and answered without interrupting his work. "I gave each of them the evening off." The voice was modulated and confident, but so low as to be almost inaudible. "What with the weather being so clement and their tasks so tiresome."

Abel spluttered. "I beg your pardon! What is the meaning of this outrage? I gave no such order." The Director was now feeling an increasing sense of unease which was rapidly transforming into anger. It began to dawn on him that this may be a perilous situation. "Who the devil are you, man?" he demanded.

The technician gently replaced a test tube in a wooden rack and turned to face the two men, whipping the white lab coat from his shoulders as he did so. "I am, Van Hoon!" he declared dramatically, bowing as one would before starting a Viennese waltz. The Dutchman removed a small white linen cap from his head and a tumble of blue-black hair cascaded onto his shoulders. Both men took an involuntarily step backwards. Professor Abel gave out a small gasp. The man before him was the most striking individual he had ever set eyes upon. Over six feet tall, with the lithe frame of an athlete and the confident bearing of one high born. Fractal scarring etched the left-hand side of his face, a treelike pattern that stretched downwards to his neck. Abel recognised the scarring for what it was, the effect of early-onset leprosy. The Professor recoiled inwardly at the thought. The Director of one of London's most highly regarded scientific institutes would have been utterly amazed had he known that Van Hoon had developed an anti-bacterial solution that controlled the spread of his condition. The Leper had contracted the disease whilst in Argentina through exposure to an infected Armadillo upon which he had been practising one of his passions, that of taxidermy. He would also have been astonished had he known that rather than abhor his condition, Van Hoon actually embraced it and regarded it as a blessing. The enigmatic Croesus kept a household whose inner guard consisted entirely of lepers, each of whom had been plucked from East London's leper hospitals. Each of these *Pestilent*, as Van Hoon referred to them, had their condition contained, through Van Hoon's scientific genius, and were used by their employer as spies and enforcers working within the dark underworld of London. As Van Hoon was often heard to say, "Who is going to stop and question a leper?"

Despite Van Hoon's leprous scarring, the most startling feature of this stranger's handsome face were his eyes, one of which was a hypnotic emerald green, the other a dead milky-white orb. Wiggins threw Van Hoon a withering look. "What are you doing here, Van Hoon?"

The Dutchman's face exploded with a wide, playful grin. "Why, good afternoon, Chief Inspector. Please forgive my little pretence. You know I find it irresistible to stage a little drama, a bit of theatrical scene stealing, you might say. A mutual friend recommended that I attend and that I may be of some use."

"Of course, MacDonald," reasoned Wiggins.

"You know this man, Inspector?" interjected Abel, looking accusingly from the police officer to Van Hoon. Wiggins nodded. "I do indeed, no need to call your guards, Professor. Mr Van Hoon is an old friend of the Police Force, and, I must inform you, a most talented scientist."

Van Hoon bowed once again in acknowledgement. "Surely, you mean *the* most talented scientist, my dear Chief Inspector?" countered Van Hoon with a wink of his emerald green eye. The leper turned towards Abel. "My goodness! What a glorious set of mustachios, Prof. You don't mind if I call you Prof, do you? Of course, you don't. You simply must tell me what brand of mustachio wax you use. It really does produce such resplendent results!"

Wiggins could see that Abel was dumbstruck. "Why exactly are you here, Sir?" he inquired purposefully, trying desperately to exert some dominance over this startling interloper.

By way of answering, Van Hoon lifted the test tube of ochre-coloured liquid and held it to a powerful desk lamp. "Why to help you, of course, Prof. See how the solution appears cloudy in the light, gentlemen?"

Both men peered at the liquid. Abel's scientific mind had now been diverted from the bizarre presence of this remarkable looking stranger to focus upon the experiment displayed before him. "I see, Sir, but I do not see the relevance. What is the purpose of this exhibition?"

Van Hoon poured the contents of the test tube into a beaker and handed it to the Director. "Be extremely careful, Prof Abel. You have in your grasp a contaminated solution of the bubonic plague virus."

Professor Abel was visibly shaken by Van Hoon's words. "But I simply do not understand. Is it your contention that the sample of virus that we keep in this secure environment has in some way been contaminated? This is preposterous! Impossible, I will not have it, gentlemen!"

Van Hoon laughed. "None the less, Sir, I can categorically assure you that not only has it been contaminated, perhaps diluted would be the more accurate description, but also that some of the virus has been removed. Approximately half of the volume of the sample you once had has been replaced with another liquid." The Professor looked closely at the sample. Wiggins could sense that the calm authority of Van Hoon was beginning to sow a seed of doubt in Abel's mind. He peered intently at the contents.

"Urine, Professor," declared Van Hoon. "Human urine, no less." Wiggins exchanged a knowing glance with Van Hoon. "And I would wager that we already know the identity of the donator."

Chapter 7 - The Prospect

"An evening digging through the filth," declared Pyke with undisguised relish, rubbing his hands together in anticipation. The action created a noise that Constable Murray found unpleasantly reminiscent of two sandpaper blocks rasping together. "Ain't nothing quite like dredging through the dirt of this fine City in search of information, Murray old boy." Pyke clapped his hands together and his face lit up in gleeful expectation of the evening's work that lay ahead of them.

Pyke, Murray, and Bunce sat in the rear of a Police Wagon driven by the redoubtable Constable Sykes. "Let's begin down Limehouse, Sykesy," instructed Pyke. "Last we heard of King, he was down Shadwell ensconced in that Opium House of his in the Basin. I reckon it's as good a place to start as any."

"As you wish, Sarge. Shadwell Basin it is," confirmed Sykes, releasing the brake of the large black van, and pulling out on to the Embankment.

Murray looked at the shoes he was wearing. Both he and Bunce were dressed in civilian clothing, or '*in civvies,*' as Pyke had ordered. Murray looked at his colleague and sensed that Bunce also felt a certain unease embarking upon such a mission out of uniform. He had not expected to feel as exposed as he did, realising that the dark blue serge offered greater psychological protection than he had ever before realised. Pyke seemed to have instinctively read his colleague's thoughts. "Can't be havin' you lads walking into dens of iniquity in full mufti now, can we? The places would clear in an instant. Would be like the Mary Celeste before you could say, Jack Robinson. Besides, so long as we are armed with warrant cards and pistols, we have nothing to fear."

Bunce swallowed what appeared to Pyke to be an extremely sharp object. The younger of the two constables was less experienced than Murray. Meanwhile, Murray's mind kept drifting to the fate of his colleague and friend Constable William Potts, shredded to death at the hands of the savage maniac, Doctor Joseph Bleak. He looked across at Jem Pyke who was fishing a cigar out of some unseen pocket and wondered, not for the first time, at how this man could have single-handedly confronted and conquered the inhuman Beast. He had witnessed the battle first hand, but still, he found it incomprehensible that such bravery existed within a human heart.

Murray coughed, and, in an effort to break the tension asked, "Have you met the new Super, yet, Sarge?"

Pyke shook his head whilst re-lighting that afternoon's cigar. He threw the spent vesta through the open window of the van and screwed his eyes against the ensuing billow of smoke that blew back in his face. "Not yet, me old china, but I have a feeling that particular meeting ain't too far off."

"I hear he's from somewhere up North," chipped in Bunce, glad of the distraction the conversation was affording. Pyke grunted. "So, I believe, though what a Northerner can possibly know about policing this cesspit, I'll never know. All stolen bicycles, flat caps and cats in trees up there I'd imagine," winked Pyke. Murray and Bunce both stifled a snigger. "Hopefully, he'll leave us alone to deal with the day-to-day while he pushes a pen and handles the Commissioner and the politicians."

"I've heard he's a bit more hands-on than that, Sarge. Nosher reckons he's a bit of an 'ard nut who likes to get his hands dirty," added Murray.

"Bleedin' hell, that's the last thing we need," puffed Pyke. "We'll just have to show him how the land lies, lads. Happens he won't last the course. Old Mac left a large pair of boots to fill, make no mistake."

A brief silence filled the wagon. "Why didn't the Guvnor get the job, Sarge?" enquired Bunce, scratching his scalp through his flimsy curls. "Surely, Mr Wiggins is more than qualified?"

Pyke leant forward towards Bunce until his oft-broken nose almost touched that of the young Constable and, feigning deadly seriousness, rumbled, "Because he couldn't stand to be too far away from them lovely curls of yours, sonny." Pyke grabbed Bunce by the back of the neck and playfully ruffled the young man's hair.

"Stop it, Sarge, leave off," urged Bunce, attempting to squirm out of Pyke's grasp. Pyke and Murray laughed, and Bunce sat back in his seat, arms crossed, his stern, reddening face failing to disguise his chagrin.

"Here we are, lads," announced Sykes over his shoulder. "You want me to wait here, Sarge?"

"Pull around the corner out of sight, Sykesy, and keep the engine idling. We ain't gonna be long," replied Pyke springing out of the van. Murray could sense that Pyke was in his element, searching for leads amongst the dregs of London's dockyards, revelling in the underlying danger. The three policemen walked down Russell's Wharf, a chill wind blowing up from the Thames, bringing the smell of mud and waste to their nostrils. Pyke raised his collar against the unfriendly weather. "Handy for the Prospect of Whitby," he half-shouted to his companions indicating the welcoming lights of the old wharf-side pub. "Maybe we can grab a quick half on the way back to Sykesy. We are out of uniform after all. What do you say, lads?" Two non-committal shrugs from his companions did little to dampen Pyke's spirits.

He led them down the narrow wynd of Pelican Steps to the shingle beach which crunched underfoot, and up some river eroded timber steps leading to Pakapuh, the erstwhile opium house, restaurant and brothel that had been the last known hideaway of Mr King. A short pier ran outward from the building, its stout timber posts driven deep into the riverbed. Pyke noted the numerous chains that hung from the underside of the pier, swaying with the ebb of the river, clanking together in a ghostly xylophonic symphony. He knew exactly what those chains had been used for over the years. A tremor of disgust rippled through him as he thought of the countless poor souls who had come to an unimaginably horrific end at the hand of the merciless Chinaman and the embrace of the rising tide of the Thames.

Pyke tried the rear door of the premises and was surprised to find it yielded at his touch. One slight push and the door fell inwards, parting easily from its hinges. Pyke quickly realised that the door had previously been breached by some great force and that someone had merely propped it against its splintered jamb in a pretence of it being affixed. This was an unexpected finding and his senses were now on full alert, his army training springing immediately to the fore. He looked at his two companions and put a finger to his lips to indicate that they should proceed in silence. His fingers pointed over each shoulder indicating to the constables that they should position themselves behind him forming an arrowhead. The first room of the building was ostensibly a restaurant, a front for the true, nefarious purpose of the establishment. The room looked as if a hurricane had struck it. Every item of furniture was smashed and broken, the serving counter obliterated into shards of timber. The door from the restaurant to the kitchen lay on the floor as if it had been wrenched from its frame by a battering ram. Pyke scanned the area quickly, signalling that Murray and Pyke draw their pistols and stay close. The kitchen was also in ruin with every utensil, pot and pan scattered around the room and shelves ripped from walls. Four large carving knives were impaled almost up to their hilts in a robust timber column which supported the upper floors. Pyke's eyes widened, and his lips pursed at this sight. He reached out, grasped one of the knives, tensed his muscles and pulled with all his might. The knife was so deeply embedded that it did not budge, the timber gripping its long blade as a miser would a farthing. '*Bleedin' King Arthur couldn't pull that bugger out of there,*' thought Pyke, reminiscing of the stories his blacksmith father would tell him as a child about Excalibur and the unyielding stone. Pyke wondered at what sort of monstrous force could have driven these knives home so deeply. '*Surely nothing human?*'

His thoughts were interrupted by the nearby muffled sound of shambling footsteps. The three police officers turned about face, pistols raised towards the diminutive figure of an old oriental woman approaching from the rear room. Her tiny slippered feet shuffled forward in short skating steps that kicked remnants of broken glass and crockery before her. Pyke nodded to his colleagues and indicated that they should lower their firearms, confident that this hunched, frail woman offered no threat. The little lady looked up at the face of Pyke and then in turn to those of Bunce and Murray. She smiled broadly, her two remaining teeth resembling chipped shards of amber. She bowed at each, in turn, her slits of eyes almost lost within her heavily wrinkled skin. Skin that resembled a deeply cracked walnut shell. Pyke indicated the destruction that surrounded them. "What happened here, mother?"

The old crone chuckled, increasing the countless deep lines that tapestried her flat, round face. "Big boy, he come back. He velly angry." Her laugh increased in pitch as she continued, her words and laughter intermingling. "He shout and shout for Mr King, but Mr King he not here. Big boy get mad and break the house. You wan' egg fried rice? I get you egg fried rice. Velly good. Velly tasty tops."

Pyke shook his head. "Not hungry, darlin' and who is this Big Boy you speak of and why exactly was he after King?"

The old lady squealed with laughter and clapped her hands. "Big Boy Chin. He tear the place up. Velly funny. Velly funny!" She was now bent double, her tiny, heavily veined hands clasping her knees.

Pyke turned to Murray and Bunce. "Hercules Chin, King's giant assassin. We thought him to be dead. Last time I saw that monster, he was falling backwards into the Thames with one of me' bullets in his chest."

"Can't be true Sarge, can it?" questioned Bunce. He could feel a shudder of primitive fear travel the length of his body at the mere mention of Chin's name. The thought that the Chinese Grendel may still be stalking the streets of the City made his scalp crawl. If he were alive, how could it be that no one had alerted them to his presence? A man of his monstrous size could surely not hide from six million people. He felt a cramp grab and twist his stomach at the prospect. "He's dead ain't he? Tell me he's dead Sarge."

Pyke stared once more at the deeply embedded knives. "I wouldn't rule anything out where that brute is concerned." He felt a vigorous tugging on his sleeve and looked down to see the beaming face of the old Chinese lady. "No eggs! Big Boy smash dem eggs," her voice rising in hilarity. "Noodles! I make you *best* noodles police man!" she urged, nodding enthusiastically.

Pyke shook his head. He was worried. '*Why was Hercules Chin pursuing King? How could he have survived being shot at such a close distance? What did this all mean? Where was the giant now?*' He realised that he needed Wiggins to help him make sense of this new development. A sudden thought hit Pyke "Was Chin alone, mother?" he asked. The wizened, shrunken woman shook her head "No understand. You wan' noodles?"

Murray intervened, “More than one?” he asked raising his fingers and counting down from five.

“Two! Yes, two!” exclaimed the old woman, dancing tiny hops of glee. “Big Boy and one more Big Boy, but not so big. His face all messed up ugly. Bad face. Bad eye. Bad neck,” she feigned disgust and drew a finger across her throat. “He even more ugly than Big Boy!” she squealed with laughter, delighted at her own observation.

Pyke groaned “Not one, but two giant monsters on the loose. Just what we bloody need.”

“Sounds like Chin’s companion has a scarred throat by the motions she’s making, Sarge,” added Murray. Bunce winced involuntarily at the image. “Perhaps an ex-convict?”

A sudden surge of dread hit Pyke. A thought had sprung into his head. He looked around, instinctively on alert. “Is Big Boy still here, Mother?” he whispered, indicating to the old lady that she should also lower her voice.

The old lady merely laughed. “You want pipe, boys?” she asked. “Fat Boy, he in back, he make you pipe. Velly good pipe. Even better than noodles!” The old lady grabbed Pyke’s wrist and pulled him through into what he instantly recognised as an opium den. He was surprised at the strength of the old crone’s grasp. The room was dark, clad in timber panels and lined with wall-mounted bunks from floor to ceiling. Each bunk was draped with a sepia stained curtain. Every surface in the room was stained with the deep brown oily residue typical of an opium den. The room stank of dampness, depravity, opium, and despair. The floor was littered with shabby discoloured cushions forming additional space for the helpless and doomed. The room, however, was sparsely occupied. Only a handful of addicts lay scattered around the den, all in various states of consciousness, some completely comatose. Pyke guessed that King’s departure had cauterised the opium den’s supply of the drug and that business was gradually ebbing towards a deathly extinction. In a corner of the room, squatting behind a low table, sat the almost spherical figure of Wang the pipe master. He lifted his rotund head at the entrance of the police officer. His heavy eyelids raised to reveal a pair of opaquely glazed eyes, pupils dilated to pinpoints. He held out a long cherry wood, flute shaped opium pipe, its end chamber already full of poisonous cargo, and turned it, offering the reed-like stem towards Pyke. “You wan’ pipe? Best pipe in London. First pipe always free for Policeman.”

Pyke raised an eyebrow inquisitively at the Chinaman’s last comment, trying to contextualise its relevance. “Not for me, fat boy. What I need is information.” He crouched down in front of the oily ball of blubber. He could hear Bunce behind him coughing and spluttering at the heavy, acrid odour of opium. Pyke looked into the vacant eyes of Wang. “Where is King? Where is Chin?”

Wang rocked back and forth slightly, his clouded mind trying to comprehend the simplest of questions. He knew that King had gone, fled to the all-enveloping safety of Chinatown. He also remembered that Chin and the other giant had quarrelled. He recalled how, after Chin had ripped the building apart looking for Father King, the two giants had sat on the pier, their backs so big and wide that they seemed to block out the entire view of the South Bank. He remembered how the pale, heavily scarred man had lost patience with Chin's childish truculence and had eventually stalked off leaving the Chinaman sitting alone. After that, all was cloudy. He had a hazy memory of smoking opium with Chin. He also had a vague vision of a giant forearm, tightened by a leather strap, veins bulging, being pierced by a brass hypodermic. Blood and ecstasy. He remembered thinking '*Big Boy is back.*' He remembered feeling happy. He hiccupped and locked eyes with Pyke, attempting to focus and eventually doing so through one eye. "King gone. He go and no come back. Big Boy, he come looking. He gone too, all gone. Just me and grandma left."

Pyke could sense that Wang was lying. He grabbed Wang's tunic fiercely and slid the drug peddler's great bulk, effortlessly, towards him. "All of that I know, sunshine. You ain't making me feel very kindly disposed towards you." He gritted his teeth together and twisted the flimsy collar tightly. "Where *exactly* did he go?"

Wang shakily wiped beads of sweat from his fat rumpled brow. "He just go. He don't tell me. King never tell me anything. Me only make pipe. Me no need to know. He and all the others, they just go. Even the snake go."

Pyke shook his head in exasperation. "Which way did he go then? On the river or on the street? North, South, East, West?"

Wang's eyes lit up at the rise in Pyke's voice. "River, he go up river to City in a black boat with black sails," spat out the Chinaman with a note of satisfaction in his voice, pleased that he was able to recall the details and answer one of Pyke's threatening questions. Pyke slowly loosened his grip and flung Wang backwards, causing the Chinaman to tumble comically. Pyke stood and kicked at a prone figure sprawled on the floor. The unfortunate stirred and protested in a deep, but incomprehensible rumble. Pyke bent down and lifted the figure bodily by the collar. He was surprised at the weight of the opium eater, expecting a withered and wasted frame rather than the bulk that he now supported in his hands. The hair of the wretch was drenched in sweat and was plastered to his forehead, covering his eyes. An acrid stench of damp neglect hit his nostrils along with an oiliness he found hard to place. He felt at once revulsion and compassion for the wretched figure whose bulk hung loosely in his grasp. "Out of here now!" shouted Pyke, guiding the addict to the door with a kick of his boot in his rear end. The man stumbled forth and fell through the door, picked himself up and exited the building, steadying himself on the splintered door frame as he did so. The addict turned and threw Pyke a sullen look as he made his way across the cobbles, jaundiced eyes staring from a grime-covered face. Pyke felt a spark of recognition but soon dismissed it. He had encountered thousands of low life during his career. "Get the rest of this garbage out of here," he ordered, indicating the few occupied booths to Murray and Bunce. Yet he could not quite shake the thought that the yellowed eyes were those of someone he knew.

He began to circle the opium room, pulling back greasy curtains, peering into booths, repulsed by the stench of the damp and soiled bedding within. He had an uneasy feeling. His gut was telling him that something was wrong. His instincts were on high alert. He walked up to one of the walls, stared at it, his face no more than four inches from the timber panelling. He tapped the wall with his fore knuckles, searching for a secret door or perhaps a priest hole. He shrugged. Everything seemed solid enough. He rapped upon a few other panels with the same result before spotting an inscription scratched into the woodwork of one panel at about head height. The script was in minute lettering causing him to lean further forward, squinting, his nose almost touching the panel in an attempt to decipher the scrawled lettering. He was so close he could smell the dry timber. Only the half inch thickness of the timber boarding separated him from what was within the wall. The unseen form of Hercules Chin. The giant assassin stood concealed in a void within the wall directly in front of Pyke. The two men were separated only by a few inches of wood. Chin was nearly eight feet tall and was built like a mountain. The Underworld's most feared killer, his status as King's enforcer was legendary. Some called him Monster, some called him the Chinese Giant, but all feared this most brutal of killers. Countless necks had been snapped, countless backs broken by his unforgiving hands. Hands that had no barometer of their strength. A merciless, narcotic-addled colossus whose addiction was ruthlessly controlled by Mr King.

Chin held his breath, his expanded chest pressing against the inside of the timber wall lining. He could hear the scratching of Pyke's fingernail on the other side. His Cro-Magnon forehead rested against the inside face of the wooden panelling, his yellowing emotionless eyes staring through the nothingness of the void.

Pyke decided that the lettering was some form of Chinese graffiti. He scratched at the letters with his fingernail, digging out a glutinous brown residue in the process. Chin clenched his gargantuan fists, enjoying the physical movement. His eyes were dead, polluted with opium. He decided that if he heard another scratch, he would break the panelling to pieces and shatter the policeman's spinal column. He sniffed. Dust invaded his nostrils. He felt an overwhelming urge to sneeze.

Pyke smelled his finger. Tar. He was about to scratch at the hieroglyphics again when his hand was stayed by a call from Murray. "No one out here, Sarge!"

Pyke grunted, lowered his finger, and turned once more to look at the spherical Wang. He snorted in disgust. As he strode back out into the nearly obliterated kitchen area, his feet crunching broken glass beneath the soles of his boots, he heard the pleading voice of Wang following him. "You sure you no wan pipe? First one free for all Police. Just like always."

Pyke grunted his disgust and held up one finger to the old lady. "You have one day to leave this place, understand? One day, then you go! After that, this place will be razed to the ground." The diminutive Chinese woman nodded so vigorously that Pyke supposed her head may topple from her hunched shoulders. "One day. Me savvy. One day." She laughed so hard it developed into a breathless cackle. "You say hello to Big Boy for me, Mr Police. You see him soon." Pyke felt the hairs rise on his forearms in primal expectation.

Once the three policemen had left the building, Wang, the orbicular master of the Opium Den, stood unsteadily and swayed towards the graffiti scrawled wall that Pyke had been examining. He steadied his blubberous form with one hand whilst the other pushed a concealed section of the wall panelling which slowly creaked open to reveal the monstrous Hercules Chin within. Chin stooped and clambered out of the void, shaking dust and cobwebs from his head as he did so. He grunted at Wang who returned his surly greeting with the widest of smiles. "Policemen go. You wan' pipe big boy?"

Chin nodded his assent and slumped his massive body onto a large grubby cushion. Dust sprang forth and floorboards creaked under his immense weight. As Wang prepared the narcotic, Chin's clouded mind drifted back to Father King. How, after his return to Pakapuh with Friedrich, whose name had already been lost in the mist of his opium-infused memory, he had remained at the Opium House, confused and angry. Angry that he had not found King and confused as to why his giant Ingolstadtian saviour had deserted him.

Wang placed the lit pipe in Chin's gargantuan hand. Chin drew deeply, inhaling the opium which was his anchor. The anchor that the nefarious Mr King used to secure the continued obedience of his most valuable asset. King had arrived at Pakapuh soon after Friedrich's departure, having been alerted of Chin's return by a hastily sent telegram from Wang. On seeing King an enraged Chin had confronted an impassive King, who safe in the knowledge that Chin would soon, once more, be his to manipulate. The Shang twins, King's brotherly assassins, had fired a volley of darts heavily laden with tranquilisers at Chin who, despite his great strength had succumbed almost immediately, much to the delight of an ecstatic King. Since then, a combination of Machiavellian machinations and whispers on the part of King, as well as copious amounts of opium supplied by Wang, had remoulded Chin's mind to the point whereby he had been fully absorbed back into King's Family of Death. He was once again malleable and under the complete control of London's most evil man.

The three police officers carefully made their way back down the slime covered, river worn steps of Pakapuh pier and strode along a short stretch of densely pebbled foreshore towards Pelican Steps. Each of them noticed, with some distaste, that the shingle and stones were interspersed with thousands of tiny bone fragments. Each fragment had been rounded and polished by the constant ebb and flow of the great river. Pyke glanced once more at the numerous chains that swung from the underside pier and speculated upon the torturous deaths of which these bones bore testament.

"I feel like oiling me tonsils lads," announced Pyke. "Why don't we hop into the Prospect and see if we can pick up any more information on this Chinese maniac while we're here?" Pyke did not wait for an answer and pushed open the door of the neighbouring riverside watering hole. He was hit by a wall of sound and a cloud of heat that was in stark contrast to the unseasonal biting wind that drilled through Shadwell Basin. The three-hundred-year-old pub was, much to Pyke's delight, stocked full of cutthroats, dockside rats, footpads, and smugglers. Pyke could taste the alcohol in the air, the atmosphere rich with the malty tang of spirits and ale. A thick, glaucous haze of tobacco smoke filled the room. Laughter and raucous voices mixed with a continual clinking of glass and the light tinkling of an upright piano which was squeezed into the far corner of the pub. Pyke rolled his shoulders and cracked his neck. This was his territory. Here he was the hunter, the alpha male, the top of the food chain. He already felt uneasy eyes falling upon him. He sensed a nervous tension creep around the room and tasted a frisson of danger. He turned to Bunce and Murray. "Perhaps best if you stay outside, lads. One of you get Sykesy and ask him to stand guard with you." Pyke realised that the heavy-set presence of Sykes may prove invaluable to the constables should the need arise. He raised his voice just enough for the immediate clientele to hear him. "Anyone goes outside looking nervous, sling 'em in the paddy wagon, no questions asked. If they ain't guilty of something today, they were sure as hell guilty of something yesterday."

The two constables thankfully pushed their way back out into the fresh air whilst Pyke forced his way towards the bar through the throng. His shoe leather scuffed the ancient, beer-stained flagstone floor as he located a vacant gap at the bar and squeezed himself between a giant bear of a man with a close-shaven bullet of a head and a small simian figure in an ill-fitting suit. Both shifted uneasily at the invasive presence and salutary smile of the Detective Sergeant. Pyke signalled the barmaid's attention with a loud tapping of his cygnet ring against a brass bar tap. "Pint of Best and a drop of Irish please Sally."

The curvaceous Sally flashed a smile that revealed perhaps the most rotten set of teeth that Pyke could remember setting eyes upon. An uneven row of brown-stained irregular pegs that reminded him of an evening stroll through the Great Eastern Necropolis. She quickly returned with the two glasses. "On the 'ouse Jem. We ain't seen you round 'ere a while. I heard you been Beast slayin', saving all us poor woman folk from that savage monster," she flirted, eyelashes fluttering, shoulders dipped, flashing what she considered to be here most effective smile. 'Broken brown ale bottles rather than tombstones, perhaps,' mused Pyke with a hearty thanks and a wink that he hoped Sally would not find too encouraging.

Pyke took a long draught of his beer and slammed his glass on the bar. He turned his head towards the giant lummox with the nubbin head who was determinedly trying to avoid acknowledging his presence. As he did so, the small monkey-like man in the ill-fitting suit attempted to surreptitiously slide off his barstool and make his exit. "Stay exactly where you are Boniface," ordered Pyke, without shifting his eyes from the hulk next to him. "I'll need a word with you once I've finished with Stonesy here." Boniface resumed his place at the bar and lit a small thin cigar that only added to the oddity of his appearance.

"How's Mrs Stones and all the little 'uns Stonesy?" asked Pyke adopting his usual greeting when addressing the colossal skin tanner. He took another frothy slug of ale.

"Thriving, Sergeant Pyke, thriving thanks," rumbled Archibald Stones, hoping that not too many of the raucous pub's patrons had noticed that he was in conversation with Detective Sergeant Jem Pyke. Pyke knew that Mrs Stones was probably the most fecund woman in East London, despite having, in his opinion, one of the ugliest, not to mention rankest men in all of Smithfield as a husband. "Seven and countin' Sergeant Pyke," smiled Stones revealing a set of mahogany dentures that almost fell out of his mouth as he talked. Stones saw a flicker of mirth play across Pyke's face as he pushed his ridiculous false teeth back into place. "Well you knocked me last two teeth out the other month at Grimley's abattoir if you remember rightly, Sergeant Pyke," admonished Stones. "Her indoors was less than best pleased, I can tell you that for nuthin'!"

Pyke spluttered a laugh into his whisky. "Might have done you a favour there, Stonesy, old boy. She might take a dislike to the new toothless Mr Stones. No more little Stonesys for you."

Archibald Stones threw back his enormous head and roared with laughter. Pyke could smell the filth of the tannery waft from the hulk. "What is it you want, Sergeant Pyke? If it's The Heap, just don't ask me. You know I can never betray The Heap. Ever."

"Don't fret Stonesy, it ain't The Heap I'm a hunting today. I know where I can find him if I ever need him. After all, he ain't moved his gigantic saggy arse off that bench for the last eight years as far as I can tell." Pyke threw back his beer, slammed the empty tankard on the ring stained mahogany bar and wiped the back of his hand across his mouth. He leaned further in towards the foul-smelling tanner. "It's King that I want," he hissed, his whole demeanour changing. There was no mistaking the underlying threat in Pyke's voice.

A stunned Archibald Stones dropped his glass to the flagstone floor causing it to explode into a hundred tiny shards, dark rum spattering his grubby and bloody work boots. Pyke could see the colour drain from the big man's face. He heard a rustling noise directly behind him and reached backwards without turning around, to secure the diminutive simian form of Boniface who, at the mention of the Chinaman's name, was again stealthily attempting to slip his post. "Stay right where you are monkey boy," ordered Pyke, eyes remaining earnestly on Archibald Stones' now petrified face.

"I couldn't say, Sergeant Pyke," mumbled Stones. "I'm a Smithfields man really, just popped down here for a change of scenery. I don't know nuffin' about King, so help me God!"

Pyke looked at the bar and nodded, a motion that indicated that this had been the answer he had expected. Sally placed a refilled tankard in front of him and retreated swiftly, sensing a threatening cloud of danger looming over that small corner of the bar. "You sure about that Stonesy?" questioned Pyke.

"Look, Jem," implored Stones, lowering his stinking head even closer to Pyke's ear. "You know I'd help you if I could," his voice now a whisper, barely audible above the comical clacking of his wooden dentures. "King is the evillest snake in this whole den of vipers. Ain't nobody in their right mind gonna help ya. Even if they knew where he was. Might as well put a gun in me mouth and pull the trigger right now. Dead man walking, that's what I'd be. Anything would be better than being skinned alive by that maniac or havin' every bone in me body slowly broken by that monster child of his." Pyke continued to nod and sipped at his Jameson whiskey. "Go on Stonesy," he encouraged.

"I can't say no more, Jem, honest I can't. This place is probably full of Jade Dragons. Think of me wife and kids, Jem, for Christ's sake. I ain't in that world Jem, never been a part of it I promise you. I do a bit of this and a touch of that, Jem, you knows that. But King? King is a Devil. I ain't brave enough to dance with the Devil." Pyke recognised that Stones was rambling and genuinely terrified. He also knew that the big tanner was in a much lower league than any that King would entertain, and most likely knew less about the Crime Lord's location than Pyke did himself.

Pyke, much to Stone's relief, proceeded to turn ominously towards Boniface who seemed to be attempting to shrink even farther into his over-sized suit. The little man's face was of a burnished, dirty umber and his scrawny neck disappeared into his collar like that of a turtle finding sanctuary within its shell. Pyke recalled that Wiggins had once commented that Boniface reminded him of National Geographic photographs of the shrunken heads prized by the wild tribes of Borneo. Boniface fidgeted and squirmed under Pyke's unrelenting stare. "You got to be pulling me chain, Mr Pyke! I know my neck is hardly what one would call substantial, yet I value it none the less."

Pyke felt slightly repulsed by the little man in the big suit and his affected manner of speech. He knew him for what he was, which was a snake in the grass of the lowest kind. A bottom feeder with affected airs and graces. "Where is King, monkey boy? I need to know, and I need to know fast."

"Some may say I resemble a simpleton, Mr Pyke, but believe me I am far from dim-witted. As such I make it my business to know absolutely nothing about that of Mr King." Boniface twitched. Pyke smelled a lead and decided to force the issue. "There's a bullseye in me pocket with your name on it if you tell me where King is."

Boniface twitched again, undecided as to how to proceed. "That may well be Sergeant, but if I were to accept, I fear there would be another bullseye, this time adorning my face." Boniface smiled, pleased with his analogy. However, Pyke could see that Boniface was tempted, perhaps even hooked. He knew Boniface would sell his own grandmother to make a few guineas. Fifty pounds was a King's ransom and would keep the little cardsharp in stake money for a year. The little man looked furtively around. He was uncomfortable with the silence that Pyke was using to tease him over the edge. Boniface thought of the money and what he could do with it, his greed was beginning to surmount his fear. "Somewhere in Soho, or maybe Chinatown, is what I heard," he mumbled, trying to mask his speech by relighting his already lit cheroot behind his scrawny hand. He pulled the peak of his fedora over his eyes as if to further disguise his deceit.

Pyke was barged in the back by a stout woman in a floral dress who looked as if she had been stuck in a pneumatic press, such was her corpulence. "Sorry Ducks," she shouted over the general tumult. She looked Pyke up and down whilst licking her ruby red lips, giving him a lascivious appraisal that made the policeman shudder.

Pyke returned his attention to the matter in hand. "You'll have to do better than that, Boniface. Give me a location. A street even," he urged. Boniface hopped awkwardly down from his stool and pulled the waistband of his fulsome trousers upwards to lift the hems from his highly polished brogues. He stood no higher than Pyke's chest, a shrunken man in an over-sized suit. He tightened his butter coloured Paisley patterned tie. "I'm not your man, Mr Pyke. Not this time. May I suggest you try upstairs? Demerara Smith is holding court on the veranda as if he were old Judge Jeffreys himself. Perhaps he can assist you with your enquiries?"

Pyke grunted as Boniface disappeared into the safety of the crowd of revellers like an ant being absorbed back into a writhing hive of scuttling activity.

As he sailed backwards through the air, his body crashing through the handrail of the balcony and plummeting towards the stone strewn mud of the Thames riverside, Demerara Smith remembered. He remembered the long voyage from Jamaica he and his mother had taken nearly forty years earlier. The dark, claustrophobic, stench laden bowels of the decrepit ocean steamer that had somehow transported them from the heat and sunshine of the Caribbean to the damp greyness of London Port. It had been a French transatlantic steamer called the Dominion, he recalled. '*It's funny what you remember when your brain is scrambled,*' he thought. He also remembered the first man whose neck he had broken, a Norwegian rival whom he had battered with a club hammer. He remembered his daughter Darlene, a smiling angel who had left him because of his drunkenness and criminal activities. Most of all he remembered the iron-like right uppercut unleashed by Jem Pyke that had started him on his way to remembering everything else.

Twenty minutes earlier Demerara Smith had been exactly where he had wanted to be, reclining in the comfort of the Prospect of Whitby's upstairs terrace, a woman on each side of him, regaling them with tales of his derring-do on the High Seas, and slinging back Jackdaw rum like there was no tomorrow. The big rum runner sat with the heels of his buccaneer boots balanced on the back of his white Great Dane, Harlequin, who lay obediently, tongue on floor, as his master roared with laughter.

"Hello, Sugar," came a familiar voice from the terrace entrance.

Demerara stopped his braggadocio and turned his gaze towards the doorway. The figure of Jem Pyke leant against the door frame, one thumb hooked in his waistcoat pocket, brown Derby tipped forward to half shield his face from view. "Jem Pyke, as I live and breathe!" Smith beamed his widest smile disclosing a scattering of gold teeth. "Step into my office, my friend. Pull up a chair, man." The big Jamaican's left hand went instinctively to his side. The movement did not escape Pyke's attention. '*Gun or knife?*' thought Pyke warily. He knew how dangerous an opponent Smith could be. Drunk or sober, he was a big man with no scruples and a bloody, violent past. A cutthroat of the first order, feared throughout Docklands London, and beyond.

"Clear the decks, girls! Me and me old shipmate here have business to discuss, do we not, Jem?"

The two girls reluctantly departed, each sent on their way with half a crown and a slap on the buttocks courtesy of Smith. Pyke drew up a chair directly in front of the smuggler, placing his half-empty whisky glass on its graffiti scarred surface. Pyke cast a glance towards the head of the massive hound under Smith's boots. Harlequin's ebony encircled eyes looked lugubriously upwards towards the detective. Satisfied that all was well, the Great Dane licked its fleshy black lips and snorted his way back to wherever it is that dogs sleep.

Demerara Smith grabbed Pyke's glass and summarily emptied its contents onto the floor. Harlequin's enormous tongue unfolded, and the dog turned his head to one side and lapped furiously at the whisky. "Have a real drink, Jem," grinned the Jamaican filling Pyke's glass to the brim with dark, ruby tinged rum from the bottle in front of him. As he did so, Pyke caught a glimpse of a dagger hilt under the Caribbean's topcoat. *'Knife it is then,'* confirmed Pyke to himself. The two men clinked glasses together and threw back the sharp sweet liquid. Pyke could feel an instant hit of molasses rich heat as he swallowed the extremely potent rum. "What can I do for you Jem?"

Pyke looked at the grinning countenance before him. These two men had history and not all of which was good. A history that went back to a shared adolescence. Smith was two years older than Pyke, but the blacksmith's son had run with an older crowd in his youth. Pyke's physique and devil-may-care attitude had separated him from his immediate contemporaries who had universally regarded him as a threat. As such he had been drawn, when not labouring at his father's forge, to the world of the older boys. Horace Smith was the leader of a group of hoodlums with whom Jem Pyke had found himself entangled. The tallest and strongest of the group, Smith was also the only one with dark skin. Fatherless, young Horace knew no boundaries when it came to behaviour or reprisal and their youthful games and high jinks soon gave way to petty crime and feuds with other local gangs. In his childhood, Horace had always dreamed of being a Pirate, a freebooting privateer, carousing the oceans and capturing priceless treasures from the wealthy. Leslie Pyke, however, yearned for the life of a soldier and campaigns in foreign lands, a brotherhood of companions fighting for freedom, equality, and justice. Each boy had, to a certain degree, fulfilled their ambitions.

Demerara Smith hit the soft mud with a momentum that took his breath away. He lay there deeply winded, fighting for air, hoping that it would come and that his back had not been broken. He could see Jem Pyke kick through what remained of the timber balustrade, splinters of wood cascading downwards towards him. Smith's Great Dane barked ferociously as Pyke dropped from the terrace and landed onto the beach with a crunch. Smith pushed himself up onto his elbows, fighting against the foul-smelling ooze to right himself. He could hear the sucking sludge of Pyke's footsteps as the policeman made his way towards him through the low tide mud.

"Where is King?" demanded Pyke, now on top of him, Smith's collar grasped tightly in his terrific hands. "People will die, Sugar, thousands of people will needlessly perish if we don't locate him. I need to know where that evil bastard is." Pyke smashed a right hand into the Jamaican's face, dislocating his jaw. Smith, bucked and rolled, using all his strength and greater size to turn Pyke over so as he now sat on the chest of the detective. The two grappled and twisted their way through the mud, exchanging curses and brutal blows. A crowd of drinkers had spilled out of the Prospect and were forming a horseshoe around the two sprawling figures wrestling in the mud. Many more were watching from the balcony above. Murray and Bunce had made their way through the throbbing mass and were trying their best to contain the throng. Smith went for his knife.

"Don't make me do it, Jem. I'll slice your liver if I have to," grimaced the smuggler, pulling the knife to one side, ready to plunge it home. Pyke swiftly extricated his hand from underneath the Jamaican and grabbed Smith's wrist and rotated and twisted with all his strength. He felt a sudden sharp snap and could see his opponent's eyes roll upwards in agony. He shoved Smith to one side and straddled him. Two more blows to the head and Smith's tongue rolled from his mouth.

Pyke leaned forward, his nose almost touching that of his boyhood friend. Their alcoholic breath steamed and mingled, each man panting to absorb as much oxygen as they could following their exertions. Pyke whispered into a swollen ear, blood spattering from his mouth. "Tell me where he is Sugar, or God help me. I'll finish you off here in this mud."

Smith gasped for breath and spluttered, the words almost unintelligible. "He'll burn me bones and hang what's left of me out for the crows if he finds out I've talked to you, Jem. Even you don't know what that man is truly capable of," pleaded the prone Smith. "Best you hit me one more time, matey." Pyke obliged. The blow sickened both the crowd and the man who had thrown it. Murray moved toward the two prone men, intent on stopping the now inevitable slaughter. Pyke raised his hand in a halting motion and turned his ear to Demerara Smith's blood swollen lips. "Gerrard Street. Somewhere in Gerrard Street. That's all I know, Jem."

Demerara Smith's stomach lurched as he saw, through one swollen eye, the diminutive, yet unmistakable figure of Oliver Boniface withdrawing into the crowd. His hopping, lop-sided gait was unmistakable. A chill of cold steel surged through his body as he remembered that apart from his singular looks, garish dress sense and reputation as an almost unbeatable cardsharp, Boniface was best known amongst his contemporaries as having the most acute hearing of any man in East London. At that moment, Demerara Smith knew he was doomed.

Chapter 8 - The Politician

Jonathan Hardridge wiped the sweat from his brow. The pressures of his post were beginning to impact upon the well-being of the newly elected MP for Camberwell. The young MP felt he was treading water, just keeping mentally afloat, and trying to juggle workload with deadlines and deadlines with home life. So much so, that he had barely seen or spoken to his wife and family during the preceding two weeks. He was beginning to lose weight, some may have said dramatically so, due in part to the strain of his position and to his new pastime of forgetting to eat. He had even begun wondering whether his three young children would recognise the gaunt doppelganger who had replaced their father. On the rare occasion when he did remember to eat, he invariably found his appetite to be as disobliging and on the verge of nausea due to constant knotting in his stomach endured.

Several weeks earlier the officers of the sixth Cavalry Brigade, stationed just outside Dublin, had confirmed that they would refuse to enforce Irish home-rule in Ulster if a parliamentary act proposing greater autonomy for Ireland were carried. It was Hardridge's immediate superior's remit to act as a conduit between all parties concerned and to negotiate a speedy and mutually agreeable outcome to this latest rift in the already damaged relations between the two countries. Invariably, however, the right honourable Henry Falls-Sampson, a foreign office dinosaur, unjustly delegated this assignment to the less experienced Johnathan Hardridge. He was the stevedore tasked with the research and groundwork that would ultimately boost his superior's reputation and bolster his already over-inflated ego even further. If that were at all possible.

It was March fifteenth and Hardridge sat at his office desk struggling with a first draft of the White Paper, its contents as dry as a sun-splintered bone in the Kalahari Desert. His fatigue had left him unable to find the correct words to type, and he continually misspelt even the simplest of words. He pulled another sheet of foolscap from the typewriter, crumpled it up angrily and hurled it in the general direction of the waste-paper basket, where it joined a multitude of other scrunched up balls of paper. Sitting back in his chair, he clasped his hands behind his head and looked at the clock hanging on the wall above a row of filing cabinets. '*Good Lord! Ten-twenty! Moira will have my guts for garters!*' he thought with a cringe that knotted his stomach even further. This would be the fourth time this week that he had missed dinner and it was only Thursday and, understanding as his wife was as to the impact of his duties upon their domestic life, Hardridge was certain that he was walking a delicate line that urgently needed addressing. '*Soon,*' he thought. '*Perhaps tomorrow, once this damn paper is written.*'

His office was small and cramped and was situated within the very bowels of the Palace of Westminster. He shared this minute workspace with an elderly MP who, when on the rare occasion he deigned to visit his administrative place of work, did nothing more than check the likely winners in that day's issue of *The Turf*. Having selected a suitable number of losers, he would then fall asleep, snoring, and expelling wind loudly enough to wake King Solomon.

As a relatively young, and newly elected member of Parliament, Hardridge felt passionately that his calling was to represent his Camberwell constituents. However, given his freshness to the position and perhaps because of a slight degree of naivety, he seemed to have spent most of the first year of his tenure being drawn into working on consultation parties for various bills and papers in which he held little or no interest. This, combined with the fact that he and his young family lived closer to Westminster than they did to Camberwell, meant that he was spending far too much time in the belly of the House.

'*Tomorrow,*' he repeated with bold conviction to no one other than himself and the repulsive stuffed parrot that his colleague kept on his otherwise unencumbered desk. '*Tomorrow, once this paper is drafted, I shall visit Camberwell.*' He fondly imagined a day of meeting constituents, discussing local issues, getting under the skin of his people's concerns and problems. Perhaps even a pint of Best in the Old King's Head, chewing the fat with real working men. "Yes!" he decided, momentarily alarmed at the sound of his own voice in the otherwise silent confines of his small office, "Tomorrow it shall be!"

Hardridge felt better. He felt enthused, re-energised. He removed his wire-framed spectacles, rubbed at his eyes, pinched the bridge of his nose, and continued typing the document proposing Anglo-Irish commentaries and negotiations. He was now somewhat rejuvenated and the misspellings of earlier had ceased and were replaced by rapidly flowing content and diplomatic doggerel. With one final carriage return, he removed the thirty-seventh sheet of the proposal with an elaborate flourish. He then collated and stapled the manuscript and placed it in an unsealed envelope for the attention of the right honourable Henry Falls-Sampson the following morning. As he securely locked away a carbon-copy of the paper in his desk drawer the idea of seeing his family and eating some home-cooked food now leapt into his thoughts. He bounded from his chair with renewed vigour, removed his hat and coat from the peg on the back of the door and, turning briefly to check that he had not left anything behind, he threw a wave to the threadbare parrot and exited the office.

As he strode along the dimly lit basement corridor, its hard plaster walls showing sporadic patches of damp and efflorescence, he began to whistle random notes. '*Tomorrow will be a fresh start,*' he thought, his bearing buoyed by his new-found optimism. He resolved that he would purchase some flowers for Moira on the way home. '*Surely the flower girl outside the Abbey would still be there?*' he hoped, checking his watch.

Hardridge had barely placed one foot on the first step of the staircase leading up to the ground floor when he felt a presence looming behind him. The hairs on the back of his neck stood to attention and his skin prickled expectantly. He whirled quickly around. His instincts screamed danger as he saw the gleaming reflection of a steel blade flashing towards him. Instinctively he raised his arm to fend off the attack but instantly felt a scorch of searing pain as the blade pierced his chest just below his left clavicle. The blade was promptly withdrawn and quickly plunged deep into the left side of his ribcage, puncturing his lung. The young politician struggled against his attacker, but the onslaught was incessant and frenzied, and he was having great difficulty breathing. Time after time the blade struck home with sickening ferocity, penetrating his flesh and muscles, each stabbing bringing untold agony. Hardridge's legs gave way and he slumped to the floor where he came to rest in a crouched position. Still, the merciless attack continued unabated upon the now completely defenceless parliamentarian. He felt his will to resist ebb away.

"Please stop," pleaded Jonathan Hardridge in a barely audible whisper. He vainly strained to lift his arms in defence but was too weak to offer any sort of resistance. He tried to look at his assailant but the blood in his eyes made it impossible for him to distinguish any features. His chin hit his chest as his eyes closed and darkness descended upon him, "I am a father, I have chil..." he gurgled, frothy blood-streaked sputum bubbling from his mouth. The rattle of death reverberated within his chest and his head lolled to one side.

"Only one more and the assassination will be accomplished!" a voice declared as the knife was thrust deep into Johnathan Hardridge's heart rupturing the descending aorta.

The MP's blood-soaked body lay motionless at the bottom of the basement staircase. From the landing above, a bronze bust of Lord George Bentinck stared blankly down upon the gory scene. With his last faint glimmer of consciousness, Hardridge was vaguely aware of something being placed carefully upon his head. His dying thought was of a wreath of flowers bought for his wife from the flower girl on the steps of Westminster Abbey.

"Telegram from the Houses of Parliament, Sir," hollered Desk Sergeant Ash, offering the chit to Sergeant Pyke.

"Blimey!" exclaimed a surprised Pyke, "Now you've got me attention, Nosher!" Pyke had been reclining in a chair in DCI Wiggins' office, legs outstretched, his Derby tilted forward shielding his eyes. He now sat bolt upright, hat in hand.

"Havin' a bit of a kip Sarge?" joked Ash playfully.

"You would n'all if you'd had the night I've had, mate," retorted Pyke, fumbling in his inside pocket for the reading glasses he had been prescribed following his recent altercation with the Beast that had been Doctor Joseph Bleak. The punishment inflicted upon his skull during what he now referred to his 'head joust' with the maniac cannibal, had slightly impaired his sight. The repeated head-butting, he had inflicted upon Bleak during their fight had left him concussed. Pyke's eyes had remained closed for some days and had stayed swollen for a time thereafter. The now faded scarring on his eyelids and brows only heightened his air of menace. He had, in fact, suffered a vitreous haemorrhage. The injury had caused the blood vessels in his left eye to bleed into the vitreous resulting in focusing problems when switching his vision between near and far objects. Nosher stifled a chortle at the sight of London's most feared police enforcer struggling to place the delicate wire spectacles upon the bridge of a nose widened and misshapen by hundreds of blows.

Pyke grabbed the telegram from Ash's hand, glancing briefly at the Desk Sergeant's striking head of hair. Ash was as noted for his abundance of hair, which stood like an electrified haystack, as he was for his rapid-fire wit and his love of pipe tobacco, good books and cricket. Most observers found Nosher's hairstyle rather comical but for some inexplicable reason, Pyke always found it inherently annoying. A deep rumble escaped Pyke's throat as he began reading the telegram. "Jesus Christ, Nosh! Why didn't you tell me?" he shouted as he leapt to his feet. "Where's the Guvnor?"

"Probably still in bed, I'd imagine Sarge. It is only five in the morning after all," retorted Sergeant Ash.

"A murder in the Big House, mate. Send Bunce and Murray down there straight away. I'll get round the Guvnor's. Tell them we'll meet them there. Get Doc Pascoe and the forensic guys to attend as a matter of urgency."

"The weapon I would suggest gentlemen would have been a knife, dagger or perhaps an awl, of no more than ten and no less than four inches in length." Doctor Nelson B. Pascoe was briefing Wiggins and Pyke on the forensic report he had just passed to them. His permanently raised eyebrows gave his florid face the impression of perpetual surprise. "The offending blade was approximately two inches in width at its widest aspect. Young Mr Hardridge suffered a total of twenty-three entry points, all to the torso, with the majority being inflicted to the frontal plane. There was a single fatal puncture which penetrated the heart, which, I must add is an exceedingly rare occurrence indeed. Of the other twenty-two punctures, none were deep enough to be fatal although three did puncture the lungs bilaterally. The fatal wound penetrated between the fourth and fifth ribs on the victim's left side. The blade entered at a thirty to forty-five-degree angle relative to the plane of the torso and approximately two inches to the left side of the sternum. This produced a two-inch wound which resulted in the left ventricle being sliced open. The heart would have ceased to fibrillate, the wound being too large to seal upon contraction. Instead, it would have widened with each contraction so that blood was forced violently out of the wound channel under high pressure immediately following the withdrawal of the blade. This resulted in widespread blood spatter to the surrounding area as our photographs testify. There would have been massive internal and external bleeding, as his heart was essentially still pumping. This would have ultimately resulted in a catastrophic drop in blood pressure to the brain, causing almost immediate unconsciousness. Death would have followed within a maximum of three to four minutes."

"Thank you, Doctor Pascoe. You have painted a most vivid picture of this poor fellow's demise. Is there anything else you can tell us before we study your report in greater detail?" asked Wiggins.

"As I mentioned, the heart itself is relatively difficult to stab as it lies directly behind the sternum. It is partially protected by the rib cage and is totally covered by the tough connective tissue between the ribs. Indeed, it even has its own fibrous covering, the pericardium. Striking the heart itself is difficult unless of course, the perpetrator has a keen grasp of anatomy or butchery..."

"Not another bloomin' maniac Doctor!" interrupted Pyke.

"... or has higher than normal upper body strength," continued Pascoe, looking reproachfully at Pyke. The rusty haired pathologist did not like to be interrupted whilst in full forensic flow. He continued. "Although in stating such, someone with anatomical knowledge would more commonly target the throat or the major vessels that are briefly exposed directly above the top of the sternum, namely the hepatic artery, the aorta in the torso, or possibly the kidneys or the femoral arteries of each upper leg. So, bearing this in mind, I would suggest that all the evidence points to the murderer specifically targeting the heart, and to having been an extremely powerful individual. All the other anthropometric data is included within my report gentlemen, so if there is nothing else, I shall bid you good day." Pascoe raised his eyebrows in silent invitation.

"Your report is most detailed and, as always, will help inform our investigation. We will call if we require further assistance. Many thanks," complemented Wiggins. Pascoe nodded and reached the door. He hesitated and turned back towards the detectives. "There is one more thing that intrigued me about this case, gentlemen. When found, the victim was wearing a rudimentary fashioned crown. One constructed from laurel leaves."

Chapter 9 - The Boss

The early morning sun attempted to penetrate the previous night's lingering fog, casting a faded pink light that danced upon the dark grey waters of the Thames. Simeon Crook smiled as his huge wooden paddle stirred the soup of the river, making pink ballerinas shimmer, dance and then dissipate. Crook was a Thames Lighterman, a member of that ancient and ennobled Guild, as had been his father and his grandfather before him. The cargo of tobacco he was transporting from The Lady Nora, fresh into Saint Katharine's Dock from the West Indies, represented the first of many trips he was due to take to and from the ship that day. Unfortunately for Simeon Crook, his day was about to change drastically, and not for the better.

He felt a dull thud on the flat bottom of his barge. "Bleedin' driftwood," he cursed aloud. A distant foghorn boomed a haunting echo to his curse. Despite his many years upon the Thames, the warning bellow had always filled Simeon Crook with a feeling of underlying dread, a deathly chill which added to his mortal fear of drowning. Despite his chosen occupation, Crook had never learned to swim. His mind slipped to an unwelcome and all too regular image of his body sinking into the murk of the River, his legs and arms working frantically against the pull of the undertow that would eventually blanket him in airless darkness. It was a vision, a nightmare, he often dreamed.

The foghorn sang again. "Snap out of it, Crooky," he admonished himself. "Pull yourself together boy." Years of working alone on the barge had instilled in him the rather unsociable, and somewhat disconcerting habit, of talking to himself. Simeon was a solitary man. He had no wife and no children. Sadly, he would be the last of his line to ply his trade within the Guild of Lightermen.

There came another thud, this time louder and on the side of the barge. Simeon had encountered almost every conceivable article of flotsam and jetsam during his years on this busiest of rivers. He looked to his port side and distinguished the unmistakable shape of a human body floating face down in the inky water and snagged to the lines connected to the side of his barge. Simeon groaned. This was merely the latest in a line of dozens of cadavers that he had encountered during his lengthy career. He knew the required procedure all too well. He was to secure the body to his craft and take it immediately to the nearest landing point on the North side of the river. Then he was to contact the River Police at Wapping and await their appearance. On no account should the body be left unattended. Thereafter he would have to provide a statement at Wapping Police Station. All of which would eat hungrily into his day's work and therefore into his earnings from the tobacco shipment. Besides, Simeon Crook was a man of a somewhat delicate constitution, and he had never relished the process of tying a dead human body to his barge.

Simeon decided that on this occasion he would forgo protocol and simply untangle the body and push it away, allowing it to drift off into the gloom for some other poor unfortunate to find. He made his way to the centre of the boat and shoved at the shape with the tapered blade of his paddle. "Damn!" It was well and truly snagged. Simeon knelt, intent on releasing the body using his slip-joint knife. The foghorn blew once more, startling the already unsettled Simeon, sending that familiar chill of dread sizzling down his spinal cord. He crossed himself before leaning over the side of the barge and pulling once more at the sodden ropes to offer a cleaner cut. As he did so the body rolled over. Slopping water splashed his head, water that Simeon Crook felt was contaminated with death, and he found himself almost nose to nose with the bloated face of a dead man. The eyeless head lurched towards him, the swollen tongue protruding grossly out of the mouth, offering up a deathly kiss. Simeon let out an involuntary retch of revulsion and threw himself onto his back, his legs kicking, he scuttled backwards away from the cadaver. During his frenzied retreat, his prized knife of twenty-nine years had slipped from his grasp and disappeared into the maw of Old Father Thames. Simeon's heart was pounding as if it were trying to escape from his chest. His pulse raced at the sight of the stone white face of the floating corpse that bobbed in the water before him. With a sense of creeping revulsion, he could now see that the water engorged face was covered in swollen sores and necrotic buboes.

"Shittin' Hell!" gasped Crook. "It's the bleedin' plague!" For the second time that morning, Simeon Crook crossed himself and asked his Lord to protect him.

While a petrified Simeon Crook was paddling frantically towards Wapping River Police Depot, Sandy Stewart swaggered his bow-legged swagger down Wapping Wall on his way to Brussels Wharf and his early morning shift on the quayside. As the dockyard's designated knocker upper, the perennially cheerful Sandy, was always first at the gate. The prudent Aberdonian had volunteered for the position of knocker upper as soon as the previous occupant, Cedric Cantwell, had passed away the previous year. The bale of jute that had fallen onto the head of the unfortunate Cantwell, breaking his upper spine and causing an instant brain haemorrhage, had, as far as the miserly Sandy was concerned, been a stroke of good luck for both him and his wallet. Sandy was always open to earning a few extra shillings, and as one of life's natural larks, he was ideally suited to the early morning role of waking up the dockyard workers, so they had no excuse to start a shift. He whistled his way down

Wapping Wall, his long bamboo knocking stick wobbling up and down with each step as it rested lightly upon his shoulder. As he approached the iron bridge that crossed Brussels Wharf, he almost stumbled across a pair of large leather, knee-high boots that lay discarded on the cobbles. One boot stood upright whilst the other was lying on its side. Simeon looked around furtively, stooped and picked one up, surprised at its great weight. "Quality piece of work that is," muttered the Scotsman, admiring the brass buckles and embossed leather straps. He could make out images of a sailing ship and a sea monster stitched subtly into the remarkably pliable leather. Sandy again looked keenly around him, and, satisfied that he was not being watched, grabbed the other boot, and shoved both under his armpit. "Waste not want not," he smiled triumphantly to himself. As far as Sandy was concerned this was turning out to be a good day.

As he strolled on, pleased with his good fortune, he cast his eyes upwards, as he always did when crossing the quay to ensure that he lowered his bamboo stick sufficiently to pass safely below the red oxide painted, iron winding gear structure that straddled the bridge. Sandy gasped. "Holy Mother of God!" his newly prized boots clattering to the cobbles. Above him, suspended by the ankles from the overhead steelwork, hung the blackened and charred remains of a man, burned beyond recognition.

DCI Albert Wiggins and DS Jem Pyke strode purposely down the third-floor corridor of New Scotland Yard towards the office formerly occupied by ex-Superintendent Magnus MacDonald. Wiggins straightened his tie and sharpened his cuffs as they approached.

"I've heard he's from up North somewhere," snorted Pyke, barely hiding his disgust.

"So too was MacDonald, lest you forget," added Wiggins with a grin.

Pyke shrugged. "Mac was from Scotland, that ain't really up North is it? That's another country altogether. They don't even speak the King's English as far as I can make out. But I don't mind the Scots. I've Scotch blood running through my veins and what an excellent infantry, brave as lions. Could do without those itchy skirts and screeching bloody bagpipes though." Wiggins raised his eyebrows in mock disbelief at Pyke's remark. They came to a halt outside the familiar door which was now adorned with a brass plaque engraved with an unfamiliar name. Superintendent Gideon Thorne. "Ready, Sergeant?" asked Wiggins, straightening his tie.

"Ready as always, Guv," confirmed Pyke, removing his Derby, and smoothing his hair at the sides. His eyelids were puffy, and his face freshly scarred from his encounter with Demerara Smith the previous day. Pyke cupped his hand to mouth and exhaled, trying to smell his own breath. "No hint of last night's rum," he declared with a degree of relief.

Wiggins smiled and lowered his voice to a mere whisper, "If the rumours I have heard regarding Mr Thorne's proclivities are true, I don't think you have much to worry about there, Jem."

Pyke gave a considered nod. "Boozer, is he?" Suddenly the new Superintendent had leapt up a notch in his estimation. "Beginning to like the old bastard already."

At that instant, the door to the office swung swiftly open. Wiggins' raised fist hung in the air as if to perform his customary knock. Pyke swallowed, unsure as to whether the new Superintendent had heard his last remark.

"Please enter, gentlemen," invited a polite, well rounded, and deeply toned voice. The man who stood before them was as tall as Wiggins, well dressed and physically well built. Gideon Thorne stood aside and ushered them into his office. Once seated, Wiggins immediately began making a mental assessment of the man before him. He already knew, from what he had read of Thorne, that he had an exemplary record as a DCI with Manchester City Police Force. His record spoke of a man who was driven to success, ambitious and forceful. There had, however, been some inconsistencies in his history that indicated to Wiggins that perhaps he was prone to stepping outside of protocol and being liable to indiscretions. A risk-taker by all accounts. Wiggins judged that Thorne was slightly older than himself, perhaps only by a year or two, or perhaps, he considered, his presence gave him an air of greater years. His face had been handsome, but his features had a somewhat puffed, weather-beaten appearance, particularly around the brow and eyes, yet his face remained strong and characterful.

'*Boozer and bruiser,*' decided Pyke looking at the Superintendent's face. '*That boat has seen a few bars and felt the tickle of a few knuckles,*' he thought knowingly.

Thorne sat and clasped his hands together on the desk in front of him. Wiggins looked closely at those hands, without, he hoped, alerting Thorne to his interest. Large, strong hands. '*No stranger to manual labour in his youth,*' judged Wiggins. He quickly noted that Thorne's fingernails were minutely flecked with paint, and that small remnants of what resembled fine wood shavings were clogged underneath his thumbnails. Wiggins also detected a faint smell of turpentine or putty fighting against the man's Cologne. '*An amateur carpenter in his spare time perhaps?*' postulated Wiggins. '*Or perhaps some furniture restoration or some such.*'

'*Murderer's thumbs,*' asserted Pyke, looking at those same hands and recalling the old adage of his grandfather, Fraser Pyke. "Look at a man's thumbs laddie, aye look at their thumbs," the old soldier would tell him. "If a man hiz a thumbnail wider than it is lang, then a murderer he will surely be." Gideon Thorne's thumbnails were stubby and almost as wide as they were long.

Thorne sat back, ramrod straight, assessing the two men in front of him. He looked at them as if he owned them. "So, gentlemen, a pleasure to meet you both. I understand the Force, and the City for that matter, owe you both a great debt for ridding our streets of the murderous savagery of Doctor Joseph Bleak." Thorne seemed to be addressing his comment towards Pyke rather than to Wiggins.

'*They ain't your streets yet, matey. You ain't earned the right to claim them as yours. They are ours,*' thought Pyke who felt uncomfortable that Thorne's compliment seemed to have been directed solely at him. "The achievement was a group one, Sir. We are a team and we lost a lot of brave men in the process of dispatching that vile bastard," he countered. Pyke's mind turned to Jennifer Potts and her brave husband, who, along with the other constables, had lost his life during that denouement in the bowels of Tower Bridge. He also thought of the brave contribution made by Lady Constance Harkness who had put her own life at risk to help in bringing the reign of The Beast to an end.

"Of course, yes of course Sergeant," nodded Thorne in agreement. "Although I understand it was your cranium that bore the brunt of the final conflict." The Northerner's eyes surveyed the scars traversing Pyke's forehead.

'*Sheffield,*' Wiggins postulated. '*Or perhaps Bradford.*' Wiggins was trying to pinpoint Thorne's regional accent which was partially cloaked under his well-modulated voice.

"I understand the terrible loss you all feel," acquiesced Thorne, lowering his head slightly as if in homage to lost colleagues.

'*Definitely Sheffield,*' decided Wiggins, convinced that there was an underlying steel to the accent rather than the more rounded vowels of Bradford.

"I would be most grateful if you could bring me up to date with your current caseload, gentlemen. I have read the files, but always prefer to hear reports face-to-face. I find it gives me a more personal understanding of your progress and of any problems you may be encountering. I am sure you understand."

Wiggins found Thorne's smile to be edged in insincerity. He felt a natural reticence towards the man. Pyke glanced towards Wiggins who instinctively responded on the duo's behalf. He relayed the details of the two recent baffling murders, indicating that they had not yet ruled out that there may be a connection that may link them together, and informed Thorne of their latest theories and as to what evidence and witness statements they had garnered. He also detailed the disappearance of the three security guards from the Cruciform building, their ongoing pursuit of Mr King, and their suspicion that the Chinaman may have a highly infectious virus within his possession. '*You couldn't make this up!*' Wiggins decided inwardly as he relayed all the details to Thorne. Throughout Wiggins' discourse, Thorne nodded sagely, listened intently, and took copious notes in what Wiggins observed to be an extremely neat and ordered hand. He had immediately noted that Thorne's handwriting sloped leftwards, back on itself. Wiggins had made a point of studying graphoanalysis and recognised that a backwards slanting writing style often characterised an introvert whose nature is such that he feels uncomfortable in the society of others. On occasion, he recalled, individuals with left slant may often have experienced a tragedy during early life and were generally nervous of the future.

Once Wiggins had completed his verbal report, Thorne sat back in his chair and looked intently into the eyes of each of the two officers sitting in front of him. He took a breath. A pause for effect. "Well, gentlemen, you have your work cut out for you, of that I have no doubt. I am at your service." Pyke winced. "At *our* service, Sir?" asked Wiggins with the slightest tone of scepticism in his voice.

"Yes, Mr Wiggins. You will find that I like to take an active interest in particularly stimulating cases, such as the ones you have just outlined, and it seems to me that you two gentlemen have stimulation in abundance," answered Thorne, his voice taking on a slightly more forceful edge. "I am not one for being chained to inkwell and desk and as you have already noted from my fingernails DCI Wiggins, I like to get my hands dirty on occasion." Thorne flashed his insincere smile for longer than necessary. "We do things differently where I come from. Commissioner Gregson has given me free rein over this department following the unfortunate departure of my predecessor, and I intend to exercise that liberty wherever and whenever I can, and, may I say, for the betterment of the Force."

'Bleedin' glory hunter,' thought Pyke, grinding his teeth. *'He needs sorting out this one.'*

"Of course, Sir," replied Wiggins, not relishing the direction the conversation had taken. "We have an incident room set up for each ongoing enquiry, Sir. I would be only too happy to show you around at your convenience. Explain our working methods and systems of investigation."

"Capital idea!" ejaculated Thorne rising from his desk briskly. He reached for a packet of cigarettes that lay, uncomfortably so for Wiggins, at a haphazard angle, half on and half off the desk edge. The action was interrupted abruptly by a sharp knocking on the Superintendent's office door.

"Enter!" Thorne's voice was stentorian in tone, reminding Wiggins of an actor projecting forth to a large audience. The unmistakable figure of Nosher Ash stepped into the room. Ash felt momentarily unsure of himself in front of the new Superintendent and decided to cast a rusty and seldom practised salute towards his new department head. Pyke stifled a chuckle with a snorting noise to which Ash threw him a 'piss off' stare.

"Yes, Sergeant Ash, what is it?" asked Thorne.

Ash glanced momentarily towards Wiggins and Pyke. "I beg your pardon, Sir but it was actually DCI Wiggins and Sergeant Pyke I was looking for. Only, a couple of bodies have been brought into the Mortuary and I thought the officers would want to see them, considering how they were discovered," stated Ash.

"More victims in our spate of unusual murders, Mr Ash?" enquired Thorne with unconcealed delight. He cupped his hands around his cigarette as he lit it as if shielding the flame against some non-existent wind.

'*He is used to outdoor life,*' deduced Wiggins instantly.

Thorne discarded the spent match in the direction of the ashtray on his desk, missing his target, much to Wiggin's vexation. Ash glanced at Wiggins and read the situation in the detective's eyes. "No Sir. Nothing to do with the recent killings as far as we can discern at this stage. The bodies are that of an unknown person and the other of a common criminal of some repute. Unlikely that they are in any way connected to the deaths of the Deacon or the Parliamentarian," delivered Ash. "I should imagine, Sir!"

Thorne considered this information, a large leathery hand rubbing over the lower third of his weather-beaten face. "Very well. I will leave you gentlemen to your investigations. I shall look forward to reviewing your report in due course. Until then gentlemen." Thorne indicated that they may leave and turned his attention towards a bookcase that dominated one wall of his office. "Please keep me informed, and remember, I am at your service." The three officers made their leave and headed for the staircase.

"Why weren't we called to the scene, Sergeant Ash?" demanded Wiggins as they hastily descended the staircase that would lead them to the Yard's basement morgue and the domain of Doctor Nelson B. Pascoe.

"One was found bobbing about in the river by a Lighterman and brought into Wapping early hours of this morning. Pascoe has this body in the isolation room," informed Ash.

Wiggins could sense an unease about the usually ebullient desk Sergeant. "Isolation room you say? I did not know there even was such a room," added Wiggins.

"Well there is now, Sir," informed Nosher.

"There is something amiss, Ash?" questioned Wiggins.

Ash chewed his lip. "Best let Doctor Pascoe explain, Sir," he shrugged.

"Very well. You mentioned two bodies. What of the other?" enquired Wiggins.

"Found hanging upside down from the iron bridge on Brussels Wharf, burnt to a crisp by all accounts."

"Sounds bizarre enough to be another addition to our series of murders Guv," observed Pyke disappointedly. "Unusual scene, prominent position, and singularly staged, by the sound of it. Why weren't we called, Nosh?"

Ash intentionally avoided Pyke's admonishing gaze and turned his response towards Wiggins. "Local lads from the docks took the body down and moved it somewhere the women and children couldn't see it. Rather upsetting by all accounts."

"Understandable but unfortunate. The crime scene is now contaminated, compromised and of little use," bemoaned Wiggins as the three colleagues strode towards the door of the Morgue.

"Why didn't you tell Thorne about the Russian and the Kent murder, Guv?" asked Pyke, changing the subject.

"I think a serial murder case and a madman who has stolen the plague virus is enough to be getting on with, Jem, don't you agree? Besides, we have little proof that Radasiliev has committed any crime as yet. I suggest we keep our powder dry as regards the Russian, or at least until we have a little more substance to go on," commented Wiggins.

The atmosphere in the morgue was clinical, yet eerily macabre. Wiggins had always found the Morgue a sad and unsettling place. A place where he felt that human beings had ceased to be human, their souls and selves having departed their shells of bone and muscle, nerve, and tissue.

"Good morning, gentlemen," heralded Doctor Pascoe, his voice echoing off the hard, tiled walls of the examination room. Pascoe leant over a naked male body which lay on a central, polished steel mortuary table. Wiggins winced at the blackened, charred flesh which covered the cadaver. He was unpleasantly reminded of a crisped suckling pig rotating on a spit.

Ash felt Pyke's hand being placed on his shoulder from behind and immediately understood the Sergeant's physical communication. "You must have business upstairs, Nosh. That old desk of yours don't run itself," observed Pyke.

"Thanks, Jem." Ash departed through the Morgue door, this pleasant and decent man grateful to be out of the room he hated more than any other in the building.

Pascoe's permanently surprised face turned towards the remaining two officers. "Male, six feet three inches tall, late-thirties to early-forties, I would wager. Cause of death almost certainly murder by immolation. May have been of African or perhaps Caribbean descent on account of the spring-like helix-shaped hair that remains," offered the pathologist, anticipating Wiggin's questioning. "No form of identification I'm afraid, so down to you chaps to dig up a name."

"No need," came Pyke's deep rumble as he slowly approached the corpse. "His name is Horace Smith, or more commonly Demerara to those who knew him less well."

Wiggins turned towards his Sergeant. "You were acquainted with the deceased then, Jem?"

Pyke nodded sombrely. "We grew up together, Guv. Close mates when we were nippers." Pyke sniffed. "He was a rum runner, dock rat, or to hear him tell it, a pirate of the seven seas. Violent man to be sure but he didn't deserve to die in a manner such as this." Pyke raised his hand indicating the charred remains that lay before him. "Burnt Sugar, how ironic for one nicknamed Demerara."

"We will still need an official identification by next of kin or some such," interjected Doctor Pascoe.

"You just had your official identification, Doc. Old Sugar's only family is a daughter by the name of Darlene who got herself as far away from Horace as she possibly could a long time ago. The next closest thing he had to kin was a Great Dane, name of Harlequin," snorted Pyke.

Doctor Pascoe's face looked even more surprised than usual. "How can you possibly tell who this is from these charred remains Sergeant Pyke?" he asked incredulously.

"His face is frozen in a grotesquely burnt smile, and nobody had more gold in his North than good old Demerara Smith," pointed out Pyke. "Besides, you'll find a tattoo of a broken skull on the sole of his left foot." Pascoe looked at Wiggins and nodded his silent affirmation.

"When did you last see him Jem? Do you know what could have happened here, who may be responsible?" asked a concerned Wiggins, his mind racing for possibilities.

Pyke lit a cigarette. Doctor Pascoe was about to admonish him but caught sight of the anger and indignance in Pyke's eyes and thought better of it. He realised that this man had been a friend of the Detective. "Yesterday, Guv. I had a *conversation* with him in the Prospect of Whitby."

"A *conversation* you say, Jem?" Wiggins had noted the intonation of Pyke's voice.

Pyke looked to the ceiling and exhaled a plume of smoke. Pascoe looked on uncomfortably. "Well, truth be known, our conversation turned into more of a disagreement shall we say. Blows were exchanged Guv."

Wiggins approached Pyke. "You mean to tell me you had a brawl with a man in a pub and the next day the same man is found dead, hanging from a bridge, and burned almost beyond recognition!" Wiggins could not cloak his exasperation.

"Well, it wasn't exactly *in* the Pub, Guv. You see, I hit him through the terrace balustrading first, so technically we had the rumble on the beach." Pascoe stifled a laugh and returned to his examination of Demerara Smith's golden teeth. "I was in The Prospect looking for a lead on King, and Sugar, here, was looking like me best bet. Unfortunately, it all got a bit out of hand. Needlessly so I'm afraid to say."

Wiggins puffed out his cheeks with a sigh. '*Where do I go with this?*' he thought inwardly. Pyke suddenly remembered. "Sugar did say that he would burn his bones if he ever found out."

"What do you mean, Sergeant? Who would burn his bones?" Wiggins asked.

"He said that if King found out that he had informed us as to his whereabouts, that he would burn his bones. I ain't never seen old Sugar so scared. Someone must have overheard and taken this information to King," announced Pyke, smashing a fist into his open palm. "Boniface, that little monkey-faced bastard! He was there. He's got ears like a barn owl that one. I'd wager he's gone straight to King and sold Sugar down the river."

"No doubt. This is most definitely the work of our Chinese friend," came the voice of Doctor Pascoe who had just proceeded to pull an object from the throat of the unfortunate Demerara Smith. A small jade dragon rested delicately between the pathologist's thumb and forefinger.

'*The Jade Dragon. King's calling card. I will kill the yellow snake this time, I swear I will.*' thought Pyke. "This is my fault, Guv. If I hadn't behaved like a bull in a china shop and had interviewed Smith somewhere more discreet, he would still be alive."

Wiggins put his hand on one of his friend's slumped shoulders. "You must not blame yourself, Jem. By all accounts, Mr Smith led a dangerous life and moved in perilous circles. Who knows what could have occurred?"

Pyke nodded. '*I'm still going to kill that Chinese bastard,*' he thought. "Doc, was there a big black and white dog found anywhere near the scene?"

"No mention of it as far as I can recall," replied Pascoe scratching his copper wire-like hair.

"Sugar went nowhere without his Great Dane, Harlequin. That dog would have been at the murder scene, so I'm guessing Sugar was killed elsewhere and just hung up in Shadwell as a warning to others. My guess is Chinatown. That's where Smith told me King was hiding out, somewhere in Gerrard Street."

"There was mention of another body, Doctor, one fished out of the River near Wapping," enquired Wiggins turning swiftly towards the florid pathologist. Pascoe snapped off his plastic gloves and threw them in a stainless-steel bin. "Indeed, there was. An altogether more alarming case. The authorities have been informed and the Men from the Ministry will no doubt be on their way as a matter of urgency." He led the detectives towards the locked isolation room and indicated the glazed screen which formed a window in the chamber's outer wall through which the inside could be viewed. On a similar table to that hosting the charred remains of Demerara Smith lay a body wrapped in moist muslin bandages. Only the head of the body had been left unwrapped and it had been turned towards the screen to offer a view of the face of the deceased. Both detectives instinctively flinched at the sight framed in the glass panel. The victim's face was swollen and encrusted with boils and ghastly buboes.

"Rubenstein," murmured Pyke, turning his head away in disgust. "Mr Jabez Rubenstein, head of the Jewish syndicate and a prominent member of King's upper Council."

"Plague!" uttered a shocked Wiggins. "King is insane, he's only gone and unleashed the Plague!"

Chapter 10 - The Battle

"I am dreadfully sorry to have to put you through this ordeal Master Rubenstein, but you do appreciate that we require an official formal identification from the most readily available next of kin," explained Wiggins sympathetically to the young man standing before him. He observed the immediate reaction of young Arnold Rubenstein keenly. Wiggins was carefully weighing up whether he thought it appropriate to put the youngster through what he recognised would be a harrowing and potentially traumatic experience. "You understand that we suspect that the remains recovered from the Thames this morning are those of your uncle, namely Mr Jabez Rubenstein?"

Arnold Rubenstein did not speak but nodded his understanding of the task being asked of him. His deep brown eyes focussed fixedly on those of the Detective Chief Inspector. Wiggins was slightly surprised at what he perceived as the young man's unexpected stoicism. He could perceive no trace of emotion other than a steely, dispassionate determination.

"I must warn you that the body you are about to see is somewhat unusual in respect of the cause of death and you must also consider the rather bloated appearance. This is due to the body having been submerged under water for what we believe to be several days. I must also bind you to a vow of silence regarding this matter. It is of utmost importance that alarm does not spread through the City before the Authorities have had sufficient time to mitigate circumstances. Do you understand?" Wiggins continued to look closely at Arnold Rubenstein who again, merely nodded. '*This boy either has an uncommon grit for one so young,*' concluded Wiggins, '*or is in some way emotionally stunted.*'

"Firstly, I must ask you a few brief confirmatory questions," continued Wiggins. Rubenstein once again nodded his acceptance.

"Your full name and address if you please?"

"Arnold Amos Rubenstein, twenty-eight Hatton Garden, London."

"Your age?"

"Seventeen years, ten months and four days."

Wiggins raised an eyebrow, impressed at the young man's instantaneous detailed recall. "And your relationship to Mr Jabez Rubenstein, also of twenty-eight Hatton Garden?"

"Nephew."

"Thank you. We understand that you are Mr Rubenstein's nearest kin, he having had no wife nor any offspring, and having lost his only brother, your father, some five years ago in somewhat tragic circumstances. Is this correct?" Wiggins again keenly observed the young Jew, aware that this situation would stir memories within Arnold of his father's brutal death at the hand of an unknown assailant. The boy's father had been found decapitated in his money-lending house, three years earlier. His abdomen had been sliced open, his organs removed, and the cavity stuffed full to brimming with gold coins. The murder was thought to have been part of a gangland dispute over unpaid debts. The case remained open and unsolved and the file sat, to this day on Wiggins' desk.

"Correct. I am his only living relative and therefore, his next of kin," confirmed Arnold, his face emotionless.

Wiggins disguised his surprise at the boy's lack of reaction. "Thank you. And as such, I must again ask if you are willing to identify what we currently suspect to be your Uncle's remains?"

"I am."

"I cannot but help think that this course of action is a mistake or at the very least, misguided," reinforced Wiggins as he stood, like a soldier standing to attention, in front of Chief Superintendent, Gideon Thorne's desk. The two men had spent the preceding fifteen minutes debating the merits of Thorne's plan to capture Mr King.

Thorne met Wiggins' steady gaze with his own, equally rigid stare. "You forget, Mr Wiggins, that you foreswore the opportunity of acceding to my position, and, as such, also surrendered your right to question my decisions." Thorne's voice was authoritative, without being excessively loud. The voice of a man who was used to being obeyed rather than questioned.

"But, the public, Sir," implored Wiggins. "We could inadvertently create a riot. There may be loss of life on each side, possibly of innocents. Surely the more prudent course of action would be to keep watch over the area, identify a more precise location, and then carry out a raid under the blanket of darkness. Our target would be a more accurate one and our chances of success would be greater, in my opinion."

"We have no time for such delicacies, Mr Wiggins," rejoined Thorne. "If this fiend has possession of the contagion that we speak of, then we must take him into custody directly or remove him permanently from the board of play as soon as we possibly can. Time is a luxury we simply do not possess."

Wiggins silently and reluctantly conceded the point. He felt somewhat disempowered by this new, dominant presence in the Yard. He had become used to MacDonald affording him a relatively free reign when it came to making decisions and formulating strategies. The Scotsman had realised that the Great Detective's apprentice possessed a razor-sharp, highly logical mind and was more skilled in analytical and tactical police work than he could ever have hoped to be. '*Always know yer limitations laddie,*' rang through his head, and as he stood in front of Thorne, Wiggins realised that the freedom afforded him previously was now utterly gone. An intense frustration built up within him as he continued to look at Thorne. He realised that his senior officer was edging him towards making a comment that would no doubt compromise him, allowing Thorne to exert even further authority over him. He felt diminished in his position. He suspected that Gideon Thorne wanted him out and wondered for what reason. Did Thorne see him as a threat or was there some more deeply seated reason, something more sinister? He decided that this man was not to be trusted.

Wiggins took a deep breath. "In retrospect, I believe you are correct, Sir. Time is very much of the essence and the threat before us is undisputedly one of enormous import."

Thorne almost managed to mask the disappointment he felt at Wiggins' sudden submissiveness and shuffled some papers unnecessarily on his desk. "Very good. We will proceed this evening as outlined in my plan. Sergeant Pyke and I will lead the offensive on horseback whilst you will ensure that the buildings and streets are cleared of innocents and lead the team who will locate King. We must do whatever needs to be done to secure the virus."

"Yes Sir," replied Wiggins, turning on his heels and exiting Thorne's office with the most desultory of salutes.

The Battle of Chinatown, the Fleet Street Press headline would declare it in the next day's early editions. The reports would be predominantly of the most lurid type, with an underlying bias of commentary against the Metropolitan Police.

"The object, gentlemen, is to identify the precise whereabouts of Mr King and his henchmen and locate and secure the contagion, which we envisage will be either on his person or at least close at hand," outlined Gideon Thorne to the mass of police officers gathered before him. The weather-beaten Northerner sat on the back of a jet-black stallion in the cobbled courtyard of New Scotland Yard. Great plumes of breath snorted from his mount's flared nostrils as the Superintendent tried to steady its jumpiness into a stationary position.

"Our discreet enquiries," Thorne glanced pointedly at Pyke who sat calmly astride his splendid grey, Kym, alongside the Superintendent's mount, "have failed to pinpoint our target's exact location other than it being somewhere within the Gerrard Street area of Chinatown." The courtyard was filled with approximately eighty police officers drafted in from various divisions from all over the city. All were armed in some form or another.

Wiggins stood to one side of Thorne's horse, his hands clasped firmly together in front of him. He surveyed the massed ranks in the courtyard, pondering how many of these men would be returning safely to their homes, their wives, and their children this evening. At a glance from Thorne, Wiggins stepped up upon a makeshift platform and, slowly and deliberately, addressed the crowd. "You have all been fully briefed as to your individual roles within this operation. Your divisional commanders will direct your particular part of the manoeuvre. Gentlemen, I urge each one of you to remember two things. Firstly, we are to avoid a panic. Our primary objective is to locate and capture the contagion. We must do this without raising unwanted public alarm. Secondly, our adversaries are Mr King and his army of killers. As you know from your briefings, these individuals are mostly Nepalese Dacoits, Indian Thuggees and members of Chinese cults such as stranglers, garrotters, and other assorted assassins. As such, these are extremely dangerous individuals who, make no mistake, will be merciless in their actions. We *must*, however, ensure that, as the guardians of justice in this great City, we protect our citizens. I want no loss of life among our public, gentlemen, this must be clearly understood!"

"Amen!" shouted Gideon Thorne, his heavily calloused hand clutching his waistcoat over his heart. "May God go with you!"

Pyke looked skyward, unconvinced as to the sincerity of his Superintendent's demonstration of religious fervour. Wiggins watched as the crowd of men milled their way out of the yard towards their various allocated vehicles. He gave Pyke a 'take care' nod as his Sergeant gently spurred on his horse and swung in behind Thorne. Kym's dusky fetlocks pranced in anticipation as her shoes sparked against the cobbles. Pyke saluted his DCI, winked, and kicked on, and the pair trotted out of the yard heading towards Trafalgar Square and thence onwards to Wardour Street.

The ground strategy, developed by Wiggins, had been a simple but hopefully effective one. A chain of armed constables would cordon off each of the lateral exits from Gerrard Street, including the main thoroughfare of Dean Street to the North, thus turning Gerrard Street into a funnel, its entrance in the West from Wardour Street and its only exit to the east into Newport Place. Officers were also placed at strategic points atop each block of buildings. A welcoming committee of constables from 'H' Division would man the west end exit along with half a dozen mounted police. Their role was to direct innocent members of the public to safety and snare any emissaries of King who tried to make their escape through this avenue. The bulk of the taskforce would progress down Gerrard Street from the West, clearing the street of innocents and searching every property for any sign of the Chinese crime lord and his crew of deadly killers. Wiggins would lead this force of infantry whilst Thorne and Pyke would spearhead an advance force on horseback, warning the public, and, hopefully, drawing the fire of their foes, thus forcing them out into the open streets.

Thorne, who emanated self-satisfaction, sat proudly upon his steed, looking around him as if surveying an embryonic battlefield. Gerrard Street was its usual sea of frenetic human motion. The honeyed, spiced aroma of the Orient hung in the air. The Street's narrow artery was clogged, as always, with sightseers, shoppers and diners, pedlars, merchants, cutpurses, beggars and street performers, and beneath it all the killers who made up London's most merciless crime syndicate. "The ideal location, and indeed, the environment within which King could conceal himself," remarked Wiggins thoughtfully, whilst scanning the scene before him.

"How so, Sir?" asked Detective Constable Murray who stood by his side.

"Why, here in Chinatown, King is cloaked by a population of fellow countrymen. Some will no doubt be loyal to him, some will be terrified into their support, whilst others, perhaps, may be completely unaware of his existence. He can hide behind numbers, race, language, loyalty and indeed anonymity. This very street is a warren of buildings, many interlinked and many with labyrinthine basements. Remember, this is a veritable hive of illegal activity. It is also plumb in the heart of London and we all know how simple it is to lose oneself in the flood of humanity that flows constantly through the arteries of this city," elucidated Wiggins.

Murray nodded in appreciation as the difficulty and enormity of the task ahead of them began to cement itself in his mind. "So even if he is here, within this very street, one of the thousands in our city, we may still fail to capture him?" wondered Murray.

Wiggins clapped an encouraging hand to the younger man's shoulder. "Let us not lose heart before we begin. Our plan, if somewhat ill-timed in my opinion, is sound and we are many and well drilled. Besides, good will always prevail over evil. That is why we are all still here, walking Earth's good ground." Murray nodded in appreciation of Wiggins' sentiment.

Thorne, satisfied that all was in order, and that all men were correctly positioned, raised his right hand, and gently squeezed his horse to signal a gentle forward trot. Pyke followed suit, eyes scanning from left to right and back again, trying to pick out any furtive signs from amongst the crowds.

Dozens of policemen began to usher people discretely from the street, shops and houses. Voices of protestation began to swell. Properties were evacuated as efficiently as possible, given the difficulty with the language barrier. "Clear the cobbles!" came the echoing cry from Wiggins and his colleagues. "Qīngchú fāngshì."

A slender ebony cane was raised by a black, leather-gloved hand to address the door of New Scotland Yard. The cane was crowned with the likeness of a horned ram, cast in solid silver. The ram's head repeatedly butted the Oxford blue, timber door with a loud staccato rapping. Sergeant Nosher Ash stood behind his desk, debating whether to answer the knocking. His parting orders from Superintendent Thorne had been to lock down the Yard and to only open the doors on the safe return of the taskforce. Until then he was to regard the Yard as a citadel and he, as its guardian. Nosh's tongue licked along the underside of his bushy moustache before biting on his lower lip. His already slit thin eyes narrowed even further. The rapping became more pronounced, more urgent. Ash bit his lip harder and ran his great bratwurst like fingers hesitantly through his thickly thatched hair. He remained stationed behind his desk as ordered.

More knocking, this time accompanied by the shrill, frantic voice of a woman in obvious distress. "Help me! Please help me! My Baby! They've taken my little girl!"

Those words immediately dictated Sergeant Ash's course of action. Orders or no orders, Thorne or no Thorne, there was a woman in desperate trouble and in need of his assistance. The noble Ash could not ignore her pleas. "Hold on Madam, I'm coming, I'm coming," he shouted as he strode purposefully towards the double doors. He located the correct keys on his chain and unlocked, unbolted, and flung open the doors. Astounded, he stood almost nose to nose with the pale-skinned, inky eyed Russian necromancer, Luca Radasiliev.

"I was beginning to think there was no one home, Sergeant," smiled Radasiliev, his voice freakishly high-pitched, and unmistakably that of the distressed woman Ash had just heard.

"Ere, what's your game mate? I'll knock your bleedin' ..." Ash's voice trailed off into silence as the Russian slowly raised his cane, presenting the head of the ram to that of Sergeant Ash who found himself instantly transfixed. His mind whirled and spun in a heady vortex of confusion as the face of the Ram transformed slowly into a human visage. The face of a heavy-set man approaching late middle age. A kindly yet tired and forlorn looking face. A face with twinkling narrow eyes and shock of white hair. A face he recognised. His own.

"What sorcery is this?" he mumbled, unable to disengage his gimlet-eyed stare from his silvery doppelganger image. He felt dizzy and displaced, unsteady on his feet.

"Sorcery, Sergeant? Why, there is no sorcery here," answered Radasiliev, his voice now returned to its own measured, cultured tone. "You see only what you fear the most. In your case it is yourself. You fear the creeping approach of old age and of becoming redundant, forgetful and ineffective." The Russian cocked his head slightly to one side as would a playful puppy, looking beyond Ash and smiled the most charming of lopsided smiles. "I believe your nest is relatively empty."

The mesmerised Ash nodded slightly, unable to avert his gaze from the silver-headed cane, which began to liquefy and elongate, stretching upwards as though being pulled by some unseen force. As fluid as quicksilver, it stretched longer and longer still until it became more solid, more honed. Ash felt a sharp ringing in his ears, a constant tinnitus resonance that increased in sharpness as did the edges of the blade that was being forged inexplicably before him. The blade glinted, an azure blue light refracted from its edge, flashing across the big Desk Sergeant's eyes, as if the blade was winking an introduction in anticipation of some forthcoming surprise. He could see his face clearly reflected in the blade, a face that seemed to slump and grow older before his very eyes. Suddenly the blade disappeared from Ash's view as it was thrust with unbelievable force clean through his abdomen. Ash dropped to his knees, the hilt of an ebony bladed sword wedged below his rib cage, its glinting, razor-sharp tip protruding between his shoulder blades.

Radasiliev strode past the body of a quivering Sergeant Ash, tipping his sable top hat as he did so and walked authoritatively into the Station. "To die, to be *really* dead, that must be glorious!" the Russian shouted triumphantly with a flourish. As he did so, three young constables ran towards him. "Sarge!" shouted constable Perkins, aghast at what he had just witnessed, the unbreakable Nosher Ash lying slowly dying in an ever-expanding pool of blood. Radasiliev waved the three officers back with a sweeping arc of his arm. All three constables flew backwards violently as if hit by a hurricane and crashed against the rear wall of the triage room. Perkins lay unconscious while the other two each tried to rise but found themselves unable to move, frozen like carved stone statues. Radasiliev laughed at his work. "How convenient. You each fear an inability to meet your Superior's expectations. Inadequacy is such a useful trait to me."

The noise was high-pitched, a constant, almost deafening symphony of human noise. Hundreds of protesting Chinese milled out into Gerrard Street. Most protested vehemently at being dragged from their homes or places of work as Police officers invaded their properties with swift efficiency. Confusion reigned as constables piled into restaurants and kitchens, homes and bathhouses, drinking dens and opium shacks. Each was systematically pulled apart and searched indiscriminately, much to the protestations of its startled occupants. A closely-knit cordon of constables, each brandishing a baton, marched slowly down Gerrard Street, herding the human flock along the artery towards its exit. People began to push back against the cordon. Objects were thrown, bricks, items of food, and utensils from kitchens, even the occasional knife or hammer. Simmering tension caused tempers to rise, the atmosphere becoming increasingly toxic and confrontational.

Wiggins could see that the crowd now vastly outnumbered the police presence by more than ten to one and that the number of people spilling out into the street was increasing with every passing second. He recognised that soon the baying crowd would overwhelm his Force. "This is a huge mistake!" he shouted to Murray as he ducked to evade a cobblestone that narrowly missed his head. "We must stop this madness!"

Wiggins hurriedly pushed his way towards Thorne and Pyke, each of whom was struggling to control their mounts amidst the increasing human current that threatened to drown them. Wiggins was astounded at the sheer volume of people that were pouring out into the street, like rats fleeing an onrushing fire. '*Surely these people are being used as a blind. King is using these people as a human shield,*' he surmised. He looked around and found an overturned fruit cart which he clambered on top of, his leather soles slipping against its greasy timbers as he tried to gain sufficient purchase. He stood cautiously, caught his balance, and waved vigorously towards Thorne. The Superintendent turned his horse and forced his way through the crowd back towards Wiggins.

"Sir, we have to put an end to this carnage!" Wiggins shouted. "Innocent people are being trampled and crushed. Children are being caught up in this human maelstrom. It is inevitable there will be fatalities and many more injured!"

Pyke drew alongside Thorne. His stallion's eyes were wide with panic and Pyke was exerting all his strength and horsemanship in an effort to keep Kym under control. "The Guvnor is right, Sir. This was a recipe for disaster from the get-go, casualties are inescapable, look around you, Sir. Believe me, I have seen enough battlefields to know one when I see one. This can and will turn ugly in the blink of an eye."

In response, Thorne spun his horse, unholstered his pistol and fired into the air three times. There was hate, embarrassment and madness in his eyes. "Move these people out!" he yelled. As his horse turned it rose to a rampant position, its hooves clawing at thin air, trying to find purchase where there was none. An elderly man in a saffron robe and Coolie hat was caught on the head by a descending hoof and dropped instantaneously to the cobbles. Both Wiggins and Pyke could see immediately from the old man's catastrophic head injuries that he had been dead before he struck the ground. The two colleagues traded an open-mouthed look. Thorne looked downward at the prone figure of the old man, exchanged a 'what of it?' glance, shrugged, and gave his steed a powerful urging kick in the ribs forcing his charger further into the crowd.

"Bloke's a bloomin' lunatic, Guv," offered Pyke. "I've seen it before. The inner beast comes out and a red mist descends. He's gone. Lost control."

"Or else he knows *exactly* what he is doing, Jem," speculated Wiggins thoughtfully. "Go after him, stay close. I will try and clear these people to safety and attempt to regain some semblance of order."

"Aye, aye, Sir," confirmed Pyke with a glint in his eye. He manoeuvred Kym in a tight about-turn and headed after his Superintendent.

Wiggins decided that enough was enough. If this heaving throng turned against his men any further, innocent people on both sides would certainly die. He withdrew his whistle from his waistcoat pocket and gave three short shrill blasts and one loud long blast. This was the preordained signal to the cordons on the side alleyways to break and allow the crowd to spill out of the enforced funnel. The lines of blue broke, allowing the deluge of humanity to flow out of the street and into the surrounding areas. Just as Wiggins jumped down from the fruit cart, Constable Murray raced to his side and shouted, "If King was here, he sure as hell won't be any longer, Guv. Thorne letting off his gun has made sure of that. This is a disaster of an operation!"

"I fear you are correct, Murray. One could almost say that those shots may have been a signal of sorts." Just then Wiggins glanced upwards, his eye caught by a glint of light crossing his face. He immediately saw a stooped figure looking down at him from a grimy fourth-floor window of a shabby building whose ground floor appeared, from its signage, to be an oriental theatre of sorts. Wiggins could see recreations of shadow puppetry fixed to the outer walls of the building, and the door was framed by a pagoda-like structure. The figure hunched at the window was slight and partially blurred by the grime that coated the glass, but Wiggins could see enough to be convinced that he was looking directly at the fiendish form of Mr King. A tingle of anticipation rippled through his body. The skin on his arms goose fleshed causing the hairs to stand to attention. To Wiggins, it was as if time stood still. The tumult and noise around him ebbed away to a muted dull drone as his eyes met with those of the satanic mandarin. He could clearly see a smile spread across King's evil countenance as the Chinaman bowed his head in acknowledgement of Wiggins' presence. The Chinaman then clapped exaggerated fake applause towards the detective. Albert Wiggins felt a chill course through his body, his fists and heart tightening as one. "It is he, Murray. It is King." Wiggins' voice sounded internalised to him, as if he were underwater, listening to a conversation held by others. It was his voice, but not at all how he thought his voice sounded. His mind raced. Locking eyes with the Chinese madman, it was as if they were the only two people in the world, a world that had become slow and blurred, his only focus being those serpentine, inhuman eyes.

Wiggins shook his head as if emerging from under water and looked at Murray, urgency painted across his face. "It is King!" he repeated. He turned his gaze back to the window and saw nothing but the grime-stained glass. The Chinaman had gone or had never been there. "Come, follow me!" commanded Wiggins, now drawing his pistol. Murray and several other constables followed their superior officer as he began to force his way through the still swamping crowd. Pushing through the horde was like being caught in a fierce onrushing riptide. Wiggins shouted for Pyke, but his voice was lost amidst the cacophony of the street.

It was then that the double doors of the theatre suddenly flew open and at least two dozen dacoits ran out brandishing swords and machetes. They were closely followed by one of the most fearsome sights any man could ever see. The gigantic form of Hercules Chin squeezed his way out of the doorway as if removing the building as he would an overcoat, and raised himself to his full height. His enormity was somehow incongruous to his surroundings, so out of context was the huge form of the giant. The Chinese Titan threw back his head and roared at the sky.

"Jesus Christ, Sir! Am I really seeing what I think I'm seeing?" gasped Murray, his skin prickling in primal fear.

Wiggins looked admonishingly at the constable. "I would not have considered you as a blasphemer, John. I am surprised."

"So am I, Sir! But that's a bleedin' monster before us! A real-life monster!"

"Truly remarkable. Surely Hercules Chin must have perished when we riddled his body with bullets on Pakapuh pier?" questioned Wiggins.

The Dacoits began to cleave their way through the crowd to reach the oncoming policemen. Wiggins could see a second and third wave of killers following their barbaric colleagues. "Fire at the devils!" ordered Wiggins, immediately realising that he and his constables were now hopelessly outnumbered. All the while, Hercules Chin tossed aside bystanders like they were flies. The constables fired their pistols at the oncoming hoard. Bodies fell to the ground, only for others to appear in their place, leaping over the fallen assassins as if they were no more than driftwood. The Thuggees hacked with their machetes and threw razor keen knives into the phalanx of constables. Some were also armed with pistols and fired these indiscriminately in the direction of the police, paying no heed to any innocents who may have been caught up in the crossfire. Wiggins and his companions returned fire but were seriously outnumbered and disadvantaged by the innocents all around. The frightful sight that was Hercules Chin continued his ponderous advance, wading through the crowd. Wiggins blasted his whistle several times in a desperate effort to summon more officers to his side. Reinforcements struggled against the tide of the fleeing public, straining to come to their comrade's aid, fighting to breach an impregnable human wall. And then the Asiatics were upon Wiggins and his men, wielding axes and machetes, knives and garrottes, professional, merciless murderers with no fear of the law nor respect for life. Blades slashed through flesh whilst bullets pierced muscle and splintered bone. Blood spewed upon the cobbles as bodies fell to the ground. Men fought hand-to-hand, the Thuggees desperately trying to strangle the policemen with their lethal wire garrottes. Adversaries rolling together in the street gutters, locked in their private, frantic struggles for survival. Wiggins stood alongside Murray, each aiming carefully and felling the rampant dacoits on their murderous approach. Wiggin's pistol clicked, its chamber now empty. He exchanged a knowing look with Murray and braced himself grimly for the imminent onslaught of a dozen knife-wielding killers. He drew his baton, clenched his fists, thought of Mary, and offered a perfunctory prayer for his salvation.

Suddenly, from Wiggins right side charged a half-ton equine battering ram of pale grey. Its momentum was such that the dacoits into which it stormed were sent flying and were broken like straw dolls, trampled under the weight of the impact. Men screamed and yelled. Kym reared under its rider, hooves strafing at both the air and the surrounding Thuggees, splitting skulls, shattering bones, and ending lives. The stallion's eyes were ablaze with, what appeared to Wiggins to be a fit of anthropomorphic rage, its irises entirely encompassed with white sclera. Kym's coat was stained with a mixture of salt and blood and steam clouded from its body in great billows of adrenalin. And there, atop the magnificent animal, was Jem Pyke, almost standing in his stirrups, wielding his old cavalry sabre with a ferocity and accuracy that simply took Wiggins' breath away. Man, after man fell before the brutal onslaught of Pyke's sword, its blurred blade spraying arcs of crimson against the cold grey evening sky. Kym was a three-thousand-pound weapon under Pyke's guidance and Pyke was a man possessed.

"Come on ye evil little yellow-skinned bastards, let's be havin' ya!" roared Pyke, as he ploughed through the mass of King's men, wreaking havoc within their ranks. "Yer up against Jem Pyke now ladies!" Pyke's thirst for battle was as unquenchable as it was inspiring, and his intervention had given more constables the opportunity to break through to join the fray, and, together with their fearless Sergeant, the company of police presented such a threatening prospect that the remaining dacoits lost nerve and scattered, fleeing into the crowds, disappearing like rats scurrying up alleyways or into buildings.

"After them, men!" commanded a relieved Wiggins. "Capture as many of the devils as you can." The men of the Metropolitan Police fearlessly gave pursuit. Wiggins turned towards Pyke, "King is in there, Jem, I saw him with my own eyes," indicating the narrow ramshackle theatre that stood before them. "I saw him in the top floor window. King is in that building!"

Without uttering a word, Pyke pulled on Kym's reigns and galloped full pelt towards the theatre, fleetingly catching a glimpse of the gargantuan Hercules Chin as he ducked and squeezed himself back in through the doorway.

Chin knew that he must protect Father King and ensure he got him to safety. The colossus turned and lumbered towards the basement stairs. He knew that Father King would escape through the interlacing tunnels that lay deep in the bowels of the theatre.

Just as he reached the top of the basement stairs, he heard a sound he did not recognise. He turned his great Cro-Magnon browed head, frowning at the noise, trying to identify what it was and where it was coming from. The sound grew louder and louder. Closer and closer. A cacophony of iron shoes hammering upon stone cobbles like a blacksmith's hammer battering a rhythm of steel upon an anvil, louder and louder, louder and louder. Then suddenly, briefly, the sound stopped for perhaps two seconds. Two seconds in which Chin curled his perspiring lips and grunted dismissively.

An ear wrenching crash of shattering glass and rending timber followed the brief silence as the great grey stallion thundered through the front window frame of the building. Shards of glass and splintered wood peppered the giant's face, forcing him to shield his eyes from the shrapnel. Debris skidded across the floor as Kym slewed to a halt amongst destroyed tables and chairs. The great horse raised itself onto its hind legs and crashed downwards once more, its weight sending a shudder through cracking floorboards. Jem Pyke jumped from his steed, his sabre in one hand, his other fist clenched tightly enough to show his great knuckles white against his skin. Pyke's battle-scarred features, spattered with Dacoit blood, emanated sheer menace as he stood facing the giant Chinaman. "Just you and me now Tiny. Better get ready for a rumble Big Boy," Pyke spat through gritted teeth.

The Chinese giant stared down at Pyke with unfeeling monolid eyes. He knew he could easily snap this little man in two, just as he had countless others. What did he care for his boasts and threats? They meant nothing to him. Chin raised himself to his full height and expanded his great chest. He threw back his head and roared at the ceiling. A primordial, terrifying roar that blasted adrenalin through Jem Pyke's body. More than six hundred rounds of legitimate boxing in the army and numerous brutal unregulated bare-knuckle challenges, not to mention brawls and scrapes in the line of his duties, could not have prepared Pyke for Hercules Chin. There was nothing that could prepare any man for this. Almost eight feet tall, four-hundred pounds of killer stood in front of Pyke.

Pyke rushed the Giant, swinging his sabre laterally and at a low trajectory, targeting the giant's upper thighs. The swiftness and agility of Chin's movement surprised Pyke. Instead of his blade finding flesh, he found his wrist grasped in a vice-like grip. Chin's enormous hand began to squeeze and crush Pyke's wrist flexors. Pyke grimaced in pain, sweat beading on his brow. The sabre clattered to the floor under the enormous pressure exerted by Chin's grasp. Pyke lashed out with his left hand, clubbing the Giant in the groin. Chin emitted a sickening howl of pain and released his grip. As the giant doubled over Pyke saw his chance. Perhaps his one and only chance. He let fly with the hardest uppercut he had ever thrown. Beginning at his bootlaces, the punch travelled upwards, Pyke digging in his heels and rolling his bovine muscled shoulders to give the punch as much momentum and power as he possibly could. Kinetic energy exploding into a potential destructive force. His fist crashed into the huge jutting jaw of the gargantuan Chinese assassin. Pyke winced as a bolt of pain shot from his fist to his elbow and on through to his shoulder. It was as if he had hit an ingot of steel. He looked at the Titan in front of him, his dead, slanting eyes searching those of Pyke, scanning his opponent with a sense of disbelief that another man had the audacity to try and hurt him. Chin shuddered then wobbled and Pyke could feel the floorboards vibrate with the impact of the colossus' weight as he dropped to his knees. The giant was stunned. Pyke saw another chance and summoning as much strength as he had remaining, drew back his left arm, and let loose with a ferocious open-handed upward motion into the nose of the Chinaman causing it to explode upwards with a sickening crack. Chin howled in pain. He had never, in all his years of violence, encountered any man who had been able to inflict such on onslaught upon him. The revelation confused him as he felt the hot blood flow from his nose into his mouth. He felt anger. A furious anger that penetrated his habitual drug-fuelled fugue. He growled a deep-throated growl that reverberated in his throat. The Lion was hurt. The lion was furious.

Pyke's right hand was damaged and all but useless due to the searing pain running through the bones and muscles, so he swung a left hook which never reached its intended target. Chin caught the attempted blow in the palm of one spade-like hand, whilst grabbing Pyke around the throat with his other. The monster smiled as he began to rise, blood pouring from what was once a nose, lifting the struggling Pyke by the neck as he did so. "I crush you, little man, squeeze your neck so it snaps like all the others."

Pyke braced his great neck muscles and kicked frantically at the Giant, both of his feet now off the ground. "Fuck you!" he spat through gritted teeth. Chin threw back his head and roared with laughter, squeezing ever tighter. Pyke clawed at Chin's hand trying desperately to pull the Chinaman's enormous fingers away from his throat. But each thickly calloused finger was the width of a police truncheon and could not be budged. Pyke could feel his breath being taken away from him. The blood pulsing through his temples felt as though it would burst through his veins. His face was darkening to a reddish blue colour as blood pooled in the vessels circulating his head. Still, the laughing giant squeezed, tighter and tighter. Blackness began to descend upon Pyke as the oxygen in his lungs began to ebb away. His kicking became increasingly frenzied until finally, it ceased altogether. He could hear the laughter of the Giant intermingled with the wheezing of his almost completely restricted throat. All became black. All became quiet.

He could see her flame-coloured hair. Dark red silken waves upon white cotton pillows. Copper snakes that spread over a frosted cotton landscape. A deep auburn tangle cascading over an alabaster pale shoulder. He could smell her scent, fresh and fruitful tinged with an underlying earthiness. He could feel himself burying his face in the lush thickness of her tresses, breathing in that scent, revelling in the feel of her, lost to any world outside of that embrace. He felt himself shifting to be even closer to her. To engulf himself in her. He could feel himself slipping away. Then there was the sound of a distant voice. A faint echo. It was not her voice. It was Him.

Wiggins.

"Drop that man or I shoot!"

Wiggins knew the lumbering giant had no idea that his pistol was bereft of bullets.

"Drop him right now, in the name of *The* King!"

The giant Chinaman considered Wiggins curiously, then looked at the pistol trained on him. Chin's grasp gradually loosened, and Pyke felt his body slump to the ground with a crash. He gasped ferociously for air, clawing at his shirt collar, desperately gulping at the atmosphere as frantically as any dying man would when trying to cling to life. He heard a gunshot, then another and another.

Chapter 11 - The Tunnels

Wiggins produced a small silver capsule from inside his jacket pocket, flicked it open with his thumbnail and waved it under the nose of Jem Pyke. The smelling salts worked almost instantly, snapping Pyke back into consciousness. He unsteadily propped himself up on one elbow and rubbed at his bruised and burning throat, wincing in pain at the rawness caused by the constriction his oesophagus had sustained at the hand of the monstrous Hercules Chin. He swallowed several times. Each time felt as if he was swallowing shoe tacks. His right hand was severely swollen and was beginning to discolour but to his delight and amazement, it did not seem misshapen or fractured in any way.

"Try not to talk, Jem," urged Wiggins. "We must get you medical attention immediately." Wiggins knelt beside his colleague, his hand on Pyke's shoulder. Pyke shook his head. "Did you get him? Did you shoot the brute?" winced Pyke, his voice a barely audible rasping wheeze.

Wiggins winced, trying to imagine the pain Pyke must be suffering. "I admit Jem, that I was calling his bluff, you see I had no ammunition, my pistol chamber was empty. The gunshots came from behind me from some of our constables. I know that their intervention undoubtedly saved both our lives. I cannot imagine they could have missed such a large target, but the brute, as you call him, escaped down the basement stairs. He is incredibly fleet of foot for such an enormous individual. There are six armed constables in pursuit as we speak."

Pyke pushed himself erect with a grunt of monumental effort, still gasping for breath. "They will be killed, Bert. Our lads will be killed. I must go after them. That thing is inhuman in physique and thought."

"What you need to do Soldier is get to a bloody hospital! You can hardly stand man. You may have suffered permanent damage and I cannot have such a thing stinging my conscience. You need a Doctor," repeated Wiggins putting a restraining hand against Pyke's chest. He could feel Pyke's rock-hard pectoral muscles heaving for air beneath the worsted waistcoat that his Sergeant habitually wore.

Pyke shook his head. "Later, Guv. The last time I saw a Doctor he tried to bite me bleedin' face off remember? Anyway, my boys are in danger and we have a monster to slay." He gently but forcefully removed Wiggins' hand from his chest. "Remember the tale of David and Goliath, Guv? Well such things can happen, we just have to show more nounce the next time," he winked. "We have no time to lose." He looked around for his sabre and retrieved it from the dust-covered floor. He balanced it in his blood-stained hand and threw Wiggins another wink. Wiggins knew there was nothing he could do or say to stop the juggernaut that was Jem Pyke. He knew when his Sergeant's mind was set so he nodded his agreement. Both men exchanged a knowing glance and proceeded to run stutteringly, side by side, down the stairs towards the basement of the theatre.

He could see only a blurred circular shape floating high above him. A chill ran through his body causing him to shiver uncontrollably and soaking his clothes through with sweat. Gradually his eyes began to focus, and his vision cleared. Objects became more defined. Nosher Ash realised that the floating circle was, in fact, the ornate ceiling rose of the Yard's entrance foyer. He had not felt this dizzy since the Christmas Ball of nineteen-ten when he had imbibed copious amounts of cheap champagne on an empty stomach. He grunted as he propped himself up on his elbows and tried to remember how he had ended up lying on his back on the Station floor. Suddenly he recalled the eyes. Those black eyes, like rippling pools of oil embedding themselves into his brain. The Russian. Luca Radasiliev, he had been here, he remembered. Then with an icy start that froze the blood in his veins, he remembered the blade. A blade of what had appeared to be liquid steel that the Russian had plunged into his abdomen. He frantically checked his torso, unbuttoning his tunic with fingers that disobeyed him. Was his shirt soaked with sweat or with blood, he worried, looking down. There was no blade, no blood, no wound, just his rather rotund belly, still in one piece. The back of his head hit the cold tiled floor as he lay back down and exhaled a long sigh of relief. '*Thank God, I'm alive,*' he thought. '*But how?*' He had seen the blade enter his body with his own eyes. He had felt it rip through his torso and shuddered at the thought. He recalled the flesh rending agony of it tearing through his muscles and organs, scratching his bones as it penetrated him. '*How was this possible?*' he wondered.

His senses began to return to him and as they did, so too did his concern for his colleagues. Most of the Force were on duty at the Gerrard Street raid and the Commissioner and his staff were at a meeting in the Home Office. That had left only himself, a few constables and clerks and the mortuary staff. He heaved himself to his feet and re-buttoned his tunic. '*No excuse for untidiness. That Radasiliev seems to have shrunk me waistcoat,*' he thought incongruously. As his head cleared still further, he was hit by a thought that filled him with absolute dread. He realised that Radasiliev may very well still be in the building, so he quickly unsheathed his truncheon and began to take in his surroundings. He was sure he could smell the unmistakable odour of smoke.

Turning around he saw three uniformed constables sprawled on the floor against the far wall. Each appeared insensible. He rushed towards them, grabbing the beaker of water that he habitually kept on his desk counter, and sluiced the three men. They each awoke with a jerk, spluttering and wiping the unwanted water from their faces. "What was that for, Sarge!" protested one.

"Never you mind, lad, get yourselves up. We may be under attack. Stand to lads!" ordered Ash. He ran towards the firearms cupboard recessed behind his desk and reached for the key chain that always hung from his belt. For the second time that day, his fingers fumbled as if they had a mind of their own. His key chain had disappeared. "Damn Russian must have taken it!" he cursed. He tried to recall to his befuddled memory whether there were any prisoners in the cells.

He sniffed at the air. "Follow me, lads," he ordered and rushed down a corridor that took him and the three constables to the major incident room. Ash could see smoke curling insidiously from under the door. "Stand back lads!" he instructed. "One of you grab the extinguisher," pointing to the wall-mounted water siphon. "Simpson, get back to the main desk and call for the fire brigade in Horseferry Road. Tell old Joe to get a tender round here sharpish." Commands duly given, Ash carefully turned the brass doorknob which was hot to the touch and was instantly met with a backdraft of heat that blew onto his face, singing his eyebrows and straw-like hair. Holding his arm up to protect his eyes, he felt the air being sucked from the corridor into the room. He could feel the heat dissipating and, feeling rather more confident the worst had passed, he gingerly entered the room. The dry heat was stifling but the flames were restricted, somewhat inexplicably as far as Ash could see, to the main wall of the room. "Pass me the Siphon, lad and pull down those curtains, I reckon we can beat this out ourselves with a bit of luck." The three men attacked the blazing wall and with a combination of water sprayed from the hand-pumped extinguisher and some vigorous beating with the drapes, the flames were soon subdued. Burnt flakes and cinders danced around the room like a negative snow flurry. Ash stood back, breathing heavily, and looked aghast at the dripping, smoking wall. Written on the plaster in yard high charred, smouldering letters were the words; 'The Lord of Darkness is upon Us.'

"Well, I never!" ejaculated Ash wiping the sweat from his soot darkened eyes.

Wiggins and Pyke reached the bottom of the basement stairs and were faced with the entrances to three separate tunnels. "This is a veritable labyrinth, Jem," stated

Wiggins, looking around him at the brickwork walls and vaulted ceiling. "We could be led into an infernal rabbit's warren of tunnels here, an ambush awaiting at any turn."

"You go down the middle, Guv," decided Pyke. "And I'll take the right."

"No, Jem. We stay together. That way we will stand a better chance. Whatever we face, we face together," emphasised Wiggins.

"Triumph together or die together, is that it, Bert?" stated Pyke with a glint in his eye.

Wiggins smiled. "That's about the size of it, Jem. Look! On the ground over there." Wiggins indicated some disturbance amongst the dust and debris on the floor leading into the furthermost right of the three tunnels. "They went that way. Our lads must have been hot on the heels of their quarry. They all went down the same route. No disturbance at any of the other two entrances."

"Right you are," Pyke was already racing ahead and was through the mouth of the catacomb in an instant. Wiggins followed, astounded at his Sergeant's remarkable recuperative powers. The two ran apace for a few minutes, their lungs heaving, hearts beating and foreheads beading with sweat. The tunnel twisted and turned. All the while Wiggins fully expected to run full pelt into the ferocious figure of the giant Chinaman at every turn. His stomach lurched at the thought. He knew, however, that Pyke would be relishing the prospect of engaging, once again, in mortal combat with the Chinese Titan. Round two. Seconds out.

Suddenly, Pyke, who was now several yards in front of Wiggins, skidded to an abrupt halt, dust billowing at his sudden deceleration. "Damn him! Damn him to Hell!" Pyke's strained voice echoed around the tunnel. Wiggins reached the point at which Pyke had stopped and felt his stomach tumble out of his body. In front of them, barring their way was a steel plate door, barred from the other side. On the floor at the foot of the door lay the twisted bodies of six constables, all palpably dead, and all with their necks broken.

"I *will* kill him, Guv. I *will* kill him!" shouted Pyke pounding the metal door with his sound hand. "No messing this time. One fucking bullet into that yellow bastard's forehead. Job done, and he can rot in Hell." The dull sound of fist against steel reverberated around the tunnel for what seemed an age.

Wiggins knelt and examined the bodies of his fallen colleagues before crossing himself. He knew these men. He knew their wives, their families, their hopes and dreams. Tears pooled in his eyes as he looked up at Pyke. "Thorne is to blame for this debacle. Where is he? Where did our so-called *superior* officer disappear to anyway? As God is my witness Jem, I will see the end of that man and gain vengeance for these brave young men."

The diminutive Chinaman strode purposefully down the underground corridor, the staccato sound of his heels echoing sharply against its stone walls. On each side of him marched a Shang twin, the ruthless, sharp-featured brothers who acted as King's protective shadows. Behind this triumvirate followed a dozen or so dacoits, grim menace etched across their hard, weather-beaten faces. Then behind this band of hardened assassins trailed the enormous, stooped figure of Hercules Chin, his head bent forward and his shoulders brushing against the vaulted ceiling of the catacomb.

King felt amongst his emerald silk robes and found the priceless vial of plague contagion safely ensconced. He threw back his head and screeched the childlike laugh of a maniac. "Now you will see my vengeance, Mr Wiggins! Now you will see the wrath of the Golden Empire!"

Chapter 12 - The Aftermath

Wiggins met Pyke on the steps of the Yard. His staff car, a four-seater Arrol Johnston, had been parked in the station garage and Pyke had ridden Kym back from the disaster that had been Gerrard Street. The horse had been virtually traumatised by the day's distressing events, but Pyke had somehow managed to calm the grey charger on the canter back. He had whispered reassuringly in Kym's ear all the way. Steam rose from his steed as Pyke executed a swing dismount, smearing the salt-stained shoulder of the beast as he did so. "Take care of him, Fred. This old boy earned his corn today make no mistake." Pyke rubbed his swollen right hand but ignored the pain.

"Yes Sir, Sergeant Pyke!" saluted Fred, a tall gangly youth with a curly mop of hair and a feeble attempt at a moustache. "Full treatment for this hero today, Sir."

Pyke smiled his thanks to the youngster, noticing for the first time, the lad's battered old, brown derby hat and faint upper lip shadow. He chuckled inwardly as he stood face to face with the gallant horse. He stroked Kym's neck affectionately. Kym nodded his head up and down in acknowledgement. Pyke's face was clouded in plumes of condensed vapour from the horse's breath. He deeply exhaled his own breath towards the horse's nostrils and whispered in its ear. "Who's the bravest damn horse in the whole bloomin' cavalry then?"

The great grey clicked his hooves off the cobbles in appreciation, nodding his head up and down in apparent agreement. Pyke laughed and vigorously patted his stallion's crest and neck again. Fred rubbed an apple against his leather tunic and threw it towards Pyke. The detective deftly caught it and fed it to the horse. Fred smiled at the obvious bond between horse and master and felt somehow jealous of the horse.

As they entered the front desk area, Wiggins and Pyke were immediately greeted by a stammering Nosher Ash. The large, ursine Desk Sergeant looked somewhat unsteady on his feet as he wiped grimy sweat from his brow. Wiggins instantly smelled the acrid odour of smoke. Not the smell of the Cambridge tobacco that habitually accompanied Nosher, but something more biting, more acerbic. The stench reminded Wiggins of the doused bonfires he and his fellow mudlarks would light to see them through their boyhood winter nights. "What has occurred here, Sergeant?" he asked forcefully.

"Fire, Guv!" responded Nosher, breathing heavily. "We managed to douse it sharpish though, purely superficial with no real damage done. Amazing really when you…"

"Anyone injured?" interrupted an alarmed Wiggins, looking Sergeant Ash up and down, trying to establish the extent of any damage.

"Minor abrasions and sore muscles only, although that damned Russian had me convinced that he'd run through me midships with a bloody great sword!" Nosher reached for his sternum and shook his head, wincing in confusion at the memory. He also wondered at the vague memory of an indistinct vision of a cloven hoof stepping over his prone body.

"Russian? Sword?" snapped Wiggins "Do you mean Radasiliev has been here and is behind this?"

"It was him all right, Sir. I'll not forget those damned black eyes in a month of Sundays, believe you me. Like pools of oil, they were, but it was his cane, Sir! His cane turned into a huge bloomin' blade right before me very eyes, Guv, and then…" Ash struggled to continue. He looked from Wiggins to a perplexed Pyke and back again.

"Then what, Sergeant Ash? Did he possess a sword cane?" asked Wiggins, recalling the extraordinary weapon that Dante Van Hoon seemed to permanently carry on his person, the shaft of exotic Bocote wood adorned with intricate carvings denoting the Inferno's nine circles of Hell.

"Not as such, Sir," added Ash running his hand through his dense crop of hair, as was his habit. He shook his head slowly, visibly shuddering at the memory. He hesitated before continuing, realising how fanciful his words would seem. "His stick, it sort of melted away, became fluid like. Shimmered you might say, like molten metal, and then transformed before my eyes into a solid blade. Then he up and plunged it directly through me vitals!" Ash looked wonderingly at his abdomen as if he had just seen it for the first time. "Sounds preposterous like Sir, but that's exactly what happened."

Wiggins nodded and put a comforting hand on the Desk Sergeant's shoulder. "He is a manipulator of the mind like no other, Nosh. Van Hoon refers to him as a conjurer of the darkest arts and a summoner of demons."

Nosh continued to shake his head as he led the two officers into the incident room. The acridity within the room was intense and clawing, and the three men could see that all around them had been ruined by a combination of fire and water. The devastation within the room, however, was not the primary object that dominated their attention. Scorched into the walls, as if burnt into the plasterwork with a firebrand, they read the words, 'The Lord of Darkness is upon Us.'

"What madness is this?" grumbled Pyke, his teeth grinding in anger. "He is a poison, Guv. A poison I tell you."

"Ravings of a lunatic I'd wager, Jem," observed Ash scratching at his head. "Some other sort of sorcery." Wiggins had approached the wall and was peering intently at the scorched script, his nose almost touching the wall. "I think not," he observed. "Although it is difficult to see how this effect was achieved, I detect a smell of some sort of accelerant. White spirit, turpentine perhaps, or even petrol. As for the words, I cannot but think that Radasiliev does nothing without it being driven by a distinct purpose. This is most definitely a message and one directed at us."

"So, he calls himself the Lord of Darkness now does he? The man is a lunatic. A warning?" queried Pyke.

"Perhaps, Jem," replied Wiggins. "Though I would wager that his pyrography refers to another creature, perhaps one that he aspires to be?"

"What of the constables who were on duty with you, Nosh?" asked Pyke, who had decided that he had heard enough talk of demons and wizardry.

"Recovering in the big holding cell with a hot cup of Rosie, Jem. Six sugars each. No lasting harm done. Just shook up a bit." Nosh looked at the toes of his boots. "They tell me he threw them across the room with a wave of his hand and rendered them helpless. Unable to move, they said." He shook his head in bewildered disbelief. Wiggins turned quickly towards Ash, a thought having suddenly sprung into his head. "And what of Doctor Pascoe? Is he still downstairs?"

"Bleedin' Hell!" ejaculated Nosh. He looked momentarily sheepish. "Pardon me French, Sir. I'd forgotten all about the Doc!"

Pyke was already halfway down the staircase that led to the basement mortuary. Wiggins and Ash followed closely behind. Pyke burst through the double doors of the laboratory and then into the adjoining dissection room. "Doc!" he shouted. "Stop!" Doctor Pascoe was stooped over one of the polished steel dissecting tables, scalpel poised in hand. On the slab in front of him lay an immobile though obviously alert and terrified lab assistant, Edward Imrie, a nephew of Pascoe whom he had nepotistically recruited only a few weeks earlier.

Pascoe's ruddy veined face turned towards Pyke's voice, his raised eyebrows quivering like rusted woolly caterpillars upon his forehead. Wiggins could see a blankness reflected in Pascoe's eyes and leapt forward to clutch the mortician's wrist, gently removing the blade from his grasp. Pascoe looked bewilderedly, his gaze fleeting from Wiggins to the traumatised Imrie and back again. "What have I done?" he cried, his quivering face crumbling in shame.

"Thankfully, nothing," confirmed Wiggins, having swiftly inspected the prone Imrie. "It looks like we arrived in the nick of time."

Pascoe sank to his knees, trembling. "My God, Bert! I nearly cut into my nephew! What is going on here? If it were not for you, I hate to think what could have happened. What in the name of all that is holy?"

Pyke helped lift the quivering pathologist and guided him to a nearby chair whilst Wiggins sprinkled water on the face of the paralysed lab assistant. Imrie's eyes blinked frantically in an effort to communicate his alarm to Wiggins. The detective tried to calm him. "Shhh, stay calm young man, try and take long deep breaths. You'll be free of this curse soon, I am sure."

"Better check the prisoners, Guv," observed Pyke. "Did we have anyone in Nosh?"

"No. House was empty for once thankfully, Jem," informed a relieved Nosher.

"I will attend to young Edward," assured Pascoe who had now pulled himself together. "Perhaps an injection of adrenalin may bring the poor lad back to normality." The doctor busied himself shuffling through the contents of a glass-fronted cabinet and indicated to his three colleagues with a wave of his hand that all would be well and that they continue about their duties.

Wiggins looked closely at Doctor Pascoe "Are you sure you are all right, Doctor?" He realised, with a pang of guilt, that he feared leaving Pascoe alone with young Imrie. Pyke sensed his disquiet and placed a reassuring hand on Wiggins' shoulder. "The Doc is fine, Guv." Reassured, Wiggins, accompanied by Pyke and Ash, climbed the stairs, and made their way down the cell corridor. "Best check on the lads and see if they need more tea, Guv," offered Pyke.

"Of course," Wiggins acknowledged. "They must be traumatised after such an ordeal. Break out the emergency brandy if needed, but just a few drops for each."

"Hold on a second," snapped Pyke, coming to an abrupt halt halfway along the corridor. He put his finger to his lips and held his other hand out, signalling that they stop and remain quiet. "I thought I heard something."

The three policemen stood rigid, their nerves on alert. Nosher held his breath, trying to control a tobacco-induced rattle, conscious that his chest could be rather wheezy at times. A faint scratching noise could be heard emanating from one of the cells.

"What's that?" asked Pyke. "I thought you said the inn was empty tonight, Nosh?"

"It is Jem. Not a soul in there," replied a now thoroughly puzzled Ash. Not for the first time that day, he scratched his head. "Rats?" he ventured.

They heard the scratching again. This time louder and more prolonged. The first time the noise had sounded like a chicken scratching on a pane of glass. This, however, now resembled the noise of a four-inch nail being pulled across a sheet of metal. Wiggin's arms goose-pimpled at the sound. "Sounds as though it's coming from cell seven," he whispered. Pyke and Ash nodded their agreement. Each of them slowly pressed an ear to the cold steel of the cell door. As they did so a loud bang reverberated on the inside of the door causing each of the three men to flinch involuntarily at the impact and the unexpected noise.

"Open this cell, Sergeant," ordered Wiggins, standing one pace back.

"I don't understand it, Sir. No one else has a key for this cell!" offered Ash looking disbelievingly from one officer to the other. As he scratched the key against the steel escutcheon another, even louder, bang came from the opposite side of the door, closely followed by a muffled yelp of glee. The three men exchanged another look of bewilderment. Pyke drew his pistol. At Wiggins' sign, Ash swiftly pulled open the cell door. Their nostrils were first affronted by the fetid reek of scrofula. Wiggins immediately pulled a handkerchief out from his breast pocket and raised it to his nose. An indistinct figure scuttled speedily across the stone floor from the door and squeezed itself as tightly as it could into the farthest corner of the room. "Police! Police!" screeched the erratic figure. "Help! Police!"

All three men recoiled at the sight of the creature before them, a form so emaciated that its hairless head appeared bulbous and over-sized, as if trying to break through its skin. Translucent veins seemed to throb below its scalp and its dirty yellow eyes protruded unnaturally from within deeply sunken eye sockets. The creature was evidently a man but unlike any other, the policemen had ever seen. It smiled a broad, evil tinged grin at the men and then looked at its unshod, grime ridden feet, toenails blackened and cracked as if they had been fired in a kiln. "Clean them winders, Jonas Crake!" the creature cackled. "Mop them floors, Jonas Crake!" The monstrosity began to hop up and down, cackling as it did so, like some demented puppet. "Pushed them needles in her ears I did! Straight through, I did! Pop! Pop!"

Pyke looked at Wiggins, disgust painted across his face. "What the Hell is *that*?"

Wiggins already knew the answer. "This is, or perhaps, should I say, *was*, Jonas Crake, the primary suspect in the Kent parsonage murder."

"The one where the geezer stuck the knitting needles into his Old Dutch's ears, Sir?" enquired Ash, disbelievingly. He could not pry his eyes away from the grotesque sight he was witnessing. "What has happened to him? He don't look much like his photograph. He looks like a spider with four legs pulled off." Ash's face could not disguise his disgust.

Wiggins shook his head. "Corrupted in some hellish way by Radasiliev, I'd wager."

At the mention of the Russian's name, the creature that had once been Jonas Crake leapt forward and slid to its badly grazed knees. "Yes, Yes! The Master! The Master!" he laughed, holding his skeletal hands together as if in prayer. Crake began to circle the room on all fours like some caged rabid dog, sniffing and licking the ground whilst murmuring some unintelligible incantation.

"I don't understand, Sir. How did he get in here in the first place?" asked a perplexed Ash. "And in God's name, why is he here?"

Wiggins looked intently at the circling lunatic. "I would imagine that he has been placed here. Radasiliev must have removed your key chain and supplanted Mr Crake within the cell. Why? I can only surmise that this is again some sort of message. A demonstration of the Russian's powers and the ease at which he can play his tricks upon us."

At this Crake abruptly ceased his incantation, and, continuing his snuffling spiral began to recite "I am the message. I am Wiggins. I am the message. I am Wiggins!"

"What is he gibbering on about, he's off his loaf." Pyke took a step towards Crake as if to make to grab him. "He's proper doin' me crust in, he is."

Wiggins stayed Pyke with a forceful command. "Stop, Jem. He is but a vessel of Radasiliev's bile. He is correct. He is the message, and that message is patently clear." Each of the three men looked once more at the scrawny arachnid form circling the cell on its hands and knees, sniffing the floor like an emaciated hunting hound. "The threat from Radasiliev is that I am next. The Russian's will is to pollute and corrupt me to a depth whereby I become a being such as the wretched thing we see before us. Radasiliev is showing me my future."

Pyke shook his head in exasperation. He felt both abhorrence and pity towards the creature that scuttled around the cell. "I've just added that Russian to me clobbering list, Guv. I've still got one sound fist. He has got to go."

"That may well be the case, Sergeant Pyke, but what do we do with this pitiful fellow, Guv?" asked Nosh, pointing to Crake, his broad nose curled in obvious disgust. Wiggins hesitated. "I have absolutely no idea."

"Absentlutely, absentlutely, absentlutely!" Crake screeched over and over, mimicking his dead wife. Wiggins thought for several seconds without any conclusion. "Lock the door, Sergeant," he eventually ordered. "Just lock the door. We will decide how to proceed once we have given the matter further thought."

Ash turned the key in the lock with a sense of relief, leaving Jonas Crake snuffling around the cold stone floor. "I'll fetch some water and bread for the poor unfortunate."

Pyke lit a cigarette and leant against the now secured cell door. "Van Hoon time?"

"What do you mean, Jem?" asked Wiggins.

"Well, if there is anyone who may have come across anything like this in the past, I would wager a pound to a lump of gentleman's morning best, that it is Dante Van Hoon."

"And *I* am telling *you*, Commissioner Gregson, that Gideon Thorne will *not* be disciplined in any way, shape or form!" Lord Blackstock's voice was verging on cracking, his rage was apoplectic.

"But, Your Lordship, Thorne's leadership was unequivocally disastrous. We lost several good men and at the last count eleven law-abiding citizens were killed in the anarchy that he was responsible for raising," retorted Gregson, thumping his desk angrily. The commissioner was secretly enjoying the confrontation. It had been a long time since he had felt such passion coursing through his frame. He had forgotten the adrenalin rush that accompanied a venting of the spleen.

"None the less. You have my orders Commissioner. I stand unmoved on this subject. There will be no disciplinary action taken against Thorne!" reasserted the nobleman. "This directive comes straight from the Home Secretary himself." Blackstock's hands clutched the edge of Gregson's desk, his head and shoulders thrust forward aggressively. Gregson could see that his body language was confrontational, inviting retaliation. The commissioner felt a sense of slight repellence for the man before him. Although he was doubtless of aristocratic bearing, Gregson disliked the *smell* of Blackstock, his prematurely greying hair, though distinguished, had an oiliness that the Commissioner imagined seeped deeper within the man.

"But these men's families, Sir! Their sons and daughters! This department owes them a debt of responsibility. A debt of thanks! We are the Metropolitan Police for God's sake! We must be seen to be making amends for this disaster!"

Gregson was now almost nose to nose with the Under Minister, his complexion reddening with rage. "Then throw an underling Officer to the lions to appease Fleet Street," dismissed Blackstock with the wave of a well-manicured hand. He turned from the desk and stalked around the room, hands firmly clasped behind his back. "How about that Wiggins fellow? He was there in a position of some authority was he not? If we need a scapegoat, why not let it be him? Throw him under the omnibus, for want of a better term."

Gregson was completely stunned. He tried to hide his disgust at the weaselling tactics of Blackstock. The commissioner drew himself to his full height. "Because, Lord Blackstock, Detective Chief Inspector Wiggins is an exemplary officer whose bravery and competence is without question, whereas Gideon Thorne is an egomaniacal incompetent buffoon!" countered Gregson. "Your suggestion is both absurd and immoral in equal measure, Sir!"

"In that case, Sir, I will leave you to deal with the Press, but rest assured, Gideon Thorne is regarded extremely highly by those at the very peak of Government, and he is absolutely *not* to be associated in *any* way with this tragic incident. If I hear so much as a hint of blame being apportioned to Thorne, I will personally move against you, Commissioner."

'*Extremely well protected,*' thought Gregson, a sour taste rising in his mouth.

"I trust I have made myself perfectly clear? I will leave the matter in your most capable hands. Good day, Sir!" With this, the Under-Home Secretary turned on his heels and, grabbing his hat from the nearby stand, marched out of Commissioner Gregson's office. Gregson slumped into his chair. He held his hand out before him and saw that it was shaking uncontrollably with adrenalin, his curled upper lip trembled in sheer frustration. He went to the glass cabinet behind his desk and produced a bottle of Glenlivet single malt and a lead crystal tumbler. He poured two fingers of the whisky and swallowed it in a single gulp. He ran his hand through his once flaxen, now grey hair and, biting his lower lip, he picked up his desk telephone. "Get DCI Wiggins to my office, please." He replaced the receiver and leaned back in his chair, deep in thought.

Chapter 13 - The Walk

Wiggins sat in front of Commissioner Gregson, struggling to comprehend what he was hearing. "You mean to say, Sir, that there are to be no repercussions for Mr Thorne following his inept handling of the Gerrard Street operation, or dare I say, fiasco?"

Gregson noted that Wiggins had not referred to Thorne by his given rank, a mark of disrespect either consciously or subconsciously made. Knowing Wiggins as well as he did, the Commissioner decided that the lapse was entirely deliberate. "Regrettably so, Bert," replied Gregson feeling the situation called for as much informality as possible.

"But this is absurd, if I may be so bold, Sir." Wiggins continued to adopt a more formal approach to the interview. "Not only is Thorne going to escape without a stain upon his character, but the Under Secretary for the Home Office has suggested that my career be tarnished, or indeed ended, due to Thorne's gung-ho and tactically inept incompetence!" Wiggins could feel the old, long subdued, demon of anger rise in his gullet. He closed his eyes momentarily to regain his composure.

"That indeed is the suggestion, Bert." Gregson stood from his side of the desk and walked towards the window. He drew up the bottom sash and leant forward, breathing in the morning air. He could see the summer sunshine dapple the plane trees outside his office and the morning mist blanketing the already busy Thames. He tried to make the scene calm his frustrations. He turned and offered Wiggins a triple gold-banded Rothmans cigarette from a silver, engine-turned cigarette case. Wiggins took the proffered cigarette and quickly noted the ornate decoration on the embossed cartouche of the case. A hunting scene, a bloodhound, nose to the ground straining at a leash held by a great coated figure who could have been Gregson himself. His keen eye picked up the small initials etched in the bottom right-hand corner of the tableau. SH.

'*Of course. Who else?*' he asked himself rhetorically, if rather jealously. He was instantly transported back twenty-five years. He was climbing the luxuriously carpeted stairs in Baker Street, seventeen in all. A habit he had been unable to break, to this day he continued to count stairs as he climbed them. Back then, he would also count the lovingly polished brass gripper rods of each tread as he and the others raced upwards to receive orders, or downwards towards an exciting new adventure. In those days he owned nothing but the clothes upon his back, the companionship of the Irregulars, and the thrill of the chase. And his wits. His wits and guile had always been what had pulled him through adversity. Thrust him forward. Put him ahead of the pack. His intelligence had always been his greatest strength. The snap of the closing cigarette case lid instantly returned him to the unpleasant reality of his present situation.

"I, however," continued a thoughtful Gregson, "would suggest a more strategic approach in this instance. I have a sense that this influence that protects Thorne runs far deeper than we suspect. I feel an uneasy murkiness at work here. A dark shadow of secrecy. We should pick our battles carefully and choose our allies wisely."

Wiggins re-crossed his legs and inhaled the freshly lit cigarette. It caught the back of his throat and made him cough slightly. The mass-produced tobacco had a harsher quality than the Turkish blend which he favoured. "You are correct, Sir. I concur. There is something afoot here, some *hand of darkness*, if you will, that shields Thorne and protects him, whether he is aware of its existence or not."

Gregson tapped the desk forcefully three times with the tips of his fingers. Wiggins recognised this as the usual precursor to the Commissioner announcing that he had come upon a decision. "I do not intend to discipline you, Bert. It would be utterly wrong to do so." He paused before continuing. "Investigate Thorne. Strictly '*off the books*' as it were. A private investigation. There is something here that sits uneasy with me, Bert. I will support you in what little way I can, but remember, I will be unable to do so in any official capacity, other in that I will handle the Press and the official Met Police line of Gerrard Street having been the timely repression of an imminent political uprising."

"I see, Sir." Wiggins was surprised at the license Gregson had freely given him. He felt apprehensive at the prospect of secretly investigating a senior officer but satisfied that he had the trust of the Commissioner. He stood and shook Gregson's hand. "Thank you, Sir. How will I keep you apprised of my progress in this matter?"

"We will find a way, Bert. Perhaps communication through a mutual 'friend' may be in order." The statement seemed to Wiggins to have been pitched as a half question. Gregson presented the cigarette case to Wiggins once more, an unspoken communication glinting in his eye. "Take another for, later, Bert. You may well need to remember the brand should you find it agreeable."

Wiggins returned to the incident room, deep in thought. Ideas, theories, facts, and half-truths bombarded his thinking. His mind felt uncharacteristically unsettled. The room had been cleared following the fire, and he watched as two decorators worked at bringing the room back to its original freshness. "Morning, chaps!" he greeted the two workmen cheerily, always conscious that working tradesmen were the backbone of the economy.

"Morning, Guvnor," replied the elder of the two, touching the peak of his cap. Wiggins observed the men for several minutes, the smell of fresh paint playing a pleasant tune around his nostrils, bringing a sense of rebirth to the room. He watched as the younger, more agile decorator tackled the high- and low-level work, ceiling coving and skirtings, whilst the more senior painter concentrated on the broader brushwork to the walls, setting the tone of the job. '*Strategy and detail,*' he thought. 'Not unlike police work in its approach. Jem and I.

He found Pyke in the temporary incident room which had been set up in a large basement storage area. Pyke was pouring over an account of the murder of Deacon Lancaster, or '*The Loaf in the Bucket Murder*' as Jem jokingly referred to it. He glanced up to see Wiggins looking at him.

"How goes it, Sergeant?" asked Wiggins.

Pyke mistakenly interpreted Wiggins' enquiry as a question about his new surroundings, rather than, as it had been intended, an enquiry about the case. "I actually prefer it down here, Guv, those decorators seem to be taking an age," explained Pyke surveying the large, gloomy room.

Wiggins smiled as he recalled the two painters upstairs. "Fancy a stroll, Jem? I feel some bracing Thames air and a constitutional may help us disentangle the Medusal nest of vipers we have found ourselves entwined within."

"Whatever that means, it sounds good to me, Guv," replied Pyke throwing aside his paperwork and secretly hoping that there may be a visit to the Ship and Shovell at the end of proceedings. "I'll get me hat."

Wiggins relayed his earlier conversation with Commissioner Gregson to Pyke as they walked slowly eastwards down Victoria Embankment. "It's bleedin' scandalous, is what it is, Guv." Pyke was enraged. "Thorne made a right, royal balls up," he cursed, throwing a half-smoked cigarette into the Thames. Wiggins could feel himself frowning at his Sergeant's action. He realised that one more cigarette, bobbing aimlessly in an already overstressed river, pregnant with pollution, would make no significant impact upon the health of the waterway, but still, he felt a glimmer of disquiet as he watched the cigarette drift away. "As if we don't have enough on our plates already without having to deal with some shady Northerner stirring things up within our midst. I tell you, Bert, for a Scotch Farthing, I'd personally boot his arse all the way back up the Great North Road."

Wiggins narrowed his eyes against the afternoon Sun. "I tend to agree with you, Jem, but I fear we need to play the long game here and be astute. On one hand, we have two inexplicably staged murders to unravel and put to rest, whilst on the other, we still have to kill the threat of King and this deadly virus he has in his possession."

"Not to mention tracking down Radasiliev," added Pyke thoughtfully.

"Well, one thing is in our favour, at least the creature that was once Jonas Crake is now safely secured within Saint Luke's. Orderlies from the lunatic asylum transferred him there this morning. Lord only knows what the doctors there will make of him," mused Wiggins. He recalled watching as his officers had led a whimpering Crake, restrained in a straitjacket, into the waiting secure wagon earlier that day. The poor creature seemed to understand little of what was going on around him and Wiggins wondered at what sort of mental corruption could not only destroy the man's wits but also radically change his physical appearance.

"They already have Nathaniel Cripes to deal with. Imagine having to look after those two deviant maniacs." Pyke watched as two gulls pulled at either end of an extraordinarily long and elastic lugworm.

"Have you contacted Van Hoon yet, Guv?" asked Pyke remembering their conversation the day before. He looked forlornly over his left shoulder, realising that they had already passed Craven Passage, home to the Ship and Shovell pub.

"Indeed, I have. We convene at his Belgravia residence at six this evening. I have invited Doctor Watson. I trust you have no objections?" responded Wiggins who had now stopped and was admiring Cleopatra's Needle with its two, flanking faux-Egyptian sphinxes.

"No objection whatsoever. I look forward to seeing the old warhorse again," enthused Pyke.

Wiggins gazed at the ancient Egyptian obelisk. "Remarkable that an object that is three and a half thousand years of age stands here upon the bank of the Thames, almost unnoticed amongst the clamour and madness of this modern metropolis, don't you think, Jem?"

Pyke was still lamenting the absence of a pint of Fullers in the Admiral's pub. "I'll wager the chaps that carved it would have no notion that it would end up here," he observed, feeling that his response was in some way inadequate and fearing that he was about to receive a lengthy lecture on the history of the enigmatic monument.

Wiggins laughed in agreement. "The needle is in fact misnamed," commenced Wiggins as they resumed their stroll. "Given that the obelisk was hewn a thousand years before the reign of Cleopatra, during the eighteenth dynasty under the rule of Pharaoh Thutmose the third."

'*Here we go,*' thought Pyke. '*Ancient history. How does he know such facts?*' He had once heard that someone learned had referred to history as being '*of no import other than to inform us as to how to proceed in the future,'* an axiom that he tended to agree with. However, over the course of the next fifteen minutes, he was to be regaled with Wiggins' potted history regarding the Needle, the interpretations of its hieroglyphics and various theories as regards its origins and the significance of its dimensions. They walked past Waterloo Bridge, Somerset House, and King's College and on into the quiet haven of Middle Temple Gardens where Wiggins selected a bench under an impressive willow tree and sat down. Pyke followed suit, looking northwards up towards the cut-through leading to Milford Lane and onward to the haven of the old timber clad inn, the Cheshire Cheese. *'All these fine drinking emporiums and we're sat out here like a pair of maiden aunts,'* he lamented.

The two sat in silence for a few moments, Pyke sensing that Wiggins had something to tell him. Something he was battling with. Pyke let the silence drift, knowing that Wiggins would be unable to sustain it. Finally, he was proven to be correct.

"I am to investigate Thorne," Wiggins announced abruptly, picking an invisible thread from his trouser leg. He cupped his hand to his mouth and coughed as though the act would somehow stifle the admission. "Completely unofficially, you understand. Commissioner's orders, Jem, but all will be denied if Thorne is alerted to my task."

Pyke took a moment to absorb the revelation. "You mean, we, Guv. We are to investigate Thorne. I will not see you bear this burden alone."

Wiggins swallowed sharply, his gaze fixed firmly ahead. A sharp breeze blew in from the river and stung his eyes. "This will be dangerous Jem. Our careers could very well be at risk."

Pyke shrugged. "When has it ever been any different, Bert? Where you go, I go. No matter what the danger. No matter what the risk. I'll be there."

Wiggins nodded and dug his fingernails deep into the palms of his hands. "Of course, Jem. I should have expected nothing less from you." The two exchanged a brief silence, each deep in thought. "I must admit I am rather apprehensive at the prospect of investigating Thorne. He seems extremely well connected and indeed protected by those at the highest levels. There is also an underlying menace about the man which I do not relish."

Pyke snapped his fingers. "Wilson Brown!" he declared, a conspiratorial smile playing across his rugged face.

Wiggins frowned. "Who?"

"Wilson Brown. The most anonymous man in London. He's a private detective. Very private. Operates out of Denmark Street. The most normal looking of men, so much so that people tend not to see him at all. He's like an invisible man. Outwardly he is unremarkable in every way. He drifts quietly around London unnoticed, spying on unfaithful husbands and treacherous wives."

"How is it that I am unaware of this individual?" asked a puzzled Wiggins.

Pyke laughed. "Because he's Wilson Brown, Guv. Only those who have use of him know of him."

"And I gather that you are on intimate terms with this Mr Brown?" Wiggins was now interested. He could see a plan of action mapping out before him. Pyke leant back on the bench, stretched his legs, and crossed his ankles. "Just so happens Wilson Brown owes me a rather large favour."

"How large?" asked Wiggins.

"Large enough for me to get him on board, Guv," grinned Pyke broadly. "Brown is our man. He could walk into Scotland Yard and tap Thorne on the shoulder, and he wouldn't notice. If there is anything to find on old Gideon, Wilson Brown will uncover it."

"He must be made aware that there is the very likely possibility that there will be danger involved," underlined Wiggins, his brows knitted with concern. Pyke slapped Wiggins on the back in an effort to lighten the mood. "He thrives on it, Guv. No point being invisible if there ain't no thrill to it, now is there? Speaking of danger, what's the danger of you buying me a pint of Best? The Cheese is but two minutes' walk from where we sit, and I feel a thirst that needs slaking before we meet with Van Hoon. Besides, with Brown on the case, we have something to drink to."

"Very well," agreed Wiggins. "Some Dutch courage you might say!"

Chapter 14 - The President

Sir Edward John Poynter suddenly realised that his immobility was caused by his wrists being tightly bound behind the trunk of a tree. He wrenched at his bindings, only to find that they dug deeper into his wrists while the rough bark of the tree tore at his skin. His eyes suddenly flashed open as if awoken by a scream from some traumatic nightmare, little realising the nightmare was one that he was about to endure. The President of the Royal Academy was stripped naked save for a course sheet of jute which loosely swaddled his genitalia. Only that, and his abundant grey beard, hid the modesty of his naked eighty-three-year-old body. He was frail and shivered uncontrollably in the early chill of the morning. His feet were wet from the dew-laden grass underfoot and felt numb with cold.

Lord Poynter had no recollection of how or why he found himself to be in this terrifying and embarrassing situation. There was a dull ache at the nape of his neck, but apart from the pain he felt emanating from his wrists caused by the tightness of the bindings, he did not feel unwell. He did, however, feel unbearably exposed. He recalled having been knocked unconscious many years before. As a young man, he had fallen from his Polo pony on the playing fields of Ipswich School and had suffered a concussion. The present vague giddiness he felt was redolent of how he had felt after that fall. He looked frantically around him, or at least, as far as his arthritic neck would allow, and found that he was tied to a tree in some unremarkable, and as far as he could tell, unidentifiable woodland. He had no idea where he was, nor what time of day it was. His instinctive vulnerability changed sharply to fear and then shockingly to intense, sudden pain as an arrow exploded into his upper thigh, pinning it to the underlying tree. He screamed uncontrollably as pain seared through his leg as the entry point pulsed and trembled. No noise had accompanied the arrow as it had hurtled towards him, only the sound of its sickening thud as it thrust into the rectus femoris muscle of his right thigh. His hands instinctively tried to make their way to the pain but only rasped upon the raised ridges of tree bark causing the skin to break and bleed. He was gasping in disbelief at the horrific situation in which he found himself, eyes wide with terror, gulping air into his lungs, his stomach churning, when a second, unannounced arrow rammed home, this time pinning his right bicep to the trunk of the tree with a nauseating crunch of splintered humeral bone. The agony was unbearable. His jaw clenched in pain and he bit the tip of his tongue clean through.

"Help! HELP!" He screamed as loudly as his lungs would allow, blood now escaping from his injured mouth. His voice echoed around the silent wood. Panic and shock were beginning to set in as his eyes darted from tree to tree trying to locate the direction from which the arrows had come. It was then that he suddenly spied his assailant. The figure stood approximately thirty yards in front of him. His assailant was dressed in a long beige robe, secured at the waist with a belt. The hood of the robe obscured the bowman's face, almost entirely camouflaging him among the surrounding trees and foliage. He seemed as though he were part of the forest, a grim wood sprite intent on destruction.

"Mercy, please show me mercy! I beseech you! I have done nothing to deserve this! I am a decent, good family man," Poynter shouted towards the hooded figure. He felt a churning nausea rise from his gut. His assailant began to reach once again for the quiver slung over his left shoulder. At that point, Poynter knew, with sickening certainty, that his life was about to end, and urine began to trickle involuntarily down his inner thighs. An arrow was carefully withdrawn and notched upon the bowstring and arrow rest, and with amazing velocity, it ripped clean through the left rib cage of Sir Edward John Poynter who threw his head back against the tree in sheer agony. The robed figure began walking steadily and slowly towards the pinioned Lord. A further two arrows thudded into Poynter's body in rapid succession, one to the upper right pubic region, ripping through the small intestine, and the other a few inches below and to the right.

"Argh! Lord have mercy!" screamed the aristocrat, tears of desperation running down his cheeks. His head slumped towards his chest, his entire body coated in beads of icy perspiration. There was extraordinarily little blood loss from the puncture wounds, only an excruciating throbbing pain that wracked his body. The hooded attacker continued to walk calmly towards the tree, crisp foliage crunching ominously underfoot until he was less than a yard away from where Poynter hung as limply as would a straw-stuffed scarecrow.

The robed assassin pulled at his victim's hair lifting his head from his chest. "Do you remember me, Mr President?" asked the attacker slowly removing his hood to reveal his face. His voice was a deep rasping whisper. Through tear-reddened, throbbing eyes Poynter spoke in a stuttering, barely audible, whispering death rattle. "No," was all he managed to muster. He shook his head slightly. He could feel the Earth spin around him in a vortex of pain and disbelief. He realised that he was teetering on the very edge of consciousness and about to slip into Death's embrace. Sliding towards being part of the past. An obituary.

"I suspected as much, Mr President, you never once looked favourably upon myself or my work and now you have become my latest, and arguably greatest work of art," snarled the bowman angrily. "There are merely a few final brushstrokes that I need to make to complete this masterpiece."

The attacker reached towards Poynter and, with some considerable effort, pulled out the first arrow in a twisting motion, ripping flesh as it was withdrawn. He then sadistically plunged the arrow directly and forcibly back into the same gaping entry wound from which it had been extricated. The Lord writhed in excruciating pain and screeched in horror at the sadistic cruelty being inflicted upon him. The pain was such that he longed for death to take him, welcomed blessed oblivion. Each of the other arrows was then in turn systematically removed and re-entered loosely, deliberately encouraging blood to flow in copious amounts. As the blood flowed, his life ebbed away. Sir Edward John Poynter thought of the unfinished oil painting which currently sat in the studio of his three-storey townhouse in Albert Gate. Arthritis and dwindling eyesight had robbed him of his lifelong technique, but he had gradually accepted the new freedom of expression his knotted joints and blurred outlook afforded. He began weeping with sadness, knowing that the canvas would never be finished. His final dying thoughts were of his beautiful wife Agnes and their three beloved daughters. He died praying that they would not see him again.

Chapter 15 - The Negotiation

The four men sat in the library of Dante Van Hoon's Belgravia mansion. The huge gothic house stood virtually unseen, surrounded as it was by a high, ivy infested, red-bricked wall topped with ornate cast-iron railings. The finials of the railings were fashioned after unicorn heads and aggressively spiked to discourage any unwanted visitors. The surrounding wall offered up one, carriage-wide gate, which provided not only a sole point of entry but also, as a perceptive observer may have noted, a solitary point of exit. The mansion's gardens were immaculate in both their design and planting and had been maintained to an exceptionally high horticultural standard. The borders were shrouded by exotic trees and populated by a diverse collection of tropical shrubs and plants. Huge date palms sat alongside banana plants, delicate red Japanese Acers were interwoven amongst majestic cypresses, and willowy eucalyptus trees swayed in the lightest of breezes. A towering wall of black bamboo sheltered a group of woolly trunked, prehistoric Trachycarpus. Banks of ferns, lilies and giant gunnera resembling spiked, felt-covered umbrellas, gave the overall impression of a grove within an exotic tropical jungle, supplanted amidst the most exclusive part of London.

The fabric of the villa was an extravaganza of turrets, rotundas, flying buttresses and balconies. Turkish inspired copper minarets festooned a roof that was sloped at a precariously steep pitch. The roof itself was covered in dull grey slates reminiscent of the armoured protective scales of a pangolin. The front elevation boasted two dozen, large, shuttered sash windows set in stone mullions which framed a central stucco portico of enormous stature. Each side of the portico was guarded by a marble statue of a lion in rampant pose, their paws clawing at unseen adversaries. Four terrazzo steps, inlaid with shards of sparkling agate and marble, led to a gigantic bronze door inlaid with elaborate Arabesque figures and occult symbols and motifs.

Internally the house was, if anything, even more impressive than its outward appearance. At the centre of the grand, double height, stone walled entrance hall stood an enormous, stuffed grizzly bear, its lips drawn back to reveal huge snarling teeth, its claws bared in an unexpectedly intimidating greeting to visitors. The foyer was dominated by a sweeping bronze staircase, its twin newel posts each in the form of a dragon holding a limp lion in its gaping jaws. The walls that flanked the staircase were decorated with elaborately detailed medieval tapestries which hung from brass rails.

Several hardwood framed glass cases positioned throughout the mansion betrayed the unusual obsession of its master. Taxidermy. Within these presentation cases were preserved exhibits of a multitude of exotic creatures gathered from around the globe, many long extinct. Sloe-eyed lemurs stood alongside lugubrious sloths. A South American peccary vied for attention with a huge, oily pelted Tapir. Armadillos, monkeys, and possums stood in lifelike repose alongside a resplendently graceful okapi.

All houses have their own distinct and individual aroma and this gothic mausoleum was no different. Incense could be seen burning from wall-mounted sconces dotted high around the dressed stonework walls. Each sconce was fashioned in the shape of a different animal head, here a snake, there a lion, an eagle, a peacock and an ape. The atmosphere was dense with the scent of the aromatic eastern oils of patchouli and sandalwood.

The vast library, in which the four companions were gathered, was as fully stocked as one could imagine a private collection could ever be. Floor to ceiling mahogany bookcases groaned with volumes ranging from priceless William Caxton prints to the most modern of scientific reference books and academic treatise. There was an entire section devoted to medical and scientific literature through the ages and another to Astronomy. The walls throughout the mansion were adorned with ornately framed oil paintings of flora and fauna from the widest reaches of the planet. An eclectic array of portraits, landscapes, religious iconography, and anatomical representations were interspersed with old masters by Giotto and Piero di Cosimo, which in turn hung alongside more modern impressionistic and avant-garde works by Berthe Morisot and Kazimir Malevich.

Doctor Watson stood at a large alabaster surrounded inglenook fireplace, admiring a grandiose Louis the sixteenth boule clock, its numerals replaced by facsimiles of the twelve apostles. Over time the hands of the clock pointed to each in turn as if representing Jesus blessing his disciples. Watson thoughtfully tapped his pipe on the heel of his shoe to remove the dottle from his last smoke, allowing it to drop neatly into the hearth. He inwardly conjectured that one could roast a brace of fully-grown pigs within the massive fireplace.

The lean, straight-backed figure of Dante Van Hoon strolled around the room, obviously absorbed in inspecting his priceless literary collection. "You know gentlemen, I agree wholeheartedly with George Gissing in that I know every book I own by its particular smell, and I have only to put my nose between the pages to be transported and reminded of a myriad of memories," he announced as he ran a finger delicately along a row of tomes. He stopped at a particularly thick and aged looking volume. The Dutchman drew it carefully from the shelf and flicked it open, uncannily to the page he sought. He turned his remarkable face towards Wiggins and Pyke who sat in opposing, cracked leather chesterfield chairs which guarded the enormous inglenook.

"We indeed have a dilemma on our hands gentlemen," announced the leper, his blue-black hair tumbling over his dead blanched eye and the leprous fractal scarring that marked the left side of his striking face. "As we can all testify, King is as dangerous an animal as stalks our metropolitan jungle. A merciless maniac who will stop at nothing to get precisely what he desires. He has somehow managed to escape from the combined forces of the Metropolitan Police, and, we suspect, has in his possession a quantity of deadly contagion that could wipe out half the denizens of London. I cannot but help think that you have done the correct thing in seeking my counsel."

Mayerhofer, Van Hoon's Russian wolf husky, raised its enormous head from where it had been slumbering at Sergeant Pyke's feet and glanced inquisitively towards its master. "I know my pet, I know. There is no need to worry," consoled Van Hoon, reaching down to scratch the wolf under its chin. "I will let no harm come of you my precious." The great hound's head returned to its now favoured position between Pyke's boots and cast a forlorn look upwards at the Detective Sergeant. Pyke smiled reassuringly, though nonetheless hesitantly, at the beast.

"If as you suspect, Mr Wiggins, that King indeed intends to initiate a mass infection, we must act quickly to prevent any spread," added the leper. He sat down on a velveteen chaise longue and opened the book he had taken from the shelf and read aloud. "The outrageous tribe that is a dragon to those who flee, but a lamb to any who show their teeth or their purse." Snapping shut the tome, he rested it thoughtfully upon his lap. "How appropriate."

"Dante's inferno?" enquired Wiggins.

"Not quite my friend. Dante's Paradiso, but apt none the less. I think we have to face this dragon head on, either with our teeth bared or our purse opened," affirmed Van Hoon.

"We certainly need to do *something*," interjected Doctor Watson. "It seems to me that the very lives of the upper echelons of the land may soon be under threat, not to mention the stability of the commercial hub that is the City. The whole affair would be earth-shattering in its consequence and the greatest disaster this country has seen … well, since the last great plague that is," underlined the Doctor, his great moustache dancing a rhythmic semaphore to his speech.

"I say we open discussions with our armed forces and piece together a joint offensive and simply blast the Chinese devil out of whichever rat hole he's currently festering in," growled Pyke banging his fist off the arm of his chair. Mayerhofer lifted his head at the noise with weary curiosity.

"We have to find the fiend first," attested Watson. "Remember, his opium den in Shadwell, Pakapuh, is currently an empty shell, reportedly half ripped asunder presumably by that giant monstrosity of his, Hercules Chin. He has also successfully flown his second rat hole in that ramshackle theatre in Gerrard Street." Watson continued to address the assemblage. "We have to consider the possibility that King will attempt to flee the country, perhaps leaving a pall of death in his wake." A reflective silence descended upon the four friends, each mentally recalling the tragic events of what the London Press had so dramatically referred to as the Battle of Gerrard Street. Eventually, Watson broke the contemplative silence. "I would wager that a private charter from somewhere on the Thames could see him safe passage to the Mediterranean in a matter of days."

Wiggins stood and walked towards one of the large sash windows that overlooked an immaculate croquet lawn. "Perhaps, Doctor, but I think he will not flee these shores yet. I feel that King's vile ego will want to observe the scourge work its path through our people. We all agree that King is doing this for some personal gain, but I also believe he will wallow in sadistic pleasure at the death and suffering he will ignite. Although he is evil enough to want to kill thousands of innocent people for his own entertainment, there must undoubtedly be something that he wants. An outcome he desires or needs."

"Or perhaps that a greater Power desires or needs?" interjected Van Hoon. "Remember, King is the Golden Empire's most valued emissary and as such is in the vanguard of their plan to destabilise Western governments."

Wiggins nodded thoughtfully. He addressed the others, his hands clasped firmly behind his back. "If we can discover his exact purpose, we may be able to end this without risking any further misery and bloodshed," he reasoned. "Jem, we must again find his location. Use every means at your disposal, every informant, nark and street corner Johnnie. Every bartender, beggar and thief you know. We simply must find out where this fiend's new lair is."

"I'll put the word out, Guv, but I agree with John. He may be planning to flee the country." Pyke nodded towards Watson. "I can also get my own Boys' Brigade on it," responded Pyke enthusiastically, trying to lift Wiggins' spirits. "They're a bit more streetwise than Willy Smith's lot I have to say, and they are as eager as can be."

At the mention of Pyke's gang of street urchins, Wiggins' memory briefly flitted back twenty-five years to a time when he, then an orphaned mudlark, led the Great Detective's Baker Street Irregulars. He often revisited those care-free days, remembering the fresh air of freedom and nostalgia. Digger, as he was known back then, and his 'unofficial division' provided Him with eyes and ears that no one else possessed. They knew every back alley, molly house, opium den, pub and warehouse in London, every inch of the Thames water frontage, every boatyard, dry dock and rat run along its course. Each case was an adventure. Someone, or something, to find. The thrill of the hunt. Trailing a suspect, sometimes for hours and days on end. Digging for treasure in the bowels of Gotham's darkest underbelly. His brief reverie was interrupted by the voice of Doctor Watson.

"Why it sounds as if you have your very own gang of Irregulars at your disposal young Wiggins?" chuckled the Doctor, his eyes displaying a knowing twinkle. "It only seems like yesterday when you yourself were..."

Wiggins coughed to interrupt the good doctor but could not but help look admiringly upon his old mentor. He felt great pride in being associated with this valiant man who had re-entered his life so heroically in what Wiggins privately referred to as the '*Northumberland Avenue Incident*' no more than a handful of weeks earlier, saving him from an unexpected, although very public attack on his life by several of King's hired Dacoit killers.

Wiggins' thoughts were interrupted by a gentle rapping upon the library door which was acknowledged by Van Hoon. "Enter."

One of Van Hoon's Pestilent entered the library carrying a tray. Van Hoon's own leprosy was contained by medication of his devising. It afforded him unprecedented access to the denizens of London's leper houses. His Pestilent were his personal army of untouchables who could come and go whenever, and wherever, he required them to, without fear of interference. What foolhardy individual would dare interfere with a leper? The robed figure seemed to drift into the room rather than walk, its pock scarred face concealed from view by the drooping hood of its cassock. Wiggins noted a yellow macramé belt securing the garment at the waist. Accompanying the leper was a beautiful, slightly built oriental girl carrying a tray of refreshments. She bowed to the room and knelt in front of the tray of green tea left by the wraithlike shrouded figure. "No need for ritual formality my dear," offered Van Hoon. "These good men are my friends and therefore Chakai and not Chaj is called for here today." She proceeded to carefully pour four cups of tea, bowed, and made to leave the room. "Thank you, Jiao," acknowledged Van Hoon.

"Fear not gentlemen. I believe I have the means by which to meet with King and perhaps broker a trade," conjectured the Dutchman, for once his habitually frivolous mien bore a serious, business-like undertone. Jiao shuddered at the mention of King's name and cast her eyes floorward. Van Hoon looked from Watson to Wiggins, to Pyke, then back to Wiggins, his one emerald green eye dancing with excitement at the prospect of the plan he was hatching. "But I must do this alone. Sola Gratia! King is a truly dangerous and intelligent adversary and will immediately be alive to any police presence or skulduggery. To interfere may prove disastrous to many innocent souls."

"And why should we trust you, Van Hoon? The lives of possibly hundreds of thousands of people would lie in your hands," pointed out Pyke, stubbing out his cigarette with excessive force into a crystal ashtray inlaid flush with the table surface.

Van Hoon bristled and straightened his back. "I may be many things Sergeant, but my word is my currency. Without it, I am as nothing. And besides, is it not best to deal with the Devil you know?"

The two locked stares, the hard-jawed pugilist, and the leprous, enigmatic Dandy. Neither broke their gaze. The sense of tension in the room was palpable before Watson decided to broker the underlying hostility. "We have no option but to trust Mr Van Hoon on this occasion. After all, we have been recommended to do so by one whom we all respect above any other, and I am sure that we can all justifiably testify to his integrity and effectiveness in the past. Why, in the case of the Ripper himself."

Wiggins interrupted quickly, "Van Hoon's intervention in the case of Doctor Joseph Bleak also stands testament to his word being his allegiance. But just how do you propose to draw out this devil, Van Hoon? We have seen in the past that his ingenuity is only rivalled by his malevolence."

"That must remain *my* secret, and mine alone Inspector, but rest assured, I have a certain *something* that he needs just as much as he has something that we desire," announced the enigma in the most sinister of tones. The eyelid of the leper's dead phantom eye licked across its ghoulish eyeball. Wiggins felt the merest of internal shudders as, for only the second time during his intermittent association with the Dutchman, he sensed exactly why this enigma was regarded as one of the most universally feared men on the planet.

The discrepancy in stature between the two figures was striking as they stood together on the perimeter of the throng of people lining Park Lane promenade. This was where the two men met, once every six months, for their customary exchange. One was tall, upright, and slim with broad shoulders and flowing dark hair, the other, a wisp of a man, diminutive of build with shoulders little wider than his prominent bald head, but with a face that emanated evil on a blood-chilling scale. They stood together in silence watching the impromptu parade unfold in front of them.

In front of the pair, a tall broad-shouldered black gentleman, extravagantly dressed in a long mink coat, fingers caparisoned with expensive gold jewellery, stood in a slowly moving car, waving his straw boater grandiosely at the cheering crowd which threatened to engulf the vehicle. The charcoal blackness of his skin only enhanced the ivory whiteness of his huge, beaming smile. Conversely, his unsmiling, white wife sat demurely at his side.

"Do you not think it strange that a man of his race and colour can be so very powerful, Mr Hoon?" asked King in a disjointed monosyllabic manner whilst craning his neck to peer at his fellow spectator. "Very few men possess such power."

"The name, as you are well aware, is *Van* Hoon," smiled the blue-black haired Dutchman, as if chastising a naughty schoolboy who had pushed just a little too far. "Power, my little yellow friend, such as that you seem to so desperately crave, invariably corrupts the soul of those who most desire it, don't you agree?" Van Hoon swung his cane in the direction of the parade. "I must admit however that he is indeed a charismatic and dominant presence, but one I fancy, that will prove a short-lived curiosity in our rapidly changing age. A zeitgeist of the post-Victorian era to which we all, even you King, belong." The Chinaman remained inscrutable, his face unchanged and seemingly disinterested. King's silence compelled Van Hoon to push his companion further. "I have often wondered, my friend, of your story. No doubt the affectatious soubriquet you have chosen to adopt bears no relation to your actual name?" prodded Van Hoon, enjoying the thrust and parry of this verbal jousting. He, of course, knew quite well the real identity of the self-proclaimed Mr King and was reasonably well informed of the Chinaman's history.

The Chinaman chuckled a high-pitched giggle. "Me only have one name, Sir." His face changing instantly from submissive to dissident. "Or should I state that I have no requirement, nor any inclination, to possess any name other than the one I have chosen," King replied, in an altogether more articulate manner than the mock broken Anglo-Chinese he had previously adopted. "A degree of anonymity brings with it a greater degree of fear and respect don't you agree, Mr *Van* Hoon? King, and King alone, suffices whereas you, I fear, have two too many names in my humble opinion. Dante this and Dante that, Prince Francis of Transylvania, John the Outcast, the list is tiresomely long. As long, no doubt, as your list of enemies."

Van Hoon smiled. The two adversaries stood studying the near hysteric adoration displayed amongst the crowd swamping the car. "Names are merely reference points for others, King. I have had many, each as good or as bad as the other. Van Hoon serves me well for the time being. As regards enemies. I have none. Not a one. The very concept of having adversaries presumes a certain equality of opponent. Such a thing would obviously be unimaginable. There may, of course, exist an inordinate number of individuals who suffer from misplaced envy and an overindulged opinion of their worth, but they could hardly be regarded as my foes. To regard oneself as such would be to exercise misplaced confidence on a quite absurdly delusional level."

"And what then, am I, Van Hoon, a friend or a foe?" grinned King sardonically, as the crowd clapped enthusiastically at the oncoming cavalcade.

Van Hoon was conscious of the presence of two of King's Burmese thugs lurking behind them. "Friend or foe, which, is entirely up to you, my dear King. I have no preference either way as the question you ask is of no consequence to me. But to business. I, as always, have something that you need, and you, I suspect, have something that I desire."

King raised an eyebrow, realisation dawning in his razor-sharp mind. He thought carefully for a moment. "I see. Perhaps we have the beginnings of a power struggle, Mr Van Hoon. You seem to be cognisant of matters which should be beyond your knowledge."

Van Hoon turned towards the Chinaman and lifted his pink, penny round spectacles to reveal his extraordinary eyes. He looked directly at King for the first time in their exchange. "Ah! But my dear King, you see, there is very little that occurs in this fine city, of which I am not, as you say, cognisant. Even matters that you consider to be entirely your own, are also known to me. I realise that this news must be rather unsettling for you. You see, with time, comes not only knowledge but also its bedfellow, power. And I can assure you, Mr King, that I have been around long enough to have amassed an almost unlimited amount of both."

King grunted dismissively and sniffed the air with distaste.

Van Hoon, content with his retort, returned his attention to the parade and quickly became conscious of a young girl, no older, he judged, than seven years of age, who stood in front of him. Her hand was firmly clasped in that of her mother's, but her body was twisted around, her cherubic face staring at the striking Dutchman. Van Hoon smiled, realising that the girl had no doubt noticed that one of his eyes was the most pellucid emerald green, whilst the other was a milky white corpse of an eye, like that of a shark about to kill. The Dutchman replaced his spectacles and bowed towards the girl then crouched down to engage with her at a more comfortable level. King looked on with distaste. Van Hoon placed an artistic finger to his lips to signal a conspiratorial silence and with the other hand, magically produced a flower from somewhere upon his sartorially resplendent person. The girl's chestnut eyes widened with amazement and her face beamed a euphoric smile as the enigma that was Van Hoon laced the dahlia head into her cascading brown hair. Her mother glanced behind her, conscious that something was occurring, and scowled menacingly at Van Hoon. "Wotcha' doing there?" rasped the woman.

The Leper stood upright, removed his cobalt blue top hat and bowed the deepest of bows. "I do beg your pardon Madam, but I felt that this beautiful young lady here deserved the compliment of the world's most beautiful flower. Beauty begets beauty. I see now, of course, whence the lucky child inherited her exquisite features. Don't you agree, Mr King?" King, disinterested, grunted once more. The woman attempted to remain as though concerned whilst also trying to conceal her embarrassment at the compliment behind an uncontrollable blush. The little girl played with the bloom in her hair and hopped up and down in delight. Van Hoon looked on amused, cherishing a moment that he knew the little girl would remember long into her old age.

"Come away from that Dandy now, Gemma," urged the mother pulling the reluctant little girl further into the crowd. Van Hoon was visibly struck by the girl's name. He winked at the girl called Gemma, waved adieu and reluctantly watched as the girl and her mother melted into the crowd.

With a sigh, he returned his gaze to the procession and pointed his cane nonchalantly toward the scene of mass adoration. "His charisma and notoriety attract people of all colours and faiths, causing them to flock to him like some present-day messiah. Now, *that* is a great power, my little golden friend, great power indeed. To have, and to comprehend this power, and to use it significantly, is a rare gift. It is not only his own race that gravitates towards his presence like moons around worlds but men and women of all ages and denominations. He is that rarity amongst men, the first and possibly the last of his kind."

"As are you, I suppose," spat King contemptuously.

"Perhaps," replied Van Hoon, his mind seemingly elsewhere.

"He is a big black man who can fight. No more than that," scoffed the Chinaman dismissively.

"I beg to differ. His success has ensured that he has within his hands the potential to change the way men regard his race. My fear, however, is that he will be engulfed in a tide of meaningless adoration, money and debauchery that will wash the opportunity from him."

King shrugged. "I care not of such fripperies, Van Hoon. "We have business to attend to. You have the serum as usual I assume?"

The leper was deliberately evasive. "I believe Mr Johnson is en-route to Paris to battle another fighter, remarkably, one of the same surname *and* colour. How extraordinarily splendid that two impressive specimens of the same race shall fight for the heavyweight championship of a world governed predominantly by the power and wealth of white Illuminati."

"I tire of this diversion. The serum if you please," demanded King, his impatience now verging on irritability.

"Despite his advancing years, I suspect the pugilist will have little difficulty overcoming the brawler. He may even carry the challenger for several rounds," pondered Van Hoon stroking his angular chin thoughtfully.

"So, you enjoy the thrill of physical confrontation then, Van Hoon?" enquired King, a sinister smile playing across the meanness of his thin-lipped mouth.

"There is nothing intrinsically wrong with pugilism as a sport. Nor indeed can I make a case against one fighting for what one believes in for that matter ... that is if the stakes are even and nothing underhand is afoot."

"Ah! I see. Equal stakes, you mean?" realised King.

"As I said earlier, I have something you *need*, and you have something I *desire*. Shall we walk a bit and discuss the matter further?" suggested Van Hoon.

King nodded his agreement, and the two men turned from the throngs that had now rendered the boxer's motorcade immobile. Van Hoon waved happily to the little girl with the gleaming chestnut eyes whom he had glimpsed amongst the crowd, as he and the Chinaman turned to walk slowly up Park Lane towards Marble Arch. The noise and clamour of the crowd began to subside behind them, and London became theirs once more.

"Perhaps without the bodyguards, King," suggested Van Hoon indicating with the tip of his ornately carved sword cane towards the two Orientals who skulked in and out of his peripheral vision. King considered for a few seconds then nodded and dismissed the Shang twins with a wave of his tiny hand. The pair withdrew as one into a side street, disappointment etched across their identical, slate sharp features.

"May I suggest a pot of coffee in more relaxing surroundings, perhaps the Ritz may be more conducive to our negotiations than the pavements of Park Lane? It is but a few hundred yards to Piccadilly and they do serve the most divine petit fours and a particularly rich Moroccan coffee blend which I am sure will be to your taste." King nodded his assent. He was growing increasingly uncomfortable with this protracted rendezvous and disliked the idea of further negotiations. However, he required the elixir. He knew that, if the situation called for it, he would himself dispatch Van Hoon with little ceremony and no regret.

The grand foyer of Cesar Ritz's masterpiece could hardly have ever played host to two more remarkable figures. Van Hoon and King sat facing each other. Each on guard. The mongoose and the snake, both abundantly wary of the other's unpredictability. They sat at a low table laden with the most precisely decorated confectionary accompanied by two small bone china cups of steaming strong Moroccan coffee. The Chinaman scooped teaspoon after teaspoon of granulated sugar into his cup. "To sweeten your sourness?" quipped van Hoon as he paid unwarranted attention to the sharpness of his shirt cuffs.

King ignored the comment and glanced sideways towards a bulky, thick-necked, Mediterranean who leaned against a nearby marble topped bar, nursing a glass of what looked like mineral water. "One of yours?" enquired the Chinaman with a nod of his head.

"Hardly," lied a dismissive Van Hoon.

"I grow weary of this charade, Van Hoon, pass me the elixir or I shall kill you now and simply take it," hissed King, his serpentine eyes narrowing to hatred filled slits, and his hand reaching inside his silk robes.

"And then what, King? Deny yourself any further dosage? Do you really want to feel the brutal hand of father time descending upon you six months hence? Be sensible. How do you find the coffee? I find lately that it is my only vice."

King snorted in disgust and sipped his sweetened coffee. Van Hoon smiled whilst tapping his index finger on the end of his cane. King replaced the delicate bone china cup unsteadily upon its saucer, spilling some of its contents onto the table. He looked at Van Hoon, realisation dawning in his now heavy-lidded eyes. The room began to swim and spin around him. He attempted to stand, leaning heavily on the table with one hand as he reached into his robes for a poison-tipped Sumerian dagger concealed within its folds with the other. He fumbled then fell to the floor dragging the coffee cup and saucer with him. "Damn you, Van Hoon. Damn you to all ten courts of Hell!" he whispered before falling into unconsciousness.

Van Hoon stroked his shoulder-length hair and with a half-smile playing across his lips, he signalled to Ilhan, his bovine Turkish chauffeur who stood at the bar. Ilhan gulped back the last of his mineral water, bit the flesh from a segment of lemon rescued from his glass, and lumbered across the room. The Turk was a short, though powerfully built man, who gave the appearance of being almost as wide as he was tall. His shaven head bore a tattooed pattern of interwoven serpents which encircled his neck and coiled onto his scalp. The serpents represented the secret sign of Saint John the Apostle. The Turk effortlessly lifted the diminutive Chinese crime lord onto his shoulder and carried him through the lobby of the hotel towards a cream and silver Rolls Royce parked directly outside.

Van Hoon picked up the Sumerian dagger from the floor and briefly inspected it with interest before pinioning it dramatically to the centre of the table. As he sauntered through the lobby towards the foyer door he glanced back over his shoulder, relishing the attention he was receiving from the uniformly slack-jawed hotel patrons, and announced to the Concierge, "Henry, so kind as always. The cakes looked simply *delightful*. I think you will find the note pinned to the table to be sufficient recompense for its damage." He turned and bowed to the stunned assembled crowd, "Adieu et bon chance, Messieurs et Mesdames."

The Roi-de-Belges silver ghost tourer sped smoothly away heading along Piccadilly towards the Euston Road and through Pentonville. The car's engine was so refined as to be almost silent. Van Hoon sat in the rear, the unconscious figure of London's most merciless and universally feared crime lord slumped beside him on the car's spotless red leather interior. Van Hoon could not resist the temptation to pat the satanic figure on his shining bald head as one would a puppy. The tourer pulled through Islington and headed North through Holloway and on into Highgate village. Van Hoon smiled lopsidedly and rolled down the window, enjoying the freshness of the afternoon air as the car left the dirt of London for the more bucolic surroundings of the City's outskirts.

A rivulet of water squeezed its way through a crumbling mortar joint to hang from the moss-covered masonry, suspended precariously in droplet form like a tear about to fall from the stone cheek of a monumental statue. The drip stretched to a quivering breaking point then plummeted downwards, splashing onto the forehead of the motionless Chinaman. Splash followed splash as one drop of moisture followed another. The Chinaman's dark unconsciousness began to give way to an indistinct dream of water dripping from a verdigrised copper pipe, the noise echoing around a huge cavernous chamber was accompanied by the agonised screaming of a man in torment. A rat gnawing through flesh, its twitching snout buried in viscera. A giant, grinning monster with bloodshot, dark ringed eyes hooded by a Neanderthal brow, applauded the scene. Somewhere in the distance was the maniacal cackling of the very devil himself. The drip dropped and exploded, each time louder than the last until it sounded like the banging of a bass drum. He dreamt of skin peeling from a petrified face, a monstrous albino snake, its head as large as a fist, entwined around a flayed man's neck, tightening with his every tortured scream.

King awoke. His head pounded. He could feel the drumbeat of his heart pulsing painfully through his temples. He was conscious of a pervading smell of rot and decay begat of mildew and damp. Slowly, he opened his eyelids, gradually becoming aware of the dimness of his surroundings. He lay on a cold bare floor, amidst a host of ancient stone sarcophagi. Allowing his eyes to adjust to the darkness, he wiped moisture from his forehead, sat upright and rubbed the back of his neck, trying to ease the incessant pounding upon the inside of his skull. He stood unsteadily at first and brushed dried earth from his stained silken robes, trying to survey his surroundings. His eyes began to adjust to the dim murkiness that surrounded him, and he soon realised that he was standing within some form of mausoleum. He turned quickly towards the sudden metallic click of a cigarette lighter. A small flame sprang forth in the gloom and was transferred to the wick of a candle. The candle was lifted to under-light the unmistakable face of Dante Van Hoon, leering at him from out of the darkness. The Dutchman's remarkable eyes focussed intently upon the Chinaman. The candlelight danced across the fractal scarring that dominated the left side of the leper's face and traced its way down his neck. The flickering light gave the disfigurement the impression of being as some otherworldly tree, afire, indelibly etched upon the leper's skin.

Van Hoon smiled. "Hello again, Mr King. I apologise for the intimate nature of the venue, but I felt that our situation warranted absolute privacy, and surely there can be nowhere as private as the home of the dead. Don't you agree?"

"Where have you brought me, Van Hoon?" demanded King, the bile building in his malevolent chest. He was apoplectic with rage.

"We are in the deepest vaults of the oldest mausoleum under the Egyptian Walk of the Western Cemetery in Highgate to be absolutely precise," replied Van Hoon indicating the stone vault surrounding them. "A magnificent example of its kind, don't you agree? A suitably gothic resting place for its recipients who were a particularly unpleasant dynasty of my erstwhile acquaintance. Habitual child snatchers and aspiring vampires. A dreadful lot. You would have liked them."

King ignored the inference and looked around him. "You think that I would be intimidated by a collection of long-dead corpses?" He seethed with anger. "I will have you, Van Hoon. You are a dead man," he spat, the invective brutally pouring from his thin-lipped mouth. "Just pray that I find it within myself to allow you to die … easily!"

Van Hoon threw back his head and roared with laughter. He dabbed theatrically at his eyes with a lace trim handkerchief and leaned forward, elbows on his knees, and stared intently into the oblique eyes of the satanic Chinaman. A large stone angel loomed behind the now deadly serious face of the Leper. "Do not *ever* threaten me, King," he growled. "I care not one iota who you are or *what* you are. Whether friend or foe, it is of no import to me," Van Hoon's voice was now lowered, forceful and intense.

"I have danced with demons and fought with emperors. I have flown with angels and prayed with saints." As he leaned closer Van Hoon's oyster coloured dead eye seemed to drill into the mind of the Chinaman. King could smell the menace emanating from his rival. "I have sung with poets and caroused with Kings. Laughed with paupers and cried with royalty. I have loved and loathed, killed and created. I have starved in deserts and feasted in palaces. I have been threatened by monsters and creatures of the night, yet I have lived longer than any man. I have heard these words a hundred times before, yet here I sit, hearing them once more, this time from your insipid lips."

King masked his disquiet. Van Hoon's speech had chilled even him to his evil bones. However, he disguised his unease and sat, seemingly unaffected by Van Hoon's discourse. "Forgive me if I appear unimpressed. No matter what you may or may not have done in the past, today is the here and now, and I promise you that I will kill you by my own hand."

"Be that as it may, I believe it is time we put our cards on the table," asserted Van Hoon, his face now only inches from that of the Chinaman. "You have the plague virus. You threaten to infect and kill tens of thousands of people. Perhaps, even more, will die."

The evillest of smiles crept slowly across King's satanic face. "What care I of these white cattle? They live in their filth, let them die in their filth. They are of no importance."

Van Hoon blinked. Inwardly he was aghast at the reaction of the abhorrent Chinaman. '*Here indeed is a creature without a shred of God's mercy,*' he thought. "Then why bother to kill them at all if they have no importance?" sneered Van Hoon angrily. "I have what you need, here in my pocket, right this instant. Enough elixir to last you a dozen lifetimes, enough to stop the ageing process forever if you wish. Free of any charge. It is yours in exchange for the virus, plus any derivatives that you may have developed," reasoned Van Hoon.

King raised one pencil-thin eyebrow. The vilest of smiles played across his face. "But who is to say that I have not already unleashed the plague? It may already be beginning to infect the scum of this City." He cackled at the thought.

"I think not," stated an outwardly confident, though inwardly uncertain Van Hoon. He knew that King's ultimate aim was to destabilise Europe and open the way for the Golden Empire to usurp power. He also knew that King was sadistic enough to use the virus simply for his own pleasure.

King remained silent.

'*A seasoned negotiator,*' recognised Van Hoon. "I also have Jiao, of course."

King raised his other eyebrow.

"Your daughter, King. The young woman who fled your unspeakable cruelty and abuse to seek sanctuary amongst my Pestilent," taunted Van Hoon.

"She is of no import to me. The cuckoo has chosen its nest. You may keep the traitorous fledgling," spat King. He paused and stroked his small goatee. "However, there is something else that you and your associates can supply that will convince me to hand over the virus."

Van Hoon felt a surge of electricity pulse through his veins. "And pray tell what this may be?"

"The Chiswick Papers. Get me the Chiswick Papers, plus the elixir in your pocket and you can have the virus. All of it. Every, last drop," proclaimed King, now heading cautiously for the vault door. "My word is also my currency. I will be in contact to make the necessary arrangements. Now please open this door and do give my regards to that whore of a daughter of mine."

Van Hoon blew out the candle. Only the dead could look upon the enormous smile that cut across his chiselled face.

Chapter 16 - The Debt

The evening had passed, and night's dark shroud began its gloomy descent upon the Kent countryside. Van Hoon knew roughly where Friedrich's self-styled 'Garden of the Dead' lay and was trying to bring to mind the exact location when he suddenly spied a turn off to an unmarked Lane shrouded under the shadow of a large Yew Tree. "Turn left here!" he announced sharply, tapping Ilhan's robust shoulder with the head of his cane. The Turk swung the Rolls abruptly onto the lane and then drove carefully for what seemed like over a mile of a stone- strewn, rutted path that narrowed until it was no more than a track bordered on each side by overgrown hedgerows. Ilhan garnered the impression that he was navigating through a tapering tunnel. Van Hoon sank back into the comfort of the Roi-de-Belges Silver Ghost's leather interior, satisfied in the knowledge that they were in the correct place. Ilhan's gloved hands gripped the steering wheel tightly, carefully negotiating his way and praying that a stray thorn would not scratch the exterior cream paintwork of the Rolls and that no stone would burst a tyre.

"Capital, here we are!" declared a delighted Van Hoon who gently stroked the head of his Wolf, Mayerhofer, who lay snoring beside him on the red leather. The track had opened out to reveal an imposing church, long since abandoned. The monolith rose before them, a black, foreboding silhouette against the blackness of the night. A cloud shifted and a haze of moonlight cast down upon the crumbling façade of the building, a gothic monstrosity of enormous proportions. The Church was surrounded by dense forest and hedgerows and as such was hidden completely from any nearby roads or pathways. A small, neglected graveyard lay to the front of the Churchyard, its ancient headstones stood at obtuse angles and its monuments and mausoleums were stained with lichen and overgrown with ivy. Van Hoon recognised this place for what it was; Friedrich's Garden of the Dead.

Van Hoon signalled Ilhan to remain in the car and awoke Mayerhofer with a prod in the ribs. Man, and wolf exited the car and picked their way through the cemetery. Van Hoon tipped his hat to a gigantic crow that sat cawing upon a stone Celtic cross. The bird dipped its head as if in silent salute and flapped off into the night. Dried leaves crunched underfoot, and Van Hoon could sense movement betwixt the tombstones. Fleeting movement of flitting shapes, silent unknown shadows. Mayerhofer snarled and growled, saliva dripping from his jaws as his hackles rose.

Van Hoon felt an unfamiliar uneasiness at these undefined, spectral shapes. Bats frittered around him, their squeaks echoing through the night, adding to the eeriness of the cemetery. Mayerhofer began to mewl in apprehension and confusion.

Van Hoon reached for the huge hoop of iron that served as a door knocker and slammed it against the massive arched oak door. There was a groove where the knocker had struck home over hundreds of years. The sound reverberated around the Churchyard causing some other crows to take flight. Almost immediately the door began to slowly open. Van Hoon was struck by the impression that whoever was opening the door was struggling to do so. Eventually, a sturdily built man with a shock of black hair and brazil nut eyes unveiled himself in the doorway backlit by glimmering candlelight. "The Master is not receiving visitors," stated the manservant and began to push the door shut as if this was a statement that warranted no response.

"But I am sure that Herr Friedrich will make an exception for an old friend such as I," smiled a beatific Van Hoon who produced a bronze coloured calling card and offered it to the doorman.

Bartram was Friedrich's only companion, a loyal and unswerving major-domo whose service had been long and devoted. To him, his Master was everything. He looked closely at this unexpected visitor. He raised a candle towards him. The face was as striking as any he had ever seen. One eye so radiantly green that it resembled a cut emerald, the other a dead blanched white. The candlelight danced upon the fractal scarring that decorated one side of that face. A face that radiated such intelligence and confidence that Bartram instinctively knew that this was a man of immense power and influence. A man who was accustomed to getting his own way. Bartram looked down at what he recognised as an untethered wolf which sat at Van Hoon's side looking expectantly at the manservant. The unflappable Bartram shook his head and looked at the card. "If you wouldn't mind stepping into the hallway, Mr Van Hoon, I will enquire of the Master." He looked conspiratorially at the Dandy as he ushered him in. "An old friend you say?" an eyebrow raised. "The Master does not receive anyone and is not, how can I put it, currently *prepared* for any callers. However, I shall endeavour..."

Bartram was cut short by a roar from within. It emanated from behind another great panelled door, some ten feet in height and half as wide. "What is it, Bartram? Send them away, whoever it is!" Van Hoon recognised the stentorian voice and smiled.

"A Mr Dante Van Hoon, Sir. An old friend by all accounts," shouted back Bartram, leaning his head towards the firmly closed door.

A pregnant silence filled the vast stone-vaulted nave of the derelict Church. Van Hoon looked around him nonchalantly and began lowly whistling the refrain from Beethoven's ninth symphony. '*One more minute and I will burst in there and surprise him with the biggest greeting he has seen since that lightning storm,'* he thought to himself.

"Send him in!" came the bellow from within.

"But, Sir," stammered Bartram. "Your present...*condition*, Sir!"

"Do as I say, Bartram," came the steadfast reply.

Van Hoon was ushered into a vast, cold room furnished with basic but over-sized furniture. The room was dominated, if such can be said, by two things. Firstly, a gigantic, though empty stone fireplace set into one wall of the room. The second dominant feature being the figure who occupied one of the chairs guarding the fireplace. Friedrich was a veritable giant. A naked giant. His appearance was striking, with most perhaps regarding it as grotesque. His grey skin was a patchwork of abhorrent scarring and his sallow yellow eyes stared out from under a heavy, leaden brow. The size of his head denoted immense intelligence and the musculature of his great body spoke of enormous strength. His thin black lips cracked open. "Sit." He indicated the chair opposite him with a gigantic hand, scarred at the wrist. "It has been a long time, Van Hoon."

Van Hoon bowed slightly and sat, feeling as if he were a child in an adult's chair. Mayerhofer lay next to him and rested his head on the stone-cold floor next to Van Hoon's feet. Whilst Friedrich continued to stare into the void of the fireplace, his chin resting thoughtfully on one huge hand, Van Hoon's eyes were fixed firmly on the face of the giant. After all, everything about Friedrich's anatomy was enormous.

"Are you cold? You must be cold. I could ask Bertram to light a fire if you so desire?" rumbled Friedrich finally turning his gaze upon Van Hoon.

Van Hoon was about to answer in the negative when the attentive Bartram burst into the room clutching an enormous smoking jacket. He proceeded to insist, much to Van Hoon's enjoyment, and Friedrich's annoyance, that his master stand and allow him to enwrap his frame with the jacket. With a satisfying, "now then," Bartram tied the jacket's cord around his Master's prodigious waist and with a nod and a crisp click of his heels, made swift his departure. Friedrich shrugged his shoulders. "He is efficient." The statement hung in the air, Van Hoon silently nodding his understanding whilst trying to stifle a smile.

Friedrich broke the silence. "And how fares Mayerhofer?" he enquired indicating the Wolf with a nod of his head.

"Irreversibly transformed, I'm afraid," replied Van Hoon, looking down at the wolf. "We have tried various routes back to normality over the years, most of them of a chemically-based nature, but alas, no success. I fear that, given that the incident occurred fifty years ago, poor Wolfgang is now more canine than human and would find the shock of readjustment too much to cope with." With this, the Wolf lifted itself from the stone floor and began to pad uneasily around the room. He found an appropriate looking corner, lifted his leg, and, having relieved himself, returned to his place at his master's feet. Van Hoon coughed, "as if to illustrate my point. I do so apologise, my friend."

Friedrich waved a dismissive hand. "It is of no matter. A pity. He was a brave man and a good friend," lamented Friedrich, looking into the ice-blue eyes of the Wolf, trying to find some remnants of humanity.

"And he remains both brave and a good friend," grinned Van Hoon scratching an appreciative Mayerhofer under the chin.

Friedrich looked directly at Van Hoon. "Why are you here? You know that I have no contact with the world outside of my Garden of the Dead."

"So I thought," parried Van Hoon. "Although I have heard recently that you befriended a certain Chinese Giant?" He paused, searching for a reaction. There was none. "Hercules Chin?" prompted the Dutchman.

Friedrich grunted. "A mistake on my part. I thought I recognised a soulmate, a fellow put-upon wretch." A deep rumble rolled within Friedrich's throat. "I believed I could save him, or at least help him, but his mind is such that coherent thought seems beyond him. His brain is drug-addled, and his intelligence is infantile. Combine that with an incendiary temper and the strength of an ox and you have an untameable beast. I thought I could fashion him into a right-thinking man, but he is beyond all help." The giant paused for a moment, looking at the vaulted stone ceiling above him. "Surely you did not come to see me after fifty years to talk of this opium-soaked fool?"

Van Hoon leant forward in his chair. His remarkable eyes engaged those of Friedrich who could feel the intensity of Van Hoon's stare probe his soul. "I come to ask of you a service. Payment of the debt."

Friedrich nodded his great head, a tight-lipped grin of realisation spread across his face. "Budapest," he stated.

"Budapest," confirmed Van Hoon.

Friedrich recalled that night, half a century ago. The savagery, the blood, the pain, the death. He looked at Van Hoon. "The Debt would be paid in full?"

"The debt will be paid in full," acknowledged Van Hoon.

"Then I agree. What is it that you need me to do?"

Van Hoon smiled a smile like a razor cut. "I only ask that you look after something for me."

Chapter 17 - The Trade

Arnold Rubenstein was beginning to feel as if he were an old hand at this larceny lark. He had always been aware of the rumours that had surrounded his late Uncle Jabez. '*Perhaps a propensity for illicit activity runs in my blood,*' he thought, somewhat warming to the concept, as he furtively made his way along Whitehall Place towards Trafalgar Square. The hour was late, and the air was damp and heavy, laced with a dense night fog that seemed to soak him through to the marrow. Not for the first time, he clutched nervously at the brown leather briefcase, gripping the handle for all his worth.

Although Van Hoon had stipulated the hour of their meeting, and Trafalgar Square as its location, he now realised that the Dutchman had not been completely precise as to where they were to rendezvous. At this hour, the Square was sparsely populated with late-night stragglers trying to locate a cab or night omnibus. Others, he suspected, may have rather more predatory intentions.

Just how Van Hoon had initially located him remained a mystery to young Rubenstein. The Leper had arranged for him to be taken to his Belgravia mansion by the fearsome-looking Turkish chauffeur, Ilhan, a few days earlier. He had been awestruck at the opulence of Van Hoon's home. Rubenstein had seen great wealth during his young life but nothing to compare with the grandiose luxury of the Dutchman's residence. The exotic stuffed animals, the grandeur of the furnishings, and the sheer visual extravaganza it presented were a feast for every sense. Initially, the wraithlike robed servants had unnerved him, but a few moments spent in the presence of the enigma that was Van Hoon had eased any of his lingering concerns.

Van Hoon had offered him his hand. "Let me extend my sincerest condolences to you, Master Rubenstein. Your Uncle's passing was indeed regrettable," consoled Van Hoon as diplomatically as he possibly could considering the circumstances. The Dutchman knew only too well the extent of the elder Jew's criminal activities and his association with the devilish Mr King.

"Why thank you, Sir," stammered Arnold, staring at the remarkable figure that stood before him. He found himself hypnotised by Van Hoon's eyes, one a swirling pool of absinthe green, the other a blanched milky white, and by the fractal leprotic scarring that exploded down the left side of his face and neck like forked lightning.

Van Hoon answered the boy's unasked question. "I have only partial sight from the left one but there are other senses that a man can develop, given sufficient time, to more than compensate for such a minor deficiency. Come, sit." He indicated that Arnold join him on a long Louis the fourteenth chaise longue by patting its plum-coloured velvet upholstery. Van Hoon lifted a small brass bell from a side table and rang it with a flick of his lace cuffed wrist. Almost immediately, a diminutive robed figure glided into the room and placed a laden silver tray on the low, amber embossed table in front of them. A translucent, cobalt blue butterfly flittered between the two men, its iridescent wings dancing in the half light. The insect eventually alighted on the leper's neck, seemingly attracted by the small silver dagger-shaped earing suspended from Van Hoon's left earlobe. Rubenstein then noticed that there were dozens of the creatures dotted around the room. Van Hoon noticed the lad's obvious fascination. "Are they not beautiful? They are the flowers of the sky. I regard them as the souls of the departed. The most delicate of God's creatures. The fabric between life and death is thinner in places than one would ever imagine," he added enigmatically. Rubenstein nodded in awed agreement as another butterfly, almost pure sugar white except for its pale grey wingtips, landed upon the silver tray.

"Ah! My lady comes to say hello," smiled the leper, tenderly extending a finger on to which the white lady flittered. "Stem ginger and bay leaf tea, young Sir? I can highly recommend it. Excellent for the digestion and circulation of the blood. Most efficacious. It is my only vice." Rubenstein looked hesitantly at the tray and then to the silently departing robed figure.

"It is perfectly safe," declared Van Hoon, reading the young man's disquiet at being served tea by what, to all intents and purposes appeared to him to be a leper. The Dutchman poured the tea into two willow pattern china cups and sat back, thoughtfully assessing the young man seated beside him. "Do you know how your Uncle met his untimely demise, Arnold? I may call you Arnold, may I not? I feel that we have made such a connection after all."

Rubenstein nodded. "Yes, Sir. Only yesterday I identified Uncle Jabez's body for Chief Inspector Wiggins. It was apparent that he had died from some fast-acting disease, as I had seen him only days earlier and he was looking hale and hearty." Arnold swallowed sharply. "It was not at all pleasant, Mr Van Hoon," his gaze falling to the floor.

"Quite so. Unfortunately, your Uncle was murdered, and that disease you referred to is The Plague. It was administered by a Chinese devil who goes only by the surname of Mr King, a sadistic killer whom I have a particular interest in, how shall I put it ... eliminating," stated Van Hoon with a raised eyebrow and a slight tilt of his head.

"The Plague! How can this be? The Plague was wiped out many years ago. And for what possible reason, Mr Van Hoon? I know my Uncle was no angel, but it seems preposterous to infect him with The Plague?" entreated a disbelieving Rubenstein.

Van Hoon shook his head, hesitating as to how to best answer the young man's questions. "Firstly, because unbeknown to the general populace, the Plague contagion has been kept alive by men of science for many years. They have controlled it in order to study its chemical properties, but they have never destroyed it. And secondly, simply because Mr King could. He wanted and needed to see its effects upon someone before he let it loose on the entire population. Unfortunately for you, he chose your Uncle." The Dutchman let the resultant silence that followed settle before continuing. "I need your help to stop King."

Rubenstein's thoughts were interrupted suddenly and brought back to the present as a hard shoulder contacted his. The impact had been so unexpected and forceful that it threw him staggering backwards. His heel caught a kerbstone and he toppled, his coccyx hitting the paved ground with a painful thud, causing him to wind himself. The briefcase snapped free of his grip and skidded off into the gloom. Arnold scrambled after the case, desperate to retrieve it. A figure loomed before him, a hazy silhouette backlit through the fog by distant streetlamps. "Apologies young, Sir," laughed a gruff rumble of a voice. "It seems as though you lost your footing. I must apologise. Please let me help you up."

The indistinct figure offered a hand which Rubenstein thankfully clutched. As he was hoisted upwards, the stranger's other fist came crashing into his jaw, knocking him sideward. "Grab the case, Mitch! Let's scarper!"

Rubenstein was dazed and as he knelt on his hands and knees, he heard the scuffle of shoes as the impromptu thieves began to flee into the darkness. "No!" screamed Arnold, "My case!" he cried, tears of frustration welling in his eyes. Suddenly the mist seemed to sweep aside as if it were a curtain pulled by an unseen cord. A tall lean figure appeared from nowhere and swung a cane with unbelievable speed and force. The wooden shaft hit the fleeing Mitch square on the back of his neck, knocking him forward to the ground. He toppled as if poleaxed, unconscious before his head cracked upon the paving slabs. Arnold winced as he heard the crack of skull connect with stone. He wondered if indeed his assailant may have received a mortal blow. The lithe stranger then pirouetted with the precision of a prima ballerina, twirled his cane, and let loose an immediate jab that struck the second thief square between his eyes. The robber stopped dead in his tracks, standing erect but appearing to be out cold. Van Hoon tilted his head slightly to one side as if examining his victim with interest. He smiled, satisfied, and gently pushed the thief backwards with the lightest of touches from the heel of his cane. The second cutpurse fell to the ground beside his companion. Van Hoon dusted himself off and straightened his top hat. "Good evening, Master Rubenstein. Such a pleasant night for a stroll. Ilhan, please retrieve the case." Rubenstein could just make out a bulky figure stooping to recover the briefcase.

"Marvellous, time for some light refreshments, don't you think?" concluded Van Hoon as he pulled Arnold upright with both arms. "I know a little Italian café but a mere stone's throw from here. They serve coffee that is beyond poetry."

The rendezvous had been arranged. The venue, London's most magnificent secular public building, The Natural History Museum in Kensington. The Cromwell Road was, as always at noon, a flowing, multi-currented river of humanity, each stream of people flowing seamlessly in all directions. Nonetheless, even here the tall, striking figure of Dante Van Hoon attracted attention as he cut a stylish swathe through the throngs making his way towards the Romanesque splendour of Alfred Waterhouse's architectural masterpiece. Both women and men cast admiring glances at the picture of sartorial elegance that was Van Hoon as he glided gracefully up the stone entrance steps and through the main front doors. Behind the balletic leper stomped the bullish figure of Ilhan who lumbered up the steps, making the contrast between the two seem almost comical.

The concierge greeted Van Hoon with a slight bow and a tug on his peaked cap. "Afternoon, Sir," greeted the doorman looking at his watch. "Your visitors are awaiting you in the Reptile and Amphibian Exhibition Hall as arranged. They frightened the life out of me if truth be told Sir," his voice lowered in a conspiratorial fashion. "The area has been sealed off from the public as you requested. It has caused no amount of a nuisance with Joe Public wanting to see that stuffed Dragon lizard, I can assure you." The concierge looked accusingly at Van Hoon.

"Excellent, Henry!" responded Van Hoon flashing a smile that could charm birds from trees. His emerald eye glinted and his blue-black, shoulder-length hair caught the noonday sun as it shone across the main hall foyer. "I am sure the Board of Directors are more than happy with the recompense they have received for the brief use of the chamber." Van Hoon turned to Ilhan who had just arrived at his elbow, his burnished, bullet shaved head barely reaching the jacket shoulder of Van Hoon's plum-coloured morning suit. Van Hoon indicated to the Turk with a wave of his hand, "Give, Henry, here a gold sovereign for his invaluable assistance will you, dear chap," instructed Van Hoon as he strode towards the stone steps that led to the

Reptile Hall. Ilhan produced the gold coin from a zipped money belt concealed under his waistcoat and flicked it spinning towards Henry. The concierge gratefully caught the spinning coin and tusked it immediately into his waistcoat pocket. Henry watched as the figure of Van Hoon disappeared down the stone steps. Suddenly a thought sprang into Henry's head. 'How does he know my name?' he wondered, scratching his head beneath his cap.

Ilhan secured the heavy timber doors behind him and stood facing the room, legs slightly apart and his arms folded across his barrel chest. His body language screamed 'none shall pass.' The room, like all the museum exhibition halls, was walled in dressed stone and lined with a multitude of glass presentation cases holding numerous exhibits. Stuffed examples of amphibians and lizards, reconstructions of skeletons, fossilised remains, teeth, skins and claws.

"I do hope you all have your tickets gentlemen. Ilhan shall be most displeased if you have forgotten them!" joked Van Hoon nonchalantly. He was faced with the diminutive, serpentine eyed oriental crime lord. King was accompanied by the omnipresent Shang Twins, one at each shoulder, twitching like deadly cobras, each eager and ready to strike at the merest of gestures from their master. King spat in a hate-filled, hissing, sibilant voice, "I have no time for such frivolities, Van Hoon. Let us get to the business in hand. You have the papers, I take it?"

Van Hoon seemed not to hear the Chinaman's question. Instead, he stood in front of the predominant presentation case set in the middle of the large exhibition hall. Within in it stood the stuffed remains of an adult male Komodo dragon, nearing fifteen feet in length and fourteen stones in weight. It was posed standing with its front two feet upon a sandy coloured rectangular shaped rock some three inches thick, a rat grasped underfoot within its enormous razor-sharp claws. Its extraordinarily long forked tongue was caught, frozen in time, at full extension as though the great lizard was tasting the air in celebration of its catch. Varnish surrounded its mouth representing the lizard's venomous, bacteria-laden saliva. "Such magnificent work!" exclaimed Van Hoon, producing a magnifying jeweller's loupe from within his jacket. He held the loupe by a telescopic ivory handle and leant forward, peering closely at the exhibit. "So precise! The tongue, such a difficult organ to replicate, is simply wonderful! The papillae are so wonderfully imagined. One could almost feel that the dragon was alive and, indeed, dangerous, don't you agree, Mr King?"

"The dragon is most definitely alive, and most definitely dangerous, Mr Van Hoon," replied King, rising to the bait of the Dutchman's opening gambit. Van Hoon laughed as he snapped shut the loupe and stepped towards King, his footsteps echoing around the stone walls. The Shang twins shifted uneasily, two identical, twitching killers, each longing for any opportunity to draw their blades. Ilhan felt for the pistol concealed in a shoulder holster under his jacket.

Van Hoon stood looking down at King. "Of course, I have the papers. And the elixir! The elixir you so desire." He signalled to Ilhan who obediently bounded forward and placed a box on the floor between the two antagonists. "There is enough of your 'milk' in that case to last you centuries," detailed Van Hoon. "It only pains me that it is you, and not some more deserving individual, who will benefit from my skills."

"And the document? What of the document? Where are the Chiswick Papers?" King's voice was rising in pitch, becoming tremulous with anticipation.

Van Hoon sneered and the light surrounding him seemed to dim. His scarred face suddenly took on a demonic quality as he leered at King. "The document is here. But first, I require the Virus. It is a stupidly simple equation I propose. No contagion equals no document. Your move, King."

King's eyes narrowed to indecipherable slits, his face contorted into a reflection of pure evil. Hatred for the Leper emanated from his every pore. Without breaking eye contact with Van Hoon, the Chinaman raised his skinny hand and snapped his fingers loudly. At his signal, a huge shape emerged from the shadows, like a giant mass of black smoke slowly invading the room. Hercules Chin loomed forward, his head almost brushing the vaulted ceiling. Ilhan gasped at the sight. "My! You are a big boy!" observed Van Hoon, taking a half step backwards. "I can safely state that your reputation is in no way exaggerated."

The Dutchman made a mental inventory of his weapons. A pair of Colt forty-five pistols initialled JHH on their mother of pearl inlaid handles, a gift from their notorious, bronchial owner. A Javanese Kris strapped to his upper right thigh, a catspaw ring fully loaded with lethal taipan serpent venom which sat upon his left middle finger, and his ubiquitous Bocote wood sword cane, tipped with the same deadly poison. Looking at the monster before him he felt sure that one, if not all, may be required before the hour was out.

Chin held out his hand towards King. The crime lord's hand was like that of a child's doll in comparison to that of the giant. King took a burnished metal bottle from the colossus and laid it on the floor next to the case of elixir. As he did so he opened the case to check its contents. He removed a glass flask of milky liquid from the purple velvet interior, examined it, and, satisfied with its authenticity, returned it to the box. King picked up the box and Van Hoon signalled that Ilhan take the metallic bottle.

"I trust the contagion is within the bottle, King?" enquired Van Hoon, whose gaze continued to be fixed with admiring fascination upon the glassy-eyed Giant who stood directly behind the Chinaman.

King nodded in agreement. "Of course. Even I have a reputation to maintain. And what of the Papers? You try my patience, Van Hoon. Any more prevarication and I shall unleash Chin! Now, where are the Papers?"

Van Hoon raised an inquisitive eyebrow, his pellucid green eye twinkled in the gloom. "I don't suppose you would countenance throwing the Giant, here, into the bargain, would you, old chap?" he indicated towards Hercules Chin with his cane. "He does look as if he could prove rather useful to me," Chin grunted his disquiet with a deep leonine growl.

"Hercules Chin is most definitely not, how do you say? *On the table,*" sneered King, his voice rising to a high-pitched screech.

"Pity. Such a wasted toy. Or is he merely a puppet in your hands?" A measure of regret played in the Dutchman's voice. Van Hoon had observed the opiate-induced dullness of the giant's emotionless eyes before quickly refocussing on the matter at hand. "And so, to your precious Papers, King."

"Yes! Yes! Where are they? I demand that you hand them over now," screamed an increasingly volatile King.

"As you wish, my little yellowish friend, but you really need to calm down, you'll give yourself a heart attack," spat Van Hoon. "The papers are here. They have been within sight the entire time."

King looked confused, irritated, and ready to explode with rage. "Where? God damn you! Where?"

Van Hoon moved quickly. More quickly than even the Shang brothers could ever have anticipated. More quickly than King could ever have imagined. More quickly even than the American dentist who had gifted Van Hoon the colt pistols thirty years earlier. The Dutchman spun, a blur of movement. A flash of silver and the crack of a gunshot and in less than a fifth of a second the glass case containing the Komodo dragon shattered into a thousand pieces. Shards of thick glass slid across the floor like a cataract of diamonds.

"Your document sits beneath the forelegs of the Komodo dragon, Mr King. Help yourself." Van Hoon smiled at the Chinaman, a huge sense of satisfaction surging through his body. "Rather appropriate, don't you think, given your usual, trite calling card." Van Hoon laughed uproariously. As he made his way from the chamber, he threw a small statuette of a jade dragon over his shoulder. "Make sure you tidy up, gentlemen. We wouldn't want to upset Henry, now would we?"

Van Hoon looked at the youngster with what Wiggins interpreted as a sense of pride. "I recruited young Arnold here to procure the Chiswick Papers. He truly does have the makings of a most excellent police constable, and if not that, then perhaps a master thief." Arnold Rubenstein could feel his chest swell with pride as the leper draped a fatherly arm around the young man's shoulder. They stood within the drawing room of Doctor Watson's rather opulent rented rooms on Montague Street. Wiggins looked aghast. "But how could you even consider handing those papers over to King? Those plans could one day prove to be essential to the preservation of this nation, the very lives of her people! This time you go too far, Van Hoon."

Magnus MacDonald agreed wholeheartedly, his face flushed with anger. "I agree. I cannae allow ye to do this Van Hoon. What you are suggesting is unthinkable, man. Trading the Chiswick Papers for the virus was never on the agenda. We must find another way!"

"But gentlemen, it is too late," flourished Van Hoon, "the deed is already completed. King has the Papers and we, gentlemen, have the contagion." Doctor Watson hung his head and cursed under his breath. Pyke threw his cigar into the fire and took a threatening step of intent towards Van Hoon.

"Reign yer neck in, Sergeant!" ordered the canny MacDonald, looking intently at Van Hoon. "I suspect that there may be more to this than first meets the eye."

Van Hoon raised his hands and looked at the Scotsman with mock wonder. "How perceptive of you, Mr MacDonald. You win the prize! I have always held that your intelligence belies that gruff little façade of yours." Wiggins could tell that Van Hoon was enjoying every second of his performance.

"Pray tell all, Mr Van Hoon" ordered MacDonald.

The leper began to stroll around the room as if deep in thought, his hands placed in front of his face, fingertips to the tip of his nose as if in prayer. He came to a halt, standing face-to-face with an enraged Pyke. Van Hoon calmly smiled as only the most supremely confident of men can do in such a situation. He addressed MacDonald whilst maintaining eye contact with Pyke. "Fear not, Superintendent, even I would not be so rash as to risk the security of your Nation. You see, the original papers, so expertly purloined by our young Artful Dodger here, are now safely back in the Ministry office from whence they came."

The company exchanged confused glances as Van Hoon revelled in the moment. "You see gentlemen, the documents that our gloating little Oriental friend now has in his possession are carefully transcribed copies. They have been skilfully altered by certain members of my Pestilent. They each had lives before contracting their condition and, as such, all have varied skills, among them draughtsmanship, calligraphy and engineering knowledge."

"Forgeries!" snapped Wiggins. "You have created forgeries!"

Van Hoon broke eye contact with Pyke and rotated on the spot to face Wiggins. He withdrew a solid gold cigarette case from his inside pocket. The case was embossed with a serpent entwined around a goblet. He removed a slim cigarillo and lit it with Doctor Watson's crystal desk lighter, fashioned to represent the Globe. The Dutchman offered the cigarette case towards the assemblage. "Smoke gentlemen? I have them specially imported from America, they are called Phillies as they are handmade in Philadelphia. They are rather splendid. My only vice, you understand."

Only MacDonald accepted, rolling his wheelchair close enough to Van Hoon who exhaled satisfyingly, sending a smoke ring towards the ceiling. Van Hoon continued. "Precisely, Chief Inspector Wiggins. The entire document is a very efficient forgery. The Nation's defensive and offensive plans in the event of a War in Europe remain safely under lock and key in Whitehall. King's copy is, however, to all intents and purposes, the real thing but with all the critical elements cleverly altered in some discrete way. Troop and collateral numbers, centres of operations, strategies, sea and air defences, codenames and cyphers. All altered. Scale drawings of ships and planes, submarines, military hardware and weapons. All modified with key components omitted or altered. In summary, gentlemen, our unsuspecting Mr King has a portfolio of useless documents rather than the oracle he supposes. Whereas as we, gentlemen, have the contagion." The leper dramatically pulled a sealed wooden box from his jacket with a flourish that invited praise.

Watson began a slow handclap. "Bravo Sir! Masterly! Van Hoon, you truly are a genius!" Wiggins, MacDonald, and a somewhat reluctant Pyke joined in the applause. Watson laughed uproariously and gave the leper a tremendous slap on the back. Van Hoon visibly flinched, unaccustomed to such intimate physical contact.

Wiggins could see that MacDonald was lost in deep thought. "Sir, you have misgivings, I sense?"

MacDonald looked at Wiggins and made a contemplative tutting noise. "I only think o' King and how we deal with the sleekit wee shite now. He has what he thinks are the genuine Chiswick Papers. His intention, presumably, is to pass the information to our enemies, either for personal gain or purely for the instigation of chaos and warfare. The logical course of action would be to allow him to flee, presumably to the Continent, and allow Van Hoon's misinformation to be passed to the interested foreign powers."

Watson interjected. "I tend to agree, though in doing so we let the blaggard escape the law and the retribution he so richly deserves."

"It is a case of letting the rat free to allow him to infest our enemies, gentlemen," observed MacDonald. "Once they find out that King has delivered useless information, he will be discredited, and his life will be endangered. Surely he would have to flee back to the Orient or end up a corpse somewhere in Eastern Europe." He looked around the assemblage, their general mood was one of agreement. "Then it is agreed. We allow King to flee. The realm will be safer for his passing and our future more secure from a misinformed and therefore angry enemy."

"I will order a watch on the main ports," added Wiggins. "Though there are a hundred points along the river from which he could depart under the cloak of darkness."

"Most likely he will charter a small craft from an unscrupulous master and be off within a few days," murmured Pyke.

Wiggins turned his attention to the unadorned mahogany box in Van Hoon's hand. "And what of the virus? It must either be destroyed or kept secure in such a way that it may be studied with a view to developing an antidote, or at the very least some form of preventative treatment."

"I agree wholeheartedly on both counts, Inspector," smiled Van Hoon.

"Its previous *safe* home proved to be less than secure," observed MacDonald. "Although there are places that I could recommend. Jem's oven would prove to be safer," he joked with a wink to Pyke. "It must be turned over to the authorities at once and kept under lock and key in the most secure vault in the land. Perhaps the Tower of London or the Bank of England?"

Watson rubbed his chin as if recalling a distant memory. "If you think the Tower is secure, you are sadly mistaken. Do not forget, it is not so long since the late Professor Moriarty was successful in penetrating its walls in his attempt to steal the very Crown itself."

MacDonald nodded his agreement. "Aye, if it weren't for your good self and a certain master Detective of oor acquaintance, he would have had away with the nation's jewels."

Pyke nodded. "You cannot get a safer place than the undergarments of the Old Lady of Threadneedle Street. I would recommend the Bank vaults."

The debate was interrupted by three sharp taps of Van Hoon's sword cane resounding on the wooden floor. Each of the men instantly turned their attentions towards the Dutchman. "And there I have a proposition, gentlemen. In this matter, I must ask for your absolute trust. Arnold, can you please leave the room for the time being?"

Wiggins could see Pyke shifting uncomfortably. Van Hoon's giant wolf husky, Mayerhofer, awoken by the tapping of the cane, slowly rose from the floor and padded towards the Detective Sergeant. The dog had developed an affinity for Pyke during the course of their association and began to nuzzle softly at his trouser leg. Pyke gave the wolf's head a playful rub. Mayerhofer's appearance in Montague Street had raised more than a few eyebrows amongst the street's other residents.

Van Hoon waited until Rubenstein had reluctantly left the room before continuing. "I propose that we dispose of the majority of the virus, whilst I privately retain a small sample for research purposes. I will endeavour, with the aid of a leading bacteriologist of my acquaintance, to develop an antidote. Imagine, gentlemen, if you will, a World wiped free of Plague. It shall be my greatest triumph!"

"And where will this sample be kept, pray tell?" asked Pyke relighting a half-smoked cigar. As always, he extinguished the match between thumb and forefinger and proceeded to discard it in the fire.

"A pertinent question, timely put," affirmed Wiggins.

"I did ask for your trust," Van Hoon reminded them. "I will share the knowledge of the repository with only one man. Only He and I will know its location."

Wiggins spotted that as he spoke, Van Hoon briefly threw what he judged to be an involuntary glance towards Doctor Watson. Watson seemed not to notice. A light switched on in Wiggins' head. He understood instantly. '*Who else in the World could Van Hoon trust with such a secret?*' He realised now exactly who the mysterious 'leading bacteriologist' would be. Wiggins grasped the initiative. "We agree," he announced. "But what of the disposal of what remains?"

At this, Van Hoon stood and straightened his evening coat. "Rest assured, gentlemen, the contagion will be administered into a vessel from which there is no return." He swept his arm forward in a grand gesture. "May I introduce you to a long-standing friend of mine, Herr Victor Friedrich, late of Ingolstadt."

The four men turned in unison. Even Pyke recoiled at the sight of the individual who had somehow entered the room unseen and, indeed, unheard. Squeezed into a large oxblood Chesterfield chair sat a giant whom Wiggins gauged to be approximately seven feet tall and almost half as wide. His enormous bulk was heavily clothed in greatcoat, breeches, and high leather buccaneer boots. The largest top hat Wiggins had ever seen crowned the stranger's huge head. Friedrich removed his hat in greeting. "Good day, gentlemen," rumbled a deep, yet pleasant voice. The giant's eyes were a sick, milky, yellow under a protruding Neanderthal brow and his pallid, waxy skin was deeply cut with gruesome scar tissue. The room succumbed to a stunned silence.

"The bubonic plague is the most virulent bacterial organism known to mankind, gentlemen. It can ravage a typical healthy human being in a matter of days," continued Van Hoon in a sombre tone. "As you know, Doctor Watson, the plague virus is a cunning adversary that evades detection by ingeniously modifying its molecular structure and thereby fooling the body's immune system into thinking there is nothing amiss."

"Indeed, it is a living, breathing organism that triggers the disguise you talk of when it realises it has infected a host by cleverly measuring the temperature to be thirty-seven degrees Celsius, which is the internal temperature of a human being," expanded Watson. "It is an abhorrent way to die I can assure you. Agonising abdominal pain, diarrhoea, nausea and vomiting, chills and fever, inflamed buboes in the armpits and groin regions, extreme lethargy and muscle weakness, gangrene, internal bleeding leading to circulatory shock, and ultimately, in nearly all cases, death."

Throughout Watson's and Van Hoon's medical tutorial, Friedrich sat in silence, his heavy-lidded eyes unmoving. His thin, blackened lips were slightly parted, revealing decayed teeth. Although his skin was heavily scarred and lined, he had a childlike quality both in his appearance and bearing. Wiggins wondered what dreadful accident had befallen this man. The Inspector detected an underlying sadness about the hulking figure. He felt sorry for him, like a father feels for his son when he realises his child has no friends. He also wondered as to the reason for the Giant's presence.

"Exactly! The bacterium strikes directly at the lymph nodes, and once safely inside, the virus begins to replicate and multiply," continued the Dutchman. "By the time the immune system eventually realises that something is catastrophically wrong, the lymph nodes swell up, creating nasty buboes. The bacteria then start migrating through the blood into the lungs and it is at that point…" Van Hoon paused, "…that the human body begins to effectively kill itself. The presence of so many bacteria in the bloodstream causes the immune system to overload, triggering septic shock where the body's blood vessels begin to leak, causing abnormal blood clotting and multiple organ failure." Van Hoon again paused, this time for dramatic effect.

Instantly the room fell silent, no man knowing what, if anything, to say. The silence was broken by Van Hoon who looked intently into the yellow eyes of Friedrich. "Are you certain you still want to proceed with this my friend?" he asked.

"Yes," came the measured, affirmative reply. Friedrich smiled, his thin, black lips lopsided. "Where better for the virus to rest than within the body of a man already dead."

Wiggins, Pyke, MacDonald and Watson exchanged confused looks amongst themselves, each man incredulous at the implication of what they had heard.

Van Hoon opened the small wooden box and removed a glass vial and offered it to Friedrich. "You do understand, my friend, that having not carried out any tests, I remain uncertain as to the effect that the contagion will have upon you."

Friedrich said nothing. He took the bottle in a giant grey hand and uncorked the lid. His jaundiced eyes gazed at the liquid and then fell upon the collected company. Everyone in the room was riveted to the scene playing out before them, the room sizzled with anticipation and dread in equal measure.

"I must protest!" declared a concerned Doctor Watson. "This is utter madness." He took a step forward as if to intervene. After all, he had pledged to save life, not to watch it be destroyed.

Friedrich raised his heavily calloused hand, indicating that Watson desist. The giant turned his great head towards Van Hoon and spoke, his voice surprisingly soft for such a frightening human spectacle. "What care I of consequence? My flesh and organs are long since dead. What possible damage can it inflict upon me? Does the disease not attack the lymphatic system? I am sure that if I possess such a thing, that it is no longer operational. Besides, what care I if I die? My life is empty. My days are endless. My nights without sleep. I know no joy. No happiness. Imagine an infinite life without purpose Van Hoon, how unremittingly dreadful is that?" Friedrich swirled the bottle, peering at its glutinous contents, churning behind the glass like a miniature maelstrom. Liquid doom. He lifted it to blackened lips, threw back his head and swallowed.

Van Hoon took the empty vial from the giant's hand, recorked it and placed it safely back in its box. He looked at the great pallid head, its waxy grey skin, patchworked with scars across a face whose dull yellow eyes reflected no emotion. Van Hoon considered his response carefully before speaking. "Thank you, my friend. Your deed is one of incomparable sacrifice and I shall not let you bear its consequence alone. No man has ever done more. Mankind can never repay this debt."

Friedrich grunted. "I renounced the world of men many years ago. My solitude is the greatest benefit I can offer the World of Man."

"And yet here you sit, the saviour of thousands, if not millions. You were created for a reason, and now we have discovered that very reason, together. You, the receptacle of a deadly virus that would have exterminated half the city." Van Hoon sat in front of Friedrich and pulled his chair closer to that of the giant. He stared closely at Friedrich, drilling into the evasive, jaundiced eyes of the colossus, searching for a glimpse of the tortured soul that lay behind them. Friedrich moved uneasily in his chair, uncomfortable with the unfamiliar scrutiny. "God himself would thank you, my friend."

Friedrich grunted. "I do not need God, nor his thanks. My creator abandoned me, my mate abandoned me, and the World of Men has shunned me, hunted me. I have been feared and abhorred wherever I have sought refuge."

"And now, should you acquiesce, you will remain under my protection," intoned Van Hoon. "We must ensure that you are safe and that I can observe the effects, if any, that the contagion may have upon you. I have secured a suitably private residence for your exclusive use." Van Hoon was about to continue when Friedrich stood to his full height. To Wiggins, it appeared that the giant filled the room.

"I do not need your sanctuary, Van Hoon. I did what I did, and now it is done. I alone will bear any consequence. I will return to my Garden of the Dead. Do not attempt to follow or contact me. The debt, Van Hoon, is repaid." With that, Friedrich touched the brim of his massive top hat and with the slightest of bows, departed the room as silently as he had entered.

Chapter 18 - The Beauty

It was a dusky, gloomy night and the grey industrial cityscape of the south bank of the Thames was the spectral backdrop to a tragic scene. Jem Pyke stood looking down at the lifeless body of a woman who had been washed up on the foreshore beneath the southernmost arch of Waterloo Bridge. He was studiously making notes whilst continually adjusting his new spectacles upon the bridge of his crooked nose. The haunting note of a night barge wailed through the darkness. The woman, who appeared to be no older than thirty, lay facing upwards, her body and outstretched arms forming the unmistakable shape of a cross. Water lapped at her arms making them look as though she were trying to fly away from death. Her lower body lay half immersed in the waters of low tide, her undulating red skirts were darkened with water and the river's impurities. Her curled blonde hair resembled the rays of the sun as it lay spread out in a radial corona against the pebbles and mud of the foreshore. Pyke scribbled more observations in his notebook. He felt drawn towards the obvious beauty of the woman who lay dead at his feet. He noticed that she was clasping what appeared to be a gold locket and chain tightly in her right hand. Pyke noted that she was simply dressed. '*Perhaps a servant?*' noted Pyke, under which he had written, '*Accident?*' '*poss. Suicide ... unrequited love?... attractive enough to have several admirers.*'

Pyke took off his spectacles, removed his Derby and bending down to the young woman, whispered tenderly. "I'll get you out of here madam." He looked at the pebbled spit he stood upon and found himself inexplicably concerned for her comfort.

He heard the forensic team before he saw them, the sound of pebbles crunching underfoot heralded their approach. As they neared, Pyke barked an order. "You fellows get your work done here as quickly and as respectably as possible and get this lady dry and safe."

"But she's dead Inspector," replied a bemused photographer as he began setting up his tripod, somewhat awkwardly given the pebble strewn beach.

Pyke glowered at the young man. "She's also somebody's daughter!" The photographer promptly went about his business, suitably shamed.

A hesitant Doctor Nelson B. Pascoe, arms outstretched for balance, manoeuvred carefully towards the scene over the treacherous terrain. His young assistant and junior forensic pathologist, Edward Imrie, was already busy investigating the deceased woman using the mysterious contents of a bulging Gladstone bag he had brought with him. The chastised photographer was now busily taking shots from several different angles and close-ups of the woman's face and hands.

"Death seems to be an exceptionally active fellow these past few days, Sergeant Pyke," stated Pascoe, his face reddened from his exertions.

"He does indeed, Doctor Pascoe, although I reckon your days would be somewhat emptier if we were bereft of his presence," replied Pyke still bristling at the inappropriate reply from the photographer moments earlier. "I have a feeling that he is sharpening his scythe on a hellish whetstone as we speak." He could see that Pascoe winced as he crouched down to examine the body more closely. "How's the gout then, Doc?"

"Just as Death seems to accompany you, Detective, Master Gout is my constant and unwanted companion. My ankle and great toe are continually tender and aflame. A burning bedfellow at night I can assure you. Every movement, no matter how slight, causes incredible discomfort. At times, even the touch of a silk sheet sends stinging pain shuddering through my foot." Pascoe produced a small phial from his pocket and shook it merrily in Pyke's direction. "However, a modest daily dose of liquid morphine shaves the edge off the pain. But enough of my woes, Sergeant, what can you tell me about this unfortunate young lady?"

As Pascoe looked at the body Pyke could see a compassionate sadness play across the older man's face. '*It affects us all, even old Doc Pascoe,*' he realised.

"It's more a case of what *you* can tell *us*, Doc," countered Pyke. "She was found by Eager Elsie, a Waterloo dolly-mop who plies her trade on the Bridge. She was walking her route, and spotted this unfortunate lass, lying as she does now, facing upwards and half out of the water. I was informed by Elsie that the deceased is not a known face in her line of employ. Looks to be in her late twenties to me Doc. She is simply dressed but in no way unkempt and with no apparent visible signs of injury. She looks so peaceful and beautiful. She may have fallen from the bridge above but has landed almost as though she were positioned in such a way."

"My initial observations, in tandem with what you have just informed me, point towards a simple case of suicide, poor soul," offered Pascoe in an unemotional and practical manner. "See the way she's clasping what appears to be a heart-shaped broach tightly in her hand? May have been rejected by a lover and threw herself from the bridge. However, as we know all too well detective, evidence garnered at the site and forensic examination will shed further light on the matter. We may perhaps find a cause of death not entirely associated with the taking of one's own life." He gazed forlornly at the vision of beautiful death before him. "I hope for her sake, that whatever the cause, her end was peaceful. God rest her soul."

"Amen to that, Doc," agreed Pyke replacing his Derby atop his head. "Let us know your findings as soon as you can and hopefully, we can identify this woman and return her to her loved ones, and she can rest in peace."

Doctor Pascoe eased himself into the leather bucket chair that sat in the corner of Wiggins' office. He sighed in relief as the leather gave comfortably under his weight. Wiggins and Pyke exchanged a smile, recognising the good doctor's habitual preference for the most comfortable seat in any room. Wiggins observed an aura of weariness around Pascoe, a sense of resigned defeat. "You look tired, Nelson."

Pascoe looked surprised, even more so than normal, and perhaps slightly embarrassed. "Do you think so? Perhaps I am a little under the weather," he acceded. "This damn gout doesn't help. The pain wears you down. Bloody nuisance."

Pyke leant against the frame of the office door, an unlit half-smoked cigar in his mouth. "What of our riverside beauty, Doc. Do we know any more of the poor child?"

Pascoe cleared his throat. Wiggins noted an unpleasant bronchial rattle that spoke to him of an underlying chest condition. He resolved to speak to Pascoe of his concerns later, perhaps in a more private setting. "Of her identity, we know nothing, but we have found some other evidence which will, I am sure, be of interest to you both. But first, some conjecture. Her shoulders and hair were dry and given the tide times and the approximate time of death, we can safely assume that she was placed in the position in which she was found, between five and six this evening."

"Placed?" asked Pyke, "perhaps she had fallen, no?"

"Unlikely, Jem," commented Wiggins, his forehead furrowed in thought. "Placement of the body seems more likely, particularly given the tableau shown in the photographs. There is an almost picturesque feel to the scene. A feeling dare I say it, of serenity." He slid several photos across the desk towards Pyke, who sat down and began to examine them carefully.

"You see, Jem," added Pascoe, "there were no injuries that we would normally associate with a fall from such a height. We measured the bridge and it is more than a twenty-five feet drop to the waterline where the deceased was found. There were no head injuries, no limb fractures, specifically of the upper arms and clavicle or scapula bones. Apart from bruising to both shins, there are no impact injuries or fractures to the lower limbs at all, which would rule out her having fallen or being thrown from such a height."

"You mentioned some new evidence, Nelson?" prompted Wiggins, consciously continuing to address the Doctor by his Christian name. He wanted to give Pascoe the sense that he was an intrinsic part of his team, and also to demonstrate his concern for the Doctor's health.

"Yes, of course." Pascoe leant forward in his chair with a new-found enthusiasm. He reached into his Gladstone and produced a lady's hair comb. "We found this tangled within our victim's hair. I believe it points towards confirming our theory of the scene having been staged. I think it was used post-mortem to arrange and tease the hair into a position almost like the rays of the sun."

Wiggins took the comb from Pascoe and produced a jeweller's loupe from a desk drawer. He proceeded to inspect the article minutely. "Whalebone. Of plain and simple design. No manufacturer marks or decoration. An inexpensive hair comb easily purchased from any market stall in the City. Perhaps from a street hawker. It is, however, of some age, and has been frequently used as the rounded edges testify. Most likely worn by an elderly woman, but not recently."

Pyke and Pascoe exchanged an impressed look. Wiggins caught the gesture and picked a silver hair carefully between thumb and forefinger from within the tines of the comb and held it up for the two to see. "Elementary, gentleman," he smiled knowingly.

"For a second, I thought you had done something devilishly clever!" chortled Pascoe. He wiped his forehead with a linen handkerchief and then bent to produce a second article from his bag. "This piece of paper was found within her bodice gentleman. He flattened out the creased paper on Wiggins' desk. Both policemen leant forward, interest keen within them.

Wiggins read aloud. "Great deliverance giveth he to his king; and showeth mercy to his anointed." He considered for a moment. "Psalm eighteen-fifty, if my memory does not fail me."

Pyke could not disguise his amazement. "That is some memory you have there, Guv! What does the text mean?"

A strained look spread across the Chief Inspector's handsome face. "I am unsure of its specific relevance, Jem, but one thing I am now convinced of is that this is murder, and it is connected to those of Deacon Hamilton Lancaster, the Politician Jonathan Hardridge and Sir Edward John Poynter."

"Boss?" asked Pyke, wondering at what connection Wiggins had made.

"All were elaborately staged. The scenes were carefully arranged, and the methods of murder precisely chosen. I believe we are pursuing one common killer. Perhaps this biblical message will unlock his identity."

Chapter 19 - The Key

"I am taking the key, darling," declared Wiggins, "I shan't be long. Perhaps an hour or two." He lifted the lid of the small silver box that sat on the highly polished consul table in the hallway of the Wiggins' family home. Carefully, he took out a single key, regarded it with satisfaction, playfully threw it upwards, deftly caught it and tusked it safely into his waistcoat pocket. Each time he took the key he followed the same ritual. As in many aspects of Albert Wiggins' life, ritual was important to him, so much so that in some ways it had become a burden.

Mary appeared in the doorway to the parlour, a knowing smile playing across her attractive, somewhat Plantagenet face. "But Albert, you have only just crossed the threshold. Surely the prospect of an evening with Mrs Potts and myself does not present such an unpleasant ordeal?" Mary's tone was one of slight admonishment mixed with humour.

Wiggins winced slightly. Amidst the turmoil of his day, he had quite forgotten that Mary was entertaining Jennifer Potts that very afternoon. Mrs Potts was the window of Constable William Potts, the erstwhile colleague of Wiggins who had heroically given his life during the capture of the demonic Beast that had been Doctor Joseph Bleak. Potts had died a hero, and Wiggins often thought back on the bravery that the young man had shown in using his own body as a shield to protect Lady Constance Harkness from certain death at the talons of the Beast. He pursed his lips in regret. "I am sorry, my dear. Jennifer's visit entirely escaped my memory. However, I feel that an hour or two in the 'sanctuary of thought' will help untangle this twisted skein that lies before me."

"I understand," replied Mary, taking her husband by the elbow. "At least pop your head into the parlour to say hello."

Wiggins looked startled. He lowered his voice. "You mean she is here? Already?"

"Yes dear," laughed Mary, "it is past seven after all!"

Wiggins looked forlornly at the wall clock and thought himself a fool. "Of course. Of course." He walked hurriedly into the parlour and greeted Jennifer Potts with a bow and a slight kiss to her proffered hand. "I do so apologise, Jennifer, unfortunately, I find that Business calls me away from our evening appointment."

"No matter, Albert," smiled an understanding Mrs Potts. "I am sure that Mary and I can survive the evening without you. I also suspect that you would better enjoy the noble pursuit of justice to the ignoble pursuit of gossip."

Wiggins bowed to the perception of femalekind and made his excuses, kissed his wife, and stepped out into a damp, Spring evening. The rain was light and intermittent as he walked the length of the Crescent and thence on to Baker Street. Within a mere quarter of an hour, he found himself knocking upon a comfortingly familiar ebony painted door topped with an ivory-hued fanlight. The door was presently opened by a slight man of roughly Wiggins' age. He was somewhat awkwardly caparisoned in doorman's livery, an outfit that looked rather out of time and out of place. His face, although youthful, was at odds with his general air which was of one older than his years; weary and perhaps downtrodden. At the sight of Wiggins, his gimlet eyes lit up. "Mr Wiggins! What a pleasure to see you. Come in, come in, why don't you?" The page stood aside and ushered the detective inside.

"Thank you, Billy," smiled Wiggins, gripping the loyal servant's hand and shaking a vigorous welcome. "How are you my friend?"

"All the better for seeing you, Sir." He glanced at the door of the ground floor flat. "Though Mrs Hudson ails something awful. She misses Mr Holmes dreadfully and her age…" Billy's voice trailed off and his eyes seemed momentarily unfocused, his thoughts elsewhere.

"I understand," sympathised Wiggins placing a brotherly hand on the small man's shoulder. "Can I see her?"

Billy considered thoughtfully before answering. "I think not, Mr Wiggins. She sleeps at the moment and I wouldn't want to disturb her. She should be in a convalescent home by rights, but you know what she's like, made of stern stuff. She simply refuses to leave and awaits his safe return from whatever adventures he is embroiled in across in Europe." Wiggins brows furrowed as he nodded. "Though the visits of Mrs Wiggins and Doctor Watson help enormously to rejuvenate her spirits," offered Billy, his mood suddenly lightened at the thought. The two men chatted for a few minutes of this and that, before Billy left to attend to his aged landlady. Wiggins began to climb the seventeen steps of the pristinely clean staircase that led to those rooms. Each step brought a memory. He and the other Irregulars racing, breath panting, hearts beating, each trying to be the first to reach the top of the stairs. Standing to attention in a row whilst Wiggins would relay his report to the Great Detective who would listen patiently and intently, sometimes probing with an incisive question that Wiggins always felt that he stumbled over in answering. The expectation of that precious guinea. The beatific smile and encouraging words of Doctor Watson. And then, after the inevitable parting of the ways of the Irregulars, the joy at the tutelage that He had bestowed upon him. How blessed he had been to fall under the Master's mentorship. How intense were the studies, the sciences, chemistry, biology and physics; the training of his mind to follow logical paths towards sometimes illogical conclusions; his tuition in observation, psychology, the study of people and their natures. It all came flooding back to him over the course of those seventeen steps. Each time he visited Baker Street it was the same. How he relished being in this place!

Wiggins removed the key from his waistcoat pocket and inserted it into the polished brass lock escutcheon, took a breath, turned the key, then the doorknob and entered. The sitting room was unlit. Wiggins drew only one set of curtains, just enough to let in a modicum of the evening's dusky half-light. He breathed in the atmosphere of the room, a scent of stale tobacco and burlap underscored with a lingering chemical undertone. He looked around him at the familiar surroundings. The table of test tubes and reports, bookcases crammed with textbooks and records, case files and of course His unique catalogues of all things criminal, methodically filed and forensically referenced. The Stradivarius case lying dustily on a shelf next to a bust of Napoleon. The bullet holes that spelt out VR in Mrs Hudson's much ill-treated plaster walls. The etchings of His birth County, Yorkshire, hung alongside faded theatre bills. A pile of unopened correspondence was transfixed to the corner desk, which overflowed with papers and was littered with half-squeezed greasepaint tubes. Upon the desk sat two framed photographs. The first was of a handsome, intelligent woman, whom Wiggins knew to be the famed Irene Adler, and the second was of three young men dressed for a country ball; the Holmes brothers, Sherrinford, Mycroft and young Sherlock. Wiggins picked up the frame and looked closely into the eyes of the young men. The intelligence that surged from those eyes was palpable, so much so that Wiggins imagined he could feel it invade his brain and heighten his senses. He was sure, as always, that a ruminative visit to these rooms would allow him to collect his thoughts and help him make sense of the web within which he currently struggled.

As always on these occasions, he made to sit in His chair to the right of the fireplace. As he did so, he was taken aback to find that he was not alone. In the opposite chair sat a gently snoring John Watson. The good Doctor's moustache twitched as he slept. Wiggins fondly imagined that Watson's errant moustache trembled as he dreamt of some long-remembered adventure. He sat quietly, deciding not to awaken his companion, preferring to allow the old soldier the comfort of his rest. He saw a half-empty brandy glass positioned next to a similarly diminished bottle on an occasional table next to Watson's chair. He looked at the mantlepiece, crowned by a pair a crossed Damascan steel rapiers. His eyes rested fondly on the rotary pipe-rack that sat next to the suspended Persian slipper tobacco pouch. Comfortable in His chair, he closed his eyes and relaxed, allowing his mind to find its own way to the conundrums that challenged him. The cycle of carefully staged murders that he felt sure was the work of a single perpetrator. He began to think them through, reimagining each scene, recalling details, searching for commonality, and waiting for the magic of the room to influence his thoughts.

His thoughts were interrupted. "Help, yourself young Wiggins. I am sure He would not have minded in the least." Watson had awoken from his slumber.

Wiggins was caught by surprise and threw Watson a questioning look. "Help myself, Doctor?"

"To the pipe, of course. Though ostensibly asleep, I have been observing you whilst you pursued your train of thought. Applying His methods, you might say. First, you looked at the pipe rack and then to the Persian slipper. I can only, therefore conclude that you were contemplating having a smoke. Elementary my dear Wiggins," winked Watson. "Please, go ahead."

Wiggins smiled and leant forward to shake the older man's hand. "Good to see you, John. I see all those years of collaboration went to effective use."

Watson tilted his head slightly in acknowledgement and reached inside his pocket for his own Peterson and produced a tobacco pouch. "Though I would suggest we use some of this Old Cavendish rather than whatever remains within that slipper. Drier than mausoleum dust, I should imagine." He indicated the pipe rack with an encouraging hand.

Wiggins nodded and reached for an old calabash pipe, thick with oil. He gripped it in his teeth and blew. "It's the one I remember best," he explained with a wry smile. Watson nodded sagely. Both men sat and smoked for a few minutes, comfortable in their silence. Watson produced another brandy glass from a nearby tantalus and poured Wiggins a generous measure. The evening half-light played a mellow sheen over the scene. Wiggins broke the quiet, wanting to explain his presence in the rooms. "I come here occasionally to collect my thoughts. The surroundings help me to ease my mind and clarify my judgements."

"I understand, of course," chuckled Watson raising his glass. "This room has witnessed more mysteries and bizarre tales than any other in the world, I should imagine. Perhaps it is no coincidence that it retains an ability to help one solve such cases. So much residual energy abounds within this room that it simply must have an effect. I myself come here occasionally to soak up the atmosphere and remember."

Wiggins wondered at Watson's statement and postulated that perhaps these four walls did indeed contain an energy, absorbed from the work and thoughts of the Great Detective, that someone encouraged mental stimulation and clarity.

"He thinks very highly of you of course," expounded Watson. Wiggins felt a flush rise above his collar. Whether it was caused by the brandy or the compliment, he could not tell. "You were his proudest achievement, you know. Said so himself. All the cases solved, the villains sent down, the lives and reputations saved, the scandals avoided. All of it. You were his masterpiece." Wiggins felt suddenly overwhelmed with emotion and took a swift pull on his glass to try and disguise the fact. "From uneducated guttersnipe ... you don't mind me saying, do you ... to the sophisticated, forensic thinker. You turned out to be a remarkable young man."

Wiggins recovered his composure and thanked the Doctor, "All down to the guidance and mentorship of yourself and Mr Holmes, I might add."

"Nonsense!" Watson wagged an admonishing finger. "One cannot build a wall without bricks or mortar. He could see that you had all the materials he needed to create all that you have become."

Wiggins again began to feel uncomfortable. He had never felt easy receiving praise and decided to swiftly change the subject. He described the murders to Watson, sharing details and theories that he would otherwise not divulge to anyone outside of his task force. He told of how he was convinced that the murder scenes had been carefully staged, each presenting a macabre, yet artistic tableau. He relayed the brutal and bizarre causes of death as Watson interjected with the occasional question. The light began to fade, as the two men exchanged ideas. Billy had earlier lit a fire which now cast a warming glow on the two men. The atmosphere was serene though the air was fecund with theories. A photographer, perhaps, or a theatrical individual such as a stage manager or an actor, an artist or gallery curator.

Watson was enthused, convinced that they were on the right track. He studied Wiggins profile, pipe in mouth, the glow of the fire playing against the outline of his face. "By Jove, Holmes! I think we have it you know!" he ejaculated. The sentence hung in the air between the two men, one embarrassed, one uncomfortable yet strangely proud that the other should make such a lapse. Watson apologised. "Why, I'm dreadfully sorry, old boy. The brandy, the half-light, the pipe, you know," his apology trailing off until he averted his gaze towards the fire. Wiggins smiled and standing, put a reassuring hand on his hero's shoulder. "I am truly flattered, John. You could not possibly have paid me a higher compliment."

Watson nodded and patted the hand on his shoulder. "Why don't we take a stroll in the evening air? The Barley Mow will still be open, and I believe a nightcap may be in order."

Chapter 20 - The Painter

A solitary table and a three-legged stool were all that furnished the small dilapidated room of the common lodging house in Rathbone Street in London's Fitzrovia district. The room was without gas or electricity supply. A solitary candle flickered a low irradiating light upon the gloomy scene. The tallow candle, now merely a stubby mass of melted wax, would only cast light for a few more hours before the crispy wick would fizzle into its waxy crater. The disagreeable aroma of animal fat that emanated from the melting wax was slightly masked by the smoky burning of the flame. The candle was not housed in a chamber stick nor spiked upon a pricket but stuck on an old chipped saucer decorated with forget-me-nots, part of a long-discarded tea set that had once known more sophisticated and appropriate use.

The room was bitterly cold and smelled heavily of damp and mould intermingled with the unmistakable aroma of linseed oil and turpentine. A thick layer of dust coated every surface except for a few finger trails and smudges upon a small wooden table where withered flowers drooped in a dried-out vase like sleeping unfortunates on the penny rope. The windows had mostly been barred up with timber that was now rotting with mildew and giving way in several places to the elements. Condensation dripped in icy rivulets down the remaining glass of one windowpane, pooling in small brown puddles on the brittle flaking paint of the windowsill. The air felt stagnant and noxious and dust-covered spider webs clung to each cornice creating a brown wispy curtain. In the low light, the badly stained hand-basin seemed to be streaked with several assorted colours, all merging into a composite black. It was coated in the multi-coloured dust of pigment powders, their irregular nematoid patterns interrupted by a trail of limescale that traced to the plughole from a single dripping tap.

The flickering light of the candle teased and danced around the room revealing a gallery of wondrous creations. The wooden panelled walls were adorned with magnificent recreations of famous paintings from throughout the ages. On closer inspection, these were not merely representations of Old Masters, but amazingly precise renditions of astounding accuracy, perfect recreations of the original works. A domestic interior scene by Vermeer segued into a portrait by Vermehren. An impressionistic Monet scene nestled alongside the Romanism of Mabuse. The baroque, rounded sensuality of Rubens merging with the powerful feminine sexuality of Renoir. No inch was spared from the colour and form festooned upon the battered oak panels. Even the half-rotten timbers of the ceiling were ornamented with Italian renaissance frescos of stunning beauty and fluidity of hand, the centrepiece being Michelangelo's creation of Adam. Rather oddly the left hand of Adam was depicted with only four fingers.

The silhouetted figure of a man with a mop of long wild hair sat hunched over a relatively small square of timber propped up on a makeshift easel. The man's eyes gazed into *her* eyes. He was fixated upon those astounding eyes. Dark chestnut coloured eyes that sparkled mischievously, knowingly. Burnt Sienna with a hint of Prussian blue. He was almost certain that her pupils were dilating a subconscious, stimulated signal of attraction, an eagerness of love reaching towards him, the creator. This, he told himself again, cannot possibly be true for these eyes are mere brushstrokes of oil carefully administered to a panel of poplar wood. These glabrous eyes, devoid of eyelashes and eyebrows, hypnotised and teased him like no others ever had. He felt flushed with power, knowing that he had created these eyes that now so entranced and mesmerised him.

He stood, straightening his back with a cartilaginous crack, and took a step back. He studied the pale luminescence of her skin as it glowed with an avarice sheen, enhancing her enigmatic, lopsided smile. A mysterious smile, pigmented with Naples yellow, white and Terre Verte, which expressed some secretive, as yet, untold knowledge or desire. Her head, eyes and torso were turned ever so slightly inwardly, giving a further feeling of intimacy. The woman looked stoically indifferent, and at the same time so familiar, as if he had met his subject many years before, but that was an impossibility. After all, La Gioconda was over five-hundred years old. She sat markedly upright with her arms folded in a reserved, almost guarded posture with her right hand resting lightly upon her left. She appeared ambiguous yet alive, an oxymoron recreated magnificently in oils.

The small painting was a masterpiece, a tour de force of his skills. The pinnacle of all his great artistic techniques. A triumphant visualisation of his genius. His sfumato painting technique supplemented by meticulous underpainting had created imperceptible transitions between light and shade, exactly as had the original. The paint used throughout the portrait was blended without borders or hard edges, as though painted by a hand of smoke. Ethereal brushstrokes so subtle that their application was imperceptible to the naked eye. The cascading Gaussian hair was created by applying layers of finely applied transparent colour, each only a few molecules thick. An unquestionable masterpiece indeed.

His eyes were drawn to the less detailed background which cleverly used an altogether more muted pallet, forcing the woman's undoubted beauty and mystery to be thrust further upon the viewer. He had portrayed the elements using atmosphere and light, and with a delicacy and finesse which da Vinci himself would commend. He returned his stare to her magnificent eyes, wondrous eyes that contained a secret. Is the secret hers or his? Would the secret cypher ever be found? After all, if the great Leonardo could include his initials in the Mona Lisa's pupils, then he reasoned that he could do likewise. With a single sable haired brush, the artist carefully painted the letter J within her left eye and the letter S in her right, so subtly that he expected theses daubs would never be appreciated. His very own secret. A secret between himself and La Gioconda.

Standing further back the dishevelled figure admired his final masterpiece. He sniffed, satisfied, and wiped a ragged, paint-stained sleeve across his pock-pitted nose. He began mumbling unintelligibly to himself. '*They made him a Knight of the realm? Scandalous! Sir Edward high and fuckin' mighty, what the hell did he know about art? True Art. A charlatan, a bloody parasitic unskilled amateur who clung onto the coattails of virtuosos. I'd wager he was unfamiliar with the intricacies of Rubens' Saint Sebastian. Well, he knows all about it now. Art turned into life. The impression of pain to the agonising reality.*' His ramblings trailed off into croaky, guttural laughter that descended into delusional sobbing and shoulder-shuddering tears.

Through the blur of his maniacal tears, he looked at a scrap of paper that lay upon the table. The torn remnant was surrounded by several sticks of charcoal, two table knives, which had been used as surrogate palette knives, and several brushes bereft of bristles. Written on the slip of paper in an immaculate cursive hand was a list which read:

Stoning of Saint Stephen ✓

Death of Caesar ✓

Saint Sebastian ✓

~~Dante and Virgil in Hell~~

Found Drowned ✓

A puff of sickly acetone breath from Jarvis Sickart and the candle was extinguished.

Chapter 21 - The Board

As he stood, Wiggins winced with pain and instinctively reached to rub his right knee. The painful throb was an occasional reminder of the pursuit of Doctor Joseph Bleak along Tower Bridge only months before. He had slipped awkwardly during the chase, losing his balance as his momentum had overreached his centre of mass, causing him to clatter to the ground with his right side bearing the brunt of the force. In an attempt to retain his balance, he had hyperextended his knee joint causing it to jar, twisting his anterior cruciate ligament in the process. The adrenalin that had coursed through his body and his desire to apprehend Doctor Bleak had somehow anaesthetised the pain temporarily, allowing him to maintain his pursuit that had eventually led to the demise of the vile multiple murderer. A daily regimen of applying an icepack to the affected area, and compression of the knee with a bandage, over two weeks, had helped in reducing the swelling. However, the pain still troubled him occasionally.

Wiggins straightened and walked over to the huge chalkboard that dominated his office. Upon it were displayed his ideas, press clippings, forensic reports, and crime scene photographs, all neatly pinned in chronological order. There were linking arrows of differing coloured chalks and several terms underlined or punctuated with question or exclamation marks. He termed it his 'murder gallery.' He stood there for hours at a time, scrutinising every conceivable scrap of evidence and formulating data. Time seemed to him to stand still as he ruminated over the evidence, always trusting in his investigative processes and not in assumptions. On the adjacent wall hung a large-scale ordnance street map of London with pins indicating the locations of the current crime scenes and carefully drawn arrows estimating possible routes of approach and escape. Distances and times were also annotated to the various highlighted routes.

The time was two-thirty in the morning and Wiggins lit another of his custom-made, double-banded cigarettes and studied his gallery. He realised that he was smoking far more than he ever used to, but put this down, somewhat disingenuously, to the stress and anxiety caused by his workload. The same had happened during the investigation of the Beast, and he now, to his dismay, experienced a hacking cough upon waking each morning. Mary had commented upon the cough and, as a non-smoker, encouraged him to '*break the filthy habit.*'

He sent a smoke ring spiralling towards the board and watched until it gently caressed a photograph of Emily Lorimer's face before dispersing. She looked peaceful in death, so unburdened and free. It had taken only forty-eight hours to identify 'Lady Thames' as she had been referred to within the Yard until a work colleague had recognised her photograph in the Standard. Miss Lorimer had been a chambermaid at a small hotel in Charlotte Street. She had by all accounts been a popular girl, newly arrived in London from '*somewhere up North.*' Wiggins then turned his gaze upon the bludgeoned face of Deacon Hamilton Lancaster, the forensic photograph showing a grotesque mask of lesions. He shuddered at the thought of the agonies the poor man must have endured, the terror that constituted his last moments. Wiggins hoped that his God had been merciful and compassionate.

When scrutinising the elements set out on the board, he invariably found himself having a conversation or debate with himself regarding each case. Ask a question, answer that question, mostly with another question, then shoot off at tangents only to return to the original question, hopefully with a greater understanding of each case or line of enquiry.

Deacon Lancaster, Johnathan Hardridge, Sir Edward Poynter, and Emily Lorimer, all killed arbitrarily within the space of thirteen days. Each murdered in extremely specific ways and ostensibly, in carefully selected locations. Each murder scene had the appearance of having been staged rather than being merely a random act of slaughter. The most minor of details all seemingly premeditatedly planned. Each crime scene meant something. Its particular staging described something, something as yet undiscovered. He felt sure of it. Wiggins had the sense of viewing a tableau, a scene, of a moment in time. '*A man of God, a politician, an artist and critic and a young lady,*' Wiggins mused. He could see no connection in their occupations other than they each strove to improve the lives of others through their vocations. So much was obvious in the administrations of a preacher and, also in the efforts of a politician on behalf of his constituents. '*Perhaps there is a link here?*' he postulated. He pursued that train of thought. '*Does not an artist seek to improve the World through his work? And surely a maid creates cleanliness and order? Perhaps the killer abhors or resents betterment?*' He was convinced that the same hand had slain each victim. A single killer. An individual of obsessive habit with a mercurial eye for detail. Excluding the murderous rampage of Bleak but a few months earlier, and the reign of the Ripper a generation before, he could not recall a case in which such a number of murders had been concentrated over such a brief time period. His thoughts returned to the previous night and his chance meeting with Doctor Watson. He revisited their conversation regarding possible occupations of the killer.

Suddenly and inexplicably, he became unexpectedly light-headed, so much so that he had to steady himself by resting against the wall. His skin became damp with perspiration, and he felt chilled. He felt faint. '*Surely, he wasn't coming down with something. Not now! The case was at a turning point.*' The detective then uncharacteristically lost his train of thought entirely. The contents and scribblings on the chalkboard seemed to blur and merge as if draining down a sink. He tried to focus on the board and clear his head but the images before him became unintelligible, the wording jumbled and illegible. It was as if the board itself was pushing him away, or perhaps as if some other force was pulling him away from it.

He slumped down heavily in a chair and took a few moments to regain his senses. He glanced at his watch, then at the walnut wall clock hanging beside the simply framed portrait of King George V. Inexplicably there was a thirty-two-minute time difference between the two. This was extraordinary. Wiggins was always fastidious in ensuring that each timepiece was wound daily and set at exactly the same time. As his head slowly cleared and his thoughts began to unscramble, Albert Wiggins felt an impulsive desire to visit Dante Van Hoon.

Chapter 22 - The Painting

Wiggins stood alone awaiting the Dutchman's arrival. It was three-fifteen in the morning. He had visited Van Hoon's Belgravia mansion on several occasions but had never before set foot in the room in which he found himself. A room which could be regarded as rather bland and unimposing in comparison to the extravagant flamboyance of the rest of the dwelling. The room was simply decorated and sparsely furnished with a simple desk and chair. One wall was lined with Spartan bookshelves heavy with what Wiggins had observed to be purely volumes of reference. Botanical tomes sat alongside scientific studies and monographs, religious texts and encyclopaedias of art, philosophy, and ancient cultures. A solitary painting adorned the walls of the room.

Wiggins had been escorted to the second-floor study by one of Van Hoon's Pestilent who had gestured with a scarred, pale hand that he be seated. Wiggins had noted that the servant's robe was tied at the waist by what he now recognised as the de-rigueur macramé belt. It seemed to be spun from gold fibres of some manufacture. He reminded himself to ask Van Hoon whether there was any hierarchical significance to the colour of the belts his Pestilent wore. The sleeve of the servant's robe had risen up as he stretched his arm towards the vacant chair disclosing a faintly tattooed moon motif on his forearm. Wiggins politely declined as he always preferred to stand when visiting on official police business, deeming it impolite to receive his host whilst already seated. The leper slowly nodded his head in acknowledgement and gently withdrew from the room. Wiggins stood facing the large, naively framed painting for several minutes. If the frame was simple, the painting it enveloped was entirely the opposite. Wiggins found himself absorbed and his focus drawn to every detail of what he recognised as a genuine masterpiece.

"Is it the artist or the subject matter that intrigues you?" whispered Van Hoon into the Inspector's ear. Wiggins flinched, startled at the suddenness and silence of Van Hoon's appearance.

"Mr Van Hoon, you surprised me by the silence of your arrival. I was entranced and caught rather off guard whilst studying the characters and composition of this rather splendid and somewhat intriguing painting," replied Wiggins regaining his composure.

"And pray tell, what does the great detective in you *see?*" encouraged Van Hoon signalling towards the picture. Wiggins decided to humour his host and studied the painting further for a few moments.

"The *detective* in me sees three naked male forms, one lying prone on the ground, seemingly unconscious, possibly dead, but certainly not sleeping. In the foreground, the other two males are wrestling violently with each other. The red-headed individual, who is clearly the aggressor, seems to be savagely biting the throat of his kneeling combatant in what appears, to all intents, to be a ferocious, almost animalistic, fight to the death. One can almost feel the strain of each muscle fibre and the forces at play."

"Indeed, Inspector, how keenly observed. I am impressed," complimented the Dutchman. "The anatomy and underlying musculature are certainly magnificently well rendered. One can effectively feel the kinetics as well as the kinematics between the two battling opponents. The brushstrokes are those of an absolute master of his art." Van Hoon produced a small, amethyst studded, mother of pearl snuff box from his pocket and proceeded to partake. "Do excuse me, Inspector, it is my only vice." He offered the box to Wiggins who politely declined. "Do please proceed with your critique, Inspector. I am pleasantly fascinated."

Wiggins nodded his understanding and continued his exploration of the oil. "Two other males, standing in the middle ground, watch on and seem to be conversing secretively. They look to be classical figures, perhaps Greek or Roman. One is robed in white and wears a laurel wreath atop his head, whilst the other seems to be of a rather devilish nature and is attired entirely in scarlet." Wiggins made a mental note regarding the laurel wreath, remembering that a similar such headpiece had adorned the dead body of the murdered politician, Johnathan Hardridge. "Actually, the devilish looking figure reminds me of the magical characters one sees illustrated on a Keller theatrical poster. He could equally, however, be a man of God as he seems to be wearing a Kippot or skull cap of some description. There is a winged demon that appears to be flying, or floating rather, and in the background a fiery tower or Golgotha of other naked bodies." A speculative silence descended upon the two men.

Van Hoon nodded his appreciation of Wiggins' observations. "Very good, Inspector. I am impressed. A most thorough appraisal, but do you not find that art is subjective in the extreme?" he questioned, breaking the silence. "A lady of my acquaintance once told me that she essentially thought the would-be attacker we see, was, in her eyes, kissing his lover's neck, and that the demon was sending them both to Hell as a punishment for their perceived sodomy." Van Hoon chuckled. "An idiosyncratic opinion on what, in essence, is such a simple subject matter."

Wiggins leant closer still to the painting, his arms clasped behind his back, his nose almost touching the canvas. He turned to Van Hoon. "I did notice that this is the only painting in this room. Indeed, it is the only piece of any type of artwork within these four walls, which, for your ostentatiousness, does seem rather out of character," offered Wiggins with a sardonic smile.

Van Hoon smirked. "I thought you of all people would understand, my good Inspector. As you can see, this is one of the smallest rooms in my humble home. As such, any other artworks adorning these walls would most certainly be overshadowed by Bouguereau's masterpiece and therefore, inevitably, ignored. They would become as pointless as an unreciprocated love and as worthless as an unworn crown. They would be rendered invisible, as if having never been created at all."

Wiggins could see that Van Hoon was warming to his subject, revelling in his metaphorical discourse. The leper continued. "I can imagine nothing as desolate as a painting *not* being looked at, don't you agree? Similarly, a musical instrument not being played, a book not being read, a great mind resting untaxed, or a muscle unexercised. All tragic and wasteful in the extreme. The artistic equivalent of an untouched Stradivarius, a discarded Iliad, a stagnant Socrates or an idle Herculean arm."

"I understand your reasoning, Mr Van Hoon," nodded Wiggins with pursed lips.

"I acquired it quite recently," added Van Hoon. "Well, recently for me that is. All things are relative, of course. It was painted by William-Adolphe Bouguereau in the year eighteen-fifty. He was a French academic painter of great repute and was remarkably successful financially, and critically acclaimed during his lifetime. I believe he passed away just a few years ago at a sprightly age, approaching eighty if I am not mistaken. I am drawn to the way he frequently used mythological themes to depict contemporary interpretations of classical subjects, and I feel personally very sympathetic towards this work."

"Regrettably, I am unfamiliar with the artist, Mr Van Hoon, but I can appreciate his skill in storytelling and metaphor," explained Wiggins.

"What we see here, Inspector, is a depiction of Dante and Virgil in Hell. As they watch the wrathful suffering before them, they, in turn, are observed by one of the Malebranche, the demon sentinels who guard Bolgia Five of the eighth circle of Hell.

"Dante's Inferno?" questioned Wiggins instantly.

"Excellent! You are surprisingly well informed. The painting was indeed inspired by a scene from the Inferno. It is set in the eighth circle of Hell which, as we all know, is the circle reserved for falsifiers and counterfeiters. Virgil and Dante watch on as two damned souls fight to the death. Capocchio, who was a heretic and alchemist, is attacked and bitten by Gianni Schicchi who had previously assumed the identity of a deceased man to fraudulently claim an inheritance. There have been very few paintings over the centuries depicting murder, but of those which do, this is unquestionably my personal favourite." Van Hoon laughed lightly. "I can personally testify that Bouguereau has managed to capture the likeness of the individuals to an uncanny degree.

Wiggins chose to pass over Van Hoon's enigmatic statement and continued. "Why is Virgil painted wearing a crown of laurel leaves?" he probed, intrigued. He hoped to glean some information that may shed light upon the significance of the headwear found on the murdered politician.

"A good question pointedly asked, detective. You see, during the Middle Ages, the laurel wreath represented great achievement in poetry and was used to 'crown' poets. Laurel was a symbol of the veneration of Apollo, who as we all know is the protector of art. In ancient Rome, poets wore the laurel crown to indicate divine inspiration when reciting their poetry before an audience. Virgil, in whose works Dante found abundant lessons in morality and literary perfection, is considered by many to be the supreme poet, is he not? In the opinion of the artist he therefore rightly deserves to be represented wearing the laurel wreath." The two men stood in silence for a few moments longer, Wiggins studying the painting whilst Van Hoon studied the Detective.

Van Hoon again broke the silence. "Despite the many attractions that a visit to my home would naturally offer, I can only imagine that you did not come here merely to trade artistic opinion. You call at an early hour of the morning, and at short notice, my friend. May I ask as to your purpose?"

"Of course. I apologise for calling at this unearthly hour but I just..." his voice trailed off and a perplexed look appeared on his face. He felt vaguely unclear as to his motivation for the visit. "Coincidentally, I wanted to ask your advice regarding the art world, one painting in particular. However, I feel our discourse has helped in answering what questions I may have had. It was fortunate indeed that your servant chose this specific room for me in which to await your arrival." Wiggins considered for a moment. "Almost as if he had read my mind," he joked.

"No need to apologise, Inspector. I find it rather fortunate that the older I get, the less sleep I seem to require to sustain me. And yes, my Pestilent are rather perceptive," replied Van Hoon enigmatically touching the tip of his nose twice with his left index finger. "Although one would be correct if one were to surmise that very little of any import that occurs within my home, does so serendipitously."

Wiggins was still endeavouring to decipher Van Hoon's cryptic remarks as the two men made their way from the nondescript room. As such his mind was somewhat distracted as Van Hoon led him through his vast, opulent library, past the rows of double-storey staircases, the shoes of both men crumping on the deep pile Axminster carpet. As they passed into a rosewood panelled corridor Wiggins' eye was drawn towards a small alcove in which the panelled walls were painted in gold leaf. Within the gleaming alcove hung a single framed drawing. Wiggins stopped dead in his tracks. The image in front of him was unmistakable and unfathomable. Van Hoon smiled as he saw Wiggins' reaction.

"Leonardo da Vinci's Vitruvian Man!" exclaimed Wiggins, as he regarded the drawing with astonishment.

"Indeed," confirmed Van Hoon. "The original, from Leonardo's very own hand."

"But how?" questioned a stunned Wiggins turning his attention to Van Hoon. "I have read that the original drawing has hung in the Galleria dell'Academia in Venice for over two-hundred years. Surely this is a copy. The original would be priceless, beyond value. Am I not correct?"

Van Hoon's smile widened, his absinthe green eye sparkling in delight. "You are indeed correct, Inspector. You see, both are originals." Wiggins seemed baffled, confused. Van Hoon continued. "I see you are somewhat perplexed, my friend. Let me explain. Leonardo drew two examples of Vitruvian Man. The one that you see before you is unknown to the world outside of these walls. I can see from your countenance that you are asking yourself why. Why, given the successful execution of the consummate representation of male human perfection, did Leonardo embark upon another, almost identical copy?" Before Wiggins could utter a response, Van Hoon held up a staying finger. "Because, my friend, his subject matter, his *sitter*, if you will, requested it of him."

"And you know this how?" interjected Wiggins.

Van Hoon evaded the question. "Recall if you will the face of Vitruvian Man, his countenance. It is somewhat grim. An unhappy face. A displeased face. The model for the drawing, although satisfied that Leonardo had captured the perfect symmetry and beauty of his body, was rather distraught that the great Artist had rendered him the face of a man disgruntled. Thus, you see before you, Inspector, the second Vitruvian Man, an exact duplicate in every aspect other than that the face you look upon now is more serene. More contented. At peace. More appropriate."

Wiggins looked closely at the drawing in the golden alcove and then looked back at the smiling Van Hoon. Once again, his gaze returned to the drawing, and thence back to the leper. Twice more he repeated the same action, realisation dawning within him. Astonishment flooded through Wiggins' consciousness. Van Hoon's smile turned to a self-satisfied grin as he slowly raised his arms from his sides to reflect the stance of the Vitruvian figure. "Well, Leo was looking for perfection, after all. Who else would he turn to?"

Chapter 23 - The Departure

Harry Pepper had been a seafaring man his entire life. "Man, and Boy," he would boast to anyone whom he thought was listening. "Trawlers out of Grimsby to Bear Island and Svalbard when I were nought but a lad. Hunting cod as big as a man. Hammering the ice off the lines every morning. Hard work for even harder men." Harry loved to reminisce, particularly over a rum and mild in the Prospect of Whitby. "From the West Indies, Jamaica and Haiti to Sumatra and the Spice Islands in the East. Old 'Arry has seen 'em all. I tells ya."

For the last sixteen years, Harry had been running his clipper out of Saint Katherine's Dock. Lilly's Catch was a three-masted ex-tea clipper that Harry had bought for what he had regarded as a song, this despite the price having eaten up his entire life's savings. He made his living with mostly short-haul trips to France and Portugal. Occasionally jobs to the North African coast to Casablanca, Tangiers or Algiers cropped up. Most of Harry's trade was on the black market, illicit shipments of tea, hashish, opium and sometimes even people. Slavery, although long abolished, still thrived in certain unscrupulous parts of the World.

Harry had, in truth, seen many sights in his fifty or so colourful years, but he would have freely admitted that he had never witnessed anything quite as strange as the sight currently before him. He had been approached the day before by a diminutive Chinaman who seemed to have a tight-lipped smile painted permanently across his face. Little did Captain Pepper realise that the small, eternally cheerful Oriental, was, in fact, The Poisoner, Mr King's master of toxins. If he had, perhaps he would not have taken the Chinaman's charter, nor indeed shaken his hand so readily. The proposition was a good one, however. Take a dozen passengers, plus luggage, to Dubrovnik on the coast of the Adriatic Sea. The fee offered was more than Harry had earned over the last twelve months, so it had been an easy decision. He had shaken hands eagerly with The Poisoner as soon as the sum was mentioned. This would keep old Mr McConville at the Bank off his back for a few months.

Harry was a small, yet robust man with a chiselled jaw, a weather-beaten face, and an unruly shock of rapidly greying hair. He carried a perpetual twinkle in his eye and his jaunty, optimistic manner tended to endear him to most who met him. His personality was rather at odds with that of his first mate, Dan Kelly, a tall lugubrious

Cockney of Irish extraction, whose face resembled that of a pockmarked, mournful Basset Hound.

"Get the crew and The Catch ready for the next high tide, Dan. We sail in the morning. Double bubble to all hands if we make Dubrovnik by Saturday!" announced Captain Pepper, his chest puffed with pride. Kelly shrugged his sloping shoulders as if he had heard the most inconsequential news imaginable and shuffled off to rouse the crew from whichever den or lodging house, they currently occupied, and to make the necessary preparations.

The morning was hazy and the hour early. Five bells had yet to be struck and Captain Pepper stood dockside, watching as his human cargo made their way up the gangplank of Lilly's Catch. Beside him stood first mate Kelly, hands in pockets. Two large black sedans had drawn up to the quayside. First to exit the convoy were the Shang brothers, identical, razor-featured killers. An air of threat and underlying menace surrounded the inseparable twins. The Shangs surveyed the scene and, happy that all was safe, indicated to within the Sedan's interior.

Mr King then emerged, walking in his tiny steps towards the boat. Harry realised instantly who his ultimate client was. King! The most evil and merciless man in London. He felt a shiver of trepidation and wondered if the vast sum of money, now sitting securely in the ship's safe, would prove to be worth the risks that were now racing through his mind. As King glided up the gangplank, his small feet seemingly not touching the timbers, he turned his head towards Captain Pepper and nodded a greeting that chilled the old sailor to his marrow. 'He has the eyes of a snake,' thought Pepper as he recalled the rumours that he had heard about King, namely that his tongue was forked, that he flayed men alive and fed their skin to a ghost python, that he tortured children and captured their tears in ampules, and his unimaginable experiments with ingastration. Looking into the eyes of the crime lord he had no doubt that all these tales were true. He could almost hear the Chinaman slither across the ship's timbers as he felt an acidic taste at the back of his throat.

King was followed by the buxom Madame Huai and the little Poisoner who had brokered the deal, ushering several dacoit Thuggees who carried trunks and luggage, each straining under the weight of their loads. Pepper and Kelly looked at each other. "What have you gotten us into this time, 'Arry?" muttered the doleful Kelly. "This is the most dangerous cargo we've ever had. Rather a ton of Moroccan hashish and a barrel of hungry tigers than this lot, Skipper."

Pepper agreed but tried to lift his morose first mate's spirits. "Think of the readies, Danny boy. Think of all the carousing and gallivanting you can do with that money, lad."

"I'll be drinking and dancing with the Dead more like," shrugged the mournful Kelly.

It was then that Harry caught sight of the vision that paled all others. The second sedan's suspension lifted as the biggest thing that Harry had ever seen, stepped out of the car. "Lord, preserve us! It's Hercules Chin!" gasped Pepper, his mouth agape. Kelly's jowly face seemed to quiver as he crossed himself several times. "Sweet Mother of Christ preserve us," he muttered.

The colossal Chinaman grunted as he squeezed his way uneasily out of the car. Harry's imagination conjured up an image of a man peeling off an over tight and wet waistcoat. The giant lumbered past them, his great boots thudding on the dockside cobbles. He passed so close to the two sailors that they could each smell him, a mustiness of serge mixed with a medicinal scent of opium, sweet and sharply floral. Chin turned his head and looked down at the two men with his dead yellow eyes. Harry could see no emotion under that great pronounced brow. 'If the eyes are the window to the soul then this one is soulless indeed,' thought the old seaman. He recalled to mind having seen the zombie creatures of the voodoo lords of Hispaniola. As Chin stepped upon the gangplank, Harry was convinced that the decking would snap, such was the cracking and groaning that the timber made with each of the Giant's steps.

Harry looked at Kelly. "Let's try and make it to Dubrovnik by Friday, shall we, Dan?" Kelly nodded slowly, a haunted look in his eyes.

Once onboard, King and his entourage took up residence in four cabins. The Poisoner and Madame Haui shared one whilst the Dacoits shared another. King had a separate cabin that linked to a further one shared by Chin and the Shang twins. Chin sat on the floor leaning against a bed of insufficient size or strength and, looking out the cabin porthole at the crewmen busily untying sheets and lines and readying for sail, remembered Father King's last words to him. "Once we land, kill them all. Each and every last one of them."

Chapter 24 - The Critic

Pyke waited patiently in Wiggins' office whilst his superior officer was immersed in deep conversation on the telephone. Wiggins had noticed Pyke entering five minutes earlier and had waved two fingers aloft signalling that he would not be very much longer with the call. Pyke stood by an open window subliminally surveying the comings and goings on Victoria Embankment, all the while listening intently to one half of the conversation taking place behind him.

"It is a rather ingenious if abhorrent, concept I agree, Mr Fry, but when you describe the work to me from your viewpoint, and, understanding the clues our murderer has left behind at the scene of the stoning, the relevance is all together, staggeringly obvious. The data had merely to be reviewed and analysed by an expert such as yourself. We are most grateful." Wiggins paused for several seconds, his gaze landing upon Pyke, who had now turned around.

"Yes … yes, I will, Mr Fry, I shall see you tomorrow at eleven-thirty." He glanced down at his notepad. "Thirty-three, Fitzroy Square you said? Yes, I shall be there punctually, and thank you once again, your input thus far has been both enlightening and invaluable. Yes, and a very good day to you too." Wiggins hung the telephone's voice piece in its cradle, straightened the pad of paper he had been writing on, and turned his attention towards Pyke, whom he indicated should sit. "I find that if one appeals to people's vanities, they cannot help but be effusive and forthcoming in their thoughts and opinions. In this instance, it has reinforced my conclusion that all four murders are without a doubt the work of the same killer."

"Who were you speaking with, Guv?" asked Pyke, his interest now firmly piqued.

"I was just having an exceedingly enlightening exchange regarding our crime scenes with a Mr Roger Fry. Are you at all familiar with the name?"

"Afraid not, Sir," came Pyke's bluntly honest response. He withdrew a tobacco knife from his pocket and began to idly scrape dirt from beneath his fingernails. Wiggins winced in barely concealed disgust. "Who is he?" asked Pyke.

Wiggins took a piece of foolscap from his desk and consulted it. "I had Sergeant Ash do a bit of research on our friend, Mr Fry and he is a well-renowned artist and a leading art critic. A highly regarded member of the Bloomsbury Group, a set of writers, intellectuals, philosophers, and artists. Seemingly their prime objectives are the creation and enjoyment of aesthetic experiences and the continual pursuit of knowledge. A commune of like-minded Bohemians, you might say."

"Fancy!" mocked Pyke, theatrically. He snapped shut his pocketknife and placed it on Wiggins' desk. He then playfully spun the knife, watching it rotate until it slowly came to a stop.

"Indeed, he is," responded Wiggins, somewhat too sharply.

Pyke could see that the spinning tobacco knife had irritated Wiggins. "Sorry, Guv," he smirked as he pocketed the knife.

Wiggins returned to business. "Over the years Fry has established a reputation as an art scholar without peer, particularly of the Old Masters, and is indeed a highly regarded artist in his own right. I thought it may be helpful to consult with him, and so it has proved. He was very approachable and only too willing to answer some questions that I had been mulling over since my visit with Van Hoon yesterday." Wiggins deliberately did not refer to his encounter with Doctor Watson in Baker Street. He wished to keep his visits to his sanctum secret.

Pyke offered his boss an already lit cigarette before lighting one for himself. "You visited Van Hoon?" he enquired, surprised and a little disappointed that he had not been invited along.

"Yes, in the early hours of this morning. Ideas had been playing on my mind and I briefly consulted Van Hoon before heading home. I was curious as to whether the colour of the macramé belts sported by his Pestilent attendees denoted some sort of hierarchy within his household. A small detail but one that I have been deliberating for some time. A conundrum that now does not seem to merit a visit at that late hour at all. I must admit that the reason for being there altogether skipped my mind once I found myself engrossed in a particularly intriguing oil painting that the Dutchman happened to have on display."

Pyke took a seat, crossed his legs, and drew a hot satisfying pull on his cigarette. "I'm intrigued, Guv."

"Well, to cut a lengthy but very interesting story short, the painting hanging in Van Hoon's small study was that of a murder scene featuring numerous hidden messages and meanings, all of which Van Hoon kindly described to me in almost forensic detail. I even found myself deciphering some of the depictions under his guidance. The work, entitled 'Dante and Virgil,' was painted by William-Adolphe Bouguereau, a French artist, over sixty years ago." Pyke could feel his attention waning already but smiled and feigned interest. Wiggins continued. "The symbolism and cryptic cyphers contained within the painting got me thinking that each of our recent murders also has the feel and, indeed, the atmosphere of such a painting. The staging of each scene, its framing and composition. Hence my conversing with Fry for the past thirty minutes or thereabouts." Pyke sat in silence, ash dangling precariously from his cigarette. He felt the encroaching burn of the smouldering ember nearing his fingers and extinguished it in Wiggins' ashtray, which Pyke noticed was almost full.

"I described the first such murder we encountered in every detail to Fry," Wiggins continued. "The clearing in Highgate Woods, the buried body of Deacon Hamilton Lancaster and the scribbled note from scripture left in his pocket. I recounted the nineteen stones used to administer his bloody demise, basically every single piece of data that we collected, I imparted."

"And what did Fry have to say about it?" questioned Pyke, now lighting himself another cigarette. *'I'm smoking like a bloody Turkish chimney these days,'* he thought. *'Perhaps I best cut down a little.'*

"Well, he digested all the details and then asked me which book of the Gospels the quotation had been taken from. I informed him that it came from Matthew, sixteen; twenty-five. He then suggested that that final piece of evidence may attest to the murderer most likely being an artist who was re-enacting or rather re-staging the 'Stoning of Saint Stephen', a work by..." Wiggins examined his notes, "the Dutch master Rembrandt Harmenszoon van Rijn." He picked up a thick, well-thumbed manila folder and waved it in the air. "All the clues are here Pyke! All the evidence we have collected and collated at each scene of crime. It all points to the conceivable recreation of four famous oil paintings, each depicting a murderous act."

"So, the Rembrandt resembles our first murder scene?" enquired a now intrigued Pyke.

"Not exactly, Jem, but the scene certainly has references to the painting. Fry even stated that the passage, Matthew, sixteen; twenty-five mirrored the exact year Rembrandt painted the work. We discovered that the unfortunate victim, Hamilton Lancaster, was a Deacon did we not? Well coincidentally, so was Saint Stephen, *and* they both openly helped widowed women in times of hardship. Fry, moreover, intimated that the clearing of the murder scene in Highgate Woods may well signify the 'opening of the Heavens' as depicted by the rays of the sun in Rembrandt's portrayal. It was all there before our very eyes, Jem," declared an exuberant Wiggins. "We had only to see it!" He slapped the folder triumphantly upon his desk.

"What about the nineteen stones used in the murder though, Guv? Seemed an awfully strange number if you ask me. Any significance there?" probed Pyke further. He could feel the excitement rising within him with the realisation that this theory may just be correct.

"Interestingly, the 'Stoning of Saint Stephen' was the very first signed painting by Rembrandt, and guess what age the artist was when he completed the work? Yes!" declared Wiggins, anticipating Pyke's answer. "He was nineteen years old! A stone for each year of the artist's life, and each stone used to ultimately take the life of another. You see, it all fits!"

"So, the theory is that this killer is murdering people and staging their death scenes to recreate works of art," questioned Pyke, somewhat disbelievingly.

"Not just works of art, Pyke, but works of art where the subject matter is murder," stated Wiggins.

"And what of the other three murders, Guv?"

"I am meeting with Fry tomorrow morning at the Omega Workshops in Fitzroy Square to furnish him with all the details we garnered thus far. He has conceded that in his opinion, it is possible that the killer may have followed the same modus operandi for the other murders. It may simply be a case of matching the remaining murder scenes with other Old Masters. Then we have a definite link," responded Wiggins. "We are close Jem, I can feel it by Jove, we are so very close."

Wiggins walked purposefully around the perimeter of Fitzroy Square towards the Omega Workshops. He was excited at the prospect of meeting Roger Fry and at testing his theory that there was a link between the murders and the art world. It was a refreshing, sunny spring morning and the crisp Fitzrovia air tasted fresh and sharp in the back of his throat. As he approached the studios he thought of each murder and wondered how, on such a glorious day, there could possibly be such depravity amongst men. His thoughts turned to his mentor. He often wondered how the course of his own life would have differed had he not inhabited the Great Detective's world. For that was unquestionably what it was. His ego and confidence, his extraordinary intellect, unquenchable drive, and unique talent had made it *his* world. All others merely inhabited it. He had affected so many lives, and a generation on, he continued to do so. Wiggins suspected that the young Digger himself would perhaps have become one of the characters that he now found himself pursuing to justice, had it not been for Him and the fatherly guidance of John Watson.

The walk from his home in Manchester Square had taken him up Thayer Street and along New Cavendish Street, on to Great Portland Street towards Regent's Park and then eastwards along Carburton Street and so into Fitzrovia. The walk had taken a little less than half an hour, and Wiggins rejoiced in spending time basking in his most favoured part of the City.

Following his telephone conversation with Fry the previous evening, Wiggins had re-examined Ash's research and he liked what his desk sergeant had unearthed. Not only had Fry initiated the Omega Workshops, but he was also the essential motivating force behind its continued success. Fry's foundation aimed to bring the worlds of art and design closer together without being influenced by social reform or modern methods of mass manufacture. He took no moral high ground, a principal Wiggins strongly admired. Fry's motivation was to remove the division between the fine and decorative arts, which he regarded as a false divide. He wanted to see the bright colours and bold, simplified forms of modern art used in contemporary design. His aim was to work alongside many of his close and talented coterie of artist friends whom he had met through the Bloomsbury Group. Wiggins appreciated Fry's philosophy in so far that all works to be produced within the group were to be done so anonymously. He wanted items to be valued for their beauty and skill rather than due to the reputation of any one artist.

'*Artist,*' thought Wiggins. After speaking with Fry on the telephone he also now strongly suspected that their killer could be an artist of some description and wondered how, being someone who lives to create, could be drawn to the ultimate act of destruction, that of taking a human life.

Shaking himself from his train of thought, he found himself standing at the doorstep of number thirty-three, Fitzroy Square. An ebonised door stood out from the white stucco façade of the five-storey Georgian townhouse, a portal to the Bohemian world it harboured. Wiggins grasped the brass door knocker and rapped his habitual knock upon the door. One, two - pause - one, two, three, and waited for a few moments. The door was opened almost immediately by an exceptionally handsome young Negro dressed smartly in overalls. Wiggins noted that his flawless skin was almost blue in its blackness and that his teeth were pearly white and perfect of shape.

"Good day, Sir. My name is Sexton and I am the caretaker here. How may we help you this glorious morning?" inquired the servant, a broad smile spreading across his ebon face. Each word was pronounced perfectly with the most precise diction.

Wiggins held his warrant card at arm's length and smiled. "Good morning, Sexton, my name is DCI Wiggins from Scotland Yard CID and I have an appointment at eleven-thirty as prearranged yesterday by telephone with your Mr Fry," answered Wiggins studying the features of the strikingly good-looking individual in front of him. The Negro's angular cheekbones and strong square jawline complimented a high forehead topped with neatly cropped hair. Wiggins noted that Sexton's cheeks sported deep tribal scarification wounds that he decided enhanced rather than detracted from his appearance. He wondered at the pain that had been endured during their ceremonial infliction.

"Very good, DCI Wiggins, we have of course been expecting your arrival. Please follow me to Mr Fry's studio. I am afraid it is on the fifth floor, but Mr Fry contends that it affords the best light in the entire building and is therefore worth the climb." Sexton flashed yet another blinding, ivory smile.

"Of course, Sexton, please lead on." Wiggins found himself warming to the caretaker. "It is Mr Fry who does us the favour, after all, so ascending a few flights of stairs is the least I can do." Wiggins, who could not help but notice how swiftly and effortlessly Sexton ascended the stone stairs, as if he were being pulled upwards by some unseen, heavenly force, followed in the wake of the custodian of the Bloomsbury Group. The two men climbed the staircase, Sexton bounding upwards and Wiggins playing catch-up, so as not to lag too obviously behind. They came to a halt at the open entrance to a huge garret room which spanned the entire length of the building. The roof space was comprised almost entirely of windows and Wiggins had to initially shield his eyes from the harshness of the light that streamed into the room. At the far end of the studio, stood a slender man of average height, sporting an immaculate pin-striped black suit and a matching black Homberg hat. '*Incongruous dress for one painting indoors,*' thought Wiggins. Fry was standing in front of a large-scale easel which held a canvas upon which Wiggins could make out the bare bones of a painting.

"Mr Fry, Detective Chief Inspector Wiggins here to see you," announced the immaculate Sexton.

"Thank you kindly, Sexton," came Fry's cheerful reply, the painter still facing his canvas. "You must excuse my apparent rudeness Inspector, but I simply must place this brushstroke before I dither and change my mind. I do so detest indecision, don't you? There, done! One wouldn't want an unfortunate error caused by impatience." Fry whirled around and bounced towards Wiggins, openly offering his hand, after having wiped it on a cloth tied around his waist. "How splendid! Splendid! You look exactly as I imagined you would look, Inspector. Always nice to put a face to the voice don't you think?" asked Fry happily. The two men shook hands, Fry, rather more vigorously than Wiggins. The artist was gaunt and slender with piercing, active eyes that seemed to dart and search from under penny-round spectacles. Wiggins reckoned him to be approaching fifty years of age but with the obvious energy and enthusiasm of a man less than half his years.

"Thank you for agreeing to meet with me, Mr Fry. Our conversation yesterday was more useful than you could ever imagine," encouraged Wiggins.

"Oh, that's simply marvellous!" enthused Fry. "I thoroughly enjoyed the whole experience myself, so rather it is I who should be thanking you, Mr Wiggins. I have been looking forward to your visit all morning and to hearing more detail of the other murders you briefly mentioned yesterday. How exciting! I think you have unleashed the secret Detective within me, or perhaps I am just naturally inquisitive. A nosey old so and so!" grinned the critic. He guffawed an adenoidal chuckle. "I have taken the liberty of looking out some reference books in readiness, just in case my memory is taxed too much." Fry pointed towards an array of books on a long drafting table.

"Shall we begin, Inspector Wiggins?" he inquired enthusiastically. "Please take a seat. It would be most helpful if you were to explain each of the murders in turn. Tell me every detail, no matter how trivial it may seem to you. It is the fine details that, when combined, make a truly wonderful work of art you understand."

"Yes, of course, Mr Fry," replied Wiggins as he sat down on one of two draftsman's stools, each of which sat at opposite sides of the long table.

"Oh, do call me Roger, I insist upon it. Can you randomise the order in which the slayings occurred please, Inspector? Oh, how exciting this all is," impassioned Fry, rubbing the palms of his wiry hands together in glee. Wiggins was beginning to find the artist's overt enthusiasm infectious. Fry sat down directly opposite the Detective. Wiggins removed his moleskin covered notepad from his inside breast pocket and opened it randomly, then flicked forward one page.

"Johnathan Hardridge, aged twenty-six years, was a newly elected MP for Camberwell. He was married with three children, all girls. His lifeless body was found at the foot of the basement steps at the Houses of Parliament with twenty-three separate stab wounds inflicted upon his person. The forensic pathologist stated that only one of these wounds, that administered to the heart, was deep enough to have caused his death. Thanks to witness testimonies we know he was murdered on the fifteenth of March…" Wiggins was politely but rather abruptly interrupted by the eager critic.

"Was the poor soul wearing any head adornment, by any chance? Sorry for interrupting Inspector but was the deceased sporting a crown of laurels or bay leaves perhaps?" enquired a visibly animated Fry.

"Yes, yes he was," responded an astonished Wiggins. "How could you possibly know of this detail, Mr Fry?"

"Because, Inspector, your killer has clearly based this murder upon a painting by the French artist Jean-Léon Gérôme. The work is entitled 'The Death of Caesar' and was painted in eighteen sixty-seven if I'm not mistaken."

"That is very interesting, Mr Fry, please … please do go on," smiled a rather bemused but impressed detective.

"The painting depicts Julius Caesar being stabbed twenty-three times, as indeed it seems, was your victim. According to the accounts of the slaying upon which the painting was based, only the second blow was fatal, and that blow was directly to the heart." Fry paused for dramatic effect. "Caesar's demise befell him on the Ides of March, which Inspector, is the fifteenth of the month, the same date upon which your MP was murdered. Both, quite obviously, were politicians, and in the painting, Caesar is depicted as wearing a crown of laurel leaves, just as you informed me your victim was when found."

Wiggins nodded. "There seems to be little doubting that our killer has indeed constructed his murderous crime to recreate the painting you describe, Mr Fry," stated Wiggins.

"Indeed. Indeed. Bravo, Inspector! And please do call me *Roger*. I feel refreshments are called for at this juncture, don't you agree?" offered Fry with a kindly smile and a vigorous rubbing together of his hands. "Tea? Coffee? Something stronger perhaps Inspector?"

"Coffee would be most welcome thank you," came Wiggins' response.

As Fry picked up the telephone, Wiggins could not help but wonder at the artist's intimate knowledge of the history art. Fry seemed to be able to reference any major work as another would click his fingers. At the same time, he wondered at the dastardly mimicry of the murderer. He again studied the canvas that Fry had been working on when they had been introduced. Only a few simple brushstrokes that already implied the naked form of a reclining woman. '*How extraordinary that one man can produce such artistic works seemingly effortlessly, whilst the next man may struggle to sharpen a pencil,*' Wiggins pondered. '*What separates one from the other?' he wondered. 'Instinct? Observation? An innate ability to transfer thought, feeling and imagery from one's mind to one's hand?'*

His conjecture was interrupted by his host. "Sexton will bring our refreshments presently. Now Inspector, shall we proceed with the next murder. I am enjoying myself immensely," enthused a clearly stimulated Fry, who now sat forward in his chair, his neck outstretched like an expectant chicken searching for seed. "Is that wicked of me, Inspector? Surely I should not be so excited by such abominable acts?"

"I would say enthusiastic, rather than excited, Mr Fry. It is not the acts themselves that excite you, rather the prospect of your knowledge being of assistance in the solving of these crimes. By all means, let us continue," replied Wiggins, turning several pages of his notepad forwards then back again. "The next murder I shall describe is that of a Miss Emily Lorimer, a young lady of only nineteen years. At first, we suspected this to be a suicide, one possibly borne of unrequited love, as her body was found beneath the first arch of Waterloo Bridge on the south side of the water, her hands clasping a heart-shaped broach. Initial indications pointed to her having jumped from the bridge to her death."

"And what, may I ask, then made you suspect that the young lady was in fact murdered, rather than having taken her own life, Inspector?" enquired Fry pointedly.

"There were no injuries consistent with a fall from hight upon the body. My colleague, Detective Sergeant Pyke, having been first on the scene, was determined to find out all he could about Emily Lorimer. Who she was, who her family were, and ultimately whether she had tragically taken her own life. Or had it been an accident, or had there been foul play at work? His intuition proved to be well-founded. We checked tide times with the approximate time of the young lady's death. You see, she was found at eleven-thirty at night, still warm, by a street worker. The time and the tides did not correlate which would mean that she had been placed half in, and half out of the water during a very specific window of opportunity. You see, Mr Fry, her shoulders were still dry when she was found. She had been posed."

"Interesting. Very interesting, did you discover anything else?" asked Fry.

"Yes, we found a bone hair comb entangled in her hair, but her hair had been laid out almost perfectly as though deliberately arranged after she was deceased. There was also a scribbled note in her tunic pocket which read..." Wiggins looked down at his notepad. "*...great deliverance giveth he to his king and sheweth mercy to his anointed*, which, we have discovered, comes from Psalm eighteen; fifty."

"Aha!" Fry clicked his fingers. "Your killer is shrewd and devious in equal measure, Inspector. This really is most rewarding! You see, he wanted you to *think* it was suicide!" Fry reached for a large volume from within the pile of reference books he had assembled. The book was titled 'Social Realism in Victorian Art' and Fry leafed through its pages until he came upon a lithograph depicting the lifeless body of a woman washed up beneath an arch of Waterloo Bridge, her lower body still immersed in the waters.

"Look, there Inspector," urged Fry, rotating the book one-hundred and eighty degrees to face Wiggins, and pointing vigorously several times to the plate. Wiggins stared at the picture, taking in every detail, astonished at its similarity to the crime scene. "The resemblance is remarkable. Almost exact in every detail."

"Not only that, Inspector, but the numbers 'eighteen; fifty' are the same as the year in which our painting was completed. The work in question is entitled 'Found Drowned' and is by the English Symbolist painter, George Frederic Watts. The piece was entirely inspired by Thomas Hood's eighteen forty-four poem 'The Bridge of Sighs.' The verse tells the story of an anonymous young pregnant lady, desperate and abandoned by her lover, who commits suicide by jumping off a bridge. Was your victim by any chance, in the family way, Inspector?"

"No, no she was not, but I notice that her arms were positioned exactly like those of the girl in the painting. In the unmistakable shape of the cross. Franky, I am astounded Mr Fry, not only by the depth of your knowledge but by the fact that the painting recreated here in this book could well be one of the photographs our forensic team recorded at the crime scene that night. The likeness is uncanny." A door hinge squeaked, and Sexton entered the room and interrupted the conversation by delivering a pot of coffee for Wiggins and a glass of freshly squeezed orange juice for Fry.

"Thank you ever so, Sexton, dear boy." The caretaker bowed and placed the tray upon the table at which the pair sat, careful not to spill anything. Wiggins noted how well manicured the Negro's fingernails were. *'Odd for a caretaker,'* he thought.

"The orange juice is for me Inspector. It is my drink of choice these days. I find coffee has a very excitable effect upon my already too active nervous system. I am afraid that my heart and mind race uncontrollably if I partake. I dread to think of what effects alcohol would have upon me and my paintings." Fry lifted the glass to his lips and took a sip.

Sexton poured the black coffee for his guest. "Cream? Sugar, Inspector?" enquired the caretaker politely.

"No thank you, just as it comes please," came the Detective's reply. "It smells splendid." Sexton bowed and exited the room.

"So, let us get down to another of your murder mysteries, Inspector Wiggins," requested Fry, once again rubbing his hands together in anticipation. "I hope you are enjoying yourself as much as I am, Inspector? I must say, this is all very splendid."

"Indeed, I am Mr Fry, but we are down to the fourth and last murder. Our last victim is Sir Edward John Poynter, aged seventy-seven, and a man you must know through association, he being the President of the Royal Academy?" offered Wiggins, reaching for his coffee.

"Yes, yes! I knew Sir Edward very well indeed. Inevitably our paths crossed many times over the years, and we became close, particularly over the past few years. A tragedy. An utter tragedy. He is, or rather, was, should I say, a great advocate of what we are attempting to do within the Bloomsbury Set. In fact, I read about his demise in the Daily Telegraph with much sadness. His death is a great loss to his family and our community. Tragic. The newspaper did not disclose any details of how he died, but rather reported merely that he had been murdered."

"Yes, we insisted that the editor, Mr le Sage, not disclose any details of how Sir Edward was killed for several reasons, but I can tell you, as his friend, that it must have been a particularly terrifying and traumatic end to his life. His all but naked body was discovered bound to a tree. He had been shot five times with either a bow or crossbow. Four arrows pierced his right side, one in the upper arm, one in the upper thigh and two close together just above the groin. Only one arrow pierced Sir Edward's left side and that had entered directly under his heart." The words had barely left Wiggins' mouth before Fry responded.

"My word, what you describe is Saint Sebastian! Of course! Simple! A painting by the great Dutch artist Peter Paul Rubens. Sixteen-fourteen, or thereabouts, if I am not mistaken." Fry clapped spontaneously. Wiggins was taken aback at just how quickly the art critic had processed the information. "I must admit that your conclusions thus far have astounded me, Mr Fry, but how can you state with such certainty that this murder represents the painting you say, and indeed, that it is by the artist you name?"

"That is an excellent question, well asked, Inspector. You see, Inspector, that surprisingly there are relatively few paintings depicting the actual act of murder. There are thousands, possibly tens of thousands, however, that depict death. Probably more if one had time to catalogue them all. The subject matter of the death of Saint Sebastian, an early Christian saint and martyr, has been painted by many artists over the years, but only Rubens painted the particular pattern of arrow entry points you describe, Inspector. Andrea Mantegna, for example, painted Saint Sebastian with a multitude of arrows in the lower half of his body, whilst Giovanni Bellini portrayed him with an arrow piercing his face and exiting his throat. Rubens' and only Rubens' depiction is the same as the scene of the murder of our poor Sir Edward."

Wiggins exhaled a long, satisfying breath, one that signalled both amazement and relief. He drained his coffee.

"You know, Inspector, and this has me somewhat perplexed, but few people realise that Saint Sebastian was not in reality, murdered. He was, according to legend, rescued and subsequently healed by Irene of Rome. So, bearing this in mind, our murderer has, in fact, made a slight error of judgement, and perhaps he is not as well-versed in the history of art as he would like to appear."

"It is undeniable, Pyke!" exclaimed Wiggins enthusiastically. "Each of the four murders is a rendering that replicates *exactly* a famous work of art, each of which in turn, depicts an act of murder within its brushstrokes."

"I take it your meeting with Mr Fry was fruitful then, Guv?" offered Pyke, stubbing out a cigarette, whilst noticing for the first time that his fingertips were tinged ochre, discoloured by his incessant smoking.

"Most enlightening, Jem," confirmed Wiggins. "Saint Sebastian, the Death of Caesar, The Stoning of Saint Stephen, Found Drowned. These are the titles of the paintings our killer has used as the inspiration for his murderous spree. He has recreated each in the execution of his crimes. From the information I offered him, Mr Fry rather brilliantly pieced together the individual killings like some murderous painted jigsaw puzzle. My instinct tells me that our killer is most definitely male, an artist, and most probably a failed one. Perhaps he even knew Sir Edward John Poynter and held a grudge against him. It is imperative that we access the Academy's records for unsuccessful membership applications. I wager that therein we will find the identity of our killer."

Chapter 25 - The Son

The old man was back in the British East Protectorate. He could feel the blistering heat of the African dust plains. A suppressive, dry heat that caused a man's lungs to burn and the horizon to shimmer like the flowing waves of the nearby Tana River. He was once again part of a big game trophy hunt, organised by himself, and financed by Sir Richard Francis Burton, explorer, author and diplomat. Hunting the great white rhinoceros of the African plains.

His body may now be a useless hulk, but his memory continued to surprise him with its enduring appetite for vivid detail. Even now he could remember the smell of the dry air, the scent of the bearers, the heavy, musky aroma of the approaching beast. He could smell its fear, he could smell everyone's fear. Only he was calm.

He could picture the great animal thundering directly towards his hunting party, its colossal head down and snorting angrily. The drought-hardened plain thundered under its approach. A wayward and premature shot from an inexperienced and anxious member of the hunt had frightened the already nervous rhinoceros, prompting the charge. Two and a half tons of armour-plated muscle rampaged directly at the small party like a locomotive. The party consisted of five wealthy aristocrats and two local tribesmen who served as human mules and guides. The aristocrats wishing to add to their collections of horns and hides and the locals wishing only for the white man's coin and to put food on their tables.

The rhinoceros was incredibly fast, deceptively so for a beast so huge. It resembled a violently advancing tornado, dust pluming in huge clouds behind its terrifying approach. The rhinoceros' double horned snout slashed from side to side at the hazy air, its short stumpy legs pumping like the pistons of a steam engine. The old man could feel his heart pounding within his chest, but he remained calm. He was sure. He had confidence in his abilities. He had done this a hundred times before. He took aim with his trusted .577 black powder express gun, narrowed his left eye, and calmly caressed her trigger.

"We have Alfred Nobel to thank you know, Father." The old man's reminiscing came to an abrupt halt as he opened his eyes. He cursed under his breath, resenting being snatched from the reverie of his halcyon days to the ineffectual hell of his present. His wheelchair was being carefully pushed by his only son, who knew from experience that any sudden bumps or unexpected movements would send pain shooting through his father's dying body. The old man winced at the thought that such a reticent weakling should be his son.

It was a still afternoon and the two men were meandering their way through the sprawling and overgrown gardens of the old man's Windsor mansion, prior to lunching together. The mansion, christened Artemis House by the old man, had been financed from the proceeds of his nefarious criminal activities, aided by the many big game trophy hunting expeditions he had led and the subsequent sale of slaughtered beasts to wealthy, cowardly men. He had hated their cowardice, had often felt the urge to turn his gun from the animal to the man, putting everyone out of their misery. But he had valued their coin more than he had detested their weakness.

He studied the unmanaged gardens which were once finely manicured, and his memory floated back to his former, more humble lodgings in Conduit Street, in Mayfair. '*It must have been over forty years ago,*' he realised, shaking his great leonine head in disbelief. He looked at his trembling, liver-spotted hands and spat a tarry globule on the lawn in disgust. '*So much time passed.*'

Although still an intimidating presence, the old man had shrunk in size and his eyes were deeply sunken and darkly ringed. His once robust features were now ashen, ravaged by the cancer which had spread throughout his body. Colonel Sebastian Moran's private physician had informed him of the undoubted benefits fresh air would have upon his diseased lungs, and as such, he had demanded a daily regime of a minimum of thirty minutes exposure, no matter the elements or how ill Moran felt. Perversely, the Colonel realised, the colder the day and the poorer his constitution, the more he enjoyed the outdoors. The young man sniffed at the air, enjoying its freshness. Moran was suitably attired in a Russian fur capped Ushanka hat and a plush mohair rug warming his atrophied legs. "Alfred Nobel? What are you talking about, you imbecile?" rumbled the old man in a barely audible, gravel-tinged voice.

The young man hesitated, having almost forgotten his previous comment, so long had it been since he had spoken. "Well you see father, it was Nobel who discovered that diatomaceous sand binds Nitroglycerin together so that it can be transported safely, without fear of accidental explosion. It is therefore rendered stable and harmless until we decide upon the time of detonation. The liquid Nitroglycerin is mixed with the sandy earth and the resulting paste is formed into sticks wrapped in waxed paper."

The Old Man snorted. '*What an idiot I scioned.*' He thought to himself. "You deign to lecture *me*, Moriarty's former Chief Executioner, on the use of Nitroglycerin! Damn you, boy, your toes would curl if you knew how many men I have dispatched from their pathetic lives over the years." His words rasped to an expectorated halt as more bilious blackness was coughed from his infected body and spat onto the lawn.

"No doubt, father," stuttered the young man. Anxious to appease his brutal parent. He continued. "Each package contains enough dynamite to flatten a small house, each with attached blasting caps which will detonate using a clock timer set for the most opportune moment." The hunched young man patted Moran on the shoulders reassuringly. "Not too long now, father."

The old man vainly attempted to turn his gaze upon his son but his pained neck would not allow it. "You know, a great detective once described me as the second most dangerous man in London. I think he would now have to reconsider his opinion," laughed Moran, coughing blood into his heavily stained handkerchief.

Chapter 26 - The Proof

"Every artist signs their work do they not, Pyke?" urged Wiggins as he stood in his comrade's office. He was studying a print of an etching entitled 'Dudley Street, Seven Dials' which he noted was signed 'G. Doré,' in the bottom left-hand corner. Pyke's office was as untidy and cluttered as Wiggins' was immaculate and ordered. Pyke had noticed the print in the window of a small curiosity shop in Wharf Lane only a few days before. He had taken an instant liking to it and had bought it in memory of his late friend Mary Hallbard, the former owner and barmaid of The Grapes pub, who had been brutally murdered by Doctor Joseph Bleak a few months earlier. Mary had once run The Crown public house smack in the middle of the Seven Dials and Pyke thought the etching would make an appropriate keepsake for his office. It now hung, lopsided but loved, on the wall opposite Pyke's pedestal desk. Although the subject matter was of a different tavern, the print served to remind Pyke of his friend every day that he sat behind his desk.

Wiggins continued his line of thought. "No matter how skilled, a craftsman invariably feels the compulsion to attribute their work with their signature. That way the world can identify how masterful they are at their craft," concluded Wiggins, straightening the framed print. He leaned forward, admiring the artistry more closely. "Some theorise that artists crave love and appreciation more than most individuals. Critical acclaim is what they seek, particularly from their peers. This need is akin to that of a performer's craving for applause, or a clown's hunger for laughter." Wiggins began to stroll around the small office, warming to his train of thought, his hands clasped behind his pole straight back. Pyke recognised that Wiggin's analytical brain was in overdrive, and settled down for what he thought would be a long ride. "We have now discovered, through the assistance of the admirable Mr Fry, that each murder can be attributed to a great oil painting of particular note. So, what if our killer, as we might expect from a performance artist, also signed what he regards as his own works of art. His murders?"

"You mean that somewhere, at each of the crime scenes, he will have written his name? Isn't that tantamount to signing his own death warrant?" enquired Pyke rather sceptically as he sat with his feet resting atop his battered old desk. He had spent the previous several minutes carefully cleaning his Derby with a clothes brush, blowing away any disturbed motes of dust.

"Do you not see, Pyke, the murderer had no option," smiled Wiggins shaking his head slowly. "He simply had to sign-off his creations! You see, he craves the acclamation of his audience and seeks a perverted recognition for the devastation he has created. He needs his work to be acknowledged. I am sure of it. We must revisit each murder site with this in mind and review the cases under this prognosis."

Pyke looked at his battered and misshapen hat forlornly, '*I'll never make this look any better,*' he thought. He smiled, '*So what, it has character.*' He flipped the derby expertly onto his head, placed an unlit cigar in his mouth and grinned. "I've got me hat. Ready when you are, Guv."

Wiggins and Pyke began walking through Highgate Woods, retracing their steps from the same entrance point at Talbot Road through which Constable Bunce had guided them only a matter of days before. Pyke walked slightly in front, occasionally moving branches out of the way for his boss. Dried leaves crackled their annoyance underfoot.

"It can't be much farther now, Pyke," assured Wiggins. "It took us precisely nine minutes and twenty-two seconds to reach the clearing on our previous visit. It is now eight minutes exactly since we entered the woods and I am sure that we've made speedier progress than we did the last time."

Pyke knew by now that he should not be surprised by Wiggins' extraordinary memory and attention to every minute detail. "There's daylight just ahead Guv," remarked Pyke feeling that his statement of the obvious was somewhat inconsequential in the light of Wiggins' observation. A branch whipped back unexpectedly and struck Wiggins on the shoulder causing him to instinctively turn to face back towards the way they had come.

"Crumbs! I'm sorry about that, Guv," cringed Pyke, smiling through gritted teeth.

"It is of no consequence, Jem," reassured Wiggins. However, his sentence trailed off into a thoughtful silence. His brow lowered inquisitively. "Look, Jem," he urged, pointing back towards a large birch tree. "Do you see that huge gash in the trunk of that birch yonder?"

Pyke narrowed his eyes, following the direction of Wiggins' pointing finger. He saw the tree and the unmistakable scar in the silver bark. "That's some groper of a lumberjack right their, Guv!" joked Pyke.

"It is indeed rather odd that such a mark would be at the chest height of your average individual don't you think? If a woodsman was attempting to chop down the tree, surely, he would saw much lower to the ground, not to mention horizontal to it, and never at such an acute angle. Don't you agree?" Wiggins rubbed his chin, his mind racing.

"That is deep scarring true enough, and fairly fresh too by the looks of it. The wound is still a creamy green with no new bark formation. Look, there's another similar gash to a tree a few rows further forward and to the right, but this time it is cleaved vertically," indicated Pyke.

"How odd!" wondered Wiggins. "No matter, Pyke, as you are aware there are often strange goings-on within any woods, especially under the cover of darkness. Witchcraft, Pagan rituals, and other such Tom Foolery are rife in such locations. For instance, I hear lately of some fantastic tales of reputed witchery, rife within Epping Forest. Talk of a woman who cracks fire from her fingertips and brings death to the foliage under her feet. All nonsense of course. Nevertheless, we have urgent matters upon which to attend. Let us proceed into the grassy grove and see if we can discover a signature for our murderous artist."

The two detectives headed carefully towards the centre of the clearing. "Guv, did you know that the locals living in and around Highgate have already nick-named this place The Corpse Copse?" questioned Pyke.

"No, I did not, Jem. A strange quirk of human nature is it not, that we always seem to demand the glorification of such tragic situations. Our very own *Beast*, *Jack the Ripper*, and not forgetting our American cousins' *Demon of the Belfry*, all abhorrent murderers are given exotic names that conjure fear, and above all, that sell newsprint."

Both detectives were now studying the scene of the stoning of Deacon Hamilton Lancaster. Wiggins hunkered down to inspect the weft of the grass, whilst Pyke's boot was toeing at a few open patches of dry ground. The water pale that had been used to cover the victim's head sat safely within the forensic laboratory of Scotland Yard along with each of the nineteen stones that had been used to kill the unfortunate clergyman.

"Needle in a haystack spring to mind, Guv?" enquired Pyke sardonically, looking up at the greying sky. "Looks like rain."

"It is here I tell you, Jem, the murderer has left his mark somehow, I know it. He could not leave this area without signing off the crime," insisted Wiggins as he continued to scrutinise the scene. "We now know the painting he recreated here was Rembrandt's Stoning of Saint Stephen. We also know that painting was the very first work to be signed by Rembrandt. He was, we know, a mere nineteen years old at the time, hence, the accompanying nineteen stones used to murder the Deacon." Wiggins was going over old ground, hoping that the repetition would stimulate some novel ideas. "We also know that Saint Stephen was appointed a Deacon by the Apostles and would distribute food and charitable aid to the poorer members of his community." Wiggins' mind was now making instant connections and theories, synapses fizzing around his brain. "Deacon Lancaster also established a mission dedicated to the welfare of recently widowed women." The Inspector closely peered into the hole wherein the victim had been buried. He knew that it had already been searched with a fine toothcomb but found himself inextricably drawn towards it. "Our murderer is clever indeed and is obviously a well-educated individual. The quote on the fragment of paper left in the Deacon's clothing testifies to such. We also know that the scribbled sentence refers to a passage from Matthew sixteen; twenty-five, which coincides with the year young Rembrandt's painting was completed."

"We know all of this, Guv." Pyke felt frustrated at this re-examination of old ground. "Could we have another religious lunatic zealot like Nathaniel Cripes on our hands?" offered Pyke, still scuffing randomly at the ground, his leather boots now dusty from the dry earth. The action had become mildly addictive. So much so that he knew he was damaging his boots but found it increasingly difficult to cease. '*Need to get the dubbin wax out tonight,*' he thought.

"I think not, Jem," countered Wiggins looking up from his crouched position. "Our perpetrator has immense knowledge of the art world and, I would venture, a resounding hatred of it. Evidently, he can read and write as he leaves us clues in plain sight to test and tease our investigative prowess. I am sure that he is of the understanding, however misplaced, that he is not only superior to us, but also to his victims." Just then, as Wiggins looked up at Pyke's silhouetted figure, he noticed something in the distance. He calculated that the angle he was looking at was roughly the same as that which the Deacon had been facing when he had been stoned to death.

"What's wrong, Guv? Looks like you've seen a bleedin' ghost?" Pyke enquired as he noted the slack-jawed look of realisation spread across Wiggins' face.

"Clever, *very* clever," Wiggins mused admiringly. "Look directly behind you Jem, where the trees give way to the meadow. What do you observe?"

Pyke swivelled to face in the direction indicated, the heel of his boot grinding a cleft into the arid soil. For a few moments, he considered the treeline Wiggins had specified. "Nothing but trees, Guv!" shrugged Pyke, shaking his head. "Trees, trees and some more trees."

"Now, slowly crouch down to my level and tilt your head thirty degrees to the right, just as I am doing," requested Wiggins.

Pyke slowly stooped down until he was squatting on his haunches and scrutinised the scene intensely. Once at the same level as Wiggins, he slowly slanted his head as instructed. BAM! Everything suddenly exploded into focus and he could see what Wiggins had seen. At that precise position, the strange slashes and gouges cut into the trees they had seen earlier, now aligned perfectly to clearly spell out the initials, 'J' and 'S'. Pyke gasped, "Remarkable! Who would have thought it?"

"I knew it, Jem! We almost have our murderer within our grasp. That is his signature. Whomever *JS* is, he just had to sign his work. His ego left him no option but to crave acclamation for his atrocity," exclaimed Wiggins enthusiastically. "This game is now most surely afoot!"

Wiggins carefully unclasped the mouthpiece of the candlestick telephone which stood upon his desk. "Sergeant Ash, please put me through to Mr Roger Fry at the Omega Workshops in Fitzroy Square, I spoke with him earlier today," urged the Detective to his Desk Sergeant. The journey back from Highgate had been rapid and Wiggins had found it difficult to contain his eagerness in re-engaging with Mr Fry.

"Very well Sir, I took note of the telephone number in my ledger, 3331 Regent," replied the reliable Ash in his ever-practical manner. Wiggins heard the distinct click of the call being connected and waited a few moments before he heard the clearly intonated tones of Sexton answering the call. "Regent 3331, Omega Workshops, good day and how may we be of assistance to you?"

"Hello, Sexton, this is Detective Chief Inspector Wiggins speaking. I met with Mr Fry earlier in the day and wondered if he was still on the premises? I would like a quick word if that is possible."

"Yes indeed, Inspector, Mr Fry is still upstairs working, shall I ask him to call you back?" asked Sexton.

"Yes, please as a matter of utmost urgency if you would be so kind," requested Wiggins.

Several minutes had passed before an obviously out of breath and a frenetic Fry came on the line. "Dear, Chief Inspector, how can I be of assistance? I do hope you have another gruesome murder to describe to me, I so enjoyed our meeting earlier today. Not a wholly creditable thing to say, I must admit, but the murders certainly did stimulate my interest." Without drawing to breathe, Fry continued, "You know I really must get another telephone installed to save my legs, but they are so expensive and rather an extravagance, don't you agree?"

"Mr Fry," Wiggins interrupted, anxious to keep the artist focussed. "I do apologise for dragging you away from your work, but we now have an additional piece of evidence, one that I feel may be exceedingly significant to the case." He could almost feel Fry's excitement vibrate down the line. "At the scene of the stoning we found the initials 'J' and 'S' carved into the trees to the east of the crime scene," revealed Wiggins. He hesitated slightly, anticipation brimming within him "Are these letters in any way suggestive to you?"

Fry pondered for a moment, unsure, but searching for some vague memory. "I am unsure. How frustrating! 'J' and 'S' you say? Now let me think. Why yes, of course! Oh, why did you not disclose this information at our morning meeting Inspector?"

"As I said, Mr Fry, this is a new piece of evidence which has only recently come to light."

"How unfortunate that we did not know of this earlier. Your murderer would by now have been apprehended and be safely ensconced behind bars," lamented Fry.

Wiggins' heart leapt, "You mean you know who the murderer is?" Pyke bounded out of his chair on hearing Wiggins' question.

"Why of course, Inspector! I suspect that he is a particularly unpleasant individual with whom I was once, regrettably acquainted. If my guess is correct, his name is Jarvis Sickart. An uncreative but dreadfully persistent amateur artist who held his own talents in unwarranted esteem." Fry stroked his chin thoughtfully, reaching into his memory. Wiggins and Pyke were pregnant with anticipation. "Let me see now... Yes, yes, I do believe I recall now. I seem to recall that he resides somewhere in the Saint Giles area, Rathbone Street rings a bell of some recollection," added Fry confidently.

Wiggins smiled broadly and nodded to Pyke who made a fist and triumphantly punched at the air.

Fry continued on the other end of the line. "I don't suppose there would be any form of reward for aiding in the capture of your killer, Inspector? Our little family of Bohemians could benefit immensely from any such monies."

Wiggins offered a word of caution, attempting to rationalise the critic's information. "Mr Fry, there must be hundreds of inhabitants of London with the same initials," he offered, ignoring the request for a monetary reward. "For instance, I would wager that they may be the most common initials in the City, given the proliferation of John Smiths. How can you be sure that this is our man?"

"Yes, that is no doubt true," conceded Fry. "But surely none would harbour such an unreserved abhorrence of the established art world as does Sickart. He holds an entrenched grudge against the Royal Academy, and therefore, also against Sir Edward Poynter, whom I know he particularly resented." Wiggins could feel his pulse racing. This sounded too good to be true. Pyke could sense his boss' optimism and was prowling around the room, eager for the telephone conversation to be over.

"You see Inspector, Mr Jarvis Sickart, has been endeavouring, unsuccessfully I may add, to gain membership of the Academy for over fifteen years now. He is undoubtedly a very proficient, and indeed, talented artist, judging by the works he sends as submissions of application. However, his rather unfortunate problem is that he is devoid of creativity. Absolutely bereft of an original thought or idea. No imagination. Not one bit. Sir Edward once joked that Sickart could copy the Sistine Chapel but in no way could he even consider creating it. He is a mimic, a copyist. A forger if you will. There is no room for such individuals in the Royal Academy. That is why he has been rejected membership on so many occasions. And, that Inspector, is why Sickart has maintained a festering feud with Sir Edward. A campaign of poisonous letters and intimidating phone calls, I understand. After all, it is Sir Edward who grants the right that allows any artist to display the letters RA, after their surname, so he was seen by Sickart as the architect of his misfortune."

Wiggins was quietly jubilant. "I am forever in your debt, Mr Fry. We shall follow up your information immediately, and please, not a word of this to anyone at this time, I beseech you."

"Of course, I understand. A pleasure to have been of assistance, Inspector. Any patronage the Metropolitan Police may see fit to provide towards our little group would be most welcome."

After further thanks and thinly veiled hints at possible recompense, Wiggins replaced the telephone mouthpiece. He turned slowly towards Pyke, trying to channel an inner calm whilst adrenalin coursed through his body. "Thanks to Mr Roger Fry, tonight we are going to catch our killer. Best get your hat, Jem."

Chapter 27 - The Arrest

Wiggins and Pyke, accompanied by several armed officers, made extensive door-to-door enquiries in Rathbone Street. They tried to be as unobtrusive as possible, but it proved impossible to conceal their activity successfully. The street was depressing and downtrodden, crammed with imposing, overcrowded four-storey tenements that seemed to lean forwards from either side of the road, looming over the cobbles and preventing daylight from penetrating the street below. Each building was neglected and forlorn, with some looking so derelict as to be almost beyond habitation. A wholly depressing and oppressive place to have to exist, in stark contrast to its thriving and affluent neighbour, Fitzrovia. Under Wiggins' precise orders the team of officers had worked the street as a cohesive and communitive team, left to right, east to west, investigating each house from top to bottom as they proceeded.

"Man alive! I thought Limehouse was bad, Guv. Even the rats have rickets here," quipped Pyke as he strode by Wiggins' side.

"It is definitely one of the more unsavoury places in the City. Only one step away from the poor house here I'm afraid, and even then, I might recommend the poor house when compared with this squalor and deprivation," replied Wiggins rather sombrely. As he did so, Constable Theaker came charging towards him excitedly. As he reached Wiggins, he cupped his hand and whispered into the Chief Inspector's ear. "Number forty-nine, Sarge. I've just spoken with a M Judd Twelvetrees, a neighbour of Sickart's who lives at number forty-three. Swears our culprit lives only three doors along from him in a lodging house."

"Good work, Theaker," encouraged Wiggins, patting the young Constable on the shoulder.

"Not only that, Sir," continued the emboldened constable, "but Mr Twelvetrees described him in some detail. Our man apparently sports a shock of spiked hair. Grows upwards and not downwards, according to Twelvetrees. He also stated that Sickart often frequents the newly opened picture theatre over in East Finchley. Goes there most days, he said." Theaker referred to his notebook, trying to contain his obvious excitement. "Sickart has been telling all and sundry about the new moving pictures and how distasteful they are. Work of the devil he says. Mr Twelvetrees reckons he could well be there as we speak."

"Excellent! I presume that will be the Picturedome that opened a few years ago. Seems strange that one who doesn't appreciate the cinema, would visit it so regularly, don't you think, Jem?" probed Wiggins.

"Nothing ceases to amaze me in these modern times, Guv. Still don't quite understand electricity me! Can't see it, can't feel it, can't even smell it, but nonetheless, there it is, the greatest wonder of the age." specified Pyke.

"Right, Pyke, gather the men around, so we can formulate a plan," Wiggins ordered.

Number forty-nine was a common lodging house that encompassed four levels of accommodation. According to the testimony Mr Twelvetrees had given Constable Theaker, Sickart lived in one of the ground floor rooms. Pyke pushed open the communal entrance door and walked into a short, dark lobby. There was a door on each side of a disturbingly unstable looking spiral stairwell. The area was poorly lit and festooned with cobwebs that clung gratefully like dust-covered drapes to peeling paint and damp plaster. The team gathered behind Wiggins, who in turn stood directly behind Pyke, the eternal battering-ram in such situations. Wiggins indicated the door to the right. "Watch now, Pyke, there's not much holding that door upon its hinges," he warned. "One swift boot from you and we'll be inside. Pistols drawn, men!" commanded Wiggins.

With an almighty crack, Pyke's size nine boot crashed unswervingly through the closing stile of the door causing his leg to become lodged awkwardly. Annoyed and angry, he pulled his leg free then simply pushed his outstretched hands against the door which easily came free from its rusted hinges and crashed inwards onto the floor. The impact caused dust to billow upward and outward from the loose soil floor within, obscuring any view temporarily.

"Police! Surrender in the name of the King," shouted Wiggins into the now dust-filled room. There was no sound, no movement within. His words were met with a still, resonant silence. Only muted extraneous street noise punctured the quiet. After several seconds spent with ears cocked, Pyke and Wiggins slowly entered the room, pistols in hand. The dust gradually settled to reveal an eerie scene.

The single room was empty and felt unnaturally cold for the time of year. The furniture was sparse, only a small table and stool. Wiggins could faintly make out a makeshift bed and a small washbasin fixed to the far wall. The dwelling smelled stagnant with mildew and had a distinctive underlying aroma of linseed oil and turpentine. Wiggins noted that the room's two small windows had been boarded up with lengths of timber. He thought this decidedly odd as each window was so small that not even an infant child could have entered through it. '*Were the bars to keep its occupant in or to keep intruders out?*' he wondered. Dust covered cobwebs hung from the ceiling, dancing like the wispy hair of some hoary old hag. Pyke and Wiggins both struck matches to help illuminate the murky room. "My Lord Almighty! Look at the walls, Jem," gasped Wiggins softly in an astonished tone. The combined flickering light from their matches revealed a room whose four walls and ceiling were fully adorned with paintings, each blending seamlessly into the next. A vast fresco of art. Wiggins recognised recreations of works by Raphael, da Vinci, Giotto, Rubens, Caravaggio and Michelangelo. There were countless others he could not attribute.

"This must have taken years to achieve," wondered Pyke, his mouth agape as his eyes explored the room in all directions. The flame of his match licked his fingertips and he tossed the spent vesta aside and lit another.

"Indeed, Jem, an extremely talented hand. Let us waste no more time here. We head to East Finchley as a matter of urgency."

The flickering light from the motion picture ceased to illuminate the motionless figure of Jarvis Sickart as he sat in the comforting darkness of the East Finchley Picturedrome. The cinema was a lavishly decorated building, velvet drapes and veloured seats, gilded mouldings and ornate ceilings. Completed only the year before, this was one of the first establishments of its kind in London, its specific purpose to show moving pictures to the masses. Masses that displayed a seemingly unquenchable thirst for this astonishing new medium. The building had been part of the wave of cinema construction that had swept across the country in the first decade of this vital, new century.

Sickart had just watched, or rather to his mind, endured, a moving picture titled 'Sixty Years a Queen' starring Blanche Forsythe as Queen Victoria. He had been affronted at what he regarded as its palpable crass vulgarity and overblown exuberance. Conversely, however, the audience had applauded their appreciation enthusiastically as the screen curtains closed and had stood as one as the National Anthem was played vigorously by the string quartet in the orchestra pit. Jarvis Sickart however, remained firmly seated, distaste rising within him.

The time was six forty-five in the evening and his fellow patrons were beginning to exit the cinema, chattering enthusiastically as they headed for the nearby train station, or towards one of the many electric trams that passed along the High Road. The four musicians had now packed away their instruments and departed via the pit bleachers, off to wet their whistles until their return for the late rescreening. As Sickart was about to rise to make his leave he suddenly felt his shoulders being forcibly pushed downward with tremendous power. He was driven back down into the red velvet cushioning of the seat. "What is the meaning of..." he began to splutter.

"Shh! Please remain seated, Mr Sickart," came the rumbling request from behind. Sickart felt his stomach lurch in fear as he sensed menace in the voice emanating behind him. The flesh on his forearms goose-pimpled. He could just distinguish a faint smell of cigar tobacco and the unmistakable silhouetted shape of a Derby hat in his peripheral vision. "My name is Detective Sergeant Pyke," continued the low, threatening rumble. "And sitting to your immediate right is my superior officer, Detective Chief Inspector Wiggins. We are both from Scotland Yard, Criminal Investigations Department." The voice was slow and measured, though none-the-less, intimidating. "I warn you that we are both armed and will have no hesitation in using weapons to our advantage." Pyke tapped one shoulder reassuringly several times whilst still restraining the man in the row in front of him with his other hand. Sickart had been oblivious to Wiggins, who had been sitting at his right-hand side for the past fifty minutes. After all, the cinema's four hundred plus seats had been almost entirely sold out.

"Good evening, Mr Sickart. I would imagine that you have been anticipating our appearance," stated Wiggins prosaically.

Jarvis Sickart turned his head ninety degrees just as the house lights came flickering on. He swallowed hard but decided to make a fist of the situation. "I had expected you rather sooner Inspector, I did leave you enough clues after all," came Sickart's sardonic high-pitched reply. The artist had gotten over his initial unease and, realising his position, had reverted to a state of forced composure. As Sickart teased his unruly shock of hair, Pyke noted that the murderer's fingernails were filthy with an indescribable pigment that darkened the underside of his fingernail plates almost to the lunulae.

"I admit that you were generous with your intimations, and indeed, your clues, although given their rather cryptic and specific association with the art world, it did take us somewhat longer to decipher them than we would normally have expected," offered Wiggins in response. "I congratulate you at the unique nature of your signature of the first murder in Highgate Woods. Particularly ingenious," complimented Wiggins, turning now to face Sickart directly. The forger had a rat-like face that betrayed his fallen circumstances. Unshaven and unkempt, his oily skin covered in boils, his eyelids looked reddened and crustily painful.

"Simple really, Inspector. It is all to do with angles, perspectives and vanishing points, not to mention how one's brain interpolates information that is not actually on show," lectured Sickart patronisingly. "Had you had a modicum of artistic inclination you would have spotted it earlier." His nose sniffed the air like a superior mouse sniffing a rather offensive cheese.

"Be that as it may, I am here, and we pronounce your murderous spree to be at an end. I fully expect you to come along peacefully without the need for us to use any undue force, Mr Sickart," stated Wiggins. "I am sure you would not wish to antagonise my colleague here. Don't you concur?"

"Oh yes, yes, of course not, Inspector," answered Sickart in his oddly feminine voice. Wiggins could sense a note of satisfaction in the killer's tone. "My master-pieces are now complete, and I am ready for my acclamation. I entirely expect the newspapers to carry my name emblazoned across their front pages tomorrow morning. I expect those loathsome editors will no doubt make the all too obvious pun that my surname demands, wouldn't you agree?"

"Sick ... Art, yes of course. They must," replied Wiggins. "It would be an absolute travesty of their art for them to miss such a glaring opportunity, would it not?"

"An absolute travesty indeed," agreed a delighted Sickart. "Do you know Inspector, it seems as though Art, as I perceive it, is about to end. The full house here this evening sadly testifies that moving pictures are to be the future. The idle classes would rather sit through six reels of balderdash and flimflam rather than spend ten minutes studying the beauty of a Rembrandt or even a Cézanne for that matter." Wiggins reluctantly decided to allow Sickart to continue with what he suspected would slowly become a tirade. He nodded as much to Pyke whom he could see over Sickart's shoulder, was becoming impatient. As far as Pyke was concerned, he had heard enough about art and artists over the last couple of days to last him a lifetime. "How many people would you speculate attended the National Portrait Gallery today? For no charge, I might add ... a hundred? Two hundred? More perhaps? Yet, for less than an hour here this evening, nearly five hundred delusional fools paid hard earned money to watch this nonsense. The term 'moving' picture is, incidentally, a complete and utter misnomer! Turner expresses more *movement* in a single brushstroke than was witnessed during the dire offering screened here this evening." Pyke's eyes looked towards the ornate ceiling. *'If he starts blabbing on about this rubbish much longer, I'm going to have to give him a tap,'* he thought.

Sickart's gaunt face was now reddening with rage and the volume of his voice was rising in accompaniment with his ire. A vein in his forehead began to throb and pulse. "Sir Edward John Poynter I ask you! That supposed Knight of the Realm and his cronies disregarded my application for academy membership once too often. *He* is to blame for this! It was *he* who had the audacity to refuse to respond to my last submission, yet he recognises the charlatans that grease his untalented palm with bribes and fawning promises. He had to pay, you understand, Inspector. He just *had* to! What did he know about true art? What did he know about true beauty?"

Wiggins, much to Pyke's relief, grew tired of Sickart's diatribe. "Save it for the judge. Jarvis Sickart, you are under arrest on suspicion of the murders of Hamilton Lancaster, Johnathan Hardridge, Edward John Poynter and Emily Lorimer. You do not have to say anything, but it may harm your defence if you do not mention when questioned, something which you later rely on in a court of law. You have the right to remain silent. If you do say anything, what you say can be used against you in a court of law. You have the right to consult with a lawyer and have that lawyer present during any questioning. If you cannot afford a lawyer, which I suspect is the case, one will be appointed for you if you so desire," declared Wiggins. "Do you understand, Mr Sickart?"

"Why of course, Inspector, I understand fully," came Sickart's snapped reply. "There is, however, no *suspicion* about it. I killed each of the individuals you mention as surely as the sun will rise tomorrow morning. In killing these people, I have immortalised each of them. Instead of simply being created by the good Lord, each one is now a *creation*, each a genuine work of art that will outlive even their loved one's memories of them."

"Man alive, you don't half talk a lot o' bollocks!" interrupted Pyke as he pulled Sickart upright by the frayed collar of his outer coat. "You're going with these nice young men now, ducky." Pyke gestured towards several constables who had positioned themselves at the ends of the row of seats in front and behind. Pyke pushed Sickart towards them and indicated that they take the murderer away.

As Pyke and Wiggins made their way out of the cinema, Pyke removed his Derby and drew his hand through his hair. "Well, I can safely state, that was a lot easier than apprehending Doctor Joseph Bleak. No damage to me old noggin' at all," quipped the Detective Sergeant.

Wiggins felt inwardly elated, satisfied that they had rid the City of another homicidal lunatic, and that the relatives of his victims may find some solace in his inevitable fate. "Indeed, it was Jem, just as we suspected. By the way, what did you make of the picture anyway?" enquired an intrigued Wiggins.

"Sixty years a Queen, Guv? To be honest, I thought it was going to be about Syphilis Phyllis!"

That evening, following a celebratory meal at Simpson's-of-the-Strand with their neighbours, James and Lily, the Wiggins' had retired early. Wiggins felt elated, unable to embrace the sleep that enveloped the contented Mary lying beside him. He lay awake in the darkness, staring abstractedly at the vague outline of the plaster ceiling rose above him. There was something amiss. Something other than the joy of a successful arrest. Something more than the satisfaction of ridding the City of a mad, multiple killer. Something was gnawing at him, a distant tug on his memory that unsettled his mind. Eventually, he could bear it no longer and arose carefully so as not to disturb his wife. He grabbed his smoking jacket and, tying its cord around his waist, quickly found his slippers and eased out of the bedroom. He turned upstairs towards his loft study, treading lightly to avoid the creaking of the stairs. Wiggins knew that it was there that he would find the answer to the seed of doubt that brewed within him.

Sitting at his desk, he gazed out of the arched sash window that offered a view of the crescent's communal square, searching for inspiration. He tried to clear his mind. After several minutes, the mental fog began to clear. It was the name, Sickart. There was something about that name that rapped at the door of his memory. Sickart. Where had he heard it before?

His study held his private collection of criminal history. Case files, masses of catalogued press clippings, categorised alphabetically and filed according to each miscreant. Biographical notes on virtually every criminal of note of recent years. He scanned his shelves and bookcases, searching for inspiration. His eyes rested on a framed photograph hanging beside a shelf of monographs of various subjects including fingerprints, shoe leather, pollen genera, varieties of cigar ash, the peculiarities of the left-handed. He saw five faces looking out from the photograph, a youthful Constable Wiggins stood proudly beside Magnus MacDonald, Superintendent Gregson, the squat Edmund Reid and then the imposing Chief Inspector Frederick Abberline. His gaze lingered upon the face of Abberline, the man who had led the hunt for the Ripper twenty-five years earlier and who, on his retirement from the Force, had turned to private detection work, most notably with the European branch of the Pinkerton Agency. Then it came to him. '*Of course, the Ripper Case!*' He unlocked a large wall cabinet and withdrew one of many box files marked 'Whitechapel Murders 1888'. From the box, he removed a well-thumbed manila folder entitled 'Suspects' and placed it carefully on his desk. He scanned through the familiar biographies until he came to the one that he was looking for, that of a Walter Sickert. '*Surely this cannot be a coincidence!*' he thought, excitedly. '*The name is too similar.*' He read on, refamiliarizing himself with the content that he had read countless times before.

The German-born Sickert had been, and remained, an artist and printmaker of notable repute and a founding father of the Camden Town Group. He had taken, what the Yard had considered, at the time, to be a morbid fascination with the Ripper Case and had painted detailed reconstructions of similarly visceral crime scenes and even a rendition of Jack himself in a room rented by the artist. The dark, shrouded figure had been indistinct, leading many to speculate that this was, in fact, a self-portrait. Sickert had been regarded as a plausible suspect for the first two murders and had been questioned by Abberline and MacDonald. However, the case against him had faltered given that, at the time of the so-called 'double event' murders,

Sickert had a stone hewn alibi, having been in Dieppe painting his most famous work, 'The Red Shop October Sun.' Abberline's attention had then turned instead to the prime Ripper suspect, Seweryn Kłosowski.

'*Surely there is a connection here?*' mused Wiggins. The similarity in the surnames. Sickart and Sickert. Both were artists. He looked at Walter Sickert's birth date of 31st May 1860 and concluded that this could be a case of an embittered and twisted son seeking to bring to life, the false notoriety of his innocent, though persecuted father. He turned to his library of biographies of what he termed *individuals of interest* and pulled out a ledger marked 'S.' Finding his entry for Sickert, Walter, he read further.

"There you are!" he said to himself, smiling with satisfaction. An illegitimate son, born in France, twenty-eight years ago, name and whereabouts unknown. '*Surely this is our man, Sickart.*' Wiggins closed the file, satisfied that his hypothesis was sound, and that the connection would add strength to the conviction and establish that the motive for the crimes was one of the most twisted in the history of crime.

Chapter 28 - The Presentation

"And for selfless gallantry and bravery in the face of insurmountable odds, and with unconditional regard for the safety of the populace of this great City and that of his fellow colleagues, I am hereby honoured to present you, Leslie Jeremiah Pyke, with the King's Police Medal for outstanding bravery. We thank you from the bottom our hearts for the part you played in the apprehension and dispatch of the Beast of London."

So, pronounced His Majesty King George the fifth as he pinned the medal on possibly the proudest chest in the land. Jem Pyke, his eyes set firmly front as he had been taught, stiffly saluted his Sovereign. Unseen behind Pyke, the slight figure of young Billy Skew, standing between Red Noreen and DCI Wiggins, mimicked the action and threw his own inexperienced salute. The merest of smiles played across the mouth of the bearded Monarch as he returned the old soldier's salute. Pyke, as he had rehearsed, took two steps backwards, bowed, turned sharply, and made his way back to his seat amongst the attendant crowd. As he did so his face was awash with the most resplendent of smiles. His friends and colleagues rose as one and began to applaud. Pyke threw an embarrassed look towards Wiggins, silently admonishing his boss for what he strongly suspected was a prearranged act. Wiggins threw a wink and returned his smile, and nodding his head, completely disregarded his colleague's unspoken plea and proceeded to applaud even louder. "Bravo!"

Tobias Pullar hastily removed his white gloves and footman's livery before furtively leaving the Palace via one of the many servant's exits. He touched the peak of his cap to the household guard on duty, in a salutary goodbye, and made his way down Buckingham Palace Road as fast he could. As he did so, he examined the faces of the people around him wondering whether his appearance betrayed his guilt at having just perpetrated a monumental crime. '*Easiest fifty pounds I've ever made,*' he thought, his satisfaction beginning to drown his feelings of unease. He gloried in the realisation that he would have had to endure at least two years of servitude at the behest of His Majesty's puritanical personal staff before he would have come anywhere near earning that amount of money. '*Not at all bad for five minutes work,*

Toby me lad,' he smiled to himself. One under a table in the anteroom, one in a cistern in the lady's water closets and another in the side foyer fireplace. '*They'll blame the Irish,'* the man with the fifty pounds had said. '*You've nothing to worry about,'* he had promised. Tobias Pullar thought only of the fifty pounds, never once considering the carnage that his actions were about to unleash upon the Commonwealth.

Doctor Watson threw his head back in laughter. "I, of course, could not make head nor tail of it, all those dancing men, some with flags in their left hand, some in the right, some standing on their bally heads," he chuckled. Wiggins and his wife Mary soaked up the enjoyment of the raconteur adventurer. "Of course, He read them as you or I would read a novel by Mr Wells! Remarkable really."

"I understand from Albert, Doctor, that you are not, as previously planned, returning to Scotland, now that the Beast has been slain," stated Mary Wiggins, referring to the death of Doctor Joseph Bleak, whilst sipping at her glass of champagne. She loved the feeling the bubbles made as they effervesced against the roof of her mouth.

"Indeed, my dear lady. I have reconsidered. Scotland can wait. I have taken temporary rooms at Montague Street, nearby the British Museum in Bloomsbury. Number thirty-one to be precise, a pertinent coincidence given that it is the very same as my old regimental number," he chuckled.

The presentation party had moved into an anteroom to encourage a less formal gathering. More champagne and a wide variety of canapes were being served by attentive waiters and waitresses amid the gold gilt splendour of the eighteen eighty-four room. Jem Pyke, standing next to Red Noreen and Billy Skew, felt a surge of pride, not generated by his recent commendation, but because he stood with his new family. He smiled and looked dubiously at the tiny cracker topped with caviar which he held in his hand. As both Superintendent MacDonald and Commissioner Gregson, once more congratulated him on his award, Jem took a bite and tried to disguise his distaste at the saltiness of the fish roe, washing the remainder quickly down with a large gulp of champagne. He threw a secretive look of feigning being sick at Billy who giggled behind his hand. He looked at Noreen, her arm protectively draped over Billy's shoulders, her sparkling, green eyes glinting back at him. He could see pride reflected in those eyes, perhaps even love. He swallowed hard and returned her smile. '*How beautiful she looks,'* he thought, her dark red hair raised and shaped, her newly purchased emerald green ball gown generous in its showcasing of her curvaceous figure. Both she and Mary Wiggins had joked when they had realised that they wore colour clashing gowns. He wondered at Noreen's ability to talk with ease to people of all ranks and positions in society, how all were charmed by her looks and demeanour. She, who had but a few months earlier, been a saloon girl with no experience of circles such as these.

He bit his bottom lip. He had decided he had decided. Tomorrow he would trawl Hatton Garden and search out an engagement ring. Emerald, he resolved, to match those eyes. He would proceed to do something he certainly never supposed he ever would and propose marriage.

He looked at Billy, clinging to her side. '*A family, a proper bleedin' family,*' he thought. His mind began to wander to thoughts of responsibility and fatherhood, but they were interrupted by the sharp clink of a butter knife against crystal signalling an impending speech. The babble of conversation that filled the room ebbed away and Pyke shifted his weight awkwardly, dreading the prospect of once more being the centre of attention. Commissioner Gregson unfolded a small piece of paper then demanded everyone's attention. All eyes focused on the tall pale figure of the Commissioner. Following a preparatory cough, he began his address to the gathered company.

"Colleagues, friends, distinguished guests. May I take this opportunity to say a few words in praise, not only of today's worthy recipients of such prestigious awards, but also of our admirable police force in general. Most of us in this room have first-hand experience of the pain and loss that our positions so frequently attract. This, I am afraid, is an unavoidable symptom of our chosen profession. There are those among us, however, that raise bravery to unprecedented heights. Those among us who have, without thought of their own safety, selflessly put their own lives at risk. Those who are willing to suffer great sacrifice that others remain safe and unharmed. The term 'hero' is a much-misused epithet, but people such as Detective Sergeant Jem Pyke here, who single-handedly engaged the nightmarish Beast that was Doctor Joseph Bleak, who had for so long terrorised our City, are worthy of the title." Pyke felt the smoothness of Noreen's hand slip into his calloused palm and intertwine with his fingers in a reassuring clasp.

"People like Chief Superintendent Magnus MacDonald, battered, tortured and nearly fatally injured at the hands of the evil Mr King and his associates." Gregson cast a glance in the direction of the Scottish veteran who sat, head bowed, in his wheelchair, deep in contemplation. "Let us not forget, Detective Inspector Albert Wiggins, who unravelled the Apostle puzzle for once and for all, leading to the Beast's demise. His intelligent and preceptive detective work is true testament to a great Teacher."

"And let us thank and remember our fallen colleagues, those who tragically cannot be here with us. Those who gave up their lives that others may live." Gregson's voice cracked momentarily, and he swallowed hard, determined to continue. "Those whom today have received posthumous awards. Men like Constable William Potts who shielded the Honourable Lady Constance Harkness from certain death whilst sacrificing his own blossoming young life. I ask you all to raise your glasses, ladies and gentlemen, to our heroes, to those who are present here today and to those who are now, unfortunately, only present in our cherished memories."

As each glass in the room was raised, the door to the anteroom slid open and a footman in full livery entered. "Pray silence for His Majesty King George the Fifth of the United Kingdom and her Dominions, Emperor of India," he announced in practised, booming tones.

The stately figure of the Monarch entered, accompanied by several dignitaries and attendants. "Please everyone, do carry on as if I were not here, I merely want to add my personal thanks to you all in a more informal setting," attested His Majesty. Pyke cast his eyes towards the ceiling, wondering when his personal torture would end, and he could be released to the Albert Bar in nearby Victoria Street. Noreen somehow read his mind and gave him an admonishing dig in the ribs.

Lady Constance Harkness, whose elder sister, Agatha, had been savagely murdered by the Beast, approached His Royal Highness and with a well-rehearsed curtsey and a warm smile, engaged the Monarch. "Your Highness, how lovely to see you once again."

"The pleasure, of course, is all mine, Lady Constance," smiled the King. "How are your mother and father? Such a terrible loss to have to endure," he added, his face showing what Connie judged to be genuine concern.

"They survive, your Highness, but both are utterly devastated. My Father buries himself in his work whilst Mother…" her voice faltered.

"I understand," empathised the King, placing a comforting hand lightly on the young woman's elbow. "I must arrange to visit Viscount Harkness at the earliest convenience to personally convey my condolences." Constance bowed in acknowledgement and, regaining her composure, asked the Monarch if she might introduce him to Sergeant Pyke and his family. "Why of course, I would consider it an honour and a privilege," he added. The King turned to follow her only to find young Billy Skew standing in front of him, his eyes agog.

"And who is this fine upstanding young man?" asked the King.

"This is Billy, Sergeant Pyke's … ward," stuttered Constance, unsure as to how she should refer to the former slaughterhouse apprentice whom Pyke had taken into his home.

"Ah! Of course, Master William Pyke," stated His Majesty, kindly ruffling the lad's hair. "I believe that you were fundamental in securing the conviction of a dangerous criminal, Billy?"

Billy swallowed hard. "I don't knows about no fundament, Your Highness, Sir, but I did tell Jem 'bout that creep Cripes who's in the Loony Bin now," he stated proudly, straightening his back, and standing on his tiptoes to seem taller.

The King laughed and clapped Billy on the shoulder. "Capital, Billy! I am sure you are a brave lad and a blessing to Sergeant Pyke." Billy smiled the widest smile his skewed little face could muster. He puffed out his chest like a proud pigeon. "I do believe I may have something upon my person to reward just such a brave young man as yourself." As King George raised his hand a footman appeared at his side and handed the King a bright shining coin. "The King's silver sovereign, Billy," he smiled placing the coin in Billy's outstretched hand. Billy's eyes sparkled. "Take care of this Billy, it is very precious and there are not many about. If ever you need help from a policeman or a soldier or the like, you show them this coin, and you will be helped without question."

"Thank you again, your Highness," enthused Billy bowing awkwardly several times. "I shall endeavour to remember to do such," he added in his best English. The boy's eyes shone as he looked at the coin, turning it over and over in his hand before putting it safely in his pocket. Jem and Noreen looked on at this tableau, their hearts glowing with pride. "I'll just go and powder me nose, Jem," blushed Noreen. Pyke nodded his understanding and noticed that Mary Wiggins offered to accompany Noreen. '*Why always in twos?*' he wondered. He drifted towards Wiggins who was engaged in conversation with the widow of Constable Potts.

"Oh! And one more thing, Billy," added the King, conspiratorially as he crouched down to whisper in Billy's ear. He produced a round colourful object from an inside pocket of his waistcoat. "Something to enjoy right now, a royal gobstopper. I find them especially useful when sitting through long boring speeches. Some people of my acquaintance speak as if they've actually got a mouthful of these. I would, however, recommend that you mind your teeth, they can be rather ceramic in nature," he winked.

"Wow! Thanks, Mr King," replied Billy as he rushed off to show Jem the multi-coloured, swirl patterned boiled sweet. In his rush he tripped over Doctor Watson's foot and went sprawling on the floor, spilling his gobstopper which rolled under a drink-laden table. "My apologies, Billy," offered Watson stooping to help the child. "Damned feet always were a bit on the big side."

"Not a bother, Doctor. No 'arm done," answered Billy as he crawled under the folds of the heavy linen tablecloth that protected the table. Watson chuckled and longed for the innocence of his long-past childhood. Billy scrambled around the floor noticing that its polished marble surface was completely free from dust. '*No need to pick the sweet clean,*' he thought gleefully as he thankfully stopped the sweet's rolling progress.

It was then that he noticed the bomb.

He knew instantly what he was looking at. Attached to the underside of the table, the device was a muted grey metallic box featuring a silently ticking clock face and a complicated mass of protruding coloured wires. Billy panicked and quickly slid himself backwards on his belly, his new dress shirt riding up to his chest, his stomach squeaking against polished marble, and pushed himself out from under the table. He ran to Pyke and pulled frantically at the policeman's jacket. "Jem! Jem! Under the table," he stammered pointing excitedly "It's a bomb!"

Pyke looked at Billy with an eyebrow raised in incredulity. "You do mean a gobstopper don't you lad?" Pyke and Wiggins exchanged apprehensive glances.

"No, Jem. It's a bomb. I'm tellin' you. A real for life bomb, an' no mistake!" By now several heads had turned towards the conversation, mixtures of disbelief and rising concern playing across their faces.

"Calm down, Billy," responded Pyke putting a reassuring hand on the young lad's shoulder. He nodded towards Wiggins who strode towards the table, crouched, and lifted the tablecloth.

Wiggins swiftly returned to Pyke's side and quietly confirmed, "The lad is right. From what I could see of the clock we have approximately three minutes before the thing explodes. We need to get everyone out of here fast!" By now Doctor Watson and Commissioner Gregson were by Wiggins' side who switched instantly into command mode. "Commissioner, inform the King and get him to safety immediately. Notify the King's Guards to get everybody out into the courtyard instantly. Doctor Watson, ask Lady Harkness to take Chief Inspector MacDonald out of the building and help get everyone else clear. Jem, start moving people out now. Billy, quickly lad, go and open all the doors and run to the street outside and tell everyone to get as far away from the palace buildings as soon as possible." Everyone nodded and turned to their tasks.

Wiggins dived under the table, and, heart thumping, twisted onto his back and tried his utmost to focus his concentration on the device. Perhaps two and a half minutes left. '*No time to think only to act,*' he thought. From under the tablecloth, he could hear the noise of exiting footsteps and the low rumble of worried voices. Satisfied that everyone was on their way he returned his attention to the device and without further thought, grasped the wires in one hand, closed his eyes, thought of Mary, and ripped them asunder from the box. The single hand on the clock face stopped. Wiggins sighed with relief, adrenalin thundering through his body. Suddenly the clock hand started to silently tick again. An icy chill submerged him. "Damn!" he cursed. The face of Jem Pyke suddenly appeared next to his. "We need to get out now Bert, everyone's either safe or on their way out. Let's go!" Pyke felt a tug at his trouser leg. He looked down. "Billy, get outta here now lad!"

"I came to help, Jem," explained Billy looking nervously at the clock face. "It's gonna blow ain't it?" Wiggins leapt up, grabbed Billy, and ran full pelt for the door. "Come on, Jem. Run!" he shouted. Looking behind him, he could see Jem Pyke standing in the middle of the room as if calming himself. "Get out now, Jem!" screamed Wiggins as he surged through the doorway into the cold afternoon air. As he glanced over his shoulder the last he saw of Jem Pyke was of him turning on his heels and racing towards the rest rooms.

'*Noreen!*' thought Pyke. '*Noreen and Mary!*' Pyke looked after the fleeing Wiggins and satisfied that he and Billy were on their way to safety, exploded into a sprint through the doors leading towards the rest rooms, plucking his hat from a nearby hat stand as he did so. His knees were pumping high and blindingly fast as he charged through the anteroom and sped along the corridor leading to the rest rooms.

Wiggins pushed Billy as far in front of himself as he could and the two of them dived forward as a ferocious blast struck them in the back. The suddenly released energy sucked the air around them inwards towards the building, the resultant vacuum instantly replaced by lung scorching heat that seared their clothes and hair. Shards of glass and fragments of timber exploded into the air. Both he and Billy tumbled to a halt on hard, skin-grazing paving slabs. Wiggins turned, gasping for air, and looked around him, anxiously scanning the devastation all around. Clouds of smoke were billowing from the palace out into the courtyard. He could see the milling shapes of people, staggering around, supporting each other. Bloodied and battered, some lay prone on the ground whilst others attended to them. He was conscious of having been deafened, sounds were muted and distant as if his head were under water. The acrid smell of cordite lay heavily in the air. He stood staggeringly and lifted Billy who was picking tiny pieces of glass from his hands and face whilst shouting something at Wiggins that was barely audible. He located Lady Constance Harkness, bending over the prone body of what appeared to be an elderly gentleman who was in obvious distress with what appeared to be two broken wrists. It was then he abruptly realised that he could not see Mary. His eyes darted frantically from one group of people to the next searching for his beloved wife, all the time silently yelling her name. '*Where was she? Where had he seen her last?*' His heart was beating frantically. His stomach lurched, his head hammered, and his memory was as vague as an evening shadow. Then Doctor Watson was in front of him, blood pouring from an open wound on his forehead, grabbing his collar and mouthing the words "Mary and Jem. Where are they?"

Wiggins turned his attention to the massive smoking hole that was now where part of the external wall of Buckingham Palace had been. There were prone, gravely injured bodies strewn everywhere. He shook his head and ran towards the huge smouldering void that had spewed forth masonry and glass just minutes before. Just then a second enormous blast flung him backwards, hurling him through the air like a rag doll, colliding with a nearby water fountain. Obscurely, he noted the VR insignias on the ornately painted cast iron fixture and wondered what the Great Empress would have made of this outrageous carnage. He pushed his pain-ravaged body up and although he could hear nothing at all now, he shouted to everyone to clear the area even further, conscious that there may be the possibility of further explosions to come. Everything played out in silent slow-motion.

A third blast blew a hole the size of a horse-drawn omnibus in the Palace wall thirty feet from the first cavernous cavity. Blocks of masonry hurtled through the air like medieval cannonballs, crashing amongst the already devastated crowds, shattering bone and crushing bodies. The scene resembled some bloody medieval battlefield.

'*Mary! Where is my Mary?*' Panic and fear coursed through his veins. All he genuinely cared for was his treasured Mary. He heard a scream and quickly realised that it was his own voice, his hearing returning to his bleeding ears. Wiggins was confused, exhausted and badly bruised as he crumpled unceremoniously backwards and fell upon his backside. Minutes had passed, or was it only seconds? He could hear screams of pain and the baying of panic and fear. He felt a gentle tug on his coattails and whirled around hoping expectantly to see his wife but was faced with a tear-stained Billy pointing eagerly at the gaping maw that had been blasted out of the side of the palace. An indistinct but identifiably human shape was emerging from the dense plumes of smoke. Flames roared behind the oncoming figure as windowpanes popped from the blistering heat and spat forth splinters of glass. The shadowy shape slowly walked towards escape through the billowing smoke and tumbling rubble. Wiggins recognised the ghost standing in front of him. Jem Pyke lifted his head, his bloodied face and bloodshot eyes met those of his friend. His ripped shirt smouldered, and embers trailed smoke from his charred tweed jacket. In his arms, he carried the limp form of a woman. A woman dressed in the remains of a smouldering emerald green ball gown.

Wiggins' felt his heart explode as he looked upon the prone figure in his friend's unshaking arms. No words were necessary between the two men, their eyes locked together in a wordless exchange. Pyke extended his arms and offered the limp form to Wiggins. He nodded his confirmation at his friend's unspoken question and gently placed Mary into her husband's outstretched arms. Wiggins' tear-filled eyes looked from Mary to Pyke and back to Mary again. His breathing was convulsed, panting to get air into his lungs.

"How? How in Hell did you … get out?"

"They wouldn't dare have me in Hell. Not today," Pyke grunted. He remained standing, his imposing figure silhouetted against the inferno behind him. Wiggins could see that Mary breathed and he could feel a faint pulse of life trickling through her body. His gaze now fixed upon the lifeless, red-rimmed eyes of Jem Pyke, whose upper lipped curled and trembled into a snarl baring his teeth. Wiggins was conscious of Watson taking Mary from him and fervently treating her on the pavement, trying to revive her into consciousness. Wiggins held Pyke's stare. "Noreen? What of Noreen? Was she with Mary? We must get her man!" he made to push past Pyke who halted him with a solid ramrod palm.

Pyke looked towards the ground. "There ain't nuthin' left to get, Bert. Nuthin' left at all."

"And what size is the lucky lady's finger, might I enquire?" asked the fawning Jewish jeweller as he carefully held the emerald engagement ring, its gold clasp and band shining under the beam of his magnifying head lamp.

"The size don't particularly matter, Abe," replied an emotionless Pyke, his square chin set as hard as he could possibly make it. "Just put it on a chain long enough to fit around me neck."

Chapter 29 - The Pain

They sat together in the parlour of Pyke's house in Gravel Lane. "Every bone I ever broke, every cut I ever had, they all healed, Bert. You only need to look at my face and hands to see that. This is a cut that will never heal, a bone that will never set." Pyke looked abstractly into the open fire, seeing nothing in the flames but the twists and waves of Noreen's auburn hair. Wiggins sipped his brandy and bit his lip, for once unable to readily conjure words that would console his friend. He too was entranced by the flames dancing in the hearth. A log crackled and spat a glowing ember onto the hearthstone.

Pyke stared at the ember as it burned, fizzled, and then died. He pinched the bridge of his oft broken nose as if to staunch his grief. He imagined Noreen sweeping the hearthstone and jokingly admonishing him for his lack of home management skills. "How did you manage before I came along, Jem Pyke? This house must have looked like a pigsty," she would say in that lilting Irish accent of hers, a half-smile playing across her freckled face. He could almost see the twinkle in her greyish green eyes.

Pyke was beginning to realise that those few minutes at the Palace had turned his life upside down and inside out in a matter of seconds. Realisation of how fragile life can be bombarded his thoughts. His future now lay ruined and shattered, his hopes and dreams snatched cruelly away from him by some unknown attacker. A lunatic bomber or, perhaps, a planned Irish raid, no matter which. For what was far from the first time that day, he felt an almost uncontrollable rage well up inside him. It coursed through him like a fast-acting poison. Wiggins could see that hatred manifest itself within Pyke. He had seen it on many occasions. The intensity of his eyes, the involuntary grinding of his teeth causing his jaw muscles to twitch and spasm, and the sweat beading on his furrowed forehead. "We will get him, Jem. We will get them. Whoever perpetrated this cowardly atrocity will be brought to justice. Our justice. I promise you that." Wiggins drained his brandy glass.

Pyke looked at Wiggins. "My justice, Bert. He will be brought to *my* justice." The words were understated yet forceful. Wiggins could feel the determination and intent in Pyke's voice. This was no idle threat, nor hopeful wish. This was a statement of absolute fact. A need for vengeance. The right for vengeance.

Pyke lifted the bottle from the floor beside his chair and recharged each of their glasses. He looked again at the fire, envisioning now the aftermath of the blast. The feeling of scalding heat that had burned at his skin and scorched his clothes, the accompanying wind that had thrown bodies to the ground indiscriminately and shred clothes from their charring bodies. The visions of that day had been burned into his conscious, so profoundly, that they had etched a deep-rooted pain within him. A pain unlike any other he had experienced. A pain that he could not begin to understand how to cope with.

Pyke drew on the brandy, savouring its sharpness, determined that it would soon cloud his mind and bring temporary oblivion from his torture. He thought of the plans he had. Plans that would now never be fulfilled. Proposing to Noreen on their bench on Hampstead Heath. Plans of getting married. How she would have loved it. The two of them running the Hoop and Grapes, but a short stroll from their front door, or another such hostelry. Raising Billy as their own and raising a family in a better time and a better place. All these plans now obliterated by the lighting of fuses and the ticking of a clock. An act perpetrated with what he could only imagine had been no thought as to the carnage and destruction that would ensue. Noreen had wanted a sister for Billy, a sibling to be proud of and to care for, but that dream had been blown explosively asunder at the Palace. What should have been his proudest moment had tragically turned into his worst nightmare. A nightmare he would be destined to relive over and over, day after day. He felt as if he would never recover from this. He felt cursed.

"You get yourself home, Bert." Pyke waved towards the door. "The hour is late, and Mary will be worrying about you. She's been through a dreadful ordeal and will most probably in a state of shock. Go and tend to your lovely wife, my friend."

"Not at all, Jem. I can stay if you like. Mary will understand. Lily is sitting with her. If not for you, she would not be waiting for me at home all. The doctors said it was a miracle that she survived with only a mild concussion, a punctured eardrum, and some minor abrasions and burns. It was your quick thinking and bravery that saved her, Jem. I can never thank you enough. There are no words that can capture my gratitude." Wiggins felt a sudden pang of guilt at what he realised may be the inappropriateness of his remarks. Pyke drained his third generous glass of brandy and was feeling lightheaded and slightly drunk. A measure of spirits in Jem Pyke's parlour was liberal, to say the least. One had to have a steady hand to raise the glass to one's lips, so full was it poured.

Pyke shook his head. "I'm only too glad that she rallies and is safe and well at home, Bert." He thought idly for a moment, still staring at the dancing fire, its amber light licking shadows across his hewn face. "Me and Billy will be all right. I'll just sit here a while. Get yourself home, Bert. Give Mary a kiss from me."

"If it were not for you, old friend, I would not have a wife to kiss," emphasised Wiggins, placing a hand upon Pyke's shoulder as he stood. "I cannot thank you enough."

Pyke looked up at him and smiled. He nodded towards the door. "Get home, Bert. I ain't going to tell you again."

Wiggins again clutched at Pyke's shoulder as he cast a consoling nod towards Billy who sat, red and bleary-eyed, at the parlour table. Pyke looked at the slumped figure of Billy. "Thanks for staying awhile, Bert."

A solitary candle backlit the half-empty bottle of blended malt that had replaced the now emptied brandy. Pyke stared drunkenly at it, straining to focus on the dancing fire he could see reflected through his glass. The glowing orange flame reflections reminded him of the searing inferno that had vanquished his attempts to reach Noreen. His beloved flame-haired Noreen engulfed in flames, blown to bits. His body shuddered at the memory. He had been so close to her when the second explosion struck, blasting his body ferociously away from her, his outstretched arms grasping desperately for her as he was thrown violently against a wall. The heat had been so extreme that when he had attempted to reach her, his eyebrows and moustache had been singed almost completely off, and his clothes had burned and smoked with glowing embers. Pyke struggled to recollect how he had found Mary Wiggins. If not for the fact that he had been informed by several people who had witnessed him appear from the ravaged building carrying her to safety, he would not have known that he had been responsible for her salvation at all.

He tried vainly to shake the horrific images that haunted his every thought. The whisky was the only prescription that seemed to work. The only remedy that allowed sleep to engulf him. He gulped back another mouthful and awaited blessed unconsciousness. Pyke had not yet shed tears. Indeed, he had not yet begun to properly mourn. How could he conceivably mourn before he could avenge her murder? He had made a solemn promise to himself and Billy that this was to be the final bottle, the final drink before he began his quest to wreak his vengeance upon whoever was responsible for taking Noreen from him. Then, and only then, could he begin to grieve.

Billy sat waiting quietly, his head occasionally nodding as he tried defiantly to thwart slumber, wanting only to be there when his hero eventually fell asleep.

Chapter 30 - The Burial

Three figures stood side by side with heads bowed. They were soaked through, their clothes clinging uncomfortably to their skins, as the rain battered down upon a gloomy, miserable afternoon. Pyke and Wiggins stood either side of Billy, Pyke's steadying arm draped around the boy's slumped, juddering shoulders. The trio stood in silence as the Priest began a short funeral homily, punctuated only by Billy's intermittent sobbing and the occasional cawing of a nearby crow. They stood in Tower Hamlets cemetery wherein Pyke had purchased a burial plot when he had been promoted to Sergeant several years earlier. He had reasoned that, with an increased workload, came increased danger and a higher likelihood of being killed in the line of his duties. He had wanted his house to be in order. Today, however, the plot had been opened to bury his love, Noreen Redman.

The Palace and Scotland Yard had decreed that Noreen should receive full police honours and a formal burial, but Pyke had refused. He knew 'Red' would not have wanted any fuss. Pyke had wanted only his adopted son, Billy, and his colleague and friend, Albert Wiggins to be present at the service. There had been only four individuals of importance to him in his life and now two of them, his mother and Noreen, were gone.

The Priest began the committal. "God our Father, Your power brings us to birth, Your providence guides our lives, and by Your command, we return to dust. Lord, those who die still live in your presence, their lives change but do not end. I pray in hope for my family, relatives and friends, and for all the dead known to you alone. In company with Christ, who died and now lives, may they rejoice in your kingdom, where all our tears are wiped away. Unite us together again in one family, to sing Your praise forever and ever."

Pyke attempted to block out the Priest's words and endeavoured to remain stiff upper lipped. He looked towards the sky, rain battering down upon his face, welcoming its cleansing sting, trying to remain strong. Wiggins listened intently to the committal service, studying each word and nuance of the priest's phrasing. Billy simply stood in a stunned indeterminate state wherein all his senses were jumbled, his shoulders convulsing with a deep-throated sob that he was unable to control. It was the first funeral he had ever attended. Pyke handed Billy an extra handkerchief he had specifically brought along. The handkerchief had belonged to his late father and was initialled in light blue thread. He remembered his Uncle Ted handing it to him at his father's funeral. Wiggins clandestinely wiped a solitary teardrop from his cheek. He patted Pyke's back three times to show him that he was there for him, as always. The coffin was lowered slowly into the grave by two civic gardeners who had volunteered their services to help as pallbearers.

"For as much as it has pleased Almighty God to take out of this world the soul of Noreen Redman, we, therefore, commit her body to the ground, earth to earth, ashes to ashes, dust to dust, looking for that blessed hope when the Lord Himself shall descend from heaven with a shout, with the voice of the archangel, and with the trumpet of God, and the dead in Christ shall rise first. Then we which are alive and remain shall be caught up together with them in the clouds to meet the Lord in the air, and so shall we ever be with the Lord, wherefore comfort ye one another with these words. Amen."

Pyke threw a single red rose into the grave and holding Billy's hand tightly, turned and began to leave the scene before any earth was administered upon the coffin. Wiggins circumnavigated the grave and thanked the Priest, palming him a note, before turning to catch up with the two departing mourners.

"Why does it always rain at funerals, dad?" asked a heartbroken Billy as they walked away from the graveside.

"Well you see, its Heaven shedding tears for our loss and letting us know that God shares in our sadness, lad," replied Pyke holding together his emotions stoically.

Sniffling, Billy looked up through reddened eyes at Pyke. "Does that mean Noreen is with God then?"

"Of course, it does lad, Noreen will no doubt already be telling the big fella' to trim his beard and whiskers and to wear proper clothes instead of that tablecloth he favours," intoned Pyke in a vain attempt to lighten the mood.

"God would look just like old Doctor Watson then," chuckled Billy guiltily.

Jacob Snipe wiped the rain from the small lens of his Eastman Kodak box brownie camera with the cuff of his sleeve. He muttered to himself as he did so, "Why does it always rain at bleedin' funerals?" He peered back into the camera and cursed that the lens was clouded with condensation. Snipe was positioned surreptitiously behind a large and forgiving yew tree which provided ideal cover for his tasteless mission. Snipe had been operating as a freelance photographer for over twenty years. He was generally considered among the fourth estate as a bottom feeder, the lowest of the low. However, 'Gutter' Snipe, as the more respectable members of the Fleet Street Press referred to him, had a reputation for getting results, for obtaining photographs that no one else seemed capable of, or brave enough, to capture. Rumour had it that he had even once captured The Ripper on film, although the rumour was one most likely to have been created by Snipe himself.

Snipe had pushed up the shutter lever twice in quick succession when he saw Sergeant Pyke dropping the rose onto the coffin. He smiled a rattish sneer, '*I could write me own headline for this one,*' he thought. The trio of mourners was moving from the graveside as Snipe frantically grasped the opportunity to take some last few photographs. As he did so he felt a strident tap upon his left shoulder. His heart sank as he realised that he had been caught. He turned around slowly, hoping that he would see a Priest, a Curate or even a gravedigger. '*These religious types are usually easy to buy off,*' he thought hopefully to himself. He was sorely disappointed.

Before him stood the magnificently moustachioed Doctor John Hamish Watson, smartly attired in mourning black, a sprig of white heather garnishing his buttonhole. Although not formally invited, the veteran adventurer had felt duty-bound to attend and had been watching the internment ceremony from a suitably secluded spot. "And what have we here?" he inquired, looking from the camera to the weasel-like face of its owner. "Jacob Snipe, up to no good as always I see. What do you have to say for yourself?"

Snipe became even shiftier and frantically tried to conceal his camera under the folds of his greatcoat. "Only tryin' to earn an 'onest crust, Doctor. You know me, the soul of discretion I am."

"Attempting to profit from the misfortunes of others, more likely," observed Watson, stroking his whiskers. "I will take possession of the camera roll, Snipe, if you don't mind." Watson's voice was low yet forceful as he held his open hand out towards the photographer. Over Snipe's shoulder, he could see Pyke, Wiggins and Billy approaching the car that would transport them from the great necropolis.

"Not bleedin' likely, old man. That's me bloomin' livelihood that is," protested the lowlife journalist. Watson quickly grabbed at the brownie, snatching it from Snipe's grasp, tossed it into the air, and with a single, well-timed swing with his hound headed, ebony cane, smashed the little camera a full twenty yards into the shrubbery. Snipe shrieked, "What have you done? Me camera!"

Watson seemed not to notice the despicable little man's protestations. "Batted number three for Middlesex at Lords, don't you know? Hah! You never forget how!" he chuckled. Snipe was now on his knees crying into his hands. Watson caught a glimpse of Billy and Pyke getting into the rear seat of the sedan whilst Wiggins held the door open for them. He could see the Chief Inspector looking directly at him. Wiggins had obviously detected the fracas and raised his hat slightly in a thankful salute to Watson who in turn acknowledged the detective with his own salute.

Watson pulled Snipe to his feet, the journalist's knees now covered in mud and clinging, rotting leaves. "I suggest that you retrieve what is left of your infernal device and scuttle off back to whatever sewer pipe you crawled from. And if I see any photographs of this occasion in the scandal sheets, I shall be placing a copy directly under Sergeant Jem Pyke's nose along with a little note confirming where he can find the photographer." Snipe scampered off in search of his camera.

"Old man, indeed! If only he'd just handed me the camera roll, he would still have his equipment, how unfortunate," harrumphed Watson as he pulled on his lapels and strode off whistling the strains of Sweet Afton.

The tragedy at the Palace caused an uproar throughout London, and indeed the Kingdom. The Press were outraged and brought into question the competence, not only of the Metropolitan Police, but also the ability of the Armed Forces to keep the peace, and the Government to govern. "Palace bomb carnage! Over twenty dead! Attempt on the life of the King!" rang the clarion from every newsvendor on every corner in the City.

The clamour was such that Commissioner Gregson was ordered to face a press conference on the steps of Scotland Yard. "Less a conference, more a shooting gallery," he would say afterwards. At Gregson's side stood the stately figure of Lord Edward Grey and behind them, Superintendent Gideon Thorne and Detective Chief Inspector Wiggins. Also, in attendance was the Palace Chief of Staff, Herbert Joseph. Voices were raised, and tempers flared whilst flashbulbs flashed, cameras clicked, and pencils scratched the quickest shorthand. Before Gregson could begin his carefully written and rehearsed statement, the hounds of Fleet Street were upon him like a pack of rabid dock dogs. "Was this an attempt on the King's life? Was the King injured? Is the King Dead?"

"His Majesty was unharmed thanks to the prompt action of his staff under the direct guidance of the Metropolitan Police," answered Gregson in calm and measured tones. Before he could expand on his reply a barrage of other questions hit him like a steam locomotive.

"Who did this? Who is responsible?" asked one.

"Was it the Irish rebels?" demanded another.

"Surely Anarchists!" shouted yet another desperate to be heard over the rabble.

"Nihilists! Foreign bombers! War is coming I tell ya! War is coming!" boomed another reporter, eager to be heard.

"Could be a lone wolf. Another maniac to plague our streets like the Beast!" declared another voice from the mob.

Gregson looked to Grey for assistance, but the Statesman merely coughed into his hand and nodded that the Commissioner should respond. "We are pursuing several differing lines of enquiry and have not ruled out any of the aforementioned as the suspected source of this heinous attack upon our Society." Gregson felt inwardly pleased with his answer but somehow knew that worse was to come. The avid throng moved closer to the group lined up on the uppermost step of the Yard's East entrance. Wiggins could feel the tension. He felt a mob mentality beginning to develop and began to feel uneasy.

"What are you doing about it?" demanded a tall rangy, red-headed reporter. "Why are you all standin' 'ere when you should be hunting these anarchists?"

"Is this a campaign? Are there more targets? The public has the right to know!" bellowed a smaller, stocky newshound.

Thorne took a step forward, his bulky solidity almost pushing Gregson aside. "I can assure you, gentlemen, that every avenue will be pursued. No stone will be left unturned in our search for the culprits. No one does this in *my* City!"

Laughter coursed through the crowd. "Your City?" came a desultory voice. "This ain't your City! It is *our* City. Who are you anyway?"

"Some big-headed Northerner down to tell us how to do things, I've heard!" slammed the small stocky reporter. His taller, freckle-faced colleague slapped him on the back. "That told him, Spence! Bleedin big head."

At that Thorne bristled. His teeth clenched as did his fists. "I will see you, gentlemen, later," he boomed indicating the redhead and the little bullish journalist. The crowd was now in an uproar. Both Wiggins and Gregson raised their hands to try and convey order, but Thorne's last statement had only poured petrol on the fire. The mob of journalists surged forward as if to engulf the official representation.

Out of the corner of his eye, Wiggins saw the sash of the second-floor turret window slide upwards. A single gunshot rang out overhead. Everyone turned towards the sound, the crowd momentarily silenced, halted mid-step. A wave of relief swept through Wiggins. All eyes were focused on the brown suited figure wearing a derby hat, who now sat on the windowsill, heels kicking the brickwork, pistol in hand. '*Pyke,*' thanked Wiggins under his breath.

Pyke began in the loudest voice he could muster. "It may not be *his* City, but it sure as Hell is *mine*! You all know who I am. God knows I've pulled most of your sorry arses out of scrapes in the past, so I don't need no introduction. Now these fine gentlemen here have answered your questions and assured you that we will do everything we can to bring these bastards to justice. Believe me, neither I, nor any of my colleagues will rest until those responsible for the deaths of these innocent people are seen hanging from the highest gibbet in the Land. I don't care if they're Irish, German or from the bleedin' Moon. You have my promise. They will feel *my* rage. Now, you've all got your story. Get back to your desks and your typewriters and write your words before I lose me temper and direct that rage at you! As God is my witness, you would not wish that fate upon any man!"

A rumble trickled through the crowd. First a few, then more, then the rest turned and reluctantly made their way slowly back to their respective offices.

Chapter 31 - The Plea

He had lurched into The Hole less than an hour before and already the unbranded bottle of whisky that sat on the ring-stained table before him was half empty. No one had given a second glance to the hunched, broad-backed drunk dressed in a pea jacket with its collar pulled tightly up. To them, the stranger was merely another anonymous roughneck docker looking to drink away his coin in Limehouse's most downtrodden bar room. The Well, or the Hole as it was more commonly known, was the favoured haunt of the Dockland's most hardened drinkers. No one came here to socialise. Few talked to each other. Here gathered the alcoholics, lost souls, and those to whom fate had dealt an unforgiving hand. Here there was no life other than losing one's memory in a sea of liquor.

Rainwater had dripped from the pulled down peak of his cap as he had ordered the bottle. He had picked a single booth in the darkest recess of the room. He did not want to be recognised. He craved anonymity and quiet oblivion.

He lifted the glass to his lips, threw the stinging spirit down his throat, and poured an immediate refill. There were no rules in The Hole. Most drinkers were solitary, lost in their thoughts in what was the alcoholic equivalent of a Chinese Opium Den, each drinker occupied with their tragic past or their non-existent future, each encapsulated in a fog of alcohol.

He lifted his head and scanned the room with half-opened, red-rimmed eyes. He recognised a few faces. Inky John, a dipsomaniac, one-time printer whose sallow, liverish face stared into a void from which he saw no escape. Alf Sandalwood, a hopeless inebriate addicted to cheap women and even cheaper gin sat alone with his thoughts as company. Heaped on the floor by the bar lay the bulky figure of 'Scotch' Bob, named as much for his consumption of whisky as for his nation of birth. The unsavoury pool of liquid in which he lay turned Pyke's stomach. He reached for the bottle and unsteadily poured another measure. Before he could lift the glass to his lips, he felt an overwhelming urge to lay his head on the tabletop.

He was awakened by the rasping of stool legs across a stone floor followed by a peremptory sigh and a heavily accented voice. "And what brings Mr Jem Pyke to the Hole? I heard you rattled a few cages down Fleet Street yesterday, Jem." The bleached white smile of Spanish Jack flashed at Pyke. When Jack smiled his ivory dentures clamped together resembling two rows of uneven piano keys, one clenched upon the other. The Spaniard had once told Pyke that the false teeth had been fashioned from the ivory of a narwhal horn, a tale which Pyke regarded with some doubt as to its veracity. Jack was a well-built but supple looking man with deeply pockmarked burnished skin, and like all who frequented The Hole, a hopeless drunkard.

"To drink, Jack. Why else would I be here?" answered Pyke. His words were slurred, his heavy-lidded eyes empty.

Jack hesitated slightly before answering, taking the opportunity to swallow back a finger of unidentifiable spirit. "The last righteous man who walked through these doors was a fire and brimstone preacher who ranted about Sodom and Gomorrah. Called us rapers of women, drunkards and brigands. He was right of course, couldn't have been closer to the truth in fact. A den of the Lost this is, and all here know it. Where else would they be otherwise? There is no absolution to be found here. Drink is our religion."

Pyke nodded slowly, taking another slug of his whisky. "And the preacher? What happened to him?"

Jack nodded to a forlorn figure hanging onto the corner of the bar. "See the walking corpse drooling at the end of the bar? That dog collar was burned within an hour of him setting foot in here. That's what 'appens to righteous men here, my friend. I think it best you go home."

"I got a pain I need to drink away, Jack." Pyke confronted the Spaniard with a ramrod stare, defying him to respond.

Jack leant back and raised his hands in mock surrender. "Who am I to argue with the great Jem Pyke? Perhaps I should just step aside and let you join the fold, brother." Once again, he hesitated before continuing, taking time to pick his words carefully from the fugue of his clouded mind. "All I know is that Red would have dragged your arse out of here, amigo, and kicked it all the way home."

Pyke rose slowly, supporting himself with one hand on the table. Jack could see murder in his eyes and instinctively shrank backwards. Pyke lurched, his shoulder hitting the wall. He looked at his shoes, then at the near-empty bottle, and then at the trembling Spaniard. He remembered his oath to Billy, an oath he had already broken. Jack smiled his widest narwhal filled grin in the hope of appeasement. He could tell his life hung in the balance. Pyke broke the tense silence. "You're right, Jack." He stumbled past the nervously grinning drunkard, squeezing his shoulder in appreciation as he did so. Jack winced as the iron-like grip squeezed his shoulder.

Pyke stumbled out into the street. He lifted his face to the heavens, impervious to the rain that lashed down upon him. He looked at the doom-laden greyness of the sky and raged at the unjust God who had taken away his Love.

"There's no difference that I can see between looking after you and tending to Mr Heap," stuttered an emotional and somewhat embarrassed Billy Skew. "I cleans the place. I feeds you, tidies up after you, makes sure there's a warm house for you to come home to." He tried to suppress the tears of frustration he could feel welling up in his eyes. "At least Mr Heap paid me a shilling now and then for the privilege."

Jem Pyke was slumped, semi-unconscious in his favourite battered chair, socks off and feet stinking up the room. He had stumbled home that night just as he had done for each of the three days since Noreen's funeral. Billy continued his tear-stained soliloquy. "I hardly ever sees you, Dad," he lamented. "You're up and out before I get out of bed and you comes home late and almost always drunk. The only time I see you is when I'm struggling to get you to bed and even then, you don't really see me." Pyke's snoring was a low rumbling sound that seemed to reverberate around the room. Billy continued his one-sided conversation. "Life was good before ... well, before what happened at the King's palace." Billy swallowed hard. He was finding it difficult to continue, such was the gaping hole he felt at the loss of Noreen. He looked at Pyke slumped in the fireside armchair and sniffed, wiping away the salty trail from his cheeks. He found it hard to accept the scene before him, such was his love and respect for Jem Pyke.

"You ain't the same person you were when Noreen was here." Billy's voice now took on a stout forcefulness that he himself did not recognise. "I miss her too you know! You ain't the only one who is hurting." Billy could feel his grief turn to a wave of disdainful anger. "Noreen was like a mum to me and I only had her for a short while, but it was the best time I ever had."

He remembered her smile most of all. No one had ever smiled at him the way that Noreen had. Her emerald eyes would shine, and her nose would wrinkle, making her freckles dance. He knew that smile was only for him. A secret smile. He remembered how she would hug him and rock him from side to side, telling him tales of Irish giants, mermaids and saintly heroes, fearless warriors and wise old kings. He remembered her laugh, a raucous boom that would fill any room and infect all who heard it. A joyous laugh without boundaries. She had never mistreated him, never made him feel inadequate. Told him that she was proud of him. No one had ever said such things to him. He looked forlornly at Pyke, thinking of those stories. "You were both my heroes," he whispered to himself.

Billy wiped his crooked nose and looked forlornly at his surrogate father. He stared at what Jem Pyke had become. He was disconsolate. He saw a drunkard, interested only in his work, and slaking his unquenchable thirst. His skin had become greyer over the last three days and he seemed more lined and haggard than he had before the tragedy at the Palace. It was as if the bomb had blown the life from Jem Pyke just as it had ripped apart that of Red Noreen. He was not, in Billy's eyes, the strong presence he had once been. He was somehow diminished, emptier, and less caring. There was no longer that mischievous twinkle in his eyes, no lopsided grin, no funny faces pulled. His chin remained unshaven, not through choice but from apathy. He looked somehow older than his thirty-eight years and his eyes had become soulless and devoid of emotion. Jem Pyke very rarely became angry these days. Billy sensed that he was merely functioning.

As Pyke continued to sleep, Billy tidied away the nearly finished whisky bottle and emptied the ashtray into the hearth. "I know you can't hear me but I'm going to leave you here tonight Dad. I don't have the energy to drag you up to bed anymore. I'm tired, sick and tired of looking after you." The young boy dragged himself forlornly upstairs to bed and was asleep the instant his head hit the pillow. There would be no sweet dreams for Billy Skew. Jem Pyke opened one eye and proceeded to hold his shaking head in his hands. He now realised that of all human emotions, self-pity was the most unattractive.

Dawn broke the next morning to the sound of the costermonger's wagons trundling their steel-rimmed wheels across the cobbles of Gravel Lane towards Petticoat Market.

"Rise and shine Billy, here's your breakfast." The curtains were swished back, and the boy's bedroom filled with early morning sunshine. Billy rubbed his disbelieving eyes. He imagined that he must be having some glorious dream. "C'mon me lad, it's a blinding morning and you don't want your cuppa char going cold now do you?" Standing before Billy's sleep encrusted eyes was a clean-shaven Jem Pyke, hair slicked back with Macassar oil, holding a tray boasting two soft-boiled eggs, six toasted soldiers and a steaming hot cup of tea with three sugars.

"Milky and sweet, just the way you likes it, Billy. Set you up for the day, this will, lad," enthused Pyke. Billy rubbed his eyes again and looked, propped up on his elbows, not upon some glorious dream, but something far, far better. He knew instantly that Jem was back. Pyke had somehow managed to turn back the clock in a few short hours and pull himself away from the abyss that had threatened to destroy him. Once again, he looked alive, vital, and energised.

Amidst the long, dark night of the soul that he had endured, Jem Pyke had remembered something his old army officer, Lieutenant Partridge had said to him after a particularly gruelling skirmish on the South African Veldt. "The true measure of a man, son, can only be seen when he is in the Pit. It's how you drag yourself back from your lowest ebb that shows the World exactly who you are." Pyke had truly understood those words the previous night.

"You've got your twinkle back, dad!" enthused Billy leaping from his bed to hug Pyke, enwrapping him in the smell of cotton nightshirt and new-found optimism.

Somehow Pyke managed to keep the contents of the tray from spilling onto the carpet. "It never went away lad, it was just a bit less bright because it was unhappy. I was dwelling on what I once had instead of cherishing what I now *have*. Grief will do that to a body, lad." Billy remained clasped tightly around Pyke, not wanting the moment to end. "C'mon now, let's get these soldiers dunked before they catch a cold."

Billy whistled merrily as he made his way up Middlesex Street towards Petticoat Lane market. The day had been a good one. Not only had Jem awoken him with his favourite breakfast of boiled eggs, toasted soldiers and milky sweet tea, but his school day had been cut short due to Miss Winter having been mysteriously unavailable for the last lesson. Billy enjoyed school but like any young lad, he relished the occasional day off, especially the last lesson of the day. Every day at Sir John Cass School in the grounds of nearby Saint Botolph's Church in Aldgate, was like an adventure to the former guttersnipe. In a short matter of months, his world had expanded from the confines of Grimley's Abattoir and his enslaved indenture to The Heap, to a seemingly limitless fount of knowledge from which he could quench his thirst for learning. Billy had become absorbed in geography and history. He now realised that the World extended far beyond the reaches of the downtrodden pit of East London. He struggled with mathematics and rudimentary science, his mind unable to make numerical connections, but he revelled in images of faraway lands and ancient battles. Soldiers and heroes, civilisations and conquerors. Caesar and Alexander, Nelson and Wellington, Drake and Raleigh. He dreamt of heroism on the high seas or the battlefield like his dad. Most of all he had found that he loved to read. The startling novels of Jules Verne and H.G. Wells captivated his attention and sent his imagination spiralling to heights and worlds he would have previously thought unimaginable. The historical tales of Alexander Dumas and the strange stories of Robert Louis Stephenson excited Billy and transported him places, where good triumphed over evil and heroism, was invariably victorious. As he sauntered along the street he pulled a half-detached twig from a pavement-side plane tree and swished it to and fro, lunging and parrying, one moment imagining himself to be the intrepid d'Artagnan, then next the Jacobite stalwart Alan Breck slashing at the air.

Billy had decided to bypass the Pyke household on Gravel Lane and take a short detour through the Market in Spitalfields. He continued to whistle his way past the

Queen's Head public house, its shining green ceramic tiles reflecting a quivering, distended image of himself that always fascinated and tickled him. He enjoyed roaming through the market, trading playful insults with stallholders, all of whom knew young Billy Skew, or rather Billy Pyke, Jem's lad, as some now called him. He chewed the fat with Jim the Clock who sold second-hand watches and bric-a-brac. He pulled faces with Nick the Hat, a bull-necked, tattooed ex-sailor who boasted that there was no item of headgear beyond his supply. Straw boater or Red Indian headdress, Nick the Hat could get his hands on them all. Billy dodged his way through the thronging crowds, tipping an imaginary hat at Polly the shoelace girl and stopping to roll playfully with Cobbler, the eternally cheerful, one-eyed bulldog belonging to Charlie Chubb, self-proclaimed 'purveyor of quality footwear to the great and the good.' Charlie only kept left shoes on display, their partners securely boxed up out of reach under his trestle table. "Ain't no one goin' to steal just one shoe now, is there?" he would say.

Yes, today was one of life's good days and Billy was happy. The air seemed clearer than yesterday, the sky brighter and not so low, and the sun much, much warmer. He chose to eventually turn for home, deciding that it was time he got back to prepare Jem's supper. He was just remembering how it had felt to be hugged by Noreen when he felt a powerful arm encircle him from behind. Billy struggled and kicked backwards with his heels, the way Jem had shown him. A growl of pain from his attacker was followed by a huge, rough hand forcing a damp handkerchief over his mouth and nose. Billy fell into limp unconsciousness almost instantly.

"Glass of ginger ale for me please, Lottie," requested Pyke. The silence which accompanied his statement bordered on deafening. It spread amongst the clientele in The Grapes who, as one, became momentarily motionless, their glasses held aloft in mid-drink between table and lips. The boisterous atmosphere had abruptly segued into a staggered hush, all eyes firmly locked upon Pyke who stood nonchalantly at the bar, enjoying the moment. He had noticed the reaction of the pub clientele reflected in the long mirror behind the bar and smiled with satisfaction. The landlady, her floral-patterned apron stretched too tightly across her protesting bosom, peered at him with a questioning look. "Please don't make me have to say that again, Lottie," winked Pyke feigning a mock heart attack.

"Right you are, Sergeant Pyke, a glass of Schweppes finest ginger for you. You want ice with it darling?" inquired the landlady.

"Let's not go too far now, Lottie," replied Pyke raising his glass in a toasting salute to the reflected faces of the patrons. Some raised their glasses in perfunctory shock before the silence was eventually broken and they returned to their revelries. The symphony of dockside chatter resumed, and Jem Pyke's new-found sobriety seemed already to be yesterday's news.

"Jem, please tell me this is some prank to test me old ticker?" pleaded Lottie. Charlotte Higgins, a small, robust woman with a pugnacious face, had taken over the running of The Grapes following the brutal demise of Mary Hallbard at the hands of the murderous Doctor Joseph Bleak. "My takings will be halved if you insist on such abstinence," she joked, scratching behind her ear rapidly as would a mangy dog. She reached for her clay pipe from under the folds of her straining apron.

"Best you lower your standards of living then love," laughed the detective. "From henceforth I shall only be partaking of the grape and the grain when the situation merits it."

"My pocket is indeed sad to hear this Sergeant, but my heart is gladdened. Now ... let's not dwell any further on the matter, what I can do for you?" asked the redoubtable Lottie.

"No there's nuthin' Lottie, I just fancied a drink on me way home. Don't expect me tonight or any other, unless of course, it is on official duty. I've time to make up for and a life to sort, and besides, I've got dinner to get home to. Me and Billy have decided we're gonna take it in turns to prepare supper, and it's his turn tonight," stated Pyke, swigging his ginger ale and turning to leave. The landlady smiled. "I can just about cope with a drop in earnings Jem but whose gonna control this unruly rabble when trouble erupts?" she intoned, gesturing imploringly towards her customers.

"You always know where to get me, Lottie." He retrieved his Derby from the coat stand and put it atop his head at a jaunty angle. He winked at the landlady and gave the battered old piano sitting in the corner a loving tap as he exited the Grapes with a token wave of his hand.

Chapter 32 - The Abattoir

Billy had awoken with a splutter and a headache that felt as if Bow Bells were ringing within his skull. It had taken him a few moments to regain his senses and he began to look around him. His heart sank as he realised where he was. The passage of time had blurred how rancid and vile smelling the abattoir was. Even though he had spent most of his young life there, Billy did not recall the odour as having been quite as bilious. Hideous memories came flooding back in a reeking tide that was accompanied by a dreadful foreboding of what now lay ahead of him.

He felt sick to his stomach now he had found himself back in the only place, other than the Pyke household, that he had ever regarded as a home. This thought filled him with despair. He now knew what life could be like outside of this hell hole and he feared that he may have lost that life and that, in time, he would forget what the real world was really like. He feared that he would sink once more among the filth and servitude of the abattoir and its vile owner.

It had only been an hour since he had awoken and already, he was filthy, his skin and fingernails blackened with the blood and grease that seemed to hang in the air. The oily smell of fat and the retch-inducing smell of excrement pervaded the atmosphere. The stench, of course, was always at its most revolting when he was near the Heap. The Heap, the monstrous proprietor of Grimley's International Abattoir was master of all he surveyed. An enormously corpulent giant who presided from his makeshift, railway sleeper throne, over the most notoriously filthy slaughterhouse in all of Smithfield. For years he had sat in the same grim corner of the tannery gorging himself on the Shambles' product. This was where Billy had spent the greatest part of his childhood, in squalid servitude to the obese mass that was the Heap.

Billy looked forlornly at the Heap. He baulked at the human leviathan's grotesque gorging and his even more deplorable physical hygiene. The Heap's repulsively bloated lips were smeared with fat and his chin dripped with some indecipherable liquid. Billy could feel that his hair was oily and matted, no doubt where the Heap had rubbed it with his fat, filthy, faecal smeared hands whilst Billy had been unconscious earlier. Billy felt nauseous. The Heap's enormous bench sat in a pool of disgusting fluid. It was impossible to distinguish where blood ended, and bodily waste began. Billy rubbed at his left ankle which was bound by a manacle chained to the rearmost wall of the concrete bunker where the Heap kept court. The obese slaughterman sat there day after day, blasting out orders whilst perched upon the riveted iron bench atop a robust construction of railway sleepers and scaffold boards.

"I'm so glad you came back to us young Mr Skew," rumbled the Heap, rolls of blubbery chin fat trembling as he spoke. "We have indeed missed you. My personal hygiene has not been what it was since you were last in attendance Billy, me lad. I've missed your attentive services. Wasn't looking after myself as best I could, you understand. Heartbroken at your absence, you might say," he offered, with a wink of a small beady eye. Billy's stomach lurched in disgust. "I need you to ... take care of me, you might say," the Heap leered.

Billy shivered, repulsed by the Heap's insinuation, but decided to stand up for himself. He felt sure that it was only a matter of time before Jem would come to his rescue. He knew that Jem would figure out where he was. '*He is a policeman after all.*' At that, a thought jumped into his head. He reached into the depths of his trouser pockets and felt the reassuring hardness of the King's coin. He felt reassured. "I didn't *come back* as you state Mr Heap. I awoke with no memory of how I came to be here! Drugged I was. By one of your tanners, no doubt," barked an emotional Billy, anger rising in his skinny breast.

Billy could see a hunched old man shambling back and forth among the tanning pits. The man busied himself picking up mutton bones and other random skeletal remains and placed them in an industrial bone grinder. The Heap had been pocketing the money he made from selling the ground bone meal as fertiliser to Sussex farmers for several years. The old man raised his head and looked directly at Billy. For a moment they exchange a glance. There was no emotion in the man's mongoloid eyes. No doubt whatever humanity had resided within him had been crushed by relentless servitude enforced upon him by The Heap. Billy could see that he was a lost soul and recognised his former self in the pitiful wretch. Billy shook his head in despair.

"Not at all, Billy," chuckled The Heap with a dismissive wave of a bloated hand. "As I told you when you awoke, we were simply lucky, me lad. Archie, there, just happened to be passing when he found you all collapsed and such. All in a little heap, one might say! In Middlesex Street, you were! Passed out you were, and nobody even batting an eyelid nor lifting a helping hand to your predicament. A disgrace upon the supposedly good people of this city of ours, I say. Didn't I say so, Archie?"

The ogreish Archibald Stone nodded his slab of a head. "Spark out he was, Mr Heap. Just like you say." He grinned a toothless smile at Billy and lumbered off to tend to his guard dogs. The Heap shifted his weight from one enormous buttock to the other. "It looks to me as if that good for nothing drunken oaf, Leslie Pyke, has been neglecting you, me lad. More than likely you collapsed due to starvation and weakness due to him drinking all his money and pissing it up against a urinal wall in some God-forsaken back street alehouse, I shouldn't wonder."

"It ain't like that at all, Mr Heap, *Sir,*" interrupted Billy angrily, placing a sarcastic emphasis on the Sir. He tried separately to hold back the tears of frustration and fury that were welling up in his eyes. "Dad's changed so he has, and for the better. He's off the sauce and looking after me right and proper."

"Dad is it?" bellowed The Heap, his walrus-like chin trembling as he roared with laughter. He looked around the company of tanners, busy at their filthy tasks. "Dad, it is, lads! Do you hear? We have little Billy Pyke now!" The men jeered and laughed. Billy felt as if he wanted to kill each, and every one of them. Throw them in the tanning pits and watch them drown in shit. Or watch as their bodies were mangled in the jaws of the bone grinding machine. How he wished Jem was here. '*They wouldn't be laughing if he were here. They would all be shitting themselves.*'

"Well he wasn't looking after you, was he now? You were found lying unconscious in the blasted street, weak and wasted you were! No meat on your scrawny little bones. You'll never starve in Grimley's International Abattoir me lad I can assure you of that. Meat a' plenty here. I'll looks after you, always have, haven't I?" oozed The Heap.

"Why have you chained me to the wall then?" demanded Billy pointedly. "I feel no better than one of Archie's dogs."

"Oh, that's merely for your own safety, Billy me lad." The Heap looked surreptitiously in all directions before lowering his booming voice to a mere whisper. "There's lots of unsavoury characters around Smithfield Market I can tell you. This way, I know that you're safe from any, how should I say, meddling? Any fiddling about, you might say. Why, only last week Irish Bob's young lad was abducted. Vanished into thin air, only a little wooden toy left on the poor lad's pillow. Bereft was old Bob! Poor lad. Trust me, I will look after you right and proper, Billy me lad. Protect you. A roof over your head, plentiful meat, and the exercise of regular work. Now, let us hear no more on the subject. Can you sluice the top of me buttock crease with that mopping brush of yours, Billy? It stings something awful with the meat sweats from me lunchtime exertions, there's a good lad now." Just as Billy dipped the makeshift brush reluctantly into the pale of scummy water The Heap broke wind. Billy wretched uncontrollably at the vile, burnt rubber stench which engulfed him, and involuntarily vomited what little stomach contents he had onto the bloody, concrete floor.

"Hey, hey! Don't be sick near me food now Billy, you'd only have to wash down the meat before I eat it, and I don't want you having to do any needless tasks. Like I say, I look after you, always have and always will." Billy wiped his mouth with the back of his hand which merely served to make him look all the grubbier and more pathetic. '*Surely he'll be here soon. He must have guessed where I am by now. He is a detective after all!*'

Just then came the unmistakable barking and snarling of the slaughterhouse's two Rottweiler guard dogs. "What the? Get into your room at once, Billy, something's rattled those dogs make no mistake. Get in and lock the door behind you and stay put until I shout for you. Go, now!" ordered the Heap, obviously worried that some harm may befall his young gift horse. Billy reluctantly heaved up the chains tethering his leg and scurried as best he could the twenty or so yards to the rearmost wall of the chamber. Billy's room was no more than a tiny concrete enclave with an infested straw bed. A notch had been cut into the door of the enclave to accommodate the chains attached to the manacle tethering Billy's ankle. He sat in the little hovel, hugging his knees close to his chest. Even here, he could hear the Rottweilers manic barking and could imagine them straining at their leashes, frothing from their ugly black lips. He could also hear The Heap barking out orders. A knowing smile played across Billy's skewed face. "You took your sweet time," he said to himself.

Chapter 33 - The Fight

"You want me to put my fist through your face? Again?" spat a furious Jem Pyke through gritted teeth at the man now barring his passage into Grimley's slaughterhouse. Archibald Stone winced at the recollection of the pain he had endured during the detective's previous visit when Pyke had swiftly removed the watchman's last remaining teeth with a thunderous right cross to the jaw. The ogreish Stone rubbed his jutting chin at the memory. Pyke had an uncanny ability to twist his fist at the precise moment of impact, a punching technique which caused maximum damage to his opponent whilst decreasing the chance of fracturing any bones himself. Jem Pyke's trademark punch, known throughout London's fighting fraternity as Jem's Gem. It was a technique taught to Pyke many years before by an old boxer by the name of Geordie McPhee.

"No way Jem, you're free to enter without any interference from me. Just don't tell The Heap I stood aside," pleaded a lisping, and obviously nervous Stone as he clumsily unchained and opened the gates into the yard.

"Wise decision, Stonesy," whispered Pyke menacingly out the side of his mouth as he breezed past the lumbering watchman. "I take it he is here?"

"Don't know what you mean, Sergeant Pyke. Honest I don't," mumbled Stones looking at the dusty toe ends of his boots. That downwards glance betrayed Stone and told Pyke everything he needed to know.

Pyke rolled his shoulders and swaggered confidently across the foreyard of Grimley's towards the slaughterhouse. He was unaccompanied and had intentionally withheld information of his whereabouts from his colleagues. He saw this as a private matter. What he needed to do today, he would do alone. He wanted no rules, no restrictions and nobody to stand in his way, not today. Two vicious Rottweilers, desperately straining at their chained neck restraints, their paws frantically pawing at the dusty ground, barked, and snarled ferociously at the approaching detective as he strode unconcernedly across the yard. He did not as much as flinch as he passed the two barking dogs. Pyke leaned forward, bared his teeth, and snarled back at the dogs. The hounds went berserk.

Grimley's Slaughterhouse was widely recognised as the most revolting shit hole in all of Smithfield, if not the entire City of London. Cow and pig carcasses hung from row upon row of iron meat hooks and blood pooled onto the concrete floor due to its single drainage point being blocked with congealed blood and putrid flesh. Raw hides, scraped of rotting skin and fur, were draped over rope lines allowing them to dry before being soaked in pits filled with a steaming gravy of water, human urine and dog faeces. This concoction, used to remove the lime and soften the hides, was responsible for giving the abattoir its distinctive, stomach-wrenching fragrance.

Pyke, however, seemed impervious to the rancid stench of the abattoir as he continued purposefully across the foyer and burst his way through the inner door into the building's main processing area. His mind was filled with anger. Anger at the brutal death of Noreen, and anger at the abduction of Billy. His rage was apoplectic, and someone would feel its fire.

A group of butchers and tanners ceased their grisly chores and looked on in startled amazement at the sight of a furious Jem Pyke heading uncompromisingly for the concrete bunker where he knew The Heap would be. After all, the Heap rarely, if ever, moved very far from his scoff trough and toilet, which were, in practice, one and the same. All the workmen knew of Pyke's fearsome reputation and no man, even those armed with the tools of their trade, cleavers and tanning hooks, was brave or foolish enough to be the first to attempt to bar his progress. Each of them seemed to sense the intensity that throbbed through the Detective. Pyke came to a halt and stood motionless with his hands at his sides, his huge fists clenched powerfully in obvious rage, blood pumping through pronounced blue veins. He looked around him and called for The Heap. "Heap! Get your enormous arse out here you child-snatching scum!"

From the darkness ahead, emerged an amorphic mass of pale dimpled flesh. A corpulent arm that glistened with an oily sheen of perspiration, filth, and bloodstains, reached out of the murk. It moved like some grossly engorged maggot until a blubbery, fat hand became visible and pulled on the cord of an overhead light that dimly illuminated the sickening sight of The Heap in all his naked ugliness. His grossly oversized head was now visible, large cheek flaps giving it the appearance of a dominant and aged orangutan. Pyke's unwavering eyes met those of The Heap which were bloodshot, beady, and tremored incessantly from side to side, each pupil seemingly with a mind and agenda of its own. An ocular Saint Vitus dance.

"Where is he, you ugly fat bastard?" growled Pyke, struggling to maintain his composure. The tanners shifted nervously around him, wondering if they should attack. Only fear of Pyke held them back.

The Heap shrugged his shoulders. "Good afternoon, Leslie," came his strident reply. The Heap's voice was deep and resonant with an air of erudite authority. "You don't mind if I call you *Leslie*, do you? It is your name after all. The name I knew you by all those years ago."

"I have no time for this shit Heap, or should that be Buster? Now, where is my boy?" Pyke roared, spit spraying in anger from his mouth. "I know you have him here, you sadistic lump of lard." Pyke shot a warning look at two undecisive tanners who were edging towards him. Each stayed their hands. "Don't place no reliance on these boys, Buster. Their arses are twitching like a rabbit's nose."

The Heap laughed a deep guttural laugh and clapped his enormous hands together in applause. Hands that displayed no knuckles of any description, only deep depressions where knuckles should be. "And why would I need to, Leslie? I am after all The Heap, am I not? And the lad is my boy! Always has been and always will be," came the throaty reply.

"You miserable pile of shit! One final time, where is my Billy?" thundered Pyke taking a threatening step forward.

"I have no idea where he is. Why should I, Jem? He deserted me…" The smile on The Heap's face seemed to chill the marrow in Jem Pyke's veins.

"That's rich coming from you! You deserted your fellow soldiers when they needed you most, you worthless piece of humanity. Lance Corporal Buster Hepworth. Coward! That's what I'll put on your tombstone," snorted Pyke in disgust. "The man with a yellow streak running from his neck to his enormous saggy arse!" Anger burned wildly in Pyke's eyes. "The morning of the fifteenth of February 1900 when you fled like a chicken from a cleaver and abandoned your brothers in arms. Or have you forgotten? You were one cowardly bastard Buster, and I'd wager that you still are, you rantallion piece of shit."

The mongoloid old man stopped sluicing fluid, leant on his mop, and looked from Pyke to The Heap and back again, his interest sparked. The tanners looked from one to another, shocked at what they had heard.

"Now, now Leslie. Your language leaves a lot to be desired especially for younger ears, and besides, that was a long time ago. Water under the bridge, old boy," offered the Heap, sweat running into his tiny bloodshot eyes. Eyes that sat above drooping puffy bags tinged blue due to poor blood supply.

'*I should just shoot him now, end this charade and be done with it,' thought Pyke. 'One bullet in the forehead, quick and easy.*' He gritted his teeth together and rejected the temptation to reach immediately for his pistol. '*Too many witnesses.*' He decided to continue his shaming of the Heap, reading the disquiet in the room. "You could have made a difference! One life! Just one! If you had saved just one fucking life in Kimberley…" Pyke remembered the mist that day, a mixture of rifle smoke and artillery shells and dust from the cavalry division's charge. He remembered leading that charge on the besieged town of Kimberley during the Boer War with his brave comrades, sabre grasped in hand, and a rifle strapped to his back, the dry, hot wind rushing towards him, burning his grit infested eyes. He remembered the trumpeting of the bugles, how it had resonated in his ears and fuelled his adrenalin.

"You've gone all misty-eyed and nostalgic on me, Leslie. You want my towel to wipe those little tears of yours? You always did rather wear your heart on your sleeve, old boy," taunted the Heap whilst offering Pyke a tattered and badly soiled blanket. He looked towards his men, expecting smiles or laughter. He was met with a stony silence. He could sense their loyalty diluting, their allegiance shifting.

Pyke's lip twitched imperceptibly as he reached for his pistol. He withdrew it slowly from its concealed shoulder holster. He raised the gun steadily and aimed it directly at the centre of The Heap's forehead. He could hear the sound of metal hitting concrete as, behind him, the tanners dropped their tools and scattered for the exit. "I should have done this thirteen years ago when I saw your yellow streaked back disappearing from the battlefield." He closed one eye and aimed his pistol at The Heap's massive forehead.

"Now, now, let's not be too hasty, Sergeant Pyke." The Heap's bulbous double chin was now quivering. His mind was racing, trying to produce a solution that would stop Pyke pulling the trigger. He felt exposed, unprotected. He stumbled upon an idea. "I have a proposition that I suspect you may appreciate," he stuttered, his eyes continuing their incessant flickering.

"The only thing you have of interest to me is my lad. Hand him over now and I may yet spare your wretched, pissy life," hissed Pyke, still pointing his pistol towards the heavily breathing bulk in front of him. He slowly cocked the gun.

The Heap continued, a note of heightened desperation in his voice. "You don't want to shoot me, Jem. Remember our fight in ninety-nine? The Royal Artillery heavyweight championship? It was the year that the great, undefeated Jem Pyke was finally bested, and if I'm not mistaken, your one and only such defeat. Well, that you admit to that is," baited the Heap. He shifted slightly causing folds of fat to roll like the ebbing tide. Pyke fleetingly recalled the memory of the fight with both disgust and regret. "Yes, I do remember that bout. I'm hardly likely to forget it. I ain't never took so many low punches, thumbings and head butts. You are a dirty bastard now and you were a dirty bastard then."

The Heap ignored the taunt. "Well, my proposition is that you should be afforded the opportunity to avenge your only defeat ... and the winner keeps the boy." He smiled revealing severely stained and crooked teeth, the front two missing entirely.

"And who exactly is to be my opponent in this fight?" asked Pyke somewhat confused. He was still considering pulling the trigger.

"Why, me of course, Leslie," laughed the Heap uproariously. He tore the last remnant of meat from a leg of lamb with his teeth and tossed the stripped bone aside. "I beat you once and I shall best you again."

"Proposition accepted!" declared Pyke without hesitation. "There's nothing I'd like better than to tan your fat hide." Pyke clicked the safety catch of his pistol and returned it to its holster. He carefully removed his Derby and hung it on a nearby unencumbered meat hook, taking care not to damage its Brunswick green silk lining. He looked around him, weighing up the attitude of the tanners that had remained and decided that they were interested, attracted by the prospect of the fight. He also sensed that they could be turned against The Heap. Pyke's talk of cowardice seemed to be sitting uncomfortably amongst their number. He concentrated on his breathing, staying relaxed, knowing full well that panicking during any fight scenario reduced one's ability to gauge one's surroundings and employ effective offensive and defensive strategies. Spatial awareness was paramount in hand-to-hand combat. "The calmer you are, the more you'll see coming," Jawbone Crabtree would say.

Pyke removed his jacket and waistcoat and hung them on the same hook as his hat. He loosened his collar, exposing his bull-like neck and rolled up his shirt sleeves. He watched as The Heap heaved his enormous mass up from his bench, air and gas escaping as he did so. The squelching noises emanating from the folds and creases of his huge bulk were sickeningly unpleasant. His chronically bowed legs were almost hidden by the hanging apron of belly flesh which dangled almost to the floor. Pyke stood five feet ten inches tall, but The Heap towered above the shorter man by at least another six inches. Pyke looked past the lumbering figure of the Heap and spotted the makeshift cell that he realised must contain Billy.

He shouted in the direction of the cell. "Stand fast, Billy! This shouldn't take too long. I'll be with you in a few minutes." Billy smiled his lopsided smile.

The Heap threw his head back and roared with laughter. "Your confidence is impressive though misplaced, my friend."

Pyke snorted a wordless rebuff, stood on his toes and danced the peculiar, preparatory dance which is the want of boxers. Should any other person perform such a dance they would look comical, but for a boxer, it is the same as breathing, a natural, subconscious reflex. A preamble to battle. Foreplay to fighting. The Heap stood unmoving, looking immovable. The two men eyed each other. '*The kidneys,*' thought Pyke. '*My only hope is his kidneys.*' Pyke clashed his fists together and with a lightning dart towards his opponent, delivered two ferocious right hooks to the Heap's left side. As he did so, his earlier encounter with Hercules Chin sprang into his mind. Pain shuddered through his knuckles causing Pyke to instantaneously retreat, all the while on his toes, whilst the Heap merely laughed in disdain. Pyke could smell an atrophic stench created by the blows he had just administered. The sickening, incomparably musky odour of neglect, faeces and sweat.

"Is that it? Is that the best the legendary Jem Pyke can do? A tickle on me back?" questioned a wide-eyed Heap who raised his flabby arms and waved his hands beckoningly towards Pyke. "Come on, Jem. Bring old Heap some sugar. Where's this legendary *Jem's Gem* that I've heard so much about?" The remaining tanners smacked their meat hooks against the walls creating a drumbeat of encouragement. Some urged on The Heap, others called for Pyke.

The detective snorted again and danced around the Heap's flailing arms and administered two stinging left hooks to the same kidneys then whirled back in front of his adversary, who this time visibly winced at the impact. Instinctively, The Heap retaliated. A massive arm shot out, surprisingly quickly and a fist the size of a five-gallon pale so narrowly missed connecting with Pyke's ducking head, that he felt it whisp through his hair. Pyke lurched in close and somehow managed to bypass the folds of protecting blubberous flesh and once again struck at the most vulnerable part of any boxer, of any man. The pain that racked through The Heap was excruciating. A pain that felt like he had been electrocuted, as if his blood was turning to acid and racing through his body like a poison.

"Plenty more where that came from, Buster!" spat Pyke sensing The Heap's pain. "I could prolong this charade and pummel you for hours if needs be. I could do with the practice. Or you can tell me where my boy is!"

The Heap launched an unexpected burst of speed for a behemoth of his stature. He leapt at Pyke in an attempt to smother him, but Pyke's nimbleness of foot enabled him to evade the attack and at the same time he thrust a thundering left cross to the temple of his attacker, instantly stunning him. The Heap's enormous head flew to one side, sweat whiplashing from his brow, saliva spewing forth from his mouth.

The Heap took a step or two backwards, buying time, trying to recover from the blow. "He's my boy, Leslie!" he taunted. "Hasn't he told you of the things we used to do together, Daddy dearest? Would make a whore blush it would!"

Pyke exploded. A red mist descended. A furious barrage of combination punches battered home to the head of the Heap, instantly cracking the bridge of his nose, and opening a sickening laceration above his right eye. A recipe of sweat, blood and grime sprayed Pyke's face in pathetic retaliation. A chopping right cross administered with Pyke's elbow was followed swiftly by a stinging series of jabs before a huge left uppercut snapped the Heap's head back with a nauseating crunch. As The Heap's head bounced forwards again, the now apoplectic Pyke hammered upwards at his opponent's nose with the heel of his open palm and rammed The Heap's nose into his skull. Cartilage fragments splintered out of his eye sockets followed by geysers of blood. The fat man's legs buckled, and he slid to the ground like some huge melted candle. Pyke could not hear the shouts of protestation from the tanners behind him, nor feel their attempts to hold him back. The Heap had become the sole target of his hatred. The hatred of the faceless bomber who had blown his love to pieces and the hatred of the man before him, the abuser of his son. He pummelled ferociously at the limp figure in front of him until the massed efforts of half a dozen butchers finally hauled him away from the seemingly lifeless Heap.

"Where is my fucking boy you worthless piece of shit?" demanded Pyke through gritted teeth, as the tanners continued to strenuously hold him back from inflicting further onslaught on the Heap.

"He is here, Jem," came the rumbling reply from behind. Archibald Stones stood, key in hand, with an arm wrapped around Billy's shoulders.

"Don't hit 'im no more, Dad," pleaded a tearful Billy. "You'll kill 'im!"

Pyke rushed to Billy and hugged him tightly. "Of course, I won't son. Are you all right? Did he hurt you?"

"No. He didn't hurt me. I'm all right." Billy returned Pyke's embrace, tears running down his cheeks. He looked over Pyke's shoulder towards the unmoving Heap. Several men, including Stones, were gathered over him. Noises of concern were mumbled, and hands were on heads. The Heap lay motionless among the throng, his forehead resting on the filthy concrete floor.

Pyke began to feel sanity begin to ebb back through him. His eyes met those of the small mongoloid man. The cleaner looked scared, wary of this violent man. He looked at his feet, his body trembling, his mind struggling to process what he had just witnessed. Pyke felt empty, ashamed. He made towards the group gathered around the fallen Heap. Archie Stones turned towards his approach. "He's alive, Jem. Just, I reckon," confirmed the ogreish yard guard. "You'd best be on your way, Jem. I've sent one of the lads for old Doc Durdle. He's just down the road from here." Stones threw a forlorn look at The Heap and then pulled Pyke away from the scene. "I'll make sure he lives, Jem," Stone's voice was conspiratorial but confident. "Doc Durdle will get him sorted as best he can with the hospital, and me and the lads will keep it quiet. No need for you to worry, Guvnor. We all know what you've been through, what with Red n'all." Stones' eyes stared at his shoes as he mentioned Noreen, unable to look Pyke in the eye. "We know n'all what The Heap was like. What he made Billy do. No one here blames you for what you did to him. Lucky to be alive he is, that's what I says."

Pyke nodded his appreciation, his face still grim. "Thanks. Stonesy. You're a good man when it comes down to it. I'll see you straight, I promise."

Pyke returned to Billy. "The lads here are going to make sure everything is taken care of. Let's go home, son."

Billy drew the shiny King's guinea from the depths of his pocket. He held it up to Jem and smiled, "I didn't even 'ave to use me Royal Penny."

"Let's get you home and cleaned up." Pyke ruffled the boy's grubby hair and wondered at his son's resilience.

It was the day after the incident at Grimley's abattoir. "Why, of course, I can!" beamed an exuberant Doctor Watson. "I'm sure that Miss Newbiggin's Home for Special Cases will be more than happy to accept young Jonathon here as a new resident." Watson continued as he lit his pipe. "All sorts of things to do for a sharp young man like Jonny here. There is the learning of letters and maybe even numbers, working in the garden, home-making, little building projects and the like. I am sure he will enjoy it immensely."

The red-headed Jonathan was happier than he had ever been. He realised that he now faced a future that would not consist of endlessly sluicing the floor of Grimley's abattoir. He smiled the broadest smile Pyke had ever seen, his mongoloid eyes sparkling with unfettered joy. The little man threw an awkward salute. "Thank you, Captain Pyke!" he proudly shouted. "Thank you, Captain Billy!" Inexplicably everyone was a Captain in Jonathon's mind.

"And thank you, Captain Watson," added Pyke with a grateful nod of his head. "Another life salvaged." Watson took an appreciative puff of his pipe and chuckled his satisfaction at a job well done.

Jonathon spent the remaining few years of his life at Newbiggin's Home for Special Cases. He particularly enjoyed the garden, planting and raising vegetables. He revelled in Miss Newbiggin's weekly field trips that included the museum with the bones of long-dead creatures that fired his often-dormant imagination, the frightening wax museum, and of course, the Zoo in Regent's Park. He particularly loved the giraffes, rejoicing gleefully in their sheer height and loquacious elegance.

Pyke had persuaded Wiggins to engage the Yard's legal team to transfer the deeds of the slaughterhouse from the permanently brain-damaged and blind Buster Hepworth to the deserving, genial Archibald Stones. Under Stone's stewardship, and with the generous financial support of a mysterious benefactor, the abattoir had been transformed from the foulest cesspit in Smithfields to the most hygienic and efficient meat-house in London. The introduction of state-of-the-art machinery, automated sluicing facilities and forward-thinking processes ensured that Grimley's future looked as bright as its newly tiled walls. Such was its prominence that Stone's introduced monthly open days when, for a modest price, the public could tour the facility, wondering at the futuristic machinery and efficiency of a modern factory. Of course, Jonathon convinced a doubtful Miss Newbiggin to allow him to pay a visit. He delighted in the automatic cleaning system that he knew meant that no one would ever have to endure the hell that he had at Grimley's. He also persuaded the good Miss Newbiggin to allow him to view the additional attraction on offer at Grimley's. Within the side yard of the Works, a small, candy-striped circus tent had been erected, and for an additional shilling, the public could view the popular freakshow that was billed, *The 'Heap' - London's Fattest Man*. Within, sat on his reinforced throne of railway sleepers, was the enormous bulk of the former master of Grimley's, his near-naked, gargantuan frame quivering in endless folds of fat as he shoved endless portions of boiled chicken into his slavering maw. The brain-damaged and blinded Heap, blissfully unaware of anything around him, was a huge, though macabre attraction. Jonathon was particularly fascinated by the Giant's new glass eyes, one a brilliant absinthe green, the other as white as virgin snow.

Chapter 34 - The Equerry

He dreamt of her hair. Dark red silken waves upon white cotton pillows. A deep auburn tangle cascading over an alabaster-pale shoulder. He could smell her scent, fresh and fruitful tinged with an underlying earthiness. He buried his face in the lush thickness of her tresses, breathing in that scent, revelling in the feel of her, lost to any world outside of that embrace. He inhaled deeply and shifted himself to be even closer to her. To engulf himself in her. He was aware of a heart-wrenching sense of loss and tears forming in his eyes. He heard a voice.

"Call for you from a Mr Howe, Sarge," announced Nosher Ash prodding a drowsy Pyke on his shoulder. Pyke had been dozing, his feet kicked up on his desk, ankles crossed with his ever-present Derby tipped low over his eyes.

"Who?" asked Pyke groggily, startled out his slumber. He felt a slight resentment at Ash for having shattered his dream with an abrupt recall into reality.

"No, not *who*!" grinned the ursine Ash, "*Howe*, Sarge. *Mr Howe*. Says he knows you."

Pyke removed his hat, shook the sleepiness from his head and wiped embryonic tears from the corners of his eyes. He coughed and straightened. "I know him all right. One of me top narks. Did he say why he was calling?"

Ash smiled again, his eyes narrowed to slits of mirth. "Yes, Jem," he struggled to catch his breath and choked back a rising laugh. "Mr *Howe* did say, *why*." By now the big desk sergeant was finding it difficult to suppress his laughter at the absurdity of the conversation. "He says he reckons he's spotted your man."

"Which man? Not Pullar?" asked Pyke jumping to his feet and eagerly pulling on his hound's tooth jacket.

"Please, Sarge, no more," pleaded Ash, his florid face becoming redder with mirth. "Howe, who, why, which! I can't take no more, Jem." Ash's roaring laugh bellowed around the incident room like the noise of a rumbling avalanche. Pyke shook his head and waited impatiently for the desk sergeant to regain his composure and the power of coherent speech. "Yes, the missing Palace equerry, Jem. Tobias Pullar. This Mr Howe reckons he has eyes on Pullar right now."

The Yard's lines of enquiry to the bombing at Buckingham Palace had been multi-stranded. Foreign nihilist organisations, already under investigation, had been heavily infiltrated and key members rounded up and interrogated. The more high-profile members of the provisional Irish campaign had also been questioned and many of their known foot soldiers summarily incarcerated without charge. However, the Met's most positive trail sat closer to home. Their investigations had revealed that one member of the Palace staff, present on the day of the bombing, had failed to return to work. All other employees had been accounted for, those who had unfortunately perished as a result of the explosion and those who were still recovering from their injuries, whether in Guy's Hospital or indeed convalescing at home. The individual who had become the Yard's main suspect was a junior Equerry named Tobias Pullar. Both Wiggins and Pyke were convinced that Pullar would prove to be their man, and Pyke had put every official and unofficial means at his disposal at the heel of the hunt for the absconded Equerry.

Ash continued. "Somewhere called The Monocle Club he says. I ain't never heard of it, I must say." Ash scratched at his head.

"I wouldn't expect you to have, Nosh," winked Pyke. "It's a club for bob tails, mate. Problem is that it's a moveable feast, never in the same place for more than a couple of nights for fear of our intervention. Is he still on the line?"

"No, Jem. But he gave me the address. He said he would meet you in the alley around the back of the place in fifteen minutes." Ash handed over a piece of notepaper. Pyke scanned it briefly before scrunching it into a ball and throwing it into the wastepaper basket under his desk. "Just off Greek Street. I can be there in ten minutes. Tell Murray and Bunce to meet me there."

"Bunce ain't due in for another hour Sarge, but Murray is just behind you. What about the Guvnor? I think, given the circumstances that he should know." A brief silence hovered between the two men. "Of course, Nosh. Tell him I'm on me way," shouted Pyke, the door of the incident room slamming shut behind his exit. Murray looked inquisitively at Ash who nodded in the direction of Pyke. "Best be after him lad, no telling what he might do."

Pyke raced down the steps of Scotland Yard entrance two at a time and nearly toppled over an approaching DCI Wiggins. Wiggins stumbled backwards at the impact and found himself feeling strangely intimidated at the obvious strength and solidity of Pyke's physique.

"And where are you off to in such haste, Sergeant?" enquired Wiggins, straightening his tie.

"One of my narks says he's just spotted Puller, Guv. Me and Murray here are on our way to pick him up," answered Pyke with a nod in the direction of the trailing constable.

Wiggins evaluated the situation instantly. "You are to stay here, Sergeant Pyke. I will accompany Constable Murray," he pronounced authoritatively. "Who is the informant and how has he identified the suspect?"

"Don't' you start, Guv, I've just gone through all that rigmarole with old Nosher in there," replied an exasperated Pyke who was straining at the leash to get to Greek Street. Murray sniggered behind a cough and a covering hand. "I have to get there in ten minutes and meet Mr Howe at the rear entrance of the Monocle Club." Murray stifled another incoming fit of laughter. Wiggins raised a questioning eyebrow, whilst Pyke elbowed Murray a touch too strongly in the ribcage.

"I insist that you stay here, Jem. I am conscious of your intimate involvement in this affair and I fear for the repercussions should you encounter our suspect outside of a controlled environment," stated Wiggins emphatically.

Pyke bristled, his jaw extended. "And what of you, Sir? Are you not also intimately involved?" The two colleagues exchanged a fixed stare, which seemed to the on-looking Murray, to last an uncomfortable age.

"I am sorry, Jem, but I must insist," reinforced Wiggins. "Now tell me who the informant is and the location of the rendezvous."

"Mr Howe, the Monocle Club, rear entrance, alley off Greek Street," relented Pyke reluctantly. "Murray here knows the exact address."

"And how will I recognise this Mr Howe?" enquired Wiggins.

"Oh, you'll recognise him all right. Just think *question mark*. Ain't no coincidence his given name is Howe." Pyke stamped back up the steps and through the Yard's double doors, fuming at missing the opportunity of apprehending Pullar.

"Back so soon, Sarge?" asked a curious Ash. Pyke glared at Ash, his temper apparent to all, and brushed wordlessly past the big desk sergeant. He rumbled some incoherent oath, and violently slammed the door of the incident room behind him. Ash could hear what sounded suspiciously like a boot hitting a panelled wall.

Wiggins' staff car edged its way slowly along the narrow seediness of Greek Street. The rain was lashing at an invasive angle and a brutal wind blew in the Soho night. "There, Sir!" announced Murray, pointing to a shadow enshrouded alleyway no wider than two men.

"Stop here, Sykes," ordered Wiggins, tapping the driver on the shoulder. "Wait here for us. This shouldn't take too long."

"Right you are, Sir," responded Sykes.

Wiggins and Murray entered the narrow alleyway in single file, Wiggins in front. Gradually their eyes adjusted to the dimness of the tiny cobbled passageway, stacked as it was with boxes and beer barrels, litter and abandoned bottle crates. Human detritus also populated the alley. Wiggins could make out at least two blanket-covered forms lying motionless, almost unseen, huddled on the cold wet ground.

Slowly, from out of the shadows, emerged a curiously stooped and angular figure. A singular spectacle indeed. As the figure moved awkwardly towards him, Wiggins immediately realised what Pyke had meant when he had referred to a question mark. The individual who approached through the gloom was that of an impossibly thin and bony man. His legs and pelvic region preceded the rest of his body as he walked. His lower torso leant backwards to a seemingly unfeasible degree then curved forward to the extent that his neck extruded horizontally, and his gaunt face looked permanently downwards towards his feet. His spine was curiously both scoliotic and kyphotic. Wiggins flinched at the extent of the disability he saw before him, recognising its cause as being some chronic spinal condition, possibly a birth anomaly. The figure shuffled flat-footedly towards the two policemen, its arachnoid arms each hanging limply at its sides. Wiggins could see that each shambling step was an agony for the poor afflicted fellow. The unfortunate advanced in a shuffling motion, his sodden shoe soles never leaving the cobbles until finally he was standing virtually toe to toe with Wiggins. So close was the man that Wiggins could smell the reek of poverty emanating from the greasy, thinning hair that sparsely covered his head.

"You ain't Sergeant Pyke," croaked the figure. "Always wears brown does Sergeant Pyke. Boots or brogues, but always brown." A hacking cough broke from the figure in front of Wiggins, a hard bullet of blood veined phlegm hit the wet cobbles next to the Inspector's black patent leather shoes. "And who might you be?"

Wiggins took an involuntary half step backwards and turned his head slightly from the malodorous wretch. "I am Detective Chief Inspector Wiggins of CID Scotland Yard and this is Detective Constable Murray," explained Wiggins flashing his warrant card briefly under the informant's nose. "I take it that you are Mr Howe?"

"That's what they calls me, on account of me shape you see." Howe sniffed and wiped a ragged sleeve across his hive ridden nose. "Do I still get me ten shillings? Jem always gives me my ten shillings," hacked Howe.

"Of course," confirmed Wiggins, reaching into his waistcoat pocket. He brought out the coins and placed them in the outstretched claw-like hand of Mr Howe. Wiggins exchanged a brief glance with Murray, communicating their mutual disbelief at the sight of the unfortunate Mr Howe. "I believe you have some information for us as regards the Palace Bomber."

Howe bit one of the coins and placed them in a pocket. "I do indeed," he acknowledged." The man who planted the bomb sits within, Inspector," declared Mr Howe, painfully indicating towards the Monocle Club with his scrawny hand.

"And how do you know this?" enquired a now dubious Wiggins.

"I heard him boasting about it here in the alley, Sir. He was…" the derelict hesitated. "He was, how can I put it, Sir? …servicing two young men just behind those rubbish bins yonder. Boasting he was, as he did it. Saying how he put one of the bombs under a long table. Saying as how he got paid fifty pounds n'all."

Wiggins nodded, confident in the knowledge that only the bomber would be aware of the precise placement of the devices. He looked at Mr Howe. "And how can you describe this man to us, given your rather unfortunate affliction, Sir."

"Sir, he calls me!" Howe laughed a harsh, throat-cracking cackle. "Been a long time since anyone called me Sir." He tried vainly to lift his head an inch or so to catch a glimpse of this police officer before him. "Red shoes, Sir. The man you are looking for wears red shoes. Most uncommon that is. Laced cross fashion with a double bow. Dark Oxblood leather soles. Brand new they looks n'all. Probably bought with his ill-gotten gains, I expects."

"Thank you, Mr Howe. We are in your debt," stated Wiggins. Mr Howe snorted, turned and painfully, and slowly shuffled back off down Greek Street and disappeared, accompanied by a hacking cough into the heart of the gloom.

Wiggins ordered Murray to stand guard at the rear entrance of the building whilst he headed for the front door. He knocked on a navy-blue door and showed his warrant card to the coquettish bare-chested attendant who opened the door and ushered him quickly inside. Immediately he was approached by a slim, well-groomed, youthful looking man whom Wiggins judged to be in his forties. A vigorous handshake and a smiling greeting were followed by a discreet enquiry. "Are you here on business or pleasure, Chief Inspector?"

"Strictly business, Sir," answered Wiggins, straightening his tie.

"Pity," lamented the smiling young man, briefly looking Wiggins up and down flirtatiously. Wiggins already felt uncomfortable and decided that he needed to regain control of the conversation. "And what may I ask, is your name?"

"Friday. John Friday," he stuttered, glancing slightly to the left as to break eye contact. Wiggins recognised the tell-tale sign of someone lying. "Very pertinent, given the day of the week," he observed with a raised eyebrow. Mr Friday smiled sheepishly. "How may I help you, Chief Inspector? I do hope you are not here to cause trouble, Mr Wiggins."

"Not on this occasion, Mr Friday. Not so long as you can point me in the direction of one of your patrons, a Mr Tobias Pullar."

Mr Friday feigned deep thought, his manicured fingernails stroking his cleanly shaven chin. "I'm sorry Inspector, but as you may imagine, we tend not to use names very much at our gatherings. You see we cater for all types here. All levels of society make use of our *facilities*. I am sure you understand."

"That being the case, I would appreciate it if you stood aside and allowed me to search the premises. I might add that if I see any illegal activity within, I shall be forced to close this establishment and arrest any individual whom I perceive as being involved in any nefarious activity," asserted Wiggins striding forcefully past a protesting Mr Friday and down the entrance hall of the building. He entered a large open room filled with dozens of men dancing together whilst a string quartet played from a small makeshift corner stage. Several more men sat at a makeshift bar that had been set up along one wall of the room, sipping cocktails from martini glasses served by two bare-chested young men wearing full face make up. The atmosphere was heady and thick with a mixture of perfume and sexual anticipation. Wiggins began to scan the room for his quarry. Several booths lined one wall of the room. Wiggins edged his way towards the booths through a throng of dancing bodies, his attention drawn towards each dancer's footwear as he did so.

Holding court in one such booth sat the massive figure of Syphilis Phyllis, one-time male prostitute, and victim of the lunatic Nathaniel Cripes. Twenty stones of bright fuchsia pink befrocked heavyweight, sporting a double eyepatch, a five-day shadow, and a small King Charles Cavalier spaniel on his lap. The giant transvestite rubbed at his bristle covered chin as he regaled a small coterie of young disciples with an outrageous tale regarding three sailors and a one-legged priest. Wiggins was about to enquire as to Phyllis' health when a slightly built figure nudged him from behind. "Pardon me," apologised a high pitched, nasally voice. Wiggins turned to see a slightly built figure being absorbed into the crowded dance floor, just in time to catch a glimpse of a pair of scarlet heels. Wiggins spun and hurried after the departing figure, barging complaining dancers out of his way as he did so. "Stop! Police!" shouted Wiggins. Tobias Pullar glanced behind him before bolting for the rear door where he flung himself straight into the restraining arms of Constable Murray.

"You mean to tell me you have him in an interrogation room! Right now?" An exasperated Jem Pyke looked coldly into his senior officer's eyes. "You have the piece of shit in this building and you did not think to inform me?" He shook his head in disbelief. In that brief moment, he questioned whether he truly knew Albert Wiggins at all. Wiggins could understand his friend's disappointment, indeed his incredulity. Wiggins returned his colleague's gaze. The atmosphere between them was fractious, sizzling with underlying pressure as if a late summer storm was about to break its electrifying way through a humid, darkening sky. Wiggins broke the tense silence. "He is yours, Jem, but allow me to do this my way. The legal way." Pyke considered, grunted, and nodded.

Tobias Pullar cut as supercilious a figure as any Wiggins could recall encountering in the stark, intimidating interrogation room. His upturned nose seemed to be constantly sniffing the air above him, a habit that Wiggins found intensely irritating.

Wiggins glanced briefly at Constable Murray who stood witness at the door. "I must remind you, Mr Pullar, that you have been charged with being responsible for committing the multiple murders of ten people by means of incendiary devices planted in, of all places, Buckingham Palace. You must realise that your position is hopeless. I can only encourage you to make your peace with God and to some extent alleviate the burden on your soul by telling us who provided you with the said devices and paid you to carry out such an atrocity."

Pullar sniffed the air and brushed at his effeminately crossed legs. "And what evidence do you have, pray tell, that it was I who perpetrated this outrage, Inspector? As far as I can glean, you have only the testimony of a paid beggar who contests that he heard me admit to this heinous crime whilst under the influence of alcohol, and I must say, a particularly heady atmosphere in the Monocle Club. Hardly a cast-iron case for a guilty verdict Inspector." Pullar's voice was a nasal, adenoidal whine which Wiggins also found intensely irritating.

Wiggins leant forward, each hand on the stained table between them, a looming, and he hoped, an intimidating presence. "Let me summarise, Mr Pullar. You were employed at the Palace. You disappeared on the night of the atrocity. You emerge, considerably richer of pocket a few days later. You are heard, by a reliable informant, boasting to a pair of Nancy boys in an alley behind the Monocle Club of having made the front pages of the broadsheets." Wiggin's voice was forceful, rising in volume as he continued. "One does not need to be a mathematician to add this all up, Mr Pullar!"

"And yet you have no evidence, Inspector," laughed Pullar looking abstractly at his bright red shoes.

Wiggins decided to play a risky card. He sat down and leant back in his chair, his protracted silence forcing Pullar to look at him. "We have your fingerprints on fragments of the device." Pullar instantly looked startled. "Impossible! I wore gloves!" he shot back, instantaneously realising at once, with ice-cold certainty, that he had just signed his own death warrant.

"I think, Constable Murray, that we have a statement from the accused that is tantamount to a confession, don't you?" asked Wiggins.

"Yes, Sir" agreed the impassive Murray nodding with the slightest of smiles playing across his face.

Wiggins turned to the former Equerry. "And now, Mr Pullar, I suggest you accompany Constable Murray here to the cells whilst I write the transcript of our interview." Wiggins felt a swell of triumph rise within his heart.

Pullar fidgeted and twitched like a man electrified. "There was another, Inspector. I merely placed the devices. The intent and the plan were his, not mine! How was I to know that they were real bombs? I know nothing of such things,

Inspector! I polish silver and lay tables!" Wiggins again used silence to his advantage, sitting back with arms folded across his chest. Pullar was lured into a panic. "He was a gamine youth, Sir. Fifty pounds he gave me Sir, fifty whole English pounds."

Wiggins raised an inquisitive eyebrow. "A gamine youth, you say? A strange turn of phrase."

"Gamine, yes sir, gamine," continued Pullar, now babbling almost incoherently. "Lovely curly hair and a faultless complexion."

"And his name?" questioned Wiggins leaning closer.

"I know not, Sir. He but gave me instructions and fifty pounds," trembled Pullar.

"I will ask you once more, Tobias Pullar. Your answer may help aid your passage to a better place. His name, if you please?"

"I don't know!" screamed a now almost unhinged Pullar. Wiggins shook his head as if in regret. He settled back in his chair before giving his prearranged cue. "Would his name, by any chance be *Kimberley?*"

At that instant, it seemed as if a hurricane from hell had entered the room. Murray stepped aside as the door flew open with a tumultuous crash and swung limply, hanging by a single hinge. The tornado of rage that was Jem Pyke stormed into the room and without any preamble strode towards a petrified Pullar, who seemed to visibly shrink in size, shrieked a piercing scream that stung Wiggins' ears. Pullar cowered backwards as a vice-like hand gripped his throat and lifted him bodily off the ground and up the rear wall of the room.

"You killed my wife, you cowardly little arse bangin' bastard!" bellowed Pyke. Wiggins would later swear that Pullar's hair blew backwards at the force of Pyke's roar. "Who paid you, girlie? You have three seconds before I get my retribution! And believe me, you ain't going to like it one little bit."

Pullar gasped for air, his heels kicking at the interrogation room wall. His thin, feminine fingers clawed at Pyke's muscled hand. "I don't know!" he wheezed. Without any further preamble, Pyke's left fist drove into the man's face. To Wiggins it seemed as if Pullar's upper lip and teeth disappeared, crumpling into the wall, his face becoming part of the plaster. Pyke pulled back his fist in readiness, veins bulging against his skin. "Name!" he spat, saliva spraying into Pullar's blood-covered wreck of a face. Pullar began to whimper then sob. The anticipation of another such blow was unimaginable. Unfortunately for Tobias Pullar, before he could imagine it, it hit him, this time destroying his lower jaw into bony shrapnel.

"Name!" roared Pyke, his massive fist cocked and ready for what Wiggins recognised would more than likely be a fatal blow. Wiggins stepped forward and placed a restraining arm on the straining bicep of his bloodthirsty Sergeant. "Enough, Jem. One more blow will obliterate him. He obviously has no name for the instigator." Pyke mumbled something unintelligible and let loose his grip. A flaccid Pullar slumped to the floor. His face looked as if a dray horse had kicked it.

"Keep that beast away from me Inspector!" spluttered Tobias Puller, his knees pulled up towards his chest in an instinctively protective foetal position. His words were almost incomprehensible, lost amongst his horrific facial injuries.

Wiggins looked at Pyke and nodded "That is enough, Sergeant. Get out of here now. Go home, Jem," he added more sympathetically. He could only but wonder at the loss that Pyke was experiencing. The pain and rage that had been boiling within him for days. Pyke nodded and cast one last loathing look of disgust at the convulsing figure lying on the floor. He turned and walked through the broken door frame, and made his way towards the front desk, almost knocking over a newly arrived Constable Bunce on his way. Pullar looked up through tear-stained eyes, desperate to make sure that the walking personification of brutality had left the room. As he did so his eyes opened wide and he raised a shaking arm, pointing after the departing Pyke. "That's him," he whimpered.

Wiggins turned, startled "What do you mean?"

"That's him," gurgled Pullar, blood seeping from his mouth. "The curly-haired, gamine youth! That's him standing right there." Wiggins looked uncomprehendingly at Pullar then spun on his heels, realisation surfacing within him. His eyes locked on those of Bunce who looked horrified at the slumped form of Pullar whose limp hand pointed shakily at the tousle-haired constable. Bunce spun and ran, realisation and fear coursing through his veins.

"Stop him!" yelled Wiggins. "Stop Bunce! It's Bunce!"

Two seconds later a large uniformed shape stepped in front of Bunce and the fleeing constable's last conscious thought was that of feeling as if he had run into a mountain. Nosher Ash blew on his fist and shook his hand as if removing fresh snow. "That hurt ... a bit," he smiled, looking at an unconscious Bunce who lay spread-eagled on the floor.

Chapter 35 - The Duel

What Wiggins remembered most vividly about the duel was that final silence. An all-pervading, shocked silence that blanketed all who had been present. He had found that silence appalling.

Before that day's event, the last duel to have been fought in London had occurred in the small courtyard of what had then been the Embassy of the Texan Republic in Pickering Place, just off Saint James Street. That had been over sixty years earlier. The location of this latest and most unlikely combat was to be altogether more ecclesiastical.

"A duel!" declared Van Hoon enthusiastically. "How melodramatic! An utterly capital idea. Why, I have not presided over a duel since that of Pushkin and d'Anthès on the Black River. A most unjust outcome, I always believed, given that d'Anthès had been conducting an affair with the Russian's wife. Mind you, one must make allowances, he was French after all. A sickeningly handsome individual, and, as I remember, like most of his kind, abhorrently egotistical." Van Hoon seemed lost in the memory, as he peered at the shimmering green contents of his small fluted absinthe glass. Wiggins looked at the Dutchman and shook his head in bewilderment. '*How can he consider anyone to be egotistical when he himself has an ego the size of a small country?*' wondered the detective.

Watson's brow furrowed as he too shook his head. "I don't like it. I do not like it, one little bit gentlemen," he rumbled, his great moustache trembling as if it were as concerned as its owner.

"I and Pyke have researched the matter and it seems that there remains a grey area as regards the legality of death by duel," commented Wiggins to the assemblage. He and Van Hoon sat in the glass room of the Leper's Belgravia mansion, alongside Sergeant Pyke and Doctor Watson. "However, we are talking about taking a risk of career-threatening proportions for some of us."

Pyke grunted. He sat, legs outstretched and crossed at the ankles, observing a tiny yellow and blue, iridescent hummingbird that flitted from one tropical bloom to the next. He wondered at how simple the life of the little bird must be. A daily search for nectar amongst Van Hoon's tropical sanctuary, devoid of any predators, or dangers and without any concept of worry, grief or pressure. "And a potentially life-threatening one for one of us," he added pointedly.

Doctor Watson looked anxious. "Surely you can simply arrest the man. You have a positive identification after all, albeit extricated from the unfortunate Equerry via an inordinate amount of persuasive force." He cast an accusatory glance over the top of his half-moon spectacles towards Pyke who grunted once more, a low throaty disdainful rumble.

"I hardly think that the young man in question constitutes a threat to such an experienced soldier as yourself, Mr Pyke," observed Van Hoon, inspecting the emergent fruit on a twisted fig tree.

"That's as may be," interjected Wiggins. "However, we must remember that this young man, through his own actions, killed ten innocent people, among them Red Noreen, and injured dozens more, among them my own wife Mary. If it had not been for the bravery of our friend, Jem Pyke here, Mary, would not be alive this day." Wiggins struggled to continue. He could feel his throat restrict and tears begin to well up in his eyes. He glanced at Pyke, who remained stony-faced, a brutal figure of seething vengeance.

"But why not just let justice take its course?" argued Watson, striking a match, and raising it to the bowl of his pipe.

"Because he killed my intended wife!" roared Pyke, suddenly standing upright, his chair clattering backwards to the tiled floor. A flurry of startled butterflies fluttered into the air. "The long walk is too good for this filth." Anger and adrenalin surged through Pyke's battle-hardened body. "I'm going to kill him myself! The last thing he is going to see in this life is Mrs Pyke's son smiling at his doomed face. This is about revenge, John, and the only way I can do this without being hung myself, is by duel."

Van Hoon placed a calming hand on Pyke's trembling shoulder. Pyke was surprised at the calm strength that pulsed from the Dutchman's grip. "I will make the necessary arrangements, gentlemen. I already have a rather dramatic venue in mind," he smiled enigmatically.

"Make it somewhere high," hissed Pyke through clenched teeth.

A unanimous show of hands had decided that Van Hoon should provide the duelling weapons, two silver-plated Colt forty-five pistols. As the only one amongst the group with any previous experience of having attended a duel, the Dutchman would invigilate. Pyke nominated Doctor Watson as his Second and Sergeant Nosher

Ash, after some degree of persuasion, reluctantly consented to act as Bunce's Second. It was decided that Wiggins would act as witness and the recorder of the proceedings.

Van Hoon, somehow, magically arranged the venue. Once more Wiggins found himself completely baffled as to the extent of influence this remarkable individual seemed to extend over the highest echelons of both Church and State. All that was left to do was to convince Bunce that his participation in a duel against Jem Pyke would be to his advantage.

The prisoner was visited in his cell by Desk Sergeant Nosher Ash, who as Bunce's allocated second, explained as persuasively as he could, that a duel was his best option under the circumstances. Nosh sat beside Bunce on the cell bunk, his large powerful hands resting upon his knees. Once he had known that he was to give the young man advice he had decided to adopt a somewhat fatherly approach to the conversation. "It may not seem it lad, but you are in the fortunate position of having been given a choice. Make the long walk or take your chances against Detective Sergeant Pyke."

Bunce fidgeted with the tail end of his shirt, twisting and untwisting it in a display of sheer fear and nervous doubt. He looked at the big bear of a man who sat alongside him. The haystack shock of salt and pepper hair, the kindly, permanently half-closed eyes nestling in the rumpled face of a caring though obviously strong man. "But surely Sarge, I could throw myself upon the mercy of the court. Take me chances, like. You never know, I may come up before a forgiving Beak."

Ash patted Bunce's knee and smilingly shook his great monolithic head. "You were responsible for the outrageous murder of multiple innocent people at Buckingham Palace, for God's sake, son! They could say yours was an act of treason upon our King. Do you really think there's a judge in all the land that wouldn't don the black cap for you m'lad? They couldn't! They wouldn't dare."

Bunce wrung his shirt tail until it squeaked. "What about insanity? I could plead insanity! I can act insane."

Nosh took out his pipe and began to scrape out the dottle with a small bone-handled pipe knife. He blew it through and peered searchingly down its stem. "Your crime was precision planned, son. Couldn't be more premeditated if you tried."

Bunce cursed. The thought of coming up against Jem Pyke, even armed with a gun in his hand, was an idea that horrified the young Constable. "Here's the deal, lad," explained Ash, tamping some fresh tobacco into the bowl of his pipe. "If in you win, you go free. Simple as that. No questions asked. You have Detective Chief Inspector Wiggins' word on that, and there ain't no man in this land whose word I would trust more. This is literally a once in a lifetime offer. If I was you lad, I would grasp it with both hands. It is your only chance. It gives you a fifty-fifty chance instead of, well, no chance. Half a chance is better than none ain't it?" smiled Nosh sympathetically.

"But it's Jem Pyke for Christ sakes, Nosh! There ain't no man in London could face a vengeful Jem Pyke and come out on top. I might as well shoot meself in the head before proceedings start," lamented the trembling constable.

"That's as may be, lad," smiled Nosher lighting his pipe. The faint sizzle of the tobacco catching always gave Ash a feeling of great inner satisfaction. He sucked and exhaled an aromatic plume of purplish-grey smoke. "Think about it for a second, its pistol against pistol lad, which is a damned sight more even than if you were to go at it bareknuckle. At least you has a chance and it is your only chance to live."

Bunce thought long and hard, his face twisted in agonising indecision. Twisted as tightly as the shirt tails in his constantly wringing hands. He took an inward draught of air, filling his lungs with faux bravery that even he knew was misplaced. "All right Sarge, I reckons I ain't got no choice but to agree to duel." Nosh nodded sagely and puffed on his pipe. "Wise decision, son."

Bunce's face suddenly lit up, a thought springing to his rescue. "So long as my father can be in attendance. I wants me old man to be there to support me," asserted the young man with renewed vibrancy.

Nosh gave the proposal his usual long pause of careful consideration. "And just where exactly is your father and what does he do for himself?"

"He lives in a big house in Windsor, Sarge. He's on the Glory Road. He ain't got long to go and all he does is sleep, swallow his medicine, and breathe oxygen through a tank. He ain't no threat, Nosher, he's an old dying man. Least I can do is let him see his son go out fighting for his life."

"I see," acknowledged Ash thoughtfully. He detested the man he sat beside with a hatred he had found difficult to mask, but his kindly soul recognised this plea as being no more than a dying man's last request. As sure as Bunce's father was already on his way to meet his maker, the man's son was equally, in Ash's mind, as certain to be making the acquaintance of the tall chap with the scythe in the none too distant future.

"Agreed," resolved Ash. "Give me the address and I'll make the necessary arrangements." Nosh left the cell with a grinding of key in rusty lock '*Must get that oiled,*' he mumbled to himself.

It was dawn, and the Whispering Gallery of Saint Paul's Cathedral had never before played host to such an extraordinary gathering of individuals. Nor had it, Wiggins was sure, ever been used as the location for so dramatic and fateful an event as a duel. Seven individuals were present, each of whom entertained their own thoughts, their own worries, their own fears.

A young, fresh-faced mass murderer, his body thrumming with a fear that this would be his last day upon the earth. His father, a seventy-four-year-old, dying man, erstwhile assassin and big game hunter, poisoned not only by his disease but also by a cancerous lust for revenge over those who had thwarted his nefarious crimes. A mute Turkish manservant who had incredibly carried the old man the two-hundred and twenty-seven stairs to be present. An ageing adventurer for justice and an upright, deep thinking officer of the law, each racked with doubt as to the ethical veracity of the proceedings, both wrestling with their loyalty to a friend and colleague and with what they believed to be proper and decent. An apparently ageless, enigmatic Croesus delighted at presiding over his first duel for over half a century. And, finally, a man whose rage at the loss of his beloved knew no bounds. A man who was prepared to kill or to be killed. For Jem Pyke, either would do.

The seven protagonists now stood in dawn's gloom on the gallery running entirely around the interior of the dome of Saint Paul's. Only one man spoke. Van Hoon presented the two weapons to be used along with an unadorned but highly burnished box containing the ammunition.

"Gentleman, the two guns I currently hold are eighteen-ninety-one Colt single-action Peacemaker models. They are widely regarded as having been instrumental in cementing the weapon's legacy as the gun that 'won the West.' Rather fanciful I would contend, but it is a rather splendid weapon. Each cylinder holds a maximum of six bullets but are currently not loaded. Can I ask each principal's Second to approach and take a weapon for their principal's use?" Watson and Ash walked forward simultaneously, each grasping the gun immediately closest to them. Pyke stood unblinking, his stare never leaving that of Bunce, who stood visibly trembling. Van Hoon then opened the polished box to reveal six silver-topped brass bullets.

"Doctor Watson and Sergeant Ash, please would you load these bullets into three consecutive chambers and then present the weapons to the combatants. Principals, you will each walk backwards twelve paces so that there is a distance of approximately twenty-four yards between you." Van Hoon withdrew a gold and scarlet paisley patterned handkerchief from his waistcoat pocket. "I have here a silk kerchief which I shall drop. Once it strikes the ground the duel shall commence, and you may do as you wish in order to win the contest. This duel is deemed *à l'outrance*, which for those not familiar with French, translates as 'to the death.' Therefore, the duel will only satisfactorily end when one combatant is mortally wounded. Do we all understand?"

Six men nodded their agreement, but Bunce remained unmoving. "Bunce! Do you agree to the terms? We cannot commence until both parties have agreed." Bunce eventually nodded his head hesitantly in reluctant agreement before crossing himself and whispering a silent prayer. His father looked on with undisguised disgust.

Pyke and Bunce now faced each other and proceeded to take twelve steps backwards. Bunce's legs twitched, fighting the impulse to whirl around and sprint off down the shadowed corridor to his left. As Van Hoon released the handkerchief time appeared to visibly slow down. Wiggins studied the tableau in front of him. The dawn morning was dark, the gallery was dim, cold and empty. He could see Pyke's breath steam from his nose and Bunce's plume from his mouth. Pyke was standing completely still, his arms by his sides, whilst Bunce was a shuddering mass of nervous energy. Down drifted the handkerchief.

The first bullet from Bunce's pistol missed Pyke entirely, zinging as it did three feet above the detective's head to land deep in the plasterwork of the encircling cathedral wall. Only then did the handkerchief strike the ground. Bunce's entire body was trembling, icy cold sweat was permeating from every pore of his skin. He found it impossible to keep his shooting hand steady, it was as if an uncontrollable palsy had taken hold over him, possessing his ability to aim. He gasped and tried furiously to gulp in air. The stress of the situation was causing him to hyperventilate erratically.

Jem Pyke stood motionless as if he were one of the painted figures adorning the frescoed walls directly below where he stood. He was as still as one of the iconic statues that filled the great cathedral. His arms both hung loosely at his sides, gun pointed towards the floor. His head was tilted slightly downwards so as his granite hewn chin almost touched his chest. His eyes burned hatred from beneath his furrowed brow, a hatred that penetrated deep into the soul of the man standing twenty-four yards in front him. A man who was quaking with fear. A man whose gun now carried only two bullets. A man whom Pyke knew would be dead within two minutes.

Pyke snarled. His hatred for this man obliterated everything else in his world. He focused on this hate and that alone. He drew nourishment from his hate.

Bunce lifted the revolver once more and took careful aim, just as his father had taught him. The gun seemed to weigh a ton. '*How ashamed father must be,*' he thought as he watched his hand tremor uncontrollably. '*His father, formerly the greatest shot in the entire British Army, the sniper's sniper, the assassin to whom Professor Moriarty had turned when a faultless shot was required. And him? A useless petrified boy, terrified of pulling the trigger, unable to hold himself steady.*' He closed one eye and focussed slightly to the left of centre of his target. He could see the barrel end of the gun dance in front of him like an out of focus cork floating on a pond. His fear was such that he could not, no matter what he did, make that cork stop bobbing.

All of this Pyke knew. His left upper lip curled up to reveal his grinding teeth. His eyes probed into those of his opponent, reading everything. Pyke knew. Bunce squeezed the trigger for a second time. The recoil jolted his arm back and he felt a searing bolt of pain shoot across his wrist as it suddenly twisted. This time the bullet hit its target. Just. Pyke's right shoulder jerked back violently at the impact. The stitching of his Hound's-tooth jacket ripped apart where arm met shoulder and the bullet grazed flesh and muscle on its exit. He moved his shoulder back to its original position and remained as motionless as before. He felt nothing. No pain, only searing hatred. Still, his pistol pointed to the floor.

Pyke transferred the pistol from his right hand to his left. Bunce whimpered, and his bottom lip began to vibrate uncontrollably. He could feel the loathing of Pyke's stare piercing his soul. He could feel his father's eyes pleading for his only son to fire his gun and be victorious. He cowered. He fumbled and dropped his gun. His wrist was wracked with pain. The clatter of gun metal on marble reverberated around the great chamber. Bunce fell to his knees scrabbling for the gun which slid and revolved as he attempted to regain its control, all the time trying desperately to see Pyke's every move. Something within him screamed that if he could not see Pyke, a bullet would splinter his skull any second. The gun spun around the floor for what seemed to Bunce to be an age before he managed to grasp the grip and push himself erect. All through this pathetic scramble, Pyke had stood in the same spot, as motionless as a statue. Bunce gripped his pistol in both hands, wary of the pain reverberating through his injured wrist, and aimed for the heart of Jem Pyke. He squeezed the trigger immediately as that heart was within his sight. The boom of the gun thundered and echoed around the cathedral.

Pyke did not flinch. He did not move a muscle. He did not even blink.

Bunce gasped as he pulled air into his lungs furiously. '*My God! I've missed!*' He dropped his emptied pistol to the floor and fell to his knees, his arms held outstretched towards his opponent in supplication. He began to sob and quiver. "Please. Please don't kill me!" he begged. "He made me do it, he did! He made me do it!" he squealed pointing at his obviously disgusted father. The congregated group of men stood in silence as Pyke slowly and deliberately raised his gun. Bunce sobbed uncontrollably. Pyke looked into the eyes of his foe and indicated with a shake of his gun muzzle that Bunce should stand. Bunce wept openly. He raised himself to his feet as gingerly as would a new-born foal, his arms still outstretched, appealing for mercy. Pyke raised his gun slowly, deliberately and took aim. Bunce whimpered and closed his eyes as tightly as he could. He was frozen in utter fear. He remembered his father once telling him that '*No man hears the shot that takes his life.*'

He heard no shot. Instead, he heard footsteps. Heavy, purposeful, rushed footsteps. He opened his eyes and the sight that greeted him made his bowels loosen. Jem Pyke, gun now discarded, steamed towards him, saliva frothing through his gritted teeth, flames of hatred burning within his eyes. And then Pyke was upon him.

There was the very briefest of struggles, Bunce frantically slapping and kicking at an unfeeling Pyke as he was grabbed simultaneously at collar and groin and lifted overhead into the air. Pyke wheeled around and venomously thrust the object of his hatred headfirst over the gallery balustrade with as much force as his arms could muster. Bunce was thrown with such ferocity that the only noise to break the appalling silence of it all, was that of his flesh and bone shattering upon the marble floor ninety-nine feet below. The silence thereafter was physically palpable. Pyke now walked towards the old man, retrieving his revolver on the way. The old man sat in his wheelchair, his rheumy eyes staring malevolently at the detective. Pyke raised his revolver and pressed the muzzle against the old man's forehead.

"No, Jem!" shouted Wiggins, moving forward. "For God's sake do not do this. That is a direct order Sergeant!" Pyke either never heard, or completely ignored Wiggins' plea and very deliberately cocked the pistol.

"Go ahead you piece of filth!" snapped the old man. "Do it! Pull the trigger! You are a coward like all your kind, hiding behind a warrant card and the so-called laws of the land. Go on, pull the damned trigger!"

"No, Jem!" repeated Wiggins. "It's cold-blooded murder. I cannot protect you this time!"

Pyke paid no heed and simply pulled the trigger. A cold metallic click rang around the cathedral. The chamber was empty. Pyke snorted and threw the gun to the floor. "I moved the barrel to an empty chamber, you old fool," he grinned menacingly. Pyke turned and walked calmly towards the gallery stairwell. As he did so he reached into his rear trouser pocket, pulled out his warrant card, and threw it to the floor behind him. Wiggins watched in awestruck silence as the slim leather-bound wallet skidded across the marble and stopped at the toe of his boot.

Chapter 36 - The Envelope

The day following the duel at Saint Paul's Cathedral, Wiggins called to Pyke's home in Gravel Lane. Pyke had not appeared at the Yard that morning and Wiggins felt an unfamiliar uneasiness as he knocked on the door of the two-bedroom terraced house. He stood for a few minutes, looking around casually as if his visit was of no moment and he had time to kill. As he stood on the threshold, casually whistling, he was absorbing all the activity within the short, grey street. Gravel Lane adjoined Middlesex Street close to Petticoat Lane, and as such, traders habitually used one end of the street to park their wagons and store their wares, effectively blocking it off from any major traffic. Men and women fussed over boxes and carried crates to their pitches and stalls, all the time carrying on the habitual ebb and flow melody of the East End. Wiggins spied a group of three loafers in double-breasted pea jackets, caps pulled low, cigarette ends burning close to their conspiratorial lips. He could smell the scent of petty larceny that seemed to emanate from their bearing and behaviour. Two shoeless young lads chased after an old barrel hoop, propelling it with sticks, and nudging at each other competitively. The rattle of the hoop upon the cobbles ticked along with the clamour of the street traders' business. A gaggle of younger girls sat on some nearby steps, giggling, and pushing each other playfully. Two robust looking middle-aged women, arms folded across their ample bosoms, gossiped in their floral-patterned laundry aprons. One of the washerwomen lifted a hand to her mouth and bit a fragile clay pipe between her nicotine-stained teeth. Wiggins recognised Black Johnny, the knife sharpener, cycling his makeshift workshop precariously over the cobbles, whetstone rattling noisily in tow.

Wiggins returned his focus to Pyke's dwelling and peered in the ground floor window, but his view was almost entirely obscured by the drawn curtains within. He reasoned that Billy would be at school at this time of day but wondered why then the drapes had not been opened upon the underlying lace curtains. He rapped once more upon the door, his habitual two deliberate knocks followed by a brief silence, and then a further three rapid knocks. He waited, then, letting out a gasp of exasperation, he turned on his heels to leave. It was then he heard the heave of an upstairs sash window opening and saw the head of a young woman pop out from within the house adjacent to Pyke's.

"Here! Who's that knockin'?" asked the woman coarsely, a lit cigarette dangling precariously from her lower lip, bouncing as it seemingly conducted her words.

"Good morning, Madam," said Wiggins, a manufactured cheerfulness in his voice. He produced his warrant card. "My name is Detective Chief Inspector Wiggins of Scotland Yard. I am a colleague of your neighbour, Mr Pyke. Would you happen to know whether he is at home?"

The woman screwed her eyes against invasive cigarette smoke and moved her headscarf slightly to accommodate a stray strand of mousey brown hair. "*You're* the bleedin' detective ain'tcha? If he ain't in, and he ain't with you, then I'd expect he'd be out gallivanting. Could be anywhere knowing Jem. The nearest alehouse is The Queen's Head just on the corner yonder, but if I remember rightly the last time he went missing, young Billy found him in The Grapes down Narrow Street."

"I know of both establishments," replied Wiggins with a barely disguised grin. "Many thanks for your time, Madam." He removed his hat and bowed his thanks to the woman.

"And many thanks to you n'all, I'm sure!" she responded, affecting a mocking West End accent as best she could, and slammed down her sash window with a closing thud.

Four hours later, and more than two dozen hostelries searched, Wiggins capitulated and gave up the search for his elusive colleague and headed back to the Yard. He had tried, amongst others, The Hoop and Grapes, The Queen's Head, The Grapes, The Prospect of Whitby, The Seven Dials, The Pillars of Hercules, The Cheshire Cheese and The Ship and Shovell. He had trawled Limehouse and Spitalfields, Saint Giles and Soho. Along the way, he had tried Jawbone's Gym and even Saint Botolph's Church and grounds.

He trotted up the steps of the Yard, his mind distracted and pushed through the doors. Nosher Ash looked up from his desk and nodded to Wiggins. "He's in your office, Guv." Wiggins' eyes turned skyward as he drew in a deep breath and shook his head. Ash's shoulders juddered with an almost silent chuckle escaping his lopsided grin. Wiggins nonchalantly opened his office door and carefully hung his hat and coat on the hat stand. He could see the back of Pyke's head, neck and shoulders, sitting as he was on the chair facing Wiggins' desk. The Detective Sergeant seemed immobile, as if he were carved from stone. Wiggins circled the desk and sat down, his eyes never leaving those of his colleague. Pyke remained motionless, staring straight ahead as if he were standing to attention on the parade ground. Between them on the desk blotter, lay a white crisp envelope, annotated with Pyke's unmistakable scrawl, *Detective Chief Inspector Albert Wiggins*.

Wiggins picked up the envelope, studied it, looked at the inscrutable Pyke, and then considered the envelope once more. He tapped the side of the envelope on the desktop and then replaced it on the blotter. He adjusted its position to ensure that the envelope's corners were square to those of the blotter. The slightest of smirks played across Pyke's thin-lipped mouth. A tense silence filled the space between the two men. Wiggins slid the unopened envelope across the desk towards Pyke. "I will not accept it, Jem." The statement rang of finality, the words of a man who has made his decision and is unwilling to yield.

Pyke continued to look straight ahead. "I am no longer fit to represent this Force Sir. I have killed a man in cold blood and so brought dishonour upon the Metropolitan Police. I have compromised my commanding officer and my colleagues and friends. I have tendered my resignation to my superior officer and fully intend to leave this building a civilian, Sir." He pushed the envelope back towards Wiggins.

Wiggins considered his next statement carefully. "You punished the man who killed your beloved Noreen and multiple other innocents. The same man who very nearly killed my wife. The man who brought carnage to a Royal Palace and endangered the lives of the very Royal Family themselves. This was a man who would have faced the gallows in any case. Most would say that you are a hero rather than a murderer."

Pyke's nostrils flared ever so slightly. Wiggins detected a twitch of emotion in the granite face before him. He continued. "If it were not for your bravery, I would not have breakfasted with Mary this morning." He hesitated, once again picking up the envelope so as the letter within slid from one side to the other. "Look, Jem, what you did was lawful. We had our most trusted legal advisors investigate it in great detail. Death by duel remains legal under the statute books. You have nothing to fear from the Law."

Pyke's face suddenly became alive with emotion. "Don't you understand, Bert? It's not the Law I'm worried about. I threw a young man to his death in front of his dying father! What sort of man am I, Bert? We lock up people like me!"

Wiggins shook his head and reached for his cigarettes. "The father is a scoundrel of the highest order, a multiple murderer just like his son. A man who has extorted and tortured his way through his hatred filled life. He has but days to live. No one will weep for the passing of Colonel Sebastian Moran."

"That may be the case, Bert, but still he is a father who watched his own son be murdered. Besides, I have been giving this some thought. I'm still in touch with my old regimental Colonel and he is convinced that we will have War in Europe within the year. I ain't too old and he said he would have me back in a jiffy. Reckons I could train troops, toughen 'em up, maybe even have a role to play on the front line. Leading the charge like old times."

"Your Colonel may be letting you down with a certain degree of compassion my friend. This is a different era of warfare, Jem. This will be so far removed from the

Boer War you graced with such valour. It will no doubt be a war of iron tanks, not horses. Artillery shells, not sabres! Poisons and gases and all other chemically produced weapons will be used. A war waged not only on the ground and at sea, but for the first time, in the air. You'll be a dinosaur in a young man's conflict ... and what of Billy? What of your adopted Son?" interjected an exasperated and impassioned Wiggins? "What will become of him?"

Pyke shook his head, unable to answer. He accepted the offered cigarette and tapped it sharply three times on the corner of Wiggins' desk. "What about the lads out there, Bert?" he asked pointing at the door, trying to avoid Wiggins' question. "They will regard me with no respect after what I did. They will see me as a man to be feared, a man who can kill when his temper is hot." He lit the cigarette and, much to Wiggins' discomfort, discarded the extinguished match in the general direction of the desk ashtray, missing narrowly. Wiggins resisted the urge to immediately pick up the match and dispose of it, realising that to do so would be petty and somehow diminish the importance of their conversation.

"Every single man in the Force looks up to you, Jem. You are the most highly respected and admired Sergeant in the Met Police. Even more so after your unquestionable bravery at the Palace. Every new recruit desperately wants to work alongside you. To a man, they want to be regarded as the *next* Jem Pyke. Well, you know what? There will never be a *next* Jem Pyke, your old man saw to that when he smelted the mould you were cast from. You may not realise it, but you are an institution around here. You are also, I might add, highly regarded by the Powers that Be."

As if on cue, the office door swung inward and in stalked the tall, slightly hunched figure of Commissioner Gregson. "Detective Chief Inspector, I would have a word with you regarding..." His voice trailed off as his eyes settled upon the envelope. He instinctively grasped the scenario that was playing out before him. "Ah, I see. I was expecting this escalation of events. Coincidentally, I have just come from a meeting in Whitehall where the subject of the encounter at Saint Paul's was brought to the table and I can assure all parties that there will be no further action taken regarding the incident. The Realm is profoundly grateful that the perpetrator of the heinous bombing of the Palace has been brought to our good justice gentlemen." The Commissioner placed his briefcase at his feet with a slight sigh. Wiggins interjected. "Thank you, Sir, that is most welcome and opportune news. However, Sergeant Pyke was just telling me of his intention to leave the Force to perhaps return to Armed Service, Sir."

"Nonsense!" roared Gregson, his shock of pale hair flopping over his forehead. "You are needed most *here*, Sergeant Pyke. There are thousands who can fight at the front if needs be, but you, well, you protect our City. You protect our People and their children. Yours is the noblest of pursuits, maintaining justice. Your place is unquestionably here, Sergeant Pyke. London needs you more than some God-forsaken trench in Austro-Hungary. Let the politicians and the military take care of the Kaiser. If indeed War does come to our Country, our City will need you even more. In times of war, anarchy at home must be quelled. We stand in *that* front-line Sergeant. This is your place!"

Gregson plucked the envelope from Wiggins' desk and tore it in half and then in half again before throwing it in the wastepaper basket. "That's where that belongs," he turned to leave before hesitating. "Oh, and one more thing, the reason I came, I had a rather important visitor this morning who asked me to pass this directly to you, Sergeant Pyke." He stooped and unclasped his briefcase and briefly fumbled amongst papers before producing a wooden cigar box the size of a large bible. He placed it dramatically on the desk in front of a bemused Pyke. "A humidor of burr yew wood construct I was reliably informed. Contains two dozen Dominican Republic Romeo y Julieta premium cigars. I am told there is a note contained inside for your consideration."

Pyke looked quizzically at each of his colleagues and carefully opened the box. He took out a small plain card on which a hand-written inscription simply read. 'From your Country, with our thanks. W.S.C.'

Chapter 37 - The Asylum

Saint Luke's Hospital for Lunatics dominated Old Street. The asylum had stood on the site since being founded in seventeen-fifty-one by a group of philanthropic apothecaries. These well-intentioned benefactors established a secure facility within the heart of downtrodden Shoreditch to provide treatment for the City's pauper lunatics. It was an enormous, foreboding structure, over five hundred feet in length and constructed of clamp brick. The building loomed over the surrounding streets like a large dark bird enveloping its protective wings around its unfortunate inhabitants. A central entrance separated male wards to the left and female wards to the right and contained single-person cells for nearly three hundred patients. Patients who suffered from a wide diaspora of afflictions, and some who had merely suffered misfortunes. Raving maniacs resided alongside young women whose only misfortune had been to have fallen pregnant and suffered rejection at the hands of their families. Schizophrenics were incarcerated alongside unfortunates of feeble mind and imbeciles shared meals with the destitute.

Each cell of the Asylum had only a small window, set high in the wall, to deny inmates even the most perfunctory glimpse of the outside world. The structure was without any form of artificial heating and as such was bitterly cold in the winter and stiflingly hot in the summertime. Its wooden bedsteads were covered merely with sagging, biscuit thin, straw-stuffed mattresses. The more dangerous residents were kept in a secure Wing, permanently entombed in their cells. These violent lunatics were manacled, and their treatment was harsh in the extreme. To the rear of the main building were two large gardens. These were set to lawn with shrub filled borders and provided a calming environment in which the less disturbed inmates could exercise and take the air, one garden exclusively for male patients, the other for females. The genders were never permitted to mix for fear of unwanted relationships and procreation.

The most common treatment regimens consisted of cold plunge baths, with a keen focus placed upon the gastrointestinal system, combined with the administration of anti-spasmodic treatments, vomit-inducing emetics and purgatives. Amidst this most modern bastion of psychiatric treatment sat Nathaniel Cripes. The deviant albino killer was imprisoned within the deepest vault of the secure Wing, isolated from all other inmates. He was bound within a duck-cloth straitjacket in cell number two-hundred and sixty-six.

Psychiatrists and physicians alike had long since successfully advocated against the outdated and barbaric practice of facial restraints, and their use had been discontinued. However, an exception had been made in the case of Nathaniel Cripes. It was felt amongst the board of governors that Cripes' proclivities, and past history, warranted such a radical measure. Since having bitten the index finger of an attending doctor's hand clean off at the proximal phalange eight weeks earlier, Cripes had been locked in a face harness head cage. The iron mask encaged his entire head and resembled a birdcage or medieval torture mask, such as those favoured in the seventeenth century. There was an incorporated 'scold's bridle' tongue-piece of spikes which clasped his tongue to inhibit his religious rantings. The attendants were by now familiar with the albino's mind games and were determined to make it impossible for him to influence or endanger other inmates who may have happened to be within ear-shot. He was categorised as being of the highest level of concern and an 'extremely dangerous and insane' inmate. All human contact was forbidden him, and his one meal of the day would be unceremoniously served through a hatch at the base of his cell door by a deaf orderly known only as Dodds.

Each day Dodds would shuffle his bow-backed way past the other cells, bang on the door of Cripes' cell, stoop to draw back a small steel hatch, and slide in a plate of whatever delights the Asylums' kitchens had conjured up that day. Mostly it would be a thin broth of potatoes bulked up with rice and an occasional slice of carrot, served with a wedge of stale bread. Dodds would then rise with a groan, crack his back, mumble an unheard curse, and shuffle his way back down the corridor. One hour later he would repeat the exercise, this time to remove the plate of food that invariably lay untouched exactly where he had left it. Cripes seldom ate, and his body was now an emaciated, bony carcass. His cheekbones were jaggedly prominent, and his pink eyes cowered deep within their translucent sockets. His frame had suffered calamitous weight loss during his incarceration. Fingernails that had once been immaculately clean and shaped were now chipped and ringed with dirt and grime. He wore a soiled and tattered red-linen robe that hung loosely around his atrophied physique. A snowy white beard only added to his gaunt ghostliness.

'*Yes Lord, I hear thee,*' Cripes repeated to himself. '*My soul has been cleansed and awaits your instructions. I shall be ready for your return and my salvation heavenly father.*' He sat, as he always did, bolt upright on his cot with both feet planted squarely on the cold stone floor, ankles together with his arms bound across his chest by the straitjacket's embrace. His gaze never wavered as he sat, motionless, staring straight ahead at some indeterminate fixed point.

'*You ascended into heaven and are seated at the right hand of the Father. It will be soon that you come again in all your glory to judge the living and the dead. Your kingdom will have no end.*' His tongue accidentally grated across the sharp prongs of the metal mouthpiece causing blood to trickle from the opening of the wrought-iron mask. He relished the pain, savoured the blood, and embraced its ferrous tang. '*The love of men shall wax cold, and iniquity shall abound. All things shall be in commotion and fear shall come upon all people.*' Thoughts now raced through his tortured mind like a driverless steam locomotive. "YES!" Cripes shouted as he jumped to his feet excitedly. His tongue ripped, tore, and shredded into tatters upon the spiny barbs that embraced it. He seemed impervious to the pain. "I hear thee, our Saviour!"
He smiled, his rat-like eyes sparkling. '*Do not forsake me, Lamb of God, I await thee.*' He was euphoric.

"Old Johnny Hobo looking a bit agitated over there, don't you think Bert?" asked Claude of his fellow Asylum orderly.

"I was just thinkin' the exact same thing about Eugene mate, seems more restless than he normally is. He's been runnin' circles around that willow tree over there for a good five minutes now. Like a bleedin' whirling dervish, he is."

The pair scanned around the west gardens as the less dangerous, more predictable inmates wandered aimlessly through the grounds or sat on the lush lawn curiously picking blades of grass. The accepted protocol during leisure hour was that guards patrolled in pairs, and Claude and Bert were one of six such pairings that kept an ever-watchful eye on their patrons. It was rare for anything eventful ever to occur on such mornings. Perhaps admonishing Jacko for pleasuring himself as he ogled the female inmates in the adjacent garden, or chastising Edgar for slapping others on the forehead then screeching as he skipped joyfully off in search of his next victim. However, an uneasiness drifted in the air that morning and both guards felt strangely disquieted by the subtly erratic behaviour they were witnessing. The sun was shining but the mood had darkened considerably. A sense of pervading foreboding descended upon the gardens like a blanket of dense black thunder cloud. Birds ceased their chirruping chorus and a feeling of electricity tinged the atmosphere.

Suddenly, all the patients within view began to descend into a state of obvious distress. Their bodies began to jerk violently as if struck with some unseen electrical charge. They moved together as one, a spasmodic, rapidly twitching ballet, dancing grotesquely towards each of the prison guards dotted around the landscape.

Within his cell, Cripes' elation continued. Somehow, he could sense the change in atmosphere. '*Thank you, Master. I can feel your presence. You have come to release me into the safety of your loving bosom. It has begun. I rejoice!*'

In the garden, Claude drew his baton. "Sweet Baby Moses! What in damnation is going on here Bert?" he inquired as he turned to face his partner. Claude lurched suddenly backwards and dry-wretched as he saw Bert's head dangling limply at an abnormally acute angle. It had been twisted so violently that his ear was situated where his nose should be. "Bert!" was the last word to escape from Claude's mouth before three inmates began to dance an insane stomping waltz upon his body until he lay silent and lifeless, his form a crumpled, unrecognisable bloodied mess.

The inmates preyed upon the guards and orderlies in an uncontrollable frenzy of bloodlust. So comprehensive was the carnage, and so quickly did it occur, that it was almost cloaked in a deathly silence. So desperate were the orderlies to escape, that the only sounds were those of desperation, of muffled straining of bodies struggling against bodies, struggling to escape their attackers. The muted sound of men and women trying to fight off the inevitability of a certain gruesome death masked the silent, universal realisation that screaming would serve no purpose. Amongst this mayhem, a tall, straight-backed figure strode confidently through the chaos, lunatics parting supplicantly before him. His expensive shoes crunched the gravel path below his feet as he headed purposefully towards the entrance of the Asylum.

Inside his cell, Nathaniel Cripes could hear the alarm claxon echoing relentlessly around the prison. He could also hear screams and cries of terror reverberating throughout the corridors and halls. Bedlam within Bedlam. The lunatics were indeed taking over the Asylum. Cripes' gaze remained unflinching as a knowing smile crept across his emaciated face. He began to recite a passage from Corinthians in his head, his tongue now swollen and on fire. '*For since death came through man, the resurrection of the dead comes also through a man.*' He repeated it over and over, his twisted, sense-starved mind giving the mantra more credence with each repetition.

The prison guards proved no match for the two hundred or so, low-level security inmates within the walls of the hospital who had not been locked in their cells, inmates who had been regarded as presenting no immediate danger to themselves or others. As with their fellow patients outside, they had, simultaneously, embarked upon a random and savage rampage of killing. Batons were of little use and pistols could not be located, or indeed loaded, hastily enough to halt the oncoming human wave of crazed maniacs. Each lunatic was intent on killing any individual wearing a white coat. It was as if some Biblical plague of starving locusts swarmed through every inch of the building, destroying all in its path.

A wave of death had descended leaving dead and dying guards littering the halls like a scene from some ghoulish medieval battlefield. The floor of the refectory resembled a winter snow scene as the guards' white lab coats were scattered everywhere. In one hallway three men were skewered upon coat hooks, the scene resembling some horrific Butcher's window display. Several attendants had been drowned in the hospital's ice-cold treatment baths, their lifeless bodies bobbing face down in the briny water. One unfortunate guard was being held down by three maniacs who had attached the electrodes of an electroconvulsive therapy machine to his temples. His limbs were rigid with the massive current that surged through his agonised muscles. His screams were tortured and continuous and all the while the lunatics pointed and laughed at his contorted spasticity. Once dead, his limbs continuing their twitching dance. Satisfied, his torturers quietly sat down and gazed unfeelingly around them as if nothing untoward had occurred.

As the havoc gradually subsided, most of the inmates began to sit down, legs crossed, recumbent in apparent tranquillity. As one, they seemed oblivious to the carnage they had created, the mayhem wiped from their collective memories. The distant buzzing of electrodes and the accompanying moaning of a dying guard echoing somewhere within the passages were now all that could be heard.

Nathaniel Cripes, as he knew he would, heard the door to his cell being unlocked. It swung open for the first time in several weeks, its steel hinges squealing like a resilient pig. Through the bars that obscured his eyes, he could vaguely make out a dark shape undoing the bindings of his straitjacket then releasing the catches of his torturous head cage.

Cripes fell to his knees, euphoria surging through his emaciated form. "You came! Thank you, Master. I knew you would. Lord Jesus Christ our Saviour!" lavished Cripes upon his rescuer.

There, standing before Cripes, was the grinning figure of Luca Radasiliev.

Chapter 38 - The Slaughter

"Come," beckoned Radasiliev, offering his hand to that of the withered Cripes. "We have the Lord's words to spread and his wonders to perform." Nathaniel Cripes looked devotedly at Radasiliev. "I have dreamt of your coming, every day since my incarceration, Master." His sibilant hiss of a voice slithered from his quivering, pallid lips. "I knew you would come. I saw you every day. I heard your voice every day. I prayed that you would come, and you have. I knew you would not forsake me in my time of need."

Radasiliev placed his hand delicately upon his acolyte's head as if bestowing a blessing. Cripes felt a burning tingle singe through him. The most depraved thoughts sizzled through his brain. "I bid you rise. Rise and follow me. There is another whom we must free."

Cripes falteringly lifted his withered frame. The atrophying pain which had previously wracked his stiffened body seemed to have disappeared as if it had been cast out at the Russian's touch. Cripes' rat pink eyes gazed adoringly into the oily, sable eyes of Radasiliev. "I am yours to do your bidding, Master. Whatever you require of me you will have. Who is this other disciple, Master?"

"He is one who will also do my bidding. His name was Crake. Jonas Crake. He is a fellow wife killer like yourself, Nathaniel," observed Radasiliev, casually checking that his ruby inset cuff links were aligned properly. "He too knew the pain of a scold's tongue."

A spark lit in Cripes' mind. "Ah, he is the creature they keep in the vault cell, oh Master. I have heard them call him the Toad." Cripes let a simpering little laugh escape his nematoid lips.

"Indeed. His depravity lies deep. So deep that it shapes him, defines him, allows me to alter his physiognomy. A pet project of mine, you might say."

"And what do you require of me, my Lord?" oozed Cripes. He was eager to please his Master and resentful, and indeed fearful, that another may usurp his place in his overlord's affections.

"All I require of you my dear Nathaniel, is havoc. Pure, unadulterated havoc," replied Radasiliev, exiting Cripes' padded cell and indicating that the deviant albino follow him. Radasiliev strode into the glazed brick corridor, the heels of his shoes creating a rhythmic clacking like castanets upon the hard, polished concrete floor.

The sound transported Radasiliev back a decade, and conjured images of his own time incarcerated in a Kamchatkan prison, buried deep under the rock of a quarry pit in eastern Russia. Each day he had slaved in the quarry, pointlessly breaking rock after rock whilst chained to two other men. Each night he spent locked in a steel cell, a hundred feet below ground, with the same two men, one mute and one blind. They had received daily beatings, assaulted mercilessly by bestial guards. Hit with batons on their kidneys and the soles of their bare feet. An excruciating pain that he could still recall to this day. A pain that made one retch. His only escape was his hatred. He bathed in his hatred. Embraced his hatred like a lover. Hatred was his refuge and hatred would be his salvation. Whilst the mute and the deaf man he was chained to indulged in a nightly bout of repellent pederasty, he would lie on the concrete block that was his bed and he would hate and hate and hate. His eyes burrowed an imaginary hole of hate into the steel ceiling above his bunk, each day, drilling that hole deeper and deeper into the overlying rock, trying to create an escape route by which his soul could reach freedom. He hated until the Lord of Darkness found him, smelled his hatred, recognised him, picked him out and invaded his soul. The Beast had spoken to him, instructed him, and imbued him with his unholy powers. He was his to obey. His life had truly begun.

And so, he and Cripes strode down the corridor. The pair, one sick with evil and empowered by darkness, the other a sycophantic acolyte, picked their way, unhindered through the masses of inmates. As they did so Radasiliev casually clicked his fingers. The door of the basement cell unlocked as if by an invisible hand, its bolt sprung, its lock unlocked. A surprised Jonas Crake crept hesitantly on all fours out into the corridor, sniffing at the air like an inquisitive, hungry hound.

"Come, Jonas," instructed Radasiliev. "Join us, my friend." Crake sniffed the trouser leg of the Russian and happily fell to heel.

All the inmates were now becalmed, the violence and carnage of the previous thirty minutes seemingly forgotten. Heads lolling to one side, eyes devoid of thought or memory, they were as empty shells, inhuman and unthinking. Cripes regarded his surroundings with relish, licking his lips and wringing his bony white hands together in glee as he padded barefoot behind the tall, striking figure of Radasiliev. In his wake hopped the pitiful creature who had once been Jonas Crake. Radasiliev stopped at the centre of the large communal dining room. He surveyed the bodies of the dead orderlies and staff that littered the room, skulls crushed, necks twisted and bodies in unfeasibly contorted positions. He threw back his head and roared an animalistic, deep-throated laugh. Some of the inmates responded by twitching like dreaming dogs or searching around themselves in bewilderment, trying to identify and pinpoint the perpetrator of such devilish merriment. The toad-like figure of Crake scurried amongst the throng, seeking out the reassuring side of Radasiliev.

The Russian leapt effortlessly upon a long dining table as if lifted by an invisible hand and outstretched his arms at his sides. Inmates began to shuffle towards him, a drooling, shifting hoard of lost souls, drawn inexorably towards the magnetic Russian. Cripes looked longingly at Radasiliev in enraptured admiration. "My Master has come," he hissed to his fellow lunatics. "He is leading an army to spread our Lord's words. Rejoice in his presence!" he oozed. As he gazed adoringly at the Russian, he saw that his Master's feet had begun to quiver. Then the Russian's entire body began to vibrate, imperceptibly. Cripes' jaw dropped as he saw space appear between the soles of Radasiliev's shoes and the tabletop upon which he had stood a mere second before. "He rises!" Cripes acclaimed "Our Master rises!" Crake hopped up and down in ecstasy, his overtly protuberant eyes sparkling with excitement.

Radasiliev now floated a full three feet above the table, his body in a cruciform position, his eyes, the deepest, blackest pits, scanned the room. "Come, my children, come unto me," he preached. The inmates streamed into the room, barging into one another, seemingly unaware of each other's presence or of the dead bodies they trampled underfoot. Their blank, lifeless eyes focussed entirely on the vision of the hovering deity before them. They stood en masse, eagerly awaiting the word of their Master. They could all sense him in their heads, a cold, icy presence that made them feel apprehensive, anticipatory of events about to unfold.

Radasiliev opened his mouth, pausing for dramatic effect, relishing the power he possessed over the hoard of lunatics. Cripes was almost apoplectic with anticipation now and he could feel himself stiffen. Radasiliev gradually raised his arms from the elbows and splayed his long fingers, like the flashing rays of the sun. "Kill, my children, kill! I want you to kill each other. Every, last, one of you. When there is but one left, kill thyself!" He threw his head back and once more roared his satanic laugh. A laugh that belonged in Hell. "Let the game commence!"

As the inmates turned upon each other in a frenzy of bloodlust, Radasiliev watched with morbid fascination, relishing his power. Men openly stamped upon skulls and bit and slashed at flesh. One woman was violently ripping handfuls of hair from a fellow patient's scalp. Male inmates were sexually assaulting their female counterparts, invading them violently before killing their conquests. One particularly large and brutal inmate ripped a rib from a fellow prisoner's abdomen and stabbed it through his victim's eye socket, forcing it to penetrate the frontal lobe of the brain. Several patients ripped at the throat of another and worried over the corpse as hyenas would a fallen antelope. The whole scene was of carnage on a biblical scale. Bodies lay motionless like ghoulish mannequins, oesophagi and arteries sticking out of gaping throat wounds. Screams of pain and agony echoed around the Asylum halls. Screams that sounded scarcely human, like tortured animals whining for the pain to end.

Radasiliev surveyed the savagery and pronounced, "Embrace them, Father, for they know not what they do!" He was again transported back to the underground penitentiary in Kamchatka. The vision was the same, dozens left dead. Everyone. Guards and prisoners alike, all polluted with a murderous hatred that had ended in absolute slaughter, and in his freedom. He smiled at the memory, particularly at the appropriately grisly way in which he had forced the mute and the deaf man to kill each other.

Eventually, there was silence. Only the large brutal monster stood, an ogreish figure clutching a human rib that dripped cerebral fluid and blood onto a floor which was already awash with human juices. All others had fallen, dead or dying, convulsing and jerking. The ogre's near toothless mouth was agape, drooling, and his lopsided face was concentrated solely upon Radasiliev. The Russian sensed danger emanating from the triumphant lunatic. The taste of fresh blood had made the madman hungry for more and he slowly approached the floating figure of the Russian who smiled and began to descend from his lofty pulpit. Crake and Cripes giggled behind him, wringing their hands in anticipation of what was about to occur. As Radasiliev drifted gently towards the floor, his upper garments, jacket, vest and shirt began to burn with a fierce white light. The mindless brute shielded his eyes, such was the intensity of the light that burst from Radasiliev's torso. Suddenly the white flames were sucked inwards into Radasiliev's body which juddered slightly at their impact. Grey tendrils of smoke twisted upwards from the Russian's now bare skin. Radasiliev's entire upper body, front and back were covered in demonic tattoos. Celestial bodies, pentagrams, occult texts, and tantric spells in long-dead languages vied for space on his human canvas with images of demons, hundreds of minute screaming faces, illustrations of snakes and dragons, slaughtered angels, and scenes of unimaginable torture. Nathaniel Cripes looked upon this human fresco in orgasmic admiration.

"Join us, my Son. You are the victor. Join our family of Darkness," offered Radasiliev, his arms outstretched towards the victorious lunatic, his veins seeming to throb from a surfeit of blood within. The brute lunged towards Radasiliev, his mind empty of anything other than an overwhelming urge to kill. The very urge the Russian had implanted within him. He brandished the rib like a dagger and howled like the maniac he truly was. Radasiliev stretched his neck forward, opened his mouth unfeasibly wide like the articulated jaws of a python and screamed a silent scream. A torrent of thousands of black, bee-like insects surged from his mouth and battered into the face of the oncoming lunatic. The giant screamed in agony as the flesh was rent from his face. He fell to his knees, his hands frantically clutching at the place where his face had once been. His screams stabbed at the eardrums of Cripes who laughed hysterically. The creature that had been Jonas Crake hopped around yelping with glee at the sight of the screaming pale pink skull of the prone giant as he trembled in his final, jerking, death throes. Radasiliev smiled as though satisfied. "Come, Nathaniel. Come, Jonas. Let us leave this House of the Dead to the Police. Our work lies elsewhere."

Chapter 39 - The Blood

Edward Imrie felt repulsed at the carnage spread out before him. He looked at Doctor Pascoe, a visual plea for some sort of affirmation, some degree of validation or support. The pathologist returned the young man's gaze, his raised eyebrows almost disappearing behind his mop of a hairline. "I know, lad, I know," Pascoe's head shook in a forlorn lament. "In all my time in practice, I have never seen anything to compare with this. Absolutely nothing."

Constables and medical crew milled around the room, picking their way carefully through the massacre in search of any signs of life. Some held handkerchiefs to their faces, some leant against blood-spattered walls shaking their heads in disbelief. A forensic photographer nervously took pictures with a state-of-the-art folding pocket Kodak box camera, eager that his task be over, but mindful to catalogue the atrocity. An atrocity he certainly was not looking forward to revisiting in the dark room later that evening, nor in the gloom of his nightmares thereafter. Instinctively he felt the need to hold his children.

The tiled floor of the dining room was awash with blood. A dark, glutinous pool that seemed to cover most of the floor. The sticky ooze clung to the boot soles of all who walked in the room, creating a constant sucking sound that brought to Edward's mind an image of shoe leather peeling off melted toffee or glue. Not for the first time since he had entered the room, he felt his stomach lurch. He noticed a young constable at the far end of the room vomiting, obviously in distress. The smell in this human abattoir was now atrocious. Strewn around the room lay the bodies of over forty inmates intertangled in a mosaic of slaughter. The injuries were ghastly, and all, Imrie felt sure, had been fatal.

"A more gruesome scene, I have never before witnessed," reiterated Pascoe, shaking his head in despondent disbelief. Imrie saw an almost imperceptible tremor play across the older man's bottom lip. His eyes blinked rapidly, as they always did during times of stress. "It looks like the aftermath of a battle."

Pascoe crouched to examine a corpse that had, what he could see, was a human rib protruding from its eye socket. '*God only knows how that got there!*' he shuddered at the thought. Next to this body lay another with only a gaping hole where once there had been a face, its throat had also been torn out, as though the man had been ripped apart by a pack of rabid wolves. Limbs had been broken, heads hung at impossible angles and internal organs seemed to have half crawled from their human shelters. He shook his head again, bewildered, and muttered something under his breath. Imrie thought he recognised a half-remembered prayer from his Sunday school days at Saint Botolph's Church.

"What in Heaven's name has occurred here, Doctor Pascoe?" The authoritative voice came from behind the stricken pathologist who turned to see Commissioner Gregson, disbelievingly surveying the scene. At his side stood DCI Wiggins and DS Pyke. Pascoe stood with a grimace and a groan. His arthritic knees cracked. *'I'm not getting any younger,'* he thought to himself, recalling an image of his father rising from his fireside chair, and realising that he had probably thought the same thing to himself.

"A mass killing, no doubt about it, Sir. As far as we can see, or hear, there are no survivors. There are also the bodies of at least another twenty or so staff elsewhere in the building and in the surrounding gardens along with those of countless inmates scattered throughout the hospital, each with equally horrific injuries to those you see before you. An absolute slaughter."

"Theory?" asked Wiggins.

Pascoe coughed nervously and looked around him. "It's as though another bomb blast has occurred but there seems to be no apparent damage to the building or the surroundings and there is most definitely no smoke or even debris. No debris, that is, apart from the human debris you see littered all around you, Sir." The men purveyed the scene momentarily. "This may sound outlandish Bert, sorry DCI Wiggins, but to me, it looks as if they have massacred each other. First, they turned on the guards and orderlies, then upon themselves. I have observed countless instances of a man murdering a group of people before turning his weapon upon himself, but I have never seen the likes of what we bear witness to here."

Wiggins was about to speak when Constable Murray appeared, breathing heavily. He spotted the Commissioner and quickly saluted. Gregson nodded in recognition. "Begging your pardons, Sirs, but we have tallied the dead with the asylum records," Murray glanced down at the sheet of paper he clasped in his hand, "... and there appears to be two inmates unaccounted for."

Pyke grunted. "I'll wager we know exactly which two n'all."

Wiggins nodded his agreement. "Cripes and Crake perchance?"

"Impossible to tell until we identify all the bodies," interjected Pascoe, sagely, "and that may prove an entirely impossible task judging by the state of some of the deceased."

"Cripes and Crake are rather unmistakable individuals," scoffed Pyke, "in that one resembles a toad and the other is a pink-eyed albino who looks like he's lived in a cave all his natural-born days. I'll just take a gander, Guv. Come on Murray. You come with me." Pyke stalked off, stepping carefully between the cadavers, Murray following gingerly behind.

As Pascoe and Imrie moved amongst the carnage, looking for any residual signs of life, Gregson turned to Wiggins. "We must minimise publicity regarding this incident, whilst putting the full power of our resources behind finding the cause. What with the mad Chinaman on the loose, the bombing at the Palace, and our most recent series of murders, now thankfully solved, I cannot but feel that we are somewhat under public scrutiny at the moment, Detective Chief Inspector."

Wiggins nodded. He was deep in thought, recalling the scene of braying reporters outside Scotland Yard. "That, Sir, may prove to be an understatement."

Gregson could see a theory forming in the sharp mind of his DCI. "I know that look, Bert. What are you thinking? Is there a connection here?" The commissioner had removed his hat and was scratching his silver mane with a gloved hand.

Before Wiggins had a chance to respond, Pyke returned to the room, his boots squelching in the blood. "You were right, Guv. After a hasty search, they don't seem to be here. The Albino and the Toad have scarpered." The two detectives looked at each other and said simultaneously, "Radasiliev!"

Gregson looked from one to the other. "You mean, you think that the missing Russian diplomat is responsible for this nightmare? How can this possibly be?"

Wiggins nodded. "I would stake my reputation on it, Sir. There is no other man in London who could have made this happen."

"Then we must locate him without any further ado," came a deep rumble of a voice. The tombstone figure of Gideon Thorne stood framed in the doorway. Thorne walked deliberately through the human remains, surveying each body with an air of superior disgust. He sniffed at the air as if he were a wolf, tasting the scent of blood. His eyes narrowed almost to slits in his leathery face. "How is it that one man can inflict such debauchery?" he inquired, looking directly into Wiggins' eyes.

"Radasiliev has rather *unique* abilities, Superintendent," replied Wiggins, holding the intimidating stare of Thorne.

"I should say so!" responded Thorne looking around him and raising a sardonic eyebrow. "I should say he is the very Devil himself if he can leave such mayhem in his wake. Wouldn't you agree, Chief Inspector?" The Northerner's tone remained subdued although menacing, his pause inviting a response. Pyke bristled at Thorne's antagonistic nature. He recognised someone spoiling for a fight when he saw one and cricked his neck. Not for the first time he pictured himself teaching this brash Northerner a lesson.

Wiggins considered his response carefully. "Not the very Devil himself, Sir, but perhaps one who has a passing acquaintance with his arts and practices. An occultist of the highest degree. A man who can influence others to do whatever he wants them to do. Both myself and Sergeant Pyke can testify to his unique and disquieting abilities, Mr Thorne."

Thorne bristled somewhat at Wiggins' slight at not using his given title. Thorne paused, then grinned. A grin that made something lurch uncomfortably inside Wiggins. "That being the case, I agree with the Commissioner. We must leave no stone unturned in the search for this … this Satanic Magician."

Chapter 40 - The Brigade

Pyke left Wiggins and DS Thorne, along with Commissioner Gregson and the forensic team with a veiled comment regarding "picking up the scent of the Russian." The excuse was only partially true. Pyke found it extremely difficult sharing air space with the new Superintendent and knew that the less time he spent with the burly Northerner, the less chance there was of him losing his hair-trigger temper and launching into a verbal onslaught. He realised that the best place for him to be around Gideon Thorne was to be nowhere near him at all. Besides, he knew that Wiggins and Pascoe were far more adept than he at managing the forensics of such a slaughter, whereas he was best suited in 'trawling the filth' of London's criminal underbelly to sniff out a lead. Moreover, he had two appointments to keep. He had a liaison with Wilson Brown arranged for later that night to catch up with the private investigator as to his progress on his clandestine surveillance of Gideon Thorne. But first, he headed towards Commercial Street.

He made his excuses, telling Murray to keep him up to speed, and headed briskly down Great Eastern Street, enjoying the Spring evening glow, trying to force the horror of Saint Luke's from the forefront of his mind. A brisk fifteen-minute walk brought him to the front door of the Ten Bells public house on Commercial Street. During his walk, he had made a mental list of those most likely to help him in his search for the Russian, some of whom would be within the very pub into which he now entered. Pyke walked through the sparsely populated bar area. He scanned the room in a vain hope that he might spy the slight, primate-like figure of Boniface. Pyke was still actively searching for the quick-witted cardsharp he was convinced had been responsible for delivering Demerara Smith to his death at the hands of Mr King. Seeing no sign of Boniface, he walked up the rear stairs to the first floor. He opened the door and walked into the sweat and heat of a gymnasium.

"Well, Jawbone, I see all four of them got here on time then," smiled Pyke as he removed his Derby and deftly flung it towards an accommodating hat stand. Pyke felt relieved to be in the gym, a brief respite from the madness and carnage of his day.

"A most punctual group of young men, Jem," rumbled the deep baritone of a square-shouldered hulk of a man with hands that would each struggle to fit into a five-gallon pail.

"I calls them me Boys' Brigade. They do little errands for me, spying missions, collecting information and such. Intelligence agents. My extra eyes and ears, you might say. The unofficial Street Division of Scotland Yard. No one suspects a street urchin of being a copper now, do they? Rather fortuitous that we had arranged this little gathering. As it happens, I may have a rather perilous job lined up for these young gentlemen."

Pyke stood alongside a row of four scruffy looking young boys, each of varying height but all slim of build. Pyke had decided it was time his gang of diminutive ragamuffins learned the art of boxing, and, more importantly, the skills of self-defence. They stood in the small, grubby gymnasium accommodated in the loft space above the Ten Bells in Spitalfields. There were no obvious outward signs that a gymnasium was housed, or even existed there. It bore no name or signage of any description and all who knew of it, merely called it Jawbone's Gym. Pyke, himself a hardened boxer of hundreds of rounds in and out the ring, trained and sparred there regularly to maintain his physicality and to clear his often-cluttered mind. At this hour there were only eight bodies in the establishment.

Wall bars and full-length, mostly cracked, mirrors were mounted on one long wall. A mixture of heavy bags and ropes were suspended on the opposite side of the long room. In its centre was a makeshift boxing ring which had been marked out using lengths of Mariner's rope nailed crudely to the dark wooden floorboards. Medicine balls, batons and benches were dotted around, and a mixed set of dumbbells stood in one corner whilst a basket of skipping ropes and badly cracked leather gloves sat in the other. The gymnasium smelled damp and fungal, of sweat, liniment and the musk of men. A tattered and torn poster advertising a welterweight contest between Jim Burge and Tom Causer was pinned to the back of the entrance door. The poster had a faded telephone number scrawled across one corner in blue-black India ink, its relevance as forgotten as the two boxers. Yesterday's men. A life-size rendering of today's man, Bombardier Billy Wells, was pinned to a section of wall between two mirrors. The blonde-haired fighter posed ready for action with his gloved hands set in his orthodox stance as if addressing a doomed opponent. Someone had scrawled '*next British heavyweight champion*' at the foot of the poster.

Pyke addressed the four boys. "Lads, this gentleman here is Mr Jawbone Crabtree, trainer of champions and the owner of this here gymnasium and boxing emporium. In this establishment, he is the master of all he surveys, and that includes you." He looked pointedly at each lad in turn. They each nodded their understanding. Pyke, satisfied, continued. "The Negro fellow over yonder is Bob the Log and the elderly gentleman sitting minding his own business in the company of a dumbbell is Mr Geordie McPhee."

Jawbone Crabtree was an imposing figure of a man. Fifty-three years of age and standing six feet three inches tall in his stocking soles. A face so craggy and decorated with scar tissue that he looked as though he had been hewn from granite and sculpted by a drunkard. His nose was so flattened upon his face that from the side you could not tell whether he actually possessed a nose at all. His nickname quite obviously came from his enormous chin which looked like a piece of armour plating that had been riveted to his face. In his younger days, Jawbone had been a challenger for the heavyweight crown of Essex for a brief time but after his defeats had begun outnumbering his wins, he had decided that training fighters would be preferable to fighting them. Jawbone continued to dream that he would uncover a true contender someday. He and Pyke embraced. "Hey, look they're hugging like girls," one of the boys whispered out the side of his mouth to his nearest neighbour in line. The boys elbowed each other in amusement.

"So, this is your ragtag little gang then, Jem? Scrawny looking bunch ain't they? Need a bit of building up I'd say. This one 'ere looks like a sparra," boomed Jawbone, turning his attention to the file of youngsters whilst winking knowingly at Pyke.

"That's why I've brought them along today, Jawbone. Need you to put a little muscle on their bones. Boxer's muscle, long and lean, tough and hard, but still supple so as they keep their speed. Speed and agility are most advantageous in their particular line of business."

Jawbone nodded his enormous slab of a head sagely. "I understand. Keep 'em hard and lean, eh?" The man's voice was as deep as a high bow on a bull fiddle. Pyke turned towards the line of boys. "Now then, lads, if you would be so kind as to introduce yourselves one at a time to the man who will train you in the manly art of pugilism," encouraged Pyke.

After a few seconds of awkward silence, the tallest of the group took a faltering step forward and removed his tattered cap. "My name is Pierce Egan, but everybody calls me Piercie and I'm fourteen years old just last week, Sir. I mostly takes charge of the others on account of me being the oldest and smartest, not to mention the most handsome." His three companions made dismissive tutting noises. Piercie elbowed his neighbour. "I am too!"

"Well a very happy birthday to you, Piercie," came Jawbone's reply. "I see you do not lack in confidence, Mr Pierce."

Pierce smiled proudly and pushed out his chest. "Ain't nobody ever called me Mr Pierce afore, Sir! I might just insist upon it from now onwards."

Suddenly, eager to get in on the act, the smallest of the boys burst forward and shook hands enthusiastically with Jawbone. "Don't pay no heed to him, Mr Jawbone Sir, my name is Tom Tyne, aged eight and three-quarters, and everybody calls me

Tiny. Not on my lack of height but 'cause of me name, you see. Doesn't half pong in 'ere Mr Jawbone," added Tiny pinching his nostrils? "What's that smell?"

"Pleased to make your acquaintance, Tiny me lad. You seem a confident young fellow n'all, and I have to agree with you that the gymnasium does have a distinct aroma," smiled Jawbone. The old trainer was beginning to soften to this group of guttersnipes. "What you can smell is the odour of hard work and determination, son. You'll soon get accustomed to that *pong* as you calls it, and in time you'll even grow to love the smell of the gym just like Sergeant Pyke and every single one of my boxers does."

Tiny sniffed at the air and scrunched up his nose nonplussed, before wiping it along the back of his coat sleeve. "It stinks," he whispered to no one in particular.

Next to break rank was a skinny curly-haired boy with tanned olive skin that looked dried and wrinkled giving him the appearance of being aged before his time. "My name is John Fosbrook, and I'm twelve years old, Sir. It's nice to meet you."

"Well it's equally nice to meet you too Master John Fosbrook, but calling you that seems rather too formal don't you think? Too much of a mouthful. What do people call you then lad?" enquired the trainer. "Oh, ever so sorry Sir, everybody calls me Fuzz on accounts of me frizzy hair, like." The others giggled and Fosbrook shot them a reproachful look.

"Now that's a proper good name there, Fuzz, I like it much better than plain old John. Makes you sound exotic like Bob the Log over there," added Jawbone encouragingly. Fuzz looked nervously towards the barrel-chested Negro, who was shadow boxing effortlessly in front of the gym's full height mirrors. "Why's he called Bob the Log, Mr Jawbone, Sir?" Pyke bit his lip and suppressed a muffled laugh.

"Well, Son," began Jawbone. "How can I put it delicately? You might say he needs a more generous cut in his trousers than most gentlemen, if you get me drift."

As Fuzz struggled to decipher Jawbone's cryptic answer, the final Brigade member took a step forward. "Hello Sir, my name is Caleb Baldwin and I'm also twelve years old. Everybody…"

"…Calls you Baldy, am I right?" interrupted an expectant Jawbone. "No Sir, everyone calls me Winner," answered an indignant Caleb as his three companions sniggered apprehensively.

"Begging your pardon, Winner," apologised Jawbone. "Right, so, that's Piercie, Tiny, Fuzz and Winner then. Jem Pyke's Boys' Brigade." Crabtree rubbed his hands together. "As for me, you can call me Coach and if you show improvement and become something that resembles a boxer then, and only then, can you refer to me as Jawbone. Understood?"

"Understood!" came the unanimous and simultaneous reply.

"Right lads get changed into your shorts and whatnot, the changing room is behind that curtain over there," ordered Jawbone, indicating the rearmost part of the attic space. The boys remained standing uncomfortably where they were, looking anxiously between themselves and Pyke. Pyke cupped his hand and whispered in Jawbone's grossly misshapen ear. "That's the only clothes this rag-tag bunch have, Jawbone, and they're lucky to be wearing them. I get them each a new pair of boots at Christmastime as a work's bonus like, but apart from that, what you see is what you get. Only Winner there has family that he can claim by blood, the other three are orphans and street lads."

Crabtree looked at the Boys' Brigade. "I forgot to say, lads, if you ain't got any other clothes with you today, you'll find a large wicker basket with odd bits of clothing and such behind the curtain. Some may be too big, but they'll do for the time being. Help yourselves to whatever you need. Oh, and I never told you, boxers starting out always go barefoot, so just take off your shoes for the first few weeks." Jawbone nodded a perceptive smile at Pyke, which was reciprocated knowingly. As the boys headed off towards the curtain, Tiny turned to Pyke and asked, "Sarge, what is puGleism?" Pyke looked at the smallest member of his Brigade, "It's just a fancy term for boxing Tiny, now go and get changed."

As the group barged each other out of the way to be first to the basket, Jawbone turned to Pyke. "Seem like a fine bunch of lads you have there, Jem." The big bruiser had never married, never had children of his own. Pyke often thought this showed through in the big man's fatherly treatment of the boys who walked through his doors. Most fathers around Spitalfields wanted to imbue their sons with the confidence, discipline, and sense of responsibility that Jawbone Crabtree dispensed from his anonymous gymnasium.

"They sure are, Jawbone, and loyal as well. Piercie is a natural born leader. Good head on his shoulders." Pyke looked at Jawbone's slab of a cranium and realised the inappropriateness of his comment. "Detective Chief Inspector Wiggins says that Piercie reminds himself of him at that age, which in my book is a prodigious compliment. Fuzz is the joker of the Brigade, but don't let that fool you, he's as smart as they come. Winner, well he's fearless and not afraid of a scrap when it is required. I think he could well become a fairly proficient boxer if truth be told. And then there's Tiny, who as you have no doubt seen, is the cheeky one of the bunch, but he can run like the wind. Wings on his heels like Hermes, has little Tom Tyne. They do a lot of hard and important work on behalf of the police that the public, and most of the Force, are blissfully unaware of," explained Pyke with obvious pride. Jawbone nodded. "Here, give me a hand with this, Jem." The two men proceeded to lift the top two sections of a wooden gym horse and placed them near one end of the long gymnasium.

The boys all shuffled barefooted from behind the curtain wearing oversized shorts and baggy vests. Tiny's shorts were so big for him that they looked like full-length trousers. He had tied a rope around the waist to keep them from falling around his ankles. The foursome looked a sorry sight, almost comical.

"Now that's definitely more like it, lads. You're already beginning to look like boxers," declared Jawbone with faked sincerity. Bob the Log had ceased his shadow boxing and was wiping the sweat from the back of his broad neck with a stained grey towel. He laughed at the sight of the quartet standing before Jawbone. "Dem's a fine bunch o' athletes you have there, Jawbone." Winner turned and threw Bob a disapproving glare.

"We look bleedin' awful, that's what we look Mr Jawbone, sorry Coach, Sir," retorted an embarrassed Tiny. The boys looked at each other and began to giggle. The giggle quickly turned into a laugh, until everybody present, except the stoic Geordie McPhee, followed suit and hooted uncontrollably at the small group of misfits standing in the centre of the gymnasium. Once the hilarity had all but burnt itself out, Jawbone raised the whistle he wore suspended from his neck by a strip of rawhide and blew one shrill blast. All was quiet. "Now lads, I want you to form a queue at that end of the gym, run the length of the floor and jump over that wooden horse positioned at the opposite end. You got that lads?"

"We ain't gonna be punching each other then, Coach?" moaned an obviously disappointed Winner.

"First lesson, Mr Winner," responded Jawbone, "is that you do as I say and do not question my methods, ever! Second lesson being that learning how to punch is only one element of becoming a boxer. Now GO!" The four boys, surprised by Jawbone's shout, ran the length of the gym, heels smacking against the hardwood floor, and each, in turn, hurdled the wooden obstacle at the far end of the room.

"Right, that's enough for today lads, get changed back into your work clothes," commanded Jawbone to a shocked and surprised Boys' Brigade.

"That's it? That's all we're doing Coach, Sir?" enquired a bemused Piercie.

"Yes, Piercie, that's all I need to know until the same time next week. Do not be late lads." Jawbone stooped to pick up a discarded towel. As the bemused bunch began to head for the changing area Tiny stopped in front of Jawbone. He stared at the old man sat on a bench, curling what to Tiny looked like an unfeasibly heavy dumbbell with one arm, a half-smoked cigarette held between the fingers of his other hand. "Who's the old geezer in the corner again, Coach?" piped up Tiny.

Jawbone ruffled Tiny's head. "Well now, that 'old geezer' you describe is none other than Geordie 'Diamond' McPhee, one of the hardest men of his size and weight this country has surely known. He could chew iron and spit rust in his day." Tiny looked at the old man who had now placed the dumbbell back in its rack by its neighbours and was heading towards Pyke. "Diamond was a great Scottish middle-weight bare-knuckle champion from the eighteen sixties and seventies. A hard man he was, hence, his adopted name. I very much doubt that Sergeant Pyke has told you this but, over forty years ago, that old man fought the future heavyweight champion of the world. He never bested Gypsy Jem Mace, but some said he put up a helluva fight, blackening Mace's eye, splitting his chin, and putting him on his knees during thirty-two brutal rounds of boxing. The Diamond doesn't say much these days, never did, to be honest, but when he does say something you'd better listen because it will be words of true wisdom."

"Is that why everybody calls you Jem, then Jem? After some ancient heavyweight champion?" enquired a rather confused Tiny turning to Pyke.

Pyke gave the slightest of nods. "It is lad, and I'm proud to be associated, if only in name, with that great boxing champion." Satisfied, Tiny raced after the others. As the boys went behind the curtain to get dressed Pyke questioned Jawbone. "So why that exact little exercise?"

"Well Jem, I really wanted to see how the boys moved naturally, how they placed their feet, their gait pattern and their balance and way they leapt the horse and how they landed. As you well know, my friend, balance is everything to a fighter. Winner has a bit of a twisted hip and Piercie's left foot turns inwards slightly. Hardly surprising, given what you've told me of their upbringing and I'm guessing, lack of proper meals. I also wanted to see how they dealt with disappointment. They were all disappointed in some way or another and I can sense such things, especially in some so young, who don't ordinarily mask their feelings. That little exercise told me a lot of things about those boys, the dynamics of their group and how they each reacted individually. I have a clear plan in my head now for next week."

"That's good, Jawbone. Thanks for this." Pyke shook hands with the big trainer. Jawbone clasped Pyke's granite-like shoulder with an enormous hand. "Least I can do, Jem."

The boys emerged from behind the curtain and assembled in front of the two, ready to be dismissed. Pyke noticed that each of them, rather sheepishly, still wore their newly found vests under the shirts. McPhee approached Pyke. As he passed the boys, he playfully rubbed Tiny's head by way of a gesture of introduction. Tiny tried not to yelp as the rock-hard fingers dug across his scalp. "Fancy a wee dance, Jem?" asked the Diamond, indicating the makeshift ring whilst extinguishing his cigarette between a leathery thumb and forefinger.

"Not today, Geordie. Lots going on at work, mate and I can't be turning up looking like John Heenan after the Tom Sayers fight, now, can I? I have a City to save, Diamond," joked Pyke. '*Little does he know how true that is,*' he thought grimly.

The Scotsman turned, disappointed. “Aye, well if ya need ony help wi’ that Laddie, just gie me a shout.” He wandered cannily back to his bench and took another dumbbell from the rack. Suddenly the gymnasium door burst open with Constable Murray invading the room like an assailant. “Sergeant Pyke, you best come quick!” he shouted, gasping to find his breath. “Guvnor needs you straight away, Sir.”

‘*Wilson Brown will have to wait until another day,*’ lamented Pyke as he headed to grab his hat.

Chapter 41 - The Angel

Lady Constance Harkness, Ms Jennifer Potts and Mrs Mary Wiggins sat in the grandiose Chinese tea house within the Whitechapel Gallery. The three ladies had become firm friends since the dreadful murder of Jennifer's police constable husband, William, at the hands of the murderous Beast, Doctor Joseph Bleak. They shared an abomination of memories that would bind them together for a lifetime. At Lady Constance's behest, the Harkness family had taken Constable Potts' widow into the very heart of their home, in gratitude for his bravery in having saved Constance's life. The young Constable had sacrificed himself so that Lady Constance could live, throwing his body between her and the slashing monster. Jennifer and her baby were now regarded as members of the Harkness family and enjoyed the freedom of the house and surrounding grounds. She particularly felt an eternal sense of gratitude towards Constance who had become like a sister to her.

The three ladies met regularly, on the afternoon of each last Tuesday of the month, for what they would describe to others as their 'cultural expeditions.' However, these cultural outings also offered an ideal opportunity to chatter and gossip without fear of any reprisal or judgement. They had met at Saint Pancras Station to begin the day. Previous rendezvous had seen them attend an eclectic array of events, including the inaugural Great Spring Show, held in the grounds of the Royal Hospital in Chelsea. Mary and Constance had taken great delight in explaining the names of the various blooms to Jennifer, each vying with each other to remember Latin terminology wherever they could. Some of the names had made Jennifer laugh.

They had also watched in awe at the athleticism and beauty of Anna Pavlova and her dancing partner Vaslav Nijinsky at Covent Garden. They had gasped in amazement at the strength and grace of the dancers and revelled in the exquisite precision of the orchestra. Both Mary and Constance had attended several ballets in the past, but the experience was an entirely new one for Jennifer. She had been enthralled by the whole experience, from the mysterious, though charming, masked attendant whose chilled hand had guided her to her seat, to the final uproarious encore. She thought the applause would never end and she had left the Opera House quite giddy and light-headed. The entire experience had filled her with an emotional joy that she would never have imagined possible. The music, the movement, the costumes, and the miraculous way that the stage lights picked out every nuance of the dance drew her into a world that she had never previously encountered. The arms of Pavlova fascinated her. The way they pointed and extended, communicating a feeling or emotion to the audience through the movement and sublime positioning of muscles.

Just four weeks earlier, they had strolled through The Regent's Park Zoological Gardens, marvelling at the recently added amphibian and reptile house. None of the ladies had seen such exotic creatures outside of picture books and encyclopaedias. The queues for the new attraction had stretched almost to the elephant house, such was the public interest. Once inside the new Herpetarium, the heat and humidity had been almost unbearable. A yellow ringed python made them flinch when it slowly raised an inquisitive head and flickered a searching tongue towards them. Their apprehension soon dissolved into relieved laughter. Their meetings always included laughter. The shared and silly laughter only friends can truly appreciate. The tank containing vividly coloured tree frogs bore a sign warning the public of the deadly toxicity of the creatures within. "Does it not seem absurd that such a small and beautiful creature could be so deadly!" remarked Jennifer with a sad expression on her elfin face.

But each agreed that the star of the show had been the giant chameleon. At first, they had stared searchingly into its enclosure, looking amongst the strategically placed branches and greenery. The exhibit seemed bereft of any life until the flick of a speckled eyelid over a large orb of an eye had betrayed the reptile's presence. "This is a Pearson's chameleon and is found in the lush rainforests of eastern and northern Madagascar. The chameleon's skin tone changes according to its mood and surroundings," read Mary from the tank-side information plaque.

Constance raised an eyebrow. "If only this were a trait common in the human race. Life would be so much less complicated, don't you think?"

"Particularly where *men* are concerned!" Jennifer had laughed.

"I'll be mother," stated Mary to her afternoon companions as she reached across the table and proceeded to pour each of them a cup from a teapot decorated with oriental birds. Her hand trembled slightly under the weight of the teapot. "I read only yesterday, Constance, that your friend and fellow reformer Emeline Pankhurst was arrested and imprisoned in Leatherhead Police Station last week. How utterly awful for the Cause. Such a brave and principled lady."

"As this is our special monthly time to be together I felt I should not burden you with my concerns and disquiets ladies, but it is indeed a travesty that the leader of the Women's Social and Political Union has been arrested at all!" replied Constance, anger raising her tone such that several fellow diners stared unappreciatively in her direction.

Mary noted the disquiet in the room. "Ignore them, darling. We should all be proud of the stance that Miss Pankhurst and others like her take in our name." Jennifer nodded her agreement. Constance's thoughts turned immediately back to her elder sister, slaughtered so brutally by the same Beast that had murdered Jennifer's husband. Mary, instinctively realising the subject of Constance's thoughts, placed a sympathetic hand upon her friend's wrist.

Lady Harkness staunched a tear and smiled appreciatively at Mary. "And do you know what she is being charged with?" she continued. "I will tell you what she is charged with. She is charged with, and I quote from the Daily Herald here, 'having feloniously counselled and procured certain persons whose names are unknown to commit the bomb outrage last week at Mr Lloyd George's house.' His unoccupied house I might well add. How totally and entirely preposterous!"

"Please don't say she will be refusing food Connie?" pleaded Jennifer as she added a teaspoon of granulated sugar to her cup of tea.

"Emeline shall, I am sure, at once declare a hunger strike, I have no doubt of that. The Home Office authorities have imprisoned her on account of a speech she delivered the night following the bombing. In that speech, she declared that, when the Franchise Bill was withdrawn, she was personally prepared to accept responsibility for all acts to which women felt themselves driven, whether they be legal or otherwise. Radical but inspiring leadership."

"Well the authorities have definitely taken that at face value," opined Mary.

"I fear that if they do not set her free, she would rather die for the Cause, and if they torture her with force-feeding, that cannot last very long. If she dies, she will die a heroine and martyr with hundreds ready and willing to take her place. But that is enough of my encumbrances, this is our day to share cultural experiences, or should I say to behave like young girls once again," laughed Constance, dismissing the matter. She took another sip of tea and replaced her cup delicately back upon its saucer. "But what of you, Mary? You look remarkably well recovered following that abominable incident at the Palace." Both she and Jennifer looked concernedly at Mary Wiggins.

Mary cleared her throat slightly, rather embarrassed that she was now the focus of attention. "I was extremely fortunate, Connie," she acknowledged. "A few cuts and bruises, an occasional burn, and a mild concussion that Doctor Watson assured me would have no lasting effect. I also suffered a burst eardrum. The *tympanic membrane,* John called it. It leaves me slightly deaf in one ear, a condition that Albert joked I may find useful in some of our more heated conversations."

Mary's companions laughed. "Mr Pyke was such a hero that day," stated Jennifer.

"If not for his actions I doubt I would be here at all," admitted Mary. "That poor man, the grief he has endured at the loss of his Noreen. My heart breaks when I think of it."

A mood of gloom descended upon the three women until Jennifer broke the silence. "How, pray tell, is a certain Mr Alexander Buchanan?" she inquired with a hint of mischief about her questioning, "I could swear I saw the two of you strolling towards the West Lake the other day. Was that him or another tall, golden-haired archaeologist you were arm and arm with?" The three ladies all smiled knowingly. Constance coughed as if the precursor to some great speech. "Let us just say that, yes, we have met again, and before this unwarranted interrogation goes any further, no, we have not yet kissed and there is no arrangement between us," stated Constance in a faux official manner.

"No doubt," agreed Jennifer, "though he is extremely handsome. I should make sure you come to an understanding soon, if I were you, Connie. Before someone else snaps him up."

The trio dissolved into fits of laughter which fostered further disapproving glances from certain nearby grandes dames. After composing themselves the friends each chose a second petit fours from the Victorian what-not placed upon the table. "How is your young master, William Albert Potts faring, Jennifer?" asked Mary, using a lace napkin to dab a stray spot of clotted cream from the corner her mouth.

"He is fit and hale and hearty thank you, Mary," declared Jennifer, her face glowing with pride. "He grows to resemble his father a little more each day he wakes. His head is full of red curls just like that of his father. I know I may say this every time we meet, but, if it were not for Connie embracing me into her family in Hertfordshire when I was with child, I dread to imagine what may have befallen the pair of us. Poorhouse I would wager. Lady Constance Harkness is not only his godmother, she is William's guardian angel," beamed Jennifer proudly.

"On that note, shall we drink up ladies?" interjected Constance swiftly changing subject matter. "Since we speak of angels, let us now go and meet a true angel who resides, believe it or not, in this very building."

The three women made their way from the tea house to a small gallery attached to Hall Three to stand in front of William Blake's 'Angel of Revelation.'

"I can confidently state that this has to be one of my favourite watercolours," specified Constance to the others.

"It is rather splendid, Connie," agreed Jennifer.

"This is one of a series of eighty biblical works that William Blake painted for one of his most prominent patrons, a Mr Thomas Butts. I understand that the artist found inspiration for the subject matter in chapter ten of the book of Revelation." Constance warmed to her subject. "See the diminutive figure of Saint John, sitting, writing as he gazes up at the gargantuan angel which is represented wearing a cloud to cover his embarrassment," joked Constance with faked shock. "The angel's face appears like the rays of the sun whilst his feet appear to be engulfed in flames," she added.

"It looks as though one could touch the clouds, they are so wonderfully imagined," observed Mary. Jennifer nodded her head in thoughtful agreement.

"I recently discovered that Blake based the angel's water-spanning stance on prints of the Colossus of Rhodes he had seen whilst touring Egypt. See the wispy figures in the centremost part of the painting? The seven thunders, horsemen riding through the billowing clouds. See them?" asked Constance, eagerly.

"Yes, but I must admit that I did not notice them at first," admitted Mary, "I was so enraptured by the angel's enigmatic face, especially his astonishing eyes. Such captivating eyes."

"And to think, this painting hanging before us is over one hundred years old, and yet, it seems so contemporary, resembling modern religious symbolism of the highest order," enthused Constance.

Jennifer and Constance slowly wandered off towards other works of art, whilst Mary remained stationary, transfixed at the face of the Angel. "Are you coming, Mary dearest?" enquired Jennifer in a raised voice.

"Yes, I shall catch you up ladies, I just need a few more moments with the angel," replied Mary, all the while fixated upon Blake's marvellous watercolour, her voice trailing off to a whisper, "...with *my* Angel." Constance and Jennifer made their way into the main gallery.

Mary began to feel detached from reality, immersed as she was in the painting. She felt a sudden drop in air temperature and the hairs on her arms raised with a reflex charge of electromagnetic energy. She was now entirely alone in the small viewing gallery and she began to feel lightheaded and queasy. As she continued to be spellbound by the angel's face, it appeared to twitch indiscernibly. Mary was absorbed in that face, fascinated, captivated. Her breathing had become shallow and gasping whilst her heart thundered in response. She could not avert her gaze from Blake's painting. So captivated was she that nothing else existed in that moment but that face and those eyes. The angel's face seemed to twitch a second time, and the painting appeared to visibly grow in stature, as if Mary's pupils had dilated, demanding the entrance of as much light as possible. There was nothing but that face, those amazing eyes. They pierced her very soul. Her head was swirling in unison with the face, intermingling with the different hues in a watercolour whirlpool.

An unseen hand gently stroked Mary's cheek, then what felt like a single finger, pressed sensually against her lips, slightly parting them. She was not afraid or unnerved at the sensation but was instead excited and pleasured by it so much so that her nipples hardened under the sexually charged malevolence in the room. The angel's eyes closed abruptly then just as quickly opened wide. Grey, dark, and imposing, those eyes seemed to suck her inwards, demanding the attention of her whole being. Mary existed in a swooning, roaring silence, suddenly interrupted by the sharp, amplified sound of someone approaching from the distance. The footsteps increased in volume and seemed to belong to a particularly strident gait. The approaching footfalls sounded, not as that of a human, but of some cloven-hooved animal. '*A horse or goat perhaps?*' thought Mary, abstractly.

As if from a shadow that was not there, the tall, slender figure of Luca Radasiliev emerged and strode purposefully towards Mary Wiggins. His high-collared, waist length cape billowed as he approached, its red silk lining licking like flames around his body. He presented an ethereal figure of striking countenance and regal deportment. His black silken hair was flecked with wisps of distinguished silver at the temples, making his hair resemble a photograph of flames. His piercing black eyes sat within a face of noble features. His presence exuded confidence and extreme self-assuredness.

Still, Mary could not move. Radasiliev stood directly between her and the painting. His face replacing that of the Angel of Revelation. She could not avert her gaze. She did not care to. "Are you an angel … or a devil?" she asked Radasiliev, mesmerised. The reply that answered her question was in the unmistakable voice and intonation of her beloved husband, Albert Wiggins. "I am not a disciple of the Devil, Mary Dearest, I am his adversary!"

Mary Wiggins awoke in indelible darkness. She tried to rise but her head and knees were blocked by some unseen and immovable obstacle. She reached out her arms and her elbows and feet which were all also repelled, blocked, encased within some barrier. She rubbed frantically at her eyes in the hope that she was still not yet fully awake and remained asleep, dreaming. Still, complete darkness. She began to panic and scream for help, but her voice instantly echoed dully within her confines. She pushed in all directions with as much might as she could muster, but nothing gave. She could tell that she was surrounded by what felt like solid timber. She tried kicking her feet against the sides of her confines. Mary's senses were racing now, her mind in turmoil. She stopped kicking, realising that her actions were pointless. Other than the sound of her laboured breathing, she was swaddled in total silence. Absolute darkness entombed her. Her hands felt around in all directions, but she could feel nothing other than what seemed like a silken pillow whereupon her head rested. Realisation dawned immediately. She was lying in a coffin, but this was no safety coffin equipped with a signalling mechanism in case of premature burial. There was no cord attached to a surface mounted bell. Mary Wiggins was entombed. She began to weep and then to sob uncontrollably. She was in utter despair.

"Telegram arrived for you barely twenty minutes ago, Inspector, best read it forthwith," hinted Sergeant Ash, waving the piece of paper in the air. Wiggins read the note aloud.

MR HIGH AND MIGHTY DETECTIVE - STOP
HAVE MARY - STOP
BURIED - STOP
STILL ALIVE - STOP
YOURS LR - STOP

Wiggins reread the telegram, the paper shaking in his trembling hand. "Ash! Get Pyke here right this instant! There is no time to spare. Tell him to cease whatever matters he is currently attending to immediately. I need him here by my side right now! Luca Radasiliev has somehow managed to kidnap my wife and if this message is to be understood, time is of the essence. It seems from the wording on the telegram that the fiend has buried her alive! Find out where that telegram was placed, Nosher. Now!"

"In the process, Sir," replied a worried Nosher as he headed for the electric telegraphy machine.

Wiggins picked up his telephone and called his home number. His eyes blinked rapidly as he waited on his call being connected then slammed down the voice piece on hearing no answer. "Damn!" he spat. He then dashed downstairs, his shoe soles barely touching the stone, to find Doctor Nelson B. Pascoe in the coroner's rooms. Pascoe was seated hunched over a microscope, his left eye peering into the eyepiece. "Doctor Pascoe, do you know how long a person can survive being buried alive?" demanded Wiggins of the pathologist, as he burst unceremoniously into the room.

Pascoe, startled, lifted his head. He could hear the frantic edge to Wiggins' normally calm voice. "I can safely state that is indeed the strangest question I have been asked today, Inspector," replied Pascoe removing a thin glass slide from under the objective lens.

"Just answer the damn question, please, Doctor Pascoe!" barked Wiggins, his voice now raised.

The portly pathologist reeled at Wiggins' uncharacteristic loss of composure, instantly recognising that the detective was under severe stress. He thought momentarily. "Well Detective, I know for certain that the average casket measures eighty-four by twenty-eight inches and is twenty-three inches deep, so..." the Doctor withdrew a notepad and pencil and began frantically scribbling down numbers. "...that is, a total volume of fifty-four, point zero nine six cubic inches, or, if you prefer, almost sixteen thousand pints of air. My understanding is that the average volume of a human body is approximately one hundred and sixteen pints. That leaves nearly fifteen hundred pints of air, one-fifth of which we can safely assume is oxygen. If a person was unfortunate enough to be mistakenly buried alive, then that person would consume say one pint of oxygen each minute, so by my calculations, it would take almost five and a half hours before all the oxygen in the coffin had been consumed. Obviously, the smaller you are, the longer you will survive, and the more stressed you are the quicker your breathing would be."

"Hell, and damnation! That leaves us less than six hours to locate and apprehend Radasiliev and find Mary's whereabouts and even then, we would need to dig for at least thirty minutes, depending on how deeply she has been buried." Wiggins clasped his head on each side, pulled at his hair, then raced back upstairs, leaving a baffled Doctor Pascoe scratching his head in bewilderment. "Where in Hell's name is Pyke, Nosher?" demanded Wiggins as he reached the front desk.

"Nobody knows his whereabouts Inspector, and he's not been in work this morning at all. I've dispatched Constable Donaldson to Pyke's residence and Constables Flowers, Theaker and Sievewright are attending his usual watering holes on the off chance. Murray is also on the case. We'll locate him don't you worry about that, Sir. As for the telegram, it was placed at the London District Telegraph Company where the central office is nine hundred and ninety-nine, Cannon Street, in the very heart of the city, Sir."

"That doesn't help us in the slightest! The LDTC delivers messages to all parts of London and even to the suburbs. I was hoping it would have been sent via one of the smaller companies or stations which only deliver within a half-mile radius. That would have narrowed down our search area to some degree. Damn!" Wiggins thumped the nearest wall in frustration. He was frantic with worry, struggling to maintain some sort of productive thought process.

Ash could see that Wiggins needed help to think. "What would you tell yourself to do in such circumstances, Sir?" he asked knowing his question would instantly re-engage Wiggins' mind and make him reason more logically rather than emotionally.

Wiggins drew in several deep breaths and ran his fingers through his hair. "Firstly, Nosh, I would ask myself what precisely do we know at this stage?" He began to pace up and down the room. "One, we know that Radasiliev has Mary in his possession."

"With all due respect Sir, we don't know that for a *fact*. It is signed with the letters L and R, but we cannot at this stage state definitively that it is Radasiliev," highlighted Sergeant Ash. "He may well be bluffing, and your good lady is this very moment hanging out the washing at home as we speak. Of course, there is also the possibility that this may be a hoax."

"Ah, but we do know this as fact, Nosher. You see, he has used the exact term that Mary uses to describe me when she thinks I am getting beyond my station, *Mr high and mighty Detective*," affirmed Wiggins. "That cannot be coincidence. Secondly, we know for a fact that the telegram was sent from Cannon Street within the last hour. Give them a call and ask if any individual resembling Radasiliev has indeed used their services within the previous sixty minutes." Wiggins still wondered at how on Earth he was going to discover where his Mary was.

Just then, Constable Donaldson burst through the station doors. Donaldson was a huge man and was red-faced and breathing heavily. "No sign of Sergeant Pyke at his home address and I'm presuming Billy will be at school currently," he gasped, supporting himself with one hand against a wall.

Wiggins punched into his palm in exasperation. "There is something definitely afoot here, Nosh. Pyke is inexplicably missing, and my beloved Mary's life is hanging, God only knows where, by the thinnest of threads. Damn Radasiliev!" cursed Wiggins. Ash had never seen his superior officer in such a visibly stressed state. "Nosher, call Van Hoon at his home, Belgravia 1212, explain the situation and get him down here, right away!"

Just then Pyke burst into the station building, closely followed by Constable Murray. "Really sorry Bert, I was with me Boys' Brigade, introducing them to Jawbone Crabtree down at the gym. Thought I might get them toughened up and ready for the search for the Russian and his deviants. As soon as Murray here spotted me leaving, he grabbed me and told me what is going on. Jumped in the squad car and got here as soon as we could," offered Pyke apologetically. He was obviously disappointed he had not been present in Wiggins' moment of need.

"And that's bleedin' fast, I can vouchsafe!" ventured Murray, his face pale from the traumatic experience of having been driven at Pyke's helter-skelter speed through the packed streets from Spitalfields to Westminster.

"You are here now, Jem, and that is all that matters. Apparently, Radasiliev has abducted Mary, and we currently have not the faintest idea where she could be. He has hinted in this telegram that she may, in fact, be buried, although thankfully still alive, for the time being, if Doctor Pascoe's calculations can be relied upon," detailed Wiggins, handing the telegram message to Pyke. He was straining to keep as calm and as focused as possible. "We MUST find her, Jem. I cannot lose her!" Pyke swallowed hard, thinking of Noreen. Wiggins continued, "we have very little time to find her and no obvious clues to assist us." He put his head in his hands, cutting a forlorn figure. "What do I do, Jem? What do I do?"

Pyke took the telegram from Wiggins' clenched hand and nodded as he donned his reading glasses before studying the telegram intently. His mind was racing with all sorts of scenarios, none of which were attractive. '*What if she were buried, but not in a coffin?*' The idea was unthinkable, and he tried to dismiss it from his mind. He was desperately trying to think of where the Russian may have taken Mary. He knew that his mind could not function properly amidst such an adrenalin rush. He felt powerless and forlornly threw the telegram to the floor and looked towards Wiggins for some guidance.

Wiggins steadied himself and continued. "I have asked for Van Hoon's assistance, and for him to come here as a matter of urgency. Perhaps he can help." Suddenly Wiggins was hit with an inspirational thought. "Do you recall the Ball he organised a few months ago to help us endeavour to determine more about Radasiliev? How he utilised what he termed 'remote viewing' and all manner of paranormal techniques to uncover information? Did he not claim that he has been afforded, or developed, a gift of being able to sense people and their thoughts? And did he not attest that he can put himself within the heads of others? Of climbing inside the skin of another, metaphorically speaking?" he reminded Pyke, his mind now racing.

"Yes, all manner of wizardry," answered Pyke, clutching enthusiastically at Wiggins train of thought. "Were you not also adamant that he enabled you to actually see the face of the Beast by some such trickery, Bert? A mesmeric trance of some sort in the Wax Museum, I seem to recall. As such, I would say anything is worth trying under the circumstances."

"I agree, Jem," confirmed Wiggins, his head felt as if it were spinning, and his stomach felt as though it were full of leaden butterflies. "Where is Van Hoon?" he shouted, exasperated, at no one in particular. "Get me Van Hoon on the telephone. I need to speak to him personally and right this instant!"

Chapter 42 - The Amalgamation

Wiggins, Pyke, Van Hoon and the shrouded figure of Feather, the most trusted member of Van Hoon's Pestilent, stood together in the deepest bowels of Scotland Yard. Once he had been fully appraised of the situation, the Dutchman had specifically requested the use of the smallest solitary confinement cell available. "The smaller the space, the more conducive the atmosphere. Sensory deprivation heightens the experience, Inspector," he had explained enigmatically to Wiggins. The two had talked on the telephone barely twenty minutes earlier. Wiggins had outlined Mary's disappearance as coherently as he possibly could under the circumstances. Van Hoon could sense barely concealed panic pouring from Wiggins as he related the contents of the telegram and Van Hoon had responded by instructing both Ilhan and Feather to accompany him directly to the Yard as a matter of urgency.

The cell was barren of any furniture and smelled of a musty dampness and the underlying stale odour of hundreds of past detainees. "Guilt and fear," Van Hoon had announced as he had entered the cell. "Other than death, the most pungent and long-lasting of all odours."

"Shame and shit more like it!" offered Pyke. The room had no windows, situated as it was, below ground level. The plaster walls were stained and deeply gouged in places, a testament to a history of physical encounters, some of which Pyke could still recall. Graffiti with names, dates and curses were etched everywhere into the soft plaster.

The hooded figure of the wraithlike Feather, wearing a gold macramé belt around his waist, produced a small but deeply padded silken cushion from within his robes and placed it delicately on the floor in the centre of the cell. He took three steps backwards and seemed to dissolve into the walls of the room. Wiggins had noted the copious leprous scarring traversing a route around his emaciated tattooed forearm. The detective turned his attention to Van Hoon. "Tell us again, Van Hoon, what exactly is it you are about to do? Will it really work? This is of the utmost urgency!"

"Remote viewing gentlemen!" came the grandiose response. Van Hoon propped his ubiquitous sword cane in the corner of the room. "Seeing something from a distance is wondrous to experience gentlemen." Pyke could see that Van Hoon was, as always, relishing being the centre of attention, even in this dire scenario. There was a sense of the Grand Guignol within the cell. An anticipation of some forthcoming naturalistic horror performance.

The Dutchman paused for effect before continuing. "It is a skill often considered hokum, one debunked by the conventional scientific community, but I can assure you, gentlemen, that it is both real and attainable. Many gifted individuals are ordinarily born with this skill but very few have ever mastered it. I studied amongst the greatest Sufis and mystics of the East where I also learned the art of psychometry, which to the uninitiated, is the ability whereby a person can sense the history of an object merely by touching it." A disbelieving Pyke was already becoming frustrated with Van Hoon's epistle. He looked towards Van Hoon's attendant and strained his eyes, but he could no longer discern Feather's slender figure, as it was all but camouflaged within the dark corner where the leper stood. "It has taken me many years to master remote viewing. Perseverance is ultimately the key. It is often termed anomalous cognition or more commonly 'second sight.' Essentially, it is defined as the ability to obtain accurate information regarding a distant place, person, or an event without the use of your physical senses or any other obvious means."

"What's wrong with a decent pair of binoculars then?" interrupted a mocking Pyke. He knew that every second that went by was like a knife cut to Wiggins. "Why don't you just cut the talk and get on with it? Mary is in peril." He could see Wiggins desperately trying to stifle his emotions.

"You do know that I am a great champion of yours Sergeant Pyke, don't you? But sometimes your propensity for the obvious is what hinders you so. Let your spirit free occasionally and observe life from strange angles, from a different plane, it will only add to your already considerable canon of physical attributes," continued Van Hoon genially. "My only fear is mediocrity. I believe that one should strive to attain perfection in all aspects of one's life. Don't you agree gentlemen?"

Pyke bit his lip and leant a shoulder against the cell wall, arms crossed. "Go on then, let's see what you got up that perfectly tailored sleeve of yours, Van Hoon. Time is a scarce commodity here."

"Yes, can we please make a start please, Van Hoon?" beseeched Wiggins. "Actions speak louder than words, especially when we have so little time."

"Why, yes of course Inspector, forgive my histrionics. I can assure you that I will endeavour to utilise all my abilities to locate your wife," apologised the Dutchman. He went on, "I am afraid that if I am to attain the necessary level of meditation, I must ask you both to now leave the cell. I shall then commence proceedings. Feather will remain in the cell with me in the unlikely event that I may require any physical assistance."

Pyke's eyes raised in the direction of where the diminutive, waif-like figure had last stood. "I sense your incredulity Sergeant Pyke," stated van Hoon, "Fear not. My companion is more powerful than you can ever imagine. One should not prejudge the worth or value of someone by outward appearance alone. All my inner Pestilent are highly trained in Eastern martial arts."

"Please proceed now, Mr Van Hoon," interrupted a now obviously impatient Wiggins, eagerly anticipating what he suspected would be a bravura performance.

"Of course, Detective Chief Inspector. You and Sergeant Pyke can observe matters through the door's glazed panel, but I must warn you that what I am about to attempt sometimes takes an age, and unfortunately it is not what you would term a spectator sport. The player alone gains all the pleasure and the audience is usually somewhat underwhelmed I am afraid. Please extinguish the lights."

Van Hoon sat in silence for almost thirty minutes. Half an hour of frantic mental torture for Wiggins who could think only of his Mary, terrified and frightened in some blackened pit. He stalked up and down the cell corridor, stopping to look in through the door's viewing panel each time he passed the cell. Within the cell, Van Hoon's eyes remained tightly closed the entire time and no part of his body moved. His breathing was uniform and deliberate. He sat cross-legged, his arms fully extended, with the palms of his hands facing upwards, as if expecting delivery of some large package. Wiggins and Pyke watched the scene evolving through the small viewing hatch in the iron-clad door. The detectives' eyes had slowly become accustomed to the darkness and could easily distinguish Van Hoon's dark motionless silhouette but not that of his accompanying Pestilent.

"Anything happening yet, Guv?" whispered an increasingly impatient Pyke into Wiggins' right ear. Wiggins remained hushed, only indicating a negative by the rapid waving back and forth of his index finger. Outwardly he seemed calm but inwardly he remained frantic, his nerves frayed to the quick. In his head, he had been constructing elaborate rationalisations for why everything would turn out all right, but still, the nagging voice in the back of his mind spoke of nothing but doom ahead. Pyke meanwhile had become tormented by the recurring thought, '*what if she is buried, but not in a coffin?*'

Meanwhile, Van Hoon had attained a state of deep relaxation whereby his mind was calm, and his body felt tremendously heavy. His limbs and inner core felt leaden. His brainwaves were now in an alpha state instead of the more usual beta state, allowing his brain frequency to become a doorway into the required transcendental condition essential to progress. Nothing supernatural, he had merely educated his body to enter hypnagogic sleep whilst allowing his mind to remain fully active and focussed. He was now on the threshold of consciousness, a hinterland phase that still permitted lucid thought, lucid dreaming, hallucinations, and sleep paralysis. The enigmatic Dutchman felt as though he was sitting in a much larger space than the eight-foot square cell he presently occupied. He was now experiencing an anaesthetic sense of separation from his body, a strong floating feeling whereby everything seemed distant and detached. His aim was now to achieve mental astral projection to experience the being of another.

Wiggins and Pyke watched as Van Hoon's hands rotated ninety degrees inwards and joined, his fingers clasping tightly together. His breathing became even shallower whilst remaining controlled and uniform. He felt weightless as though he was hovering high above all else. He could see his physical body sitting far below him. He looked down upon Feather, standing in attendance in the corner of the cell, and he could see the two detectives observing the scene he was observing. Van Hoon was now experiencing subjective impressions of being outside his physical body, a transcendence of his spatiotemporal boundaries, of being in two places at the same time. He felt a sense of tranquillity and immense power.

"Anything happening now, Guv?" probed Pyke again. His patience was wearing thin at what he was increasingly regarding as nothing more than an attention seeking pretence.

"Nothing, Jem, categorically nothing happening at all. Other than the hand movements he has not moved a muscle and his eyes remain tightly closed. Nonetheless, let us not be too hasty. Despite his reputation as an extortioner extraordinaire, Van Hoon has never let us down and I have come to trust his word," replied Wiggins in hushed tones.

Van Hoon looked around and what he saw was as if he were looking at the scene through a fine sheet of gauze. Everything was ever so slightly out of focus, blurred and obscured. He looked down at his hands. No fractal scarring was present upon his skin. These were not his hands, and yet they were his hands. It felt as though he was wearing the finest of satin gloves, but gloves of skin and flesh. He could feel the inside of these strange gloves but not the outside. On the left-hand index finger, there was an ornate golden signet ring which bore an embossed crest of a dragon, with a single blood-red ruby enclosed within a circle of Jet. It was a family crest Van Hoon was only too familiar with and he instantly realised he was now seeing exactly what Luca Radasiliev was seeing. He had achieved his goal. Van Hoon was now inside the Russian necromancer.

Several minutes passed before Van Hoon's eyes suddenly snapped open and he triumphantly announced, "Mary is not dead, Inspector!"

Wiggins exploded into the cell and looked the Dutchman directly in the eyes. "How can you say that categorically Van Hoon? You have been sitting in this cell, unflinching and silent for almost two hours now man! Mary has just under three hours of air left judging by Doctor Pascoe's calculations!" he questioned angrily.

"Two hours you say? Remarkable. It seemed no more than five minutes to me! Please understand that my earthly body may very well have been stationary here as you witnessed Inspector, but have you ever endeavoured to sit cross-legged in a cold damp prison cell without moving for thirty minutes, never mind for two whole hours? Preposterously impossible! The body you saw before you was bereft of my very being. I have been elsewhere and, I might add, extremely busy. I reiterate that I know exactly where Radasiliev is and furthermore I know exactly where you can find the delightful Mary," responded, Van Hoon, calmly.

"Where?" demanded a desperate Wiggins, Pyke uttering the same question simultaneously.

"He hides within the derelict ruins of Saint Mary Magdalene Church in the civil parish of Staplehurst with your good lady wife, whom I can assure you is not buried in some coffin as Radasiliev has led you to believe. She may imagine that she is so interred, but this is a cruel illusion created in her mind by Radasiliev. He is accompanied by an unsavoury being called Crake, a scuttling insect of a creature that was once an ordinary man like yourselves, and the unpleasantly deviant Nathaniel Cripes. Believe me, you most certainly do not want to be inside that particular mind for more than one second. Hell would be a preferable option. You need to make haste to Babylon Lane until you spy the ramshackle church atop a small wooded hill to the east."

"Let's go Pyke, we have no time to get reinforcements, it is just you and I, Jem," pronounced Wiggins.

Pyke relished the prospect. "I'll get me hat, Guv."

Van Hoon followed the two detectives towards the front foyer. "I wish you Godspeed dear friends, but beware Inspector, Radasiliev is a master of the darkest arts. A conjurer of spirits and a raiser of demons. He will not be alone. His powers make him an extremely formidable opponent. I also fear that he may be the harbinger of the foulest and most malevolent creature the Earth has ever known."

Chapter 43 - The Nightmare

It had been the most harrowing journey Wiggins had ever taken. He and Pyke, in the speeding police car, Pyke driving full throttle, his knuckles whitening on the steering wheel as his teeth clenched in an involuntary grimace. Each passing minute had been an agony for Wiggins, knowing as he did, that his wife was in the hands of the devilish Radasiliev, somewhere, if Van Hoon was to be believed, within Saint Mary Magdalene Church. His one crumb of comfort came in the Dutchman's reassurance that Mary was not, as Radasiliev had sadistically led him to believe, buried alive.

Pyke had scorched down the embankment to Tower Bridge, whilst Wiggins sounded the claxon continuously. Cars, horses, and wagons pulled to the side of the road and gently strolling couples were forced to rush for safety at the threat of the oncoming police car. The Wolseley could hold ten men and as such, felt strangely empty and rather unsafe to Wiggins. Pyke's driving was fatalistic at the best of times, but it was now bordering on insane. His foot pressed the accelerator pedal hard to the floor of the car whenever possible, slowing down only to take corners or bends, usually by working down through the gears, rather than utilising the breaks. Wiggins had never experienced driving like it.

They had sped across Tower Bridge and soon the frustratingly busy streets of Bermondsey and Greenwich gave way to the quieter lanes of Crayford and Bexley. Chatham Docks, with its interminable barges and cranes, warehouses, and dry docks, in turn sped by, eventually giving way to the bucolic lanes of rural Kent. The engine screamed and wailed, pushed to its limit. Despite this, the journey seemed endless to Wiggins, '*How on earth had Radasiliev gotten Mary all the way to Staplehurst, so quickly?*' He knew that Sergeant Ash would have by now arranged for at least another squad car to follow them, and no doubt alerted the local constabulary.

Pyke skidded the car around a particularly tight bend and, as if he had read Wiggins' mind, spat out between his gritted teeth, "I doubt if any of them local boys will be up to standing against this lunatic, Guv. I hope Nosher has rallied our troops." Despite his deep anxiety, Wiggins' noticed how seldom Pyke was blinking, so intent was his concentration on his driving. He noted the speedometer needle was permanently quivering in the red zone of the dial, flirting with its top speed of forty-five miles per hour. The Kent hedgerows raced past in a green and brown blur.

Normally he would have reprimanded Pyke for such reckless driving, but now he found himself urging him to go even faster. "Hurry, Jem! Every second may count!" Pyke nodded, acutely aware of the urgency, but said nothing in reply. He was determined that Albert Wiggins would not lose his Mary, as he had done his Noreen. He could feel tears begin to well behind his eyes as he thought of his lost love. He made himself a solemn oath that, no matter what, Mary and Albert Wiggins would survive whatever lay ahead, even if he was to sacrifice his own existence. He had saved her once and now they could save her again, together.

"Here, Jem. Down this lane to the left!" snapped Wiggins consulting the map that he had been wrestling with for the previous few miles. Pyke swung the car into the lane, its rear tyres skidding on the muddy surface, and followed the single track up the hill towards the church. A crest of grass ran down the centre of the track, stones and pebbles sprayed upwards and pinged like buckshot against the car's fenders and undercarriage. Pyke's foot came down hard upon the brake and the Wolseley slid to a juddering halt a foot or so away from the gates of the churchyard, its radiator billowing steam in exhaustion. Both men sprang from the car, their boots splashing in muddied puddles. Wiggins pushed open the wrought iron gates, reluctant hinges squealed meekly in protest. Both men drew their pistols and Pyke checked the ebony truncheon strapped to his belt.

Night was beginning to fall, and dusk was giving way to a cloak of misty darkness. The moon filtered through the darkening gauze, creating a shimmering half-light that permeated the stillness of the night. Wiggins and Pyke ran past the cottage that had formally been occupied by Jonas Crake and his nagging wife. Wiggins spared the cottage a glance, imagining the horror that had occurred within. It brought to mind an image of Crake ramming two knitting needles into his wife's ears, and thence, through her brain until they had almost exited the temples on the opposing sides. Pyke also glanced at the cottage, imagining the scene and the amphibian-like Crake.

Both men ran up the gradually inclining pathway, legs and hearts pumping, into the ancient parish graveyard and towards the church. They could see flashes of bright white light pulsing from within the church, illuminating the building's cracked and broken stained-glass windows. The light cast spectral shadows across the graveyard that danced like some devilish marionettes. "What the hell is that, Guv? Looks like lighting *inside* the bloody building!" asked a bemused Pyke.

Before Wiggins could conjure up a reasonable answer, the main window above the church narthex, which contained a glass rendering of Saint Michael slaying the Fallen Angel, exploded outwards in an almighty blast of icy white fire that illuminated the night sky like an incendiary device. Wiggins and Pyke instinctively shielded their eyes and dropped to the ground with pistols poised. Shards of multi-coloured glass seemed to spin slowly before them in a kaleidoscopic whirlpool. It was as if time had slowed down, almost to a standstill. Wiggins and Pyke looked at each other in astonishment and proceeded to push themselves erect, moving at a sloth-like pace. Their bodies seemed extremely heavy as if they were wearing suits of lead. An owl hooted from a nearby oak tree, its gnarled bows reaching out like multi-jointed fingers from some monstrous black hand. The hoot of the owl seemed interminable, never ending. It fled the sanctuary of its tree, its wings flapping majestically in a slow motion. All sound around the two detectives was dull and muted. "The window, Jem! Look at the window!" Wiggin's voice sounded to Pyke as if it were travelling under water.

From the void that had once contained Saint Michael and the Fallen Angel, the two detectives could see the unmistakable figure of Luca Radasiliev floating in the air, a blinding white light throbbing behind him giving the impression of angelic wings. Flames of astonishingly bright fire emanated from the Russian's body like a magnesium fuelled halo. In his outstretched arms, he held the limp, and seemingly lifeless, figure of Mary Wiggins.

"Mary!" screamed Wiggins through blistered and mucus stretched lips, his voice muffled by the vacuous state that Radasiliev had created. Pyke could literally see the sound wave emanating from Wiggins' mouth like the blowing of smoke rings. Wiggins was frantically trying to push towards the Russian, but it was as though he was running within a vat of molasses. His feet felt heavy as though they were clad in asphalt spreader's boots. He saw how frail and small Mary looked in the arms of the necromancer. Then he heard a cracking report from his left side and could see Pyke's shoulder recoil as the muzzle of his pistol released a smoke-shrouded bullet. "Noooooo!" he could hear himself shout, "You may hit, Mary!"

He could trace the trajectory of the bullet as it vibrated slowly, pulsing through the treacle of the night air. As it approached a laughing Radasiliev, the Russian merely twisted his body to one side to allow the bullet to pass harmlessly into the brickwork of the church façade. As the bullet impacted and compressed into the fabric of the church, the lethargic spell was instantly lifted and real-time was restored. Wiggins and Pyke gasped for air, flexed their muscles, and realised that somehow some sense of normality had been restored.

Still, Radasiliev remained floating high above them. "I had expected you sooner, gentlemen," he sneered, his stygian black eyes showing no emotion. "I bid you welcome to my house!" The Russian looked skywards towards the moon and began to incantate. "Magoth excieo quod superius sicut. Magoth excieo quod superius sicut." The Russian's stentorian voice reverberated around the stillness of the graveyard. A stench of sulphur swam through the night air, and warm rain began to fall from the darkening sky.

Pyke levelled his pistol once more at the floating figure, its black cloak flapping like the wings of some gigantic bat. Just as his finger curled on the trigger, Wiggins' hand shot forth and pushed his colleague's pistol arm skyward. "I will not have you accidentally shoot my wife, Jem!" shouted the DCI, his voice hoarse with exasperation. Hot rainwater poured down his agonised features. Still, the devilish incantation continued. The Russian's chant grew louder and louder. Radasiliev lowered his gaze from the moon to bore into the faces of the two men below him. He snarled, "Mortals beware, the demons arise!" he proclaimed. The Russian's crazed laughter rose to an ear-splitting pitch before diminishing, as he floated backwards, carrying Mary back into the body of the Church.

Wiggins and Pyke heard a sharp, splintering crack from behind them, quickly followed by another, then another. Both men wheeled, their senses alert to danger. What they then saw defied belief and stretched their minds beyond all comprehension. The headstones within the graveyard were fracturing as though struck by an invisible coruscation. A great rending and crunching of granite upon granite resounded around the graveyard. Wiggins and Pyke looked at each other and then all around them.

"What sorcery is this, Bert?" asked a bewildered Pyke, crouched and ready for action.

Wiggins did not answer. He had no answer. Warm rainwater now battered against his forehead and poured down his face, his jaw was slack in bewilderment. There was no answer he could give. He watched as gravestones shattered and split all around them and began to sink into the ground. As they did so, he could see the soil of the graves move as if it were being disturbed and displaced from within. The ground began to subside and undulate around them, giving way under their feet. Both men bent their knees and outstretched their arms to maintain their balance and remain upright. To their horror, skeletal hands thrust forth simultaneously from the muddy sod of each grave, clawing at the air, closely followed by scores of shambling, earth caked, decomposed figures.

"Sweet Jesus Christ!" shouted Pyke. "The Dead are rising, Bert! The fucking Dead! What sort of nightmare is this?" He felt his blood turn to ice. Strangely, even now, with the gates of Hell seemingly opening before them, Wiggins felt a slight distaste at the use of what he regarded as inappropriate language. However, given the circumstance, he was prepared to overlook it.

"Run to the Church, Bert! Get Mary! I'll deal with this walking chamber of horrors, here!" urged Pyke, shoving Wiggins towards the chapel.

Wiggins looked at him as if he were a lunatic. "There are scores of them Jem! How can you possibly..." The sentence remained unfinished as, having shaken themselves free of what had formally been regarded as their final places of rest, the first of the reanimated cadavers stretched decomposed hands towards the two detectives. Their eyeless skulls shook, and their near fleshless bodies began to lumber towards the two detectives. Pyke unclipped the blackjack from his belt and swung at the neck of the closest corpse. Bone splintered as the billy club hit its target. The body crumpled to the ground and fell into a writhing pile of body parts, arms and legs flailing against each other as if in tormented conflict, the torso juddering beneath a headless neck.

The two detectives exchanged a look of amazement. "Well, that's new!" declared Pyke, his body now trembling with revitalising adrenalin. He wiped the hot rain away from his face. Wiggins drew his own blackjack and the two colleagues ploughed on into the advancing masses of the undead, flailing at the rancid hide and bone of the decaying creatures. Each detective weighed into the oncoming bodies, thrashing and battering their way through bone and flesh until their arms began to ache with building lactic acid. There seemed no end to the number of reanimated foes. Then came a smell so foul and so noxious that they both thought they would choke.

"Get to the Church, Bert! Run!" repeated Pyke, skeletal fingers clawing at his chest. "Get to Mary!" Wiggins nodded and wheeled towards the church, running up the approach lane, his feet slipping frustratingly beneath him in mud whilst the rain spiked at his face.

Pyke decided to draw the seemingly endless stream of undead away from the Church, his intention being to somehow lose the zombified hoard and double back to help Wiggins. "Come on, you stinking bastards, let's see how fast you can move your old bones!" Just as he threw a final invitation to the savage cadavers, he felt a rock hard, ice-cold hand grasp at his shoulder. He spun to loosen the grip and a bolt of primordial fear raced through him as he looked into the hard, grey, masonry eyes of a stone statue of an Angel, which had rendered itself free from an ornate grave memorial. Pyke's heart raced. '*This cannot be real!*' He grasped the wrist of the effigy, trying desperately to free himself, his sweat and rain covered hands slipping hotly against the stone-cold arm of the statue. The Angel raised its other arm and its granite hard fingers curled slowly around Pyke's neck. The detective struggled frantically against the unforgiving grip and swung a haymaker of a punch to the head of the animated effigy. He howled in pain at the impact, knuckles, metacarpals and phalanges crumpled in his left hand. Pyke writhed under the statue's grip, kicking desperately in an attempt to free himself. He tensed his enormous neck muscles, but his throat was being slowly constricted, and all the while those sightless stone eyes continued to bore into his soul. He could feel the deathly stroke of several cadaverous hands now clawing at his back. He felt his oesophagus narrow, muscles weaken, and his breath began to leave his lungs. Pyke began to feel faint. He knew this was the onset of unconsciousness, the forerunner to death. '*Killed by a fucking Angel!*" he thought, frantically trying, with all his remaining strength, to push himself away from the stone behemoth. His strength was failing, his will faltering. He felt for the emerald ring that hung from a fine gold chain around his neck. He could feel his eyes closing.

The grasping at his clothing suddenly ceased. A sensation as if his attackers were being plucked from him one by one. Suddenly he felt a crunching impact. An almighty crash, stone cracking against stone. The vice-like grip of the Angel loosened abruptly and he was dropped unceremoniously to the ground where he knelt and gasped for air, hands in the mud, nausea rising in his gut. He wiped the incessant rain from his eyes, shook his head and looked upwards to see the smiling face of Van Hoon's bovine Turkish chauffeur Ilhan, who stood holding a large chunk of granite headstone in his hands. The Turk pulled back his shoulders and took a second, heaving swipe at the now headless Angel, this time removing an arm from the effigy and losing the hunk of granite in the process. Pyke looked on, jaded. Granite shards rained down on his head, lacerating his face in several places.

Pyke looked around to see more than a dozen robed figures dancing among the onslaught of the undead, scything at them with clubs and machetes. An elegant massacre. '*Van Hoon's Pestilent!*' recognised Pyke, with a relieved smile. The lepers moved with almost balletic grace, picking their way through the corpses like avenging ghosts, and at the forefront of the mayhem, walking towards him, came the smiling Van Hoon, sword cane unsheathed and resting nonchalantly upon his shoulder.

"Van Hoon!" wheezed Pyke. "You came."

"But of course, Sergeant. You did not think that I would leave all this fun to you and Chief Inspector Wiggins, did you?" A frenzied corpse launched itself at Van Hoon from behind, only to receive a spinning side swipe from the Dutchman's sword cane which pierced the lumbar spinal column, slicing the cadaver in two. Van Hoon sighed at the inconvenience, withdrew a silk handkerchief, and cleaned the blade of rotting flesh. Pyke raised himself unsteadily to his feet with a helping hand from Ilhan. He looked at the fallen Angel, massaging some blood flow back into his aching neck muscles. As he did so, a crack appeared in the centre of the statue's torso and began to spread like a fracturing cobweb across its body. The fissures began to open and expand, and an intense white light blasted outwards from within the body of the statue. Pyke looked at Van Hoon, searching for an explanation. "This is not good, gentlemen," announced the Leper, for once, concern playing across his scarred face. "One might even go so far to say, a rather disturbing development."

The stone of the Angel fractured and crumbled. The three men shielded their eyes from the intensity of the burning white light which pulsated in the space where the angel had once been. Splinters of stone spat from the nebulous light and peppered Pyke, Van Hoon and Ilhan. "Take cover!" shouted Van Hoon, urgency obvious in his normally controlled voice. The trio turned to run as an explosion of white light engulfed them, kicking the breath from their lungs. They felt a blast of ice-cold fire burn at their exposed skin and were thrown forward into the muddy quagmire of the churchyard. Each man slowly stood and looked at the source of the blast. Where once had lain the shattered remains of the Angel, now stood what looked, to Pyke, like a large seed pod. The pod's skin resembled an embryotic membrane that pulsed and throbbed as if alive. Van Hoon reasserted his previous statement. "This is *definitely* not good."

Pyke looked quickly to Van Hoon and then back to the abhorrent looking cocoon in front of him. "What is it? What in damnation are we dealing with here?" As if to answer his question, the skin of the pod was pushed outwards from within, stretching the venous membrane until suddenly it split. An ashen, leathery hand appeared, tearing at the membrane with long jagged talons, peeling back the pod casing. A putrid, yellow puss oozed from the gaping tear, slopping onto the ground, bringing with it a noxious stench of hydrogen sulphide gas. "Sweet mother of Christ!" uttered Pyke in open-jawed disbelief. "The nightmare gets worse!"

A second monstrous hand tore open the rent and, out of the cocoon, emerged the most abhorrent sight Jem Pyke had ever seen. A sight he was sure would haunt his dreams to his grave. A gargantuan, naked, grey-skinned gargoyle heaved its way out of the pod. It peeled the hideous membrane from its grotesque body and swallowed it. Its mouth was a wide gaping hole. The gargoyle's eyes were a deep blood red, its vast simian nose flattened across its wide, devilish face. The head was crowned by a short stubby, gnarled horn surrounded by hard scales. The creature had long arms, as thick as small tree trunks, which reached down below its knees. Its leathery skin resembled that of an elephant and was covered in a film of viscous clear slime.

"Magoth!" exclaimed Van Hoon. "Demon Prince of the inner circle of Hell!" he swallowed in disbelief. "If Radasiliev can summon forth such filth as this, then he is indeed a more dangerous foe than even I ever imagined." Pyke could sense an element of begrudged respect in the leper's voice. Just then the creature lurched towards them, its gaping maw dripping yellow fluid. Pyke lifted his pistol and, hands shaking, put two bullets into the chest of the oncoming Demon. The monster flinched briefly, but the resultant entry points that appeared in its skin closed and healed over almost immediately. Pyke swallowed hard. The valiant Ilhan then launched his considerable bulk at the advancing monster, throwing himself like a charging bull into its fetid flesh. Magoth flung Ilhan aside as if he were a puppet. The Turk hit a nearby tree trunk with a resounding thump, unconscious upon impact.

Van Hoon drew both of his ivory-handled Colts from their holsters, spun them around his fingers three hundred and sixty degrees, and fired both at the Beast's forehead, both bullets striking home at the same spot almost simultaneously. Lighting cracked overhead, illuminating the scene in a nightmarish, staccato luminescence. The creature juddered to a halt in the created strobe light. Pyke felt an instant sense of hope. His relief, however, proved short lived. The monster shook its great head, slime flying from its dewlap jowls, and a tongue the size of that of an ox sloughed from its mouth and licked non-existent lips. The Demon's blood-red eyes bore into those of the heterochromatic Leper. Van Hoon was hit as if by an invisible force and sailed backwards through the air as if blown by a hurricane. He landed amongst a sea of writhing undead. The zombies descended ravenously upon him, pulling him towards a large open communal grave. Van Hoon's heels ploughed trenches through the rain-battered soil as he desperately kicked for purchase.

The Demon Prince then turned its attention towards a dumbstruck Pyke. It sprang at the stunned officer with surprising speed and agility, for such a bulky creature, pinioning him in a grip of iron. Pyke felt complete revulsion at the touch of the Demon. He could feel the appalling creature's glutinous skin, smell its sulphurous breath, and feel its heartbeat against his. Its huge tongue slobbered over his face, lapping at his skin like a thirsty dog. Pyke stifled a retch and strained against the Demon's grip. He threw back his head and smashed his forehead into that of the Demon. Magoth's skin resembled a thick grey rubber and the monstrous head was completely unaffected by Pyke's cranial attack. Again, Pyke tested the Demon's strength, hoping he could free himself. His thoughts now were of Van Hoon, sinking below a tide of homicidal corpses, and of Wiggins, deep within the very den of Radasiliev. Thinking of the plight of his comrades revitalised him, restored strength that he thought lost. He smashed the butt of his right elbow into what, in a human, would be the lower rib cage, but felt no reaction from the Demon. His recently injured hand ached at the force juddering through his elbow. '*What if I bite this fucking tongue?*' he thought in desperation. '*Surely that's gotta hurt it?*' He steeled himself at the prospect.

He bit deep. He bit hard. The taste was appalling. Hot brimstone jelly spurted into his mouth, blistering his palate and descaling his teeth. The Demon screeched a high-pitched scream reminiscent of a boiling kettle. Pyke felt as if his eardrums would burst. He gagged. He twisted violently and managed, with Herculean effort, to release his right hand.

"Its head, Pyke! You need to take its head!" shouted Van Hoon, his voice distant, almost lost amongst the snarling mayhem of the bodies that now almost entirely enveloped him. The Leper was valiantly thrashing at the centre of a mass of the undead who crawled over him, slashing and biting, overwhelming him with their sheer numbers. The Leper somehow, through gargantuan effort, raised himself above the sea of scrabbling bodies. He arched his back and with every last ounce of strength, threw back his arm and flung his unsheathed sword cane skyward towards Pyke, just as the mass of cadavers overcame him and engulfed him from view. Van Hoon fell backwards into the open grave, immersed in a turmoil of writhing corpses. A hive of death.

The sword cane somersaulted through the air, its blade of honed Damascus steel, catching the moonlight with each revolution. Pyke strained every sinew in his arm, reaching deep into the night. Whispering a silent prayer, he managed to clutch the handle of the blade as it soared towards him and in one continuous motion, turned and swung the sword with all the might he could muster. He felt the blade slice through the gelatinous flesh of the Demon and judder as it carved its way through vertebrae. Magoth's huge head lolled to one side, flopping ghoulishly onto one shoulder. The crimson eyes began to leak thick, mustard coloured smoke. Pyke stepped free of the half-decapitated Demon, and with a full-blooded swipe, completely cleaved Magoth's head from its shoulders. The head tumbled to the ground and rolled to a stop at Pyke's mud-covered boots. He breathed a huge sigh of relief and gave it a disdainful kick.

Satisfied that the Beast was slain, Pyke turned and ran, pistol and sword cane in each hand, towards the grave that had devoured Van Hoon. There was no visible sign of the Leper, nor his undead assailants. The grave was sealed over as if it had never been disturbed at all. He stood dumbfounded, his brain unable to process what he was looking at when he became aware of a presence behind him. He spun and threw a haymaker that flew over the ducking head of Ilhan. The mute Turk pointed frantically towards the Church indicating that Pyke should follow in pursuit of Wiggins. Pyke understood but looked with desperation at the grave at his feet. "Van Hooooon!" he shouted above the pounding rain. Ilhan shoved him, pushing him towards the Church. The message was clear. You help your friend and I will help mine. With a final look at the grim-faced chauffeur, Pyke turned on his heels and sped towards the Church.

Chapter 44 - The Spade

Ilhan scrabbled at the earth, panic rising within him. He could feel his heart thump in his chest and blood course through the swollen vein at his temple. He clutched frantically at clods of earth, sinking his fingers into the fleshy soil, dredging it aside. He worked like a tunnelling machine, all the time ignoring the rawness in his fingertips, strafed skin intermingling with the displaced soil and scree. His fingernails scraped painfully against stones and shale whilst the rain drummed down incessantly, blinding him as it cascaded down his forehead and into his eyes in muddy rivulets. The storm caused the pit to fill with a muddy, pebble laden torrent but he continued his work, disregarding the pain in his hands and the aching in his back and chest. Surely there could not now be enough time. Surely his Master was gone.

He heard a splash beside him and turned his head to see the toe of a mud-covered boot, and beside it, the flash of moonlight glinting off metal.

"Looks like you need a bit of help me old son," came a calm, almost cheerful voice from above. Ilhan looked upwards to see the backlit bulk of Nosher Ash silhouetted against a lightning streaked sky. The thunder bellowed, and the lighting cracked as the burly desk Sergeant stamped down on the blade of the spade he held and cut through the earth.

Pyke ran towards the church, his shoe leather skewing on the saturated gravel. As he approached the door, he caught a brief glimpse of a thin, pale shadow disappearing into the murk of the graveyard. "Cripes!" he cursed knowingly. He barged through the doors of the Church, timber scratching against flagstone, and skidded to an abrupt halt. Before him, face down in the aisle, lay the prone figure of Albert Wiggins, arms splayed outwards as if he had been shot. Pyke dropped to one knee. "Bert! Wake up, Guv! Don't be dead!" He shook the prone figure and turned Wiggins' limp form over onto his back. As he did so he felt a tremendous blow strike at the nape of his neck. Blackness descended like a dark curtain and he slumped forward, unconscious, atop the body of his friend.

Chapter 45 - The Choice

His head ached as it had never ached before. His skull throbbed as though it had been cracked open by some bludgeoning sledgehammer. The pain that pounded behind his eyes was palpable, intensely unbearable. A penetrating neural pulsing in his temples made him flinch in spasmodic agony. Shivering rigors trembled throughout his entire body. He cautiously ventured to open his eyelids, fully expecting light to gradually filter through his eyelashes, bringing with it even greater, more excruciating pain. No light was forthcoming. He instantly began to panic at the thought that whatever blows he had suffered had perhaps cost him his eyesight. Alarmed, he momentarily imagined a life of blindness. His heart fluttered then raced in panic. He imagined, with horror, a life without seeing his beloved Mary ever again. A life spent being a burden. He dropped his chin to his chest and gritted his teeth, trying desperately to regain some grip on the reality of his situation.

He could smell claggy dampness in the chilly air, a heavy scent of mildew that spoke of a building or room long since habitually occupied. He could hear the steady echoing dripping of water somewhere behind him, each metronomic splash resonated through his tenderised brain. His lips were brittle and cracked dry. He could taste blood in his throat and was aware of the ferrous sense of dried compacted blood lining his nostrils. He could also sense a presence. He was certain he was not alone. He stretched out his senses, trying to rationalise his circumstances, trying to remember what possible chain of events had brought him to wherever he now was. He recoiled his head violently at what felt like a hand brushing at his face. The back of his head cracked against something solid and resonant. The pain was akin to a spike being driven through his skull. '*What had happened to him? Where was he? Where was Mary?*'

He felt a hand hurriedly pull away what he now recognised to be a blindfold. The light beamed upon his skin which felt tender and brutalised. He opened one eye gingerly. The other eye, swollen shut, refused to open. The glare of the light stung his eye causing his eyelid to tremor involuntarily.

"You may have noticed Inspector that you are, how do you English say? In a spot of bother. A bit of a pickle, what?" Wiggins instantly recognised the cultivated Slavic tones of Luca Radasiliev before he could properly focus on the figure of the Russian.

He was aware that the summoner of demons stood before him, but as yet his shimmering shape was an indistinct shadow.

Wiggins attempted to move but realised that he was securely bound to what he imagined to be a wooden stake of some description. He shook his head quickly from side to side, clearing his blurred vision, and looked into the piercing, molasses-black eyes of Luca Radasiliev. The Russian held a long-barrelled handgun nonchalantly in each hand. "You may perceive, my friend that you are, somewhat ironically, secured to a crucifix."

Wiggins struggled unsuccessfully against his bindings. His arms were strapped securely by rope from shoulder to wrist to the horizontal crosspiece of the crucifix, whilst his body from neck to ankles was equally tightly bound to the vertical stake. He tested his bonds frantically and found that so tightly was he tied, he could move only his head and the fingers of his hands ever so slightly. Radasiliev smiled, an evil gash cutting across his handsomely chiselled face. He stared intently at the trapped policeman, the grin turning into a demonic snarl. The pupils of the Russian's eyes dissolved into a distinct bloody vermilion colour and Wiggins could feel the darkness of the Russian's soul begin to pollute that of his own. He shuddered. He was overcome by a sickening feeling, as if poison was being poured into his mind and was trickling through his veins, infusing his consciousness with some terrifying transfusion. He began to feel a tide of corruption and fear invade him like an infection. He looked around frantically, trying desperately to focus on anything other than the magnetic eyes of the Russian. He realised he was in the old Church. He could see a macabre backdrop of dirt festooned stained-glass windows and smoke tarnished stone arches behind the Russian, whilst to his side, he could see the vague shape of a beheaded Madonna beside which crouched the once human form of the grovelling Jonas Crake.

Wiggins endeavoured to recapture his resolve. "You do realise that you will not survive this," he stated matter-of-factly, attempting to gain some degree of control over his seemingly hopeless situation. "No matter what you do to me here today, the might of the entire Metropolitan Police Force, not to mention the British Government, will pursue you to the ends of the Earth. The good people of this Nation will not tolerate your devilment and corruption. No matter where you go, you will find no refuge."

Radasiliev laughed the laugh of a lunatic who exists beyond the reality of reason. "How appropriate that you say so, my dear Inspector." He raised his head to the vaulted ceiling, spreading his arms wide, and roared a command that echoed around the chamber "Bring in the others!" As he did so Radasiliev began to gently, imperceptibly, levitate into the air. Radasiliev now floated a full twelve inches above the cracked tiled floor of the Church. His head lowered slowly, and his crimson-eyed stare once again penetrated the one functioning eye of Wiggins. An all-saturating chill of uncertainty and helplessness seeped through the detective. A feeling of guilt and resigned futility swept over him. Just then, Wiggins became vaguely conscious of movement to either side of him, the sound of people struggling with a great weight, of heaving exertion.

"Very good, exactly where I wanted them!" declared the floating Russian. "You now have, Mr Wiggins, to the right of you a representative of your beloved Metropolitan Police in the shape of your loyal hound, Sergeant Pyke. Welcome Leslie, how rewarding to see you once more." Wiggins could hear the obviously gagged and muffled raging response of Pyke thunder beside him. "And to your left, the most beautifully appropriate member of 'the good people' of your nation. I trust I have no need to introduce you to your lovely wife, Mary."

Wiggins' eye widened as he writhed and wrenched so frantically at his bonds that they cut into his flesh. "You are a devil, Radasiliev. A scum-sucking devil beyond humankind! Let them go! If it is I you want then take me and let them go, in the name of God and all that is decent and proper!"

"God? What need have I of *your* God? Let us be improperly indecent, Chief Inspector," laughed Radasiliev raising his face heavenward. "I answer to a higher being than your God. The Lord of Darkness himself commands me and I shall be elevated to his side amongst the vipers, the demons and the other exquisite creatures of the night."

"You are a crazed lunatic! Let these people go I beseech you. I will succumb and sacrifice myself if that is what you so desire." Wiggins could hear muffled protestations on either side of him now. "Do whatever you will with me, just set them free, man!" responded Wiggins, now desperately trying to hold on to whatever degree of self he still retained. The creature that had once been Jonas Crake screeched and clapped his hands in ecstasy as a group of hooded acolytes finished positioning the crucifixes to which Jem Pyke and Mary Wiggins were securely strapped, at either side of the Inspector. These crosses were slightly shorter than the one to which Wiggins was secured and both were carefully positioned so as the temples of their prisoners' heads were almost touching the outstretched hands of the detective. Crake tumbled back and forth like an excited chimpanzee, hands slapping at the floor and howling his appreciation.

Wiggins strained and stretched out his left arm what little distance his bonds would allow. His fingertips just managed to feather Mary's hair. "Do not panic, my love. He will not prevail. I refuse to allow it." He could hear nothing but a faint whimper in return.

The levitating Russian floated serenely towards the crucified triumvirate. "Look at this glorious sight! Golgotha played out before my very eyes, how magnificent," he declared. "And when they came to the place, which is called Calvary, there they crucified him, and the malefactors, one on the right hand, and the other on the left," gloried a laughing Radasiliev. "You now have a choice to make, Mr High and Mighty Detective ... a choice of life over death."

Crake scuttled forward, gurgling and giggling, and forcibly placed a pistol in each of Wiggins' hands. Wiggins was mystified, '*Why is he arming me?*' he thought incredulously. He gripped the cold metallic handles of each gun, a misplaced optimism rising from within him as he frantically tried to twist his wrists to aim the guns towards Radasiliev. He quickly realised, that agonisingly, his bonds were so tightly and specifically tied that he was unable to redirect them away from the heads of his carefully positioned loved ones on either side of him. Gradually he began to realise the wicked game Radasiliev was about to play. His heart sank to a place so deep within him that he felt he would never retrieve it.

Radasiliev sensed his opponent's despair and revelled in it. A self-congratulatory smile spread across his pitiless face. "I crave your indulgence, Inspector. A small diversion to amuse my corrupted old soul." Radasiliev looked at the three helpless figures strung up before him. Wiggins, he could see was in abject despair, his head hung downwards, chin upon chest, defeated. His will was crushed. Mary, all but unconscious in a fear-induced state, her head laying limply upon her shoulder to her husband's left. The hate-filled eyes of Pyke drilled into those of the Russian, his nostrils flaring and his neck straining at its leather bonds, saliva darkening his gag, as he struggled every muscle in his body to split free from his bondage. His rage was palpable.

Radasiliev stared intently at Wiggins who, under the necromancer's stare, found himself cocking the hammer of each of the long-barrelled pistols he held in his hands. "You have a choice, Inspector. You can put a bullet either in the head of your trusted friend or that of your beloved wife. The choice is entirely yours."

Crake wrung his hands together wildly and cackled with glee. "Friend or wife," he muttered. "Friend or wife."

Wiggins lifted his head, his brain now alive and racing with permutations. "And if I were to refuse to either request?"

"Then it is quite simple. I shoot first your wife, then Mr Pyke, here, and finally after watching your grief until I am bored, I will then shoot you. You will all die, Inspector," rejoiced the Russian.

Wiggins could feel Pyke pushing the temple of his head forcibly against the muzzle of the gun he clutched in his right hand, trying to make the decision for his colleague. Urging him to pull the trigger. Again, Wiggins' mind raced. "I see no advantage to me in this Radasiliev. If I shoot either my wife or friend, then what happens?"

"Why, I then kill only you, of course, Inspector and the remaining member of your happy triptych will be free to go his, or her, merry way," reasoned the Russian as if the answer were the most obvious statement he could ever have uttered. "Simple."

Wiggins could feel the frantic struggling of Pyke beside him, pressing his head ever more aggressively onto the gun muzzle. Radasiliev laughed and floated closer to Pyke. Their eyes met. The hatred that emanated from Jem Pyke was as intense as the rays of the Sun. *'If I were free, I swear I'd tear your head from your shoulders you freak!'* thought a determined Pyke. He squirmed and writhed, kicked and twisted, trying desperately to bite through the gag that prevented him from speaking. Blood began to seep from his wrists and neck where he strained against his bindings.

The Russian stared deeply into his captive's eyes, "I very much doubt you could physically do such a thing Leslie, but you would give your life for others I see. I must admit that I have never felt such unexpurgated hatred flow from a single human. Your hatred gladdens and nourishes my infected soul, Sergeant. I thank you."

The Russian moved towards the wilted form of Mary Wiggins. "Such a handsome woman. You must be proud to have her as your wife, Mr Wiggins?" He flared his nostrils in an exaggerated inhalation as if searching for an elusive scent. He stopped suddenly as if hit by an unseen hand of realisation. Radasiliev placed a hand gently upon Mary's stomach and regarded her with an aura of surprised delight. "You are *with child*, handsome wife! How impossibly perfect! And then there were three!"

Pyke writhed even more furiously, leather biting through flesh and vein, he repeatedly butted the side of his head frantically against the muzzle of the pistol clasped in Wiggins' right hand. Wiggins could feel all the strength of character he possessed slowly draining from within him. His self-will had forsaken him. All self-preservation vanished, resigned in the defeat of death. He knew what he must do. His choice was that he had no choice. "May God forgive me," he choked. He looked to the heavens, tears streaming from his eyes and began to squeeze the trigger. The World stood still.

The gunshot rang out and echoed with a deathly, hollow resonance around the defiled dereliction of the House of worship. Pyke's head jolted violently backwards at the sound of the shot.

A small silver disc appeared suddenly in the very centre of Radasiliev's forehead. The Russian's eyes and mouth gaped in incredulous amazement. His body first dropped on bended knee before toppling to the ground, falling face down on the cold, hard flagstones of the church floor.

Standing directly behind Radasiliev's motionless body, Dante Van Hoon lowered the still smoking Colt forty-five he held aloft in both hands. Sergeant Nosher Ash and the devoted Ilhan stood behind him. "A rather excellent shot, though I do say so myself," declared the leper. "John Henry, himself would have been proud."

The Dutchman strode towards his captive companions, nonchalantly putting another bullet into the back of the Russian's skull as he strode over his prone body. The carcass juddered. "You never can be too sure with these types you know, even if the bullets *are* made of poured molten silver," observed Van Hoon.

At the sound of the shots, the red-robed acolytes had fled as one from the church and ran directly into the waiting clutches of a newly arrived battalion of London's finest. Van Hoon holstered his pistol and unsheathed his sword cane. He first released Wiggins who slumped, emotionally and physically drained into his arms. Van Hoon gently laid the detective down on the steps of the altar and, looking apologetically at the beheaded Madonna, administered a generous draft of brandy from a vial. He then proceeded to cut Pyke free as Ash and Ilhan untied the trusses of Mary Wiggins. Pyke rubbed his wrists where they had been sliced and gouged by his struggles for freedom.

The thing that had formerly been Jonas Crake quivered and skulked in the shadows and made its way stealthily towards the rear of the Church, eventually finding a furtive hiding place behind the very pew from which he had concealed himself from the ghastly floating man, a mere few weeks earlier. Content that he was suitably concealed from view he began to curl up into a protective foetal position and rock back and forth.

Albert Wiggins embraced his wife at the altar. Van Hoon crouched down beside them and fished a small silver cube from his waistcoat pocket, wafting it gently under Mary's nose. Her eyes fluttered open with a jolt, her mind regaining consciousness. "Why! Mr Van Hoon," she gasped looking into the remarkable heterochromatic eyes of the Leper.

Van Hoon smiled comfortingly. "May I reintroduce you to your husband, my dear," he declared, indicating Wiggins. "He truly is a most remarkable individual, I can assure you madam."

Mary turned her head towards her husband and with tears welling in her eyes asked, "Is it all over, Albert? Are we both alive darling?"

"Indeed, we are, my love. All three of us in fact. Thanks to our brave friends, we are indeed alive and, I hope, well," replied Wiggins stroking his wife's stomach. "Why didn't you tell me?"

Mary stuttered. "I wanted to make absolutely sure first, dear. I could not bear the thought of disappointing you."

Wiggins hugged his wife in his arms. "You could never disappoint me, my love." They embraced.

The onlooking Nosher Ash turned away and dabbed secretively at his eyes with his tunic sleeve. Van Hoon strode towards Jem Pyke who stood motionless over the prone form of Radasiliev. The leper turned over the Russian's body with a dismissive kick of his oxblood leather shoes. The cadaver's countenance was etched with a death grin, unlike anything Pyke had ever seen. Van Hoon produced a small brass, syphon-like gun from a concealed shoulder holster, pointed it at Radasiliev's forehead and sprayed it with what appeared to Pyke to be nothing more than common or garden tap water. Pyke stood back in amazement as the water burned fiercely through the skin with a smoking sizzle, leaving a large cavity between the points of the two silver bullets embedded in the Russian's skull. The grin on the dead man's face miraculously disappeared to be replaced by a nondescript horizontal line.

"He shall no longer rejoice in the glory of his death," declared Van Hoon, holstering his unique weapon.

"Well, I'll be! What was that?" questioned Pyke staring nonplussed at the change in Radasiliev's lifeless form.

"A mere ha'penny water pistol my good man. Holy water being its blessed ammunition," replied Van Hoon, his teeth gleaming behind a resplendently wide smile.

"But surely even holy water blessed by the Pope could not have such an effect?" argued Pyke looking at Radasiliev's dissolved head in bewilderment.

"I am entirely sure you are correct, Sergeant Pyke. This particular holy water, however, was in fact blessed by an Apostle of our Lord," replied Van Hoon enigmatically.

Pyke nodded as if in understanding, his eyes again fixed upon the gaping hole in Radasiliev's head. After a few seconds of contemplation, he thought '*but where would one find an Apostle with which to bless water in this day and age?*' He turned to where Van Hoon had stood only seconds before to find that the Dutchman was no longer there, instead he was strolling towards Wiggins, casually twirling his sword cane, and whistling the Danse Macabre.

The thing that had once been Jonas Crake's silent relief was interrupted by a gentle tap on his bony shoulder. He turned his head in dread, just in time to see the knuckles of Ilhan's fist hurtling towards his face. It was the last thing he would see for a very long time.

"I fancy we should depart now and rejoin to my Belgravia sanctum," offered Van Hoon, assisting Wiggins and Mary to their feet. "There we can provide succour and nourishment and treat your wounds."

The five companions all agreed and headed towards the church doorway which now stood open, held welcomingly by the sturdy Ilhan whilst an unconscious Crake hung limply in the Turk's grasp. Van Hoon led the way whistling as he went, followed by Wiggins, supporting his still groggy wife. Jem Pyke and Nosher Ash followed. Ilhan closed the door behind them and brought up the rear, dragging the inanimate form of Crake in one hand behind him. The creature's heels left two distinct trails in the muddy ground. "I imagine there will be room enough in the Rolls if we all huddle together," announced Van Hoon with a flourish towards Ilhan. The bulky Turk nodded his substantial head in agreement. Pyke and Ilhan exchanged a respectful glance as the Turkish chauffeur, dragging what remained of Jonas Crake behind him, passed the Detective Sergeant.

"And what of the body?" inquired Wiggins of Van Hoon as they settled into the leather luxury of the Dutchman's Silver Ghost. "What of Radasiliev?"

"I will arrange for it to be removed and properly disposed of before Dawn," declared Van Hoon. "Drive on Ilhan, and don't spare the horses, as they say."

The mutilated body of Luca Radasiliev lay motionless upon the ancient church floor. All was silent within the derelict building save the rustle of dried leaves as they spun and danced a vigorous tarantella around the corpse, propelled as they were by incoming draughts and winds that penetrated the decrepit skin of the church. The solidity of the silence was all encompassing.

The night crept on and on. Hours passed. The moon followed its arc across the darkness of the sky. A lone fox sniffed and scratched at the decaying timber of the front door of the Church. It raised its inquisitive nose into the night air, searching for an elusive and unidentifiable scent. A scent that was alien to it. It caught a whiff of something rancid, something corrupt, and something that the animal sensed was dangerous. It whined, barked timidly, whined again then ran off into the safety of the darkness. All was silent. All was still.

Radasiliev's corpse suddenly shuddered as if jolted by an unseen electric current. Slowly it rose from the floor. The leaves that had danced and twirled around it now lay motionless as if entombed in a vacuum. The Russian's cadaver continued to rise until it floated, suspended in the air, four feet above the ground. Gradually the body began to tilt on its axis until, now vertically erect, it came to a juddering halt. The wind howled in the churchyard and the dancing black limbs of the surrounding trees conducted a silent orchestra against the backdrop of a full moon. The fox shrieked the unholy scream of a banshee and the night air resounded with the unified croaks of a thousand toads.

The gaping wound in Radasiliev's head, caused by the acidity of Van Hoon's holy water, began to expand. It became a dark shadowy void, an increasing vortex of swirling blackness which spread across the Russian's face, until that face was completely engulfed by a seemingly bottomless inky pit. From inside this churning hole of blackness, a low rumbling moan began to emanate. A vortex of wind violently thundered around the church walls. Radasiliev's body convulsed as if struck by lightning then began to break and splinter and fold in upon itself. The churning blackness continued to increase in size until the dark cyclone had entirely swallowed the broken body of the Russian. As it did so, the moan became a deep-throated grunt as though someone, or something, were trying to thrust its way through the infinite obscurity of the void.

Then movement. The darkness became something more solid, more acutely formed. A fold of membrane flapped open and was pierced from within and a long, claw-like fingernail emerged from within the blackness, followed closely by the remainder of a deathly white hand that clutched at the unwilling air around it.

Chapter 46 - The Cleaners

Two figures, each dressed like undertakers, stood in the centre of the darkened, disused church. Their pointed, upturned noses sniffed at their surroundings before the taller of the two broke the silence. "Mr Van Hoon definitely specified this particular Church did he, not Mrs Critch?" enquired Mr Critch to his wife in his nasal voice.

"Indeed, he did, Mr Critch, 'tis unquestionably the Church of Saint Mary Magdalene he instructed us to attend," replied Mrs Critch in her equally adenoidal Welsh lilt. "I have it here, written on this piece of paper, directly in front of my own eyes and in his very own hand, I do Mr Critch. Mr Van Hoon even sketched a small map for us which, I am glad to say, we have followed precisely, and besides, we have passed no other church for miles. It does seem a rather God-forsaken area to be sure."

The couple had driven their anonymous black removals lorry from Southwark to Kent under the cloak of darkness. Their progress had been fortuitously guided by the lunar perigee that had illuminated their travels. They had driven for almost two hours until they had reached the civil parish of Staplehurst then onwards to Hawkenbury before proceeding along Babylon Lane until they had spotted the derelict church sitting silhouetted atop a small wooded hill. It was now three-thirty in the morning, and all was calm as they entered the chapel. Not even the stirring of a church rat broke the stillness. Both figures made their way to the spot that Van Hoon had described as needing their particular attention.

"Strange. Very peculiar indeed. There is nought here for us to cleanse that I can see. Mr Van Hoon categorically stated that there would be a '*customer*' to be attended to and removed, and that the scene was to be rendered spotless," puzzled Mr Critch as he scratched his bald, ovoid head.

"As is our speciality, Mr Critch," answered his wife.

"As indeed, you say, is our speciality, Mrs Critch. And yet, no customer is to be found."

"I concur totally Mr Critch, absolutely no call for our presence here at all as far as I can see," agreed his wife whilst crossing her arms. Each looked around them, confounded.

The door to the church crashed open and the silence was abruptly and raucously broken by a clumsy tangle of humanity and hardware. "I've got the mops and buckets mummy," boomed Leonard Critch as he stumbled boisterously into the church, sloshing water everywhere as he approached. "Shh! You could wake the very dead themselves you lumbering oaf," admonished Mrs Critch crossly.

"Sorry, mummy," whispered Leonard in his slow and deliberate fashion. He looked forlornly at his shoes, disappointed in his clumsiness. He hooked a finger childishly into the corner of his mouth.

"Doesn't look like we'll be needing these, after all, Leonard my boy," exclaimed a disappointed Mr Critch, trying to offer his embarrassed son a crumb of comfort. This was after all why the Critches were universally employed throughout the criminal subclass of London, namely for the cleaning and disposal of all manner of grisly evidence. They prided themselves on their long-held reputation of being able to cleanse any crime scene of all forensic traces, no matter how small, and of their talent for the untraceable disposal of all associated remains. The Critches' discretion was regarded by Gotham's underworld to be beyond reproach and as such, they were seldom without work.

"I just don't understand it. Mr Van Hoon is always so meticulous in all his business dealings. His information is always detailed in the extreme. He has certainly, over time, given us some of our most interesting and unique challenges," deliberated the lanky Critch, as he continued to scratch his polished head. "His exact words to us were to '*remediate the remains.*' Now I don't quite rightly know what *remediate* means but to exactly what remains was he referring, I ask you, Mrs Critch? Where in heavens name are they?"

"There are none whatsoever that we can see nor smell, and our noses have never missed a single droplet of blood, nor our eyes a stray hair or a flake of skin these past twenty-seven years, Mr Critch. We are unquestionably the most highly regarded caretakers in the business bar none," boasted Mrs Critch. They both nodded in agreement. "Perhaps 'tis some sort of test of our honesty or loyalty perhaps? Having to travel all this distance. Best we head off back home Mr Critch and best not to complain of the situation." She turned towards her lummox of a son. "Leonard, take the equipment back to the lorry and wait until we've had one final sweep lest we've overlooked something of import." The lumbering Leonard nodded happily, a relieved grin spreading across his docile face. He exited as noisily and as clumsily as he had entered only moments before. His mother shook her head at his raucous departure.

"Mr Critch, I shall check the nave again and in between each and every pew. You investigate the choir stalls and attend the confessional once more for a final check. Better to be safe than sorry where Mr Van Hoon is concerned. We must be absolutely sure before we leave that no remains are requiring our attention. I cannot imagine that our subject has simply disappeared or stood up, walked out of here and found their way home. We simply cannot incur the wrath of an upset Van Hoon. One can only imagine what *that* would look like!" remarked Mrs Critch visibly shuddering at the thought.

Mr Critch nodded sagely and headed off eagerly for the confessional stall despite having checked it less than twenty minutes before. He adored the work and the niche market he and his good wife had carved out for themselves. '*Strange,*' he thought to himself. '*There are very few religious effigies to be seen in this place, other than that headless Madonna and the three large crucifixes fixed to what appear, strangely, to be makeshift wooden trolleys.*' Mr Critch scratched at his billiard ball head. Something was not right. Something felt wrong to him. Not only was he beginning to wonder if this was the correct church but whether it was really a place of worship at all.

He continued with his search. On sliding open the dusty velvet drape of the priest's settle the sight that met the Welshman made him jump and left him momentarily startled. "Shit! Oh God, shit, sorry! My sincere apologies for the industrial language, Father. I had no idea you were back here. Scared the living daylights out of me you did, and no mistake."

An earthy aroma emanated from within the confessional box, a deeply organic odour, of sulphur, fungi and scrofula. Critch had smelt worse over the years but thought it strange that a man of God would smell as disgusting as a wet dog with a bowel complaint.

Within the darkness of the stall, sat an old man, clean-shaven except for a white moustache that traced the lines of his nasolabial folds all the way to his acutely angular chin. He was dressed all in black from head to toe with a gold, star-shaped medallion in place of his clerical dog collar. Mr Critch noted the cleric's particularly thin nose had strangely arched nostrils. His hair was immaculately slicked back forming a v-shaped hairline but contrarily his eyebrows were fulsome and unruly and extended horizontally across the bridge of his nose as one thick unbroken line. His mouth was obscured by his generous whiskers and his ears were exposed and were abnormally pointed. His ever so slightly bloodshot eyes were piercing and seemed to be pin-pointed from a light of unknown source. His skin bore a deathly white pallor and a slightly cracked, alabaster appearance.

Critch felt an inexplicable fear rise within him. As he looked at the man of God, a wave of revulsion swept over him. "Ahem, we were just passing by Father and decided to come in to say a short prayer to Saint Christopher to watch over us on our long homeward journey," explained a hesitant Mr Critch suspecting that nobody ever merely passed by this particular church positioned high on a hill as it was.

The pallid old man stared at the younger man in silence for a full twenty, unblinking seconds. "Well ... I'll ... I'll leave you be now, Father. A Priest needs his contemplation after all." '*What a stench?*' thought Critch as he turned to leave.

"I am no filthy Priest," replied the old man calmly. "I am a Count." As the old man smiled, his eyes turned a deep blood red. Mr Critch saw two long, sharply pointed front teeth projecting over the man's glistening bottom lip. It was at the point that Mr Critch whimpered.

'*What a waste of a journey,*' thought Mrs Critch as she hunkered down to gaze along the length of another row of dusty pews. '*No body to be seen.*' Her knees creaked and her hips groaned. '*What a waste of petrol,*' she groaned. '*The cost of petrol is killing our line of business,*' she bemoaned. "Nothing! Not a single thing to dispose of here, Mr Critch," she shouted towards the general direction of the choir stalls.

Silence.

"MR CRITCH!" she hollered.

Mrs Critch stood up stiffly from her enforced crouch to see an enormous wolf bounding silently towards her at an incredible speed from the far end of the aisle. Her bladder emptied involuntarily through absolute terror as the creature sped towards her. Huge paws padding furiously over the floor, its blood-red eyes emanating a lustful evil. The wolf's defined musculature rippled under its huge furry shoulders as it raced closer. In a matter of seconds, it had launched itself towards the terrified woman, its lips curled back into a gruesome snarl, revealing two long sharply pointed incisors. As it ripped at her jugular vein, she could swear she saw the image of her husband's face in the wolf's crimson eyes.

Leonard sat in the back of the lorry, waiting for his parents, amongst the buckets and mops, brooms and barrels of bleach and caustic soda. He was trying to do his numbers, counting aloud as his father had taught him. '*Look at the things Leonard and count out the numbers, just like you do the fingers on your hands and the toes on your feet,*' his father had instructed. Leonard was proud that he could now attain the lofty heights of his age, twenty-seven, although the world of reading and writing remained a complete mystery to him. How anyone could see sounds in those scratchings, loops and lines was beyond his infantile mind.

'*Three buckets. Fourteen bottles of bleach, two boxes of rags and five spare mop heads,*' he tallied, raising a finger each in turn. Daddy would be proud. Leonard continued to wait patiently. It seemed to him as though he had been waiting for an exceptionally long time, although sometimes for Leonard, time seemed to pass very slowly indeed. '*Six boxes of lint, three bags of lime, three spades and two shovels.*" Leonard was enjoying the game. '*One big wooden box, three digging forks and six garden brooms. Where were Mummy and Daddy?*'

He was running out of objects to count so he carefully took off his boots and socks and began to count. '*Ten, always ten, just like the last time,*' he thought happily. He smiled at the thought of his little piggy squealing '*wee, wee, wee,*' as it raced all the way home. Leonard chuckled and pulled his socks back on, straining to lean forward against his bulk, then pushed his feet back into his boots. A jolt of something resembling fear struck him as, unable to retie his laces, he realised that his mother would know that he had removed his boots. Mrs Critch would always get annoyed at having to tie and retie Leonard's work boots several times each day.

'*Six boxes of lint, three bags of lime, three spades and two shovels,*' Leonard repeated in his head. '*One big wooden box, three digging forks and six garden brooms, and one man with big red eyes and sharp teeth.*'

Leonard's initial welcoming smile turned to a whimper of primal terror as the fetid man leant towards him and laid an ice-cold hand upon the poor lad's trembling shoulder.

Chapter 47 - The Rendezvous

He remembered it as clearly as though it were only this morning. As he sat upon his chosen park bench overlooking Hampstead Heath, the memory was evoked so vividly in his mind, that it seemed to him almost real, as if it were occurring this very moment. Before he had met her, it had merely been an ordinary bench, just like any of the others dotted around the parkland. One where he occasionally sat and smoked a while, pondering life's imponderables and ruminating on stubbornly unsolved cases. Now it was a special bench, their bench. Two strangers had met by mere happenstance at this spot, and an unexpected love had flourished. A meeting conjured by a series of unconnected events that had changed both of their lives. A slight delay in polishing a shoe, turning left at the path rather than right, pausing to look at an industrious squirrel, all minor details, but a cumulation of little events that had led to that moment. A moment that engendered a blissful relationship that would ultimately lead to tragedy.

He looked at the dancing heads of the ruby pink cyclamen nestled under a nearby birch tree, not knowing what they were called, but admiring their beauty and delicacy, seeing their raspberry hoods delicately waft in the breeze. He half closed his eyes against the rising sun and let his memory drift back to that first meeting...

It is a bracing Wednesday morning. Frost crystallises the grass, so it crumples underfoot, and a perfectly cloudless sky of vast infinite blue spreads overhead. The place where he sits makes him feel alive, invigorated and revitalised, but most of all it is where he gains solace and peace to reminisce. He can only imagine, for he cannot remember his mother. She and his still-born twin brother had both died during what he was later to learn from his father had been an appallingly complicated childbirth, compounded by her suffering from consumption. She had known that she was unlikely to survive the birth but had held onto the hope that there was a whisper of a chance that her baby may have a luckier fate than she. She had not known that she was carrying twins, and she had not been lucky. He often questions why it was *he* who had been chosen to survive rather than his sibling. His father always struggled to talk about his lost loves, devastated as he was by their passing, preferring instead to fill his loss with a Spartan-like work ethic. Later he would tell him that his brother was to be called Thomas. He liked the sound of that. Jem and Tom. Tom and Jem. What a pair they would have made. What adventures they would have had. Is he blessed or cursed, or both in equal measure? Is he twice the person or half a person, he often wonders? As he sits on his bench his mind also turns to his fallen comrades in arms. Again, he agonises over why it was he who had somehow managed to survive the terrible atrocities of war whilst his fellow soldiers, mostly his friends, some perhaps braver and foolhardier than he, had been selected to die and to never return home. '*How can there possibly be a God?*' he ponders. A higher being that permits the young and heroic to die but allows fiends, monsters, and deviants to live and thrive. God knows he has seen enough of the latter to know that they are real. Very real. He reminisces about his father, a bull of a man who worked every waking hour at the forge he had built himself. He remembers a picture book from his childhood, a rare thing. Within it was a rendering of the god Vulcan, working his Olympian forge. It reminded him of his father, the constant roar of the furnace, the billowing of bellows and the almost relentless clanking of steel upon steel. It was here, amongst the steam and metal, that Jem Pyke had forged his own identity, his immense strength, stamina, and resolute determination.

He studies the three layers spread out in front of him, the glistening frosted grass, merging into the woods and tree canopy, which in turn blends into the cloudless blue sky. Three layers, stages of life, perhaps, of childhood, middle age, then old age and thence to Heaven. He laughs at the analogy and removes a Capstan from his engine-turned cigarette case. He taps the end of his cigarette three times upon the case to ensure a more even burn of tobacco, a habit that no man is taught, yet one which each habitually performs. Jem Pyke's reminiscing is interrupted in a most unexpected, yet gently polite manner.

"May I join you, Sir?" asked the flame-haired woman standing in front of him.

"Yes," he hesitates, startled at her seemingly unheralded appearance. Her voice is an angel's song. "Ah, why yes, of course you may, madam," replies Pyke awkwardly, standing upright, removing his Derby, and offers the woman a seat with a wave of his arm. He brushes off what little dew there is remaining on the wooden slatted seat, sits back down himself, and returns his unlit cigarette into its allotted space in its case.

Pyke smiled to himself as he recalled the awkwardness of the subsequent several minutes of that first meeting, neither individual making any attempt at further conversation. There seemed no reason to break the silence, only a repressed desire to do so. Each was caught by a silent hesitancy. He snorted a semi-laugh, recalling how desperately he had wanted to ask this beautiful lady her name. To ask her why she was there, and why so early in the morning. What did she do for a living? Where did she live? Why, what, where, how, who? A thousand and one questions he should have asked. He remembered that after several minutes she had risen to leave. They exchanged polite smiles, he half rising to acknowledge her departure, she adjusting her stole as she turned from him. He silently admonished himself at his reticence, his distrust of conversation, and made himself a promise that one day he would get answers to all his unanswered questions.

Jem Pyke had made a point of rising at five every Wednesday morning and heading off to Hampstead Heath to clear his head and recharge his rationality. Why he chose a Wednesday to visit the Heath he did not rightly know, but it seemed as good a day as any. The middle of the week he always regarded it. He had made this trip habitually each week, whenever work duties allowed, for the last several years, occasionally riding his police horse Kym, but more often, driving from Gravel Lane to the Heath. He usually spent no more than thirty minutes in his contemplation. During that time, he would smoke two cigarettes and let his mind wander down whichever path it chose.

> "May I ask your name, if you don't mind me being so bold?" enquired Pyke to his flame-haired, fellow bench sitter. He had so hoped she would be here again. They had shared the bench for the past three Wednesday mornings and neither, until now, had uttered a single word. Their mutual nervousness was compounded by an equal coyness in such matters of romancing. Pyke found his reticence whilst in the company of the opposite sex disconcerting, given his normal lack of inhibition and monumental recklessness. Somehow this woman was different, rekindling the awkwardness of his adolescence. Perhaps there was a risk here that even the foolhardy would be unwilling to take. There had of course been shy glances and the awkward but fleeting meeting of eyes but neither had yet found the correct or proper words to say. Pyke had however noticed that his normal smoking habit had now nervously increased to three cigarettes per visit.
>
> "You do not need to be *bold* to enquire my name, Sir, merely mannerly," responds the woman with a smile tugging at the corner of her mouth. "My name is Miss Noreen Redman, and I thought you'd never ask! It's been weeks now," she admonishes him with a sense of fake irritation.

Pyke rather liked the idea that she had titled herself 'Miss' and moves ever so slightly closer to Noreen. He removes his Derby and places it on the knee of the leg crossed over the other.

"I am indeed delighted to meet you, Miss Noreen Redman, my name is Mr Leslie Pyke, but me mates tend to call me Jem, on account of me detesting my given Church name," offers Pyke with a beaming smile of tartare covered teeth.

Noreen smiles, displaying perfectly aligned white teeth. "Oh, I much prefer Leslie to Jem," she leans rather conspiratorially towards Pyke, "and between you, me and this park bench, it isn't exactly the first time we have *met* is it?" They both share a knowing laugh at the thought of the past four weeks during which they have indeed met every Wednesday morning, even if it had been under a cloak of awkward and embarrassing silence.

"The colour of your hair matches your surname," states Pyke, instantly feeling rather foolish at the obviousness of the statement.

"That is as may be, but I am ever so glad that you do not resemble your surname, Mr Pyke," jokes Noreen in her lilting Irish accent.

Pyke let out a hearty laugh at the memory of him having been compared to a rather ugly fish. He lit the second cigarette of his allotted thirty minutes. He looked at their view. He loves the stillness of it, the freshness of the crisp new morning. A sea of ground-hugging haze drifts across the heath like a lace quilt. He looked at the birch trees, pale white ghosts that seem to line up before him like a spectral infantry backed by the stronger, older oaks and sycamores, motionless in the still, grey air. A soft dew blanketed everything, clinging to cobwebs, interlacing the grass of the heath. He raised his head and sniffed deeply, filling both his nostrils with the metallic ozone of the unpolluted morning. He imagined, as he so often did, that he can smell gunpowder, hear the crack of rifles and the whipping noise of displaced air as bullets whiz past his head. The birdsong breaks his imagery, bringing him back to the here and now. The beautiful, unearthly trilling of thrush and blackbird charmed his soul. The birches, no longer slender wraith-like soldiers, but merely trees, nodded gently towards him. He sat in silence. Absorbed. Content. Thinking of her.

The sun had now risen in the sky and warmed his face. A face battered and scarred yet still handsome and vital. A rather heroic, battle tarnished face, he often thought when shaving first thing every morning. His nose, broken, its bridge depressed through multiple injuries, his forehead scarred by the legacy of a hundred blows. He drew upon his cigarette and closed his eyes.

"I hope you do not find me too forward, Leslie, but may I ask why it is you come here each Wednesday morning?" enquires the flame-haired woman.

"Well, Miss Noreen, I come here to remember and to think," replies Pyke, "and I'd much rather you called me Jem, if that is all right with you Miss?"

"Of course. Jem it shall be. I shall call you whatever you wish, if it means we can chat for a few moments each week instead of suffering those wretched silences of previous rendezvous."

"So, by the same token, why then do you come here each Wednesday morning, Miss Noreen?" asks Pyke, reaching for his cigarette case.

"Me? Why I come here to forget. Isn't it remarkable that we have both met, two strangers, one who comes to this exact spot upon the Heath to remember and the other to forget. We are an odd pair, don't you think?"

"Perhaps some may think so, Miss Noreen," replies Pyke, his stomach feeling suddenly empty. "Others, I'd wager, may consider us quite a fine couple, indeed." Her eyes twinkle with a warmth that lights up his heart.

The sudden annoyance of a barking dog abruptly interrupted Pyke's memories. He found himself angry at the dog for its unknowing insensitivity. Reality encroached as abruptly as a bullet. He was sitting alone, there was no Noreen, no Red Noreen, not now, not ever again. His heart crumpled inwards at the thought that he would never again set eyes upon her beauty, feel her strength, enjoy her humour, bathe in her gorgeous, ethereal eyes. Never again hear her lilting, provocative voice, or her raucous, braying laugh. All he had was memories. Memories of her curly red hair tumbling to the nape of her back where she had prominent Venus dimples at her iliac spine. Her skin had been pale, almost translucent and had glowed with a vitality that could light up a darkened room. He found the thought that her skin no longer existed utterly unbearable. She could make Pyke laugh uproariously even at the silliest of things, it was her intonation and the looks she gave. 'God! How I miss you. My Love." He flicked away his second cigarette, stood and turned for home.

Chapter 48 - The Hunter

Doctor Watson stared studiously at the stuffed head of a water buffalo mounted on what he judged to be an oak plaque that hung over the head of a pink-veined marble mantelpiece. '*Most likely Portuguese Estremoz marble,*' he pondered. Despite the season, the fire below roared, and logs cracked, throwing forth sparks that died to acrid smelling smoking embers as they landed upon the stone hearth. The flickering flames seemed to imbue the head of the great black buffalo with a fleeting animation, alive with dancing light and shadow. Watson found the whole effect agreeably hypnotic. He imagined the great beast snorting and rolling its massive head, blinking its eyes against the dry dust of the African plains. He lowered his gaze from the enormous buffalo head to that of the sleeping figure in the brown cracked leather chesterfield chair at the side of the fireplace. The Old Man's head lay tilted forward, his rumpled chin resting upon his white-haired chest. Regular snoring was occasionally interrupted by a grunt or groan followed by a loathsome licking of his tongue across insipidly pale, cruel looking lips.

Watson patiently absorbed the scene from the twin chair opposite that of the Old Man. He observed the giant elephant gun than leaned threateningly against one side pilaster of the fireplace. Its double-chambered barrel cruelly resembling the pachyderm trunk of its quarry. He judged that should it be required, he could easily reach the gun before the Old Man. He noticed the plaid blanket that covered the Old Man's lap, thinking how scratchy it looked, and cast his mind back to the land of his Fathers, trying unsuccessfully to identify the specific tartan. '*One of the Stewart tartans,*' he suspected, '*but there are so many of that clan.*'

The Old Man shifted, a groan of pain falling from his drooling mouth. Some part of Watson found the situation soothing. The comfortable silence interrupted only by the monotone ticking of a walnut, wall-mounted grandmother clock, interspersed with the soporific droning of the Old Man's snoring. Watson found himself reminiscing of the many long, contented evenings spent with Him within the rooms on Baker Street. The rustle of newssheet, the acridity of thick tobacco smoke, the underlying scent of unidentifiable chemicals. The comfort of two people sharing the same space, understanding and content with their differences.

A sharp snort from the Old Man broke Watson's reverie. He looked across at his companion and remembered. He remembered the numerous attempts this individual had made upon his life and that of his friend. He remembered his cruelty, the fear he had instilled in all around him. He had been the most physically dangerous opponent they had ever faced. The world's greatest big game hunter. A man who had purportedly pursued a Bengal tiger single-handedly down a narrow underground tunnel. The greatest shot ever to have graced the British Army. The sniper who never missed. A man of ferocious temper and even crueller reputation. The man who hated and detested Watson above all others who remained alive. A man who now sat before him, diminished and somehow shrunken, aged and broken. Polluted with a cancer that had somehow increased his toxic hatred.

Watson flicked his cigarette butt into the open mouth of the fire and twisted the end of his great moustache. He leaned forward and grasped the silver hound's head crafted grip of his cane and prodded its brass ferrule against the slumped shoulder of the Old Man. The Old Man spluttered, his eyes rolling behind his heavily drooped eyelids.

The Old Man flinched, remembering a Prussian bullet that had lodged itself in the same spot forty-five years earlier. He could again feel the bone shatter, taste the ferrous blood in his mouth, smell the gunpowder and the fear of death encompassing him. His eyes flickered. The vague shape of a well-dressed man sat before him brandishing some sort of stick. He pawed at the stick with a great leonine hand, blotched with patches of purple and littered with liver spots, its skin brittle and cracked. He opened his eyes and laughed a coarse, deep-throated, poisoned laugh at what he saw.

"It was me you wanted dead, wasn't it," asked Watson, lowering his cane. "At the Palace. It was me."

The Old Man looked at him and smiled the smile of a demon. Watson saw blood seeping from his blackened gums. "Of course," replied the Old Man. "It was always you. All the others, all those law-abiding scum and police filth, they were, how can I put it, happy collateral damage."

Watson shook his head. "And yet here I sit, Colonel."

"Here *we* sit," corrected Moran, casting a surreptitious look at the elephant gun. Watson swiftly grabbed the giant firearm and rested it upon his lap. Moran's eyes seemed to redden with increased hatred. "Are you going to shoot me then Doctor, here in this hospice for the dying? Now, what type of sport would that be? Break that Hippocratic oath you took when you were an eager young sprat?"

"I have no need to kill you, Moran," replied Watson. "I see that Mother Nature is taking her just revenge on one of her most abhorrent creations. No doubt she regrets the moment your distasteful life came into being."

Moran roared with a burst of laughter that ended in a globule of deep black blood being expectorated into his paw-like hand. Watson winced in obvious disgust. Moran painfully drew back his arm and, lurching forward, attempted to throw the sputum at Watson. The blood landed pitifully at his own feet.

"Pathetic," observed Watson. "Your only son, broken and dead before your eyes and still you thirst for some manner of twisted revenge. In many ways, I pity you, Moran. You should welcome a hasty death."

"To Hell with Death! To Hell with you! To Hell with your pity!" roared Moran. "I need no pity. I will kill you and the guttersnipe long before I cash in my coin!"

Watson stood and brushed himself down. "I will say goodbye, Moran. I feel tainted by your presence, soiled, and violated by your insipid threats. I promise you that I will attend your funeral and will do so with a gladness in my heart that the World will finally be free of your malevolence." Watson turned for the door.

"Don't you run from me, you bastard! I'll kill you with my bare hands!" screamed Moran, his throat rattling with pneumonia.

Watson smiled and indicated with his cane, the table of pills at the side of Moran's chair. "Make sure you take your medication, Sebastian," and exited the room.

Watson tipped his hat at Moran's nurse as he stooped to enter his cab. He could still hear the throaty roar of the Colonel ringing faintly in his ears as he departed. He sat back, rejoicing in the comforting sound of crumpling leather under him, and removed his gloves. He reached into his pocket and withdrew a handful of assorted pills. He studied them thoughtfully, unsure as to whether granting the repellent Moran a hastier death had been an act of charity or an act of vengeance.

Chapter 49 - The Arrival

Harry Pepper looked into the Basset Hound eyes of Dan Kelly realising that his face would be the last thing that his first mate would see. Kelly's almost pleading stare seemed to drill into Harry's soul; why did you let them on board skipper? Surely it was always going to end this way. Kelly's dolorous face trembled uncontrollably as he was hoisted aloft by the giant Hercules Chin, his ankles clamped together in one enormous hand, his wattled neck in the other. With an almost elemental force, Chin slammed the body of the doomed sailor down onto the starboard gunwale of Lily's Catch. Harry's stomach churned as his first mate's body was broken at an unfeasible angle by the massive impact, before slipping almost apologetically over the side and into the calm waters just outside of Dubrovnik harbour.

There was carnage all around the deck of The Catch. Dacoit stranglers and Indian Thuggees had set upon Harry's crew like manic flies attacking a carcass. The cries of dying men carried on the evening breeze as crewmen were stabbed and garrotted without compunction. The scene before Harry was a frenzy of death. Within a few minutes, his entire crew lay dead around him, his deck awash in good men's blood.

Hercules Chin roared at the sky and turned his attention towards Harry who, realising that he was the last man standing, turned on his heels to dive overboard and take his chance with the sea. He had seen what this monster had done to Kelly. His stomach lurched once more as he found himself face to face with the very Devil himself, Mr King. The diminutive Chinese crime lord was flanked on either side by a razor featured Shang twin, each armed with glinting machetes. King smiled at Harry, his serpentine eyes oozing venomously. Harry expected to see a forked tongue slither from that malevolent mouth. "Down below, if you please, Captain Pepper," came King's sibilant hiss. He nodded towards the cabin, indicating that Harry descend. At once Harry understood King's intent. The safe. King wanted his charter money.

Harry descended the companionway into the Captain's cabin, the point of a machete prodding at each of his shoulder blades. He could see no possible way out of this situation. Once in the cabin, the Shang twins forced him towards the ship's safe. "The combination please, Captain Pepper," ordered King.

Harry thought fast. If he gave King the combination his life was over, his throat slit with one cut of a razor-sharp blade. He imagined watching his life spill out of him, a viscid red cataract pooling on the deck boards. He looked quickly around and there seemed no way that he could escape such cramped surroundings. The companionway was blocked by the Shang twins and up on deck awaited the behemoth that was Hercules Chin. The single porthole in the cabin was too small to allow him passage through. King seemed to read Harry's thoughts. "There is no escape, Captain Pepper. Your only hope is to give me the combination and rely on my mercy and good grace." Harry knew of King. He knew that his soul held not one ounce of mercy. He also knew that he was a sadistic torturer who liked nothing better than to flay a living man and feed his skin to his monstrous ghost python. He recalled a story, often told amongst dock folk, of King having had his heart removed, of how he was sustained, not by a beating organ, but by a spirit of unending evil. Many thought the man to be the very Devil himself and yet Harry also knew that he had no choice. He had to give the Chinaman the combination. Perhaps a swift death at the end of a machete was preferable to being broken in two by that giant monster up on deck.

"Two, two, one, zero," Harry muttered, his eyes fixed purposefully on those of the reptilian King. As soon as the words left his mouth, he felt that his life must be over.

"You are a wise man, Captain Pepper," hissed an exultant King, his eyelids licking his eyes like those of a satisfied lizard. He nodded imperceptibly and a Shang twin, slipped his machete into his belt and crouched down to open the safe. He spun the dial as indicated, heard a click as the tumblers spun, pulled down on the handle and heaved open the door of the safe. King clapped his hands in glee as an envelope heavy with money was handed to him. Much to Harry's chagrin a wooden box was also hauled from the safe. A box that Harry knew contained a sizeable sum in gold Krugerrands. Various documents and a few items of jewellery followed.

Harry grabbed his chance. The last and only chance of a desperate man. He deftly snatched the machete from the belt of the crouching Shang twin, quickly twisted behind King and held the blade so close to the Chinaman's neck that he could hear the singing rasp it made against his Adam's apple. Both Shang twins advanced liked crouched tigers ready to spring. Harry could feel King carefully reach within the folds of his robes, no doubt searching furtively for a hidden blade. "Don't do it, King," spat Harry in the crime lord's ear. Even if you stab me your throat still gets cut." King relaxed and urged the Shangs to stand their ground. Harry edged carefully backwards, blade at King's throat, and edged up the short companionway one careful step at a time. He could smell the scent of oriental spices emanating from King and felt repulsed that he was touching the diabolic creature. As he moved upwards, the Shang twins advanced steadily, murder pulsing in their eyes. The two men emerged onto the deck and Harry cast a terrified look around him. To his immense relief, he saw that Hercules Chin and King's henchmen were occupied aft tossing the remaining corpses of Harry's crew over the side. His stomach turned and a vengeful tide arose in his maritime chest. Harry shoved King forcefully back down the companionway into the path of the oncoming Shang's, jammed the machete into his belt, ran full pelt towards the gunwales, and dived headlong into the sea.

He could hear the commotion behind him as he hit the brine, voices raised and the clatter of feet upon the deck like a stampede of wild horses. Harry plummeted under the water stroking downwards as powerfully as he could, pulling at the depths with all his strength. Bullet trails fizzed through the water as the dacoits above fired arbitrarily, hoping to find their target. Harry twisted and swam like an eel under the hull of the boat, a desperate plan forming in his adrenalin pumped mind. He would find refuge under the ship in his secret smuggler's alcove. The alcove was an inverted box incorporated into the hull of the boat that was used to hide contraband from inquisitive port authority officials. The box was constructed so as it was raised above the waterline creating a safe airspace big enough to house several men. Harry was pleased with his plan. He could remain hidden within the alcove with enough air to sustain him until the Chinese hoard had departed the ship. As his head surfaced into the box, he let out a gasp. The air was fetid and stale but filled Harry's aching lungs like nectar from the Gods.

Harry shrieked and his heart leapt in his chest as he turned his head to come face to face, nose to nose with that of his erstwhile first mate, Dan Kelly. Harry stifled a scream. Kelly's corpse had somehow been sucked under the hull and been snagged within the alcove. The blood-encrusted eyes of the cadaver stared emptily into those of the shivering Harry, and Kelly's lugubrious face seemed to maintain an accusatory aspect. Harry gathered himself. "One last favour, Dan, if you don't mind, old mate." Stifling his revulsion, Harry grabbed Kelly's broken body and with as much effort as he could muster, heaved it outwards from the hull. He ducked under the waterline and watched expectantly as the bulk drifted upwards, his hope being that King's men would assume that the body was Harry's. Bullet trails broke the water and Kelly's body jerked as it was filled with a hail of lead. Harry returned to the sanctuary of the alcove and offered a prayer of thanks to Poseidon.

A cavalcade of large black cars edged up to the dockside as the two lifeboats were moored to the quay. The entourage of Eastern officialdom welcomed the disembarking assemblage of assorted Chinese killers, cutthroats and poisoners led by the diabolic King. An especially large van-like vehicle had been provided to transport the monstrous Chin. Smiles were exchanged and hands were shaken. The air was one of mutual respect, underlying fear and vaguely disguised menace blanketed by a reserved but shared expectation that this meeting would be the catalyst that would push Europe towards a war unlike any the globe had seen.

Chapter 50 - The Dragon

"How fare you with your treatment of the murderer, Crake?" asked Wiggins.

"He resides within a secure room within my home, Inspector, and is responding quite well to our administrations. We can see a semblance of humanity returning to the corrupted creature, but as to whether we can restore him to his former state, I remain doubtful. A fascinating case, nonetheless. However, that is not why I called you here today."

Van Hoon and Wiggins sat within a grand summer house located in a secluded corner of the Leper's Belgravia garden. The pavilion was an ornate structure that to Wiggins, was reminiscent of the Chinese tea houses he had seen painted on Mary's best willow pattern china. It was overhung by an enormous cherry tree that shrouded the structure in garlands of pale pink blossom. He noted that the location, picked by Van Hoon, offered complete privacy. The two men sat at a low table upon which hot drinks had been served, mint tea for Van Hoon and Turkish coffee for Wiggins. A light breeze aroused a flutter of blossom to dance in the air like snowflakes. The detective picked up the small demitasse and took a sip. "Your invitation stated it was urgent, Mr Van Hoon." He looked around him. "And presumably of a sensitive nature?"

For once, Van Hoon looked serious. He engaged Wiggins with his remarkable eyes and lowered his cup delicately upon its saucer. "I am afraid, Chief Inspector, that I have extremely disturbing news."

Wiggins was intrigued. '*What news could the unflappable Van Hoon possibly consider as being disturbing?*'

Van Hoon seemed to consider his next words carefully. "Radasiliev's body has gone."

"As you arranged," confirmed Wiggins, taking another sip of his coffee, and wondering if he found it slightly too syrupy in consistency.

"Indeed," replied Van Hoon, moving forward slightly. "However, the attendants whom I sent to dispose of the Russian's remains have been found in Saint Mary's, butchered, torn limb from limb. Their vehicle remains abandoned at the scene and their son, who acts as their assistant, is also missing."

"And your conclusion? Has Radasiliev risen from the Dead and wreaked vengeance upon these attendants?" joked Wiggins.

"I fear not, Chief Inspector. I fear we are facing something far worse than a reincarnated Luca Radasiliev. I believe that the Russian's death has conjured forth a beast of far more frightening proportions than our erstwhile demon summoner. I believe that Radasiliev was used merely as a conduit in bringing forth this creature." Van Hoon paused for effect. "One needs only to closely examine the Russian's name to understand that, my friend."

"But, who, Van Hoon, or indeed what could possibly prove more hellish than Radasiliev himself?" quizzed a now alarmed, and somewhat bewildered, Wiggins.

The leper delicately placed his cup back upon its saucer before answering. "He is the Prince of Darkness, a scourge upon this Earth. He sits at the side of Mephistopheles himself. He is Nosferatu, he is Vampyr, the King of the Living Dead, ruler of all that is evil and unholy. He is the Dracule, the Dragon, the Impaler. If Radasiliev were to have possessed the ability to somehow resurrect him, we would face a threat greater than any plague. We would face the end of days. A future whereby life as we know it ceases to exist and the surface of the Earth would crawl with the undead."

Wiggins stared at Van Hoon in disbelief. He shook his head, sat back, and crossed his legs. "This is the stuff of fantasy. Surely you do not subscribe to Mr Stoker's lurid fantasies of blood-sucking nightcrawlers and vampires?"

"Of course not, my friend. His tales of bats and mist, wooden stakes and garlic are pure fabrication and elaboration. I more than any other man, should know that," added Van Hoon stroking the scar running from one side of his abdomen to the other underneath his shirt. "Besides, Mr Stoker should have respected the confidence into which he was taken, albeit, on an evening fuelled with a rather copious supply of the finest Swiss absinthe. He does possess a most admirable tolerance to alcohol and a talent for embellishment."

Wiggins thought for a second, recalling Stoker's novel, then gasped slightly. "Are you saying..? You are Van..."

"All I am saying, Chief Inspector," interrupted Van Hoon sharply, "is that I am grateful that Mr Stoker's book is populated not only by characters rechristened with fictional names but also by a protagonist whose power bears little resemblance to the nature of the evil and pollution that the creature is truly capable of. I hope beyond hope, that I do not make the reacquaintance of this foulest of evils."

Van Hoon wrote Luca Radasiliev's name in capital letters upon a piece of paper and laid it before the detective. You see now, Chief Inspector?"

Epilogue - The Old Lady (1987)

She sat on her usual bench feeding the birds. She loved to feed the birds. Each day she would hobble from her room, out into the garden, carrying a bag of mixed seeds and nuts and perch in her habitual position opposite the little copse of silver birch trees.

Sitting back, she closed her eyes against the late morning sun, relishing the dancing, dappled patterns the light made against her eyelids. The inquisitive chirpings of the birds and the light breeze blowing through the shrubbery relaxed her weary joints. She rested. As always, her mind drifted back through her life, her family. She remembered her lost ones with affection and regret in equal measure. She also rejoiced in how lucky she had been. Realising now how her life, although shadowed at times by worry and grief, had taken many fortuitous paths over the last eight decades. When times had seemed at their lowest ebb, it was as if a benign presence had looked down upon her and circumstances had turned for the better. Her Arthur had always said, "Don't you worry, Gem love, something always turns up." And somehow it always had.

As she remembered her good fortune, she caught a faint whiff of something. '*What is it?*' she questioned herself. '*Cinnamon, perhaps cloves, or bay leaves,*' she thought. She opened her eyes, blinking against the sun. The man who sat beside her had done so silently. She shook her head in disbelief, at first unable to comprehend, then, given the wisdom of the aged, she accepted the sight that greeted her gaze.

"Why, you are ... The Dandy," she smiled. "From all those years ago. My mother told me not to look at you, but I could not help it. You were so..." her mind drifted.

"What *is* that word now?" she struggled to regain her memory. "Compelling! That's it. You were just so compelling that I couldn't help but stare."

The Dandy smiled and gently took her trembling hand in his. His touch was strong but gentle. She felt contented and safe. He looked fondly at the liver spots that adorned her almost translucent skin and lifted her hand to caress it with the gentlest of kisses. "I am so glad that I made such an impression on so endearing a little girl all those years ago."

She smiled, flattered. "But how can this be?" she asked. "You have not changed. You are no different. You are the same now as you were then, and me, an ancient crone who sits and feeds the birds," she lamented.

The Dandy shook his head whilst stroking her hand "You were beautiful then and you are beautiful now." She laughed and looked fondly into his remarkable eyes. A brief silence wafted between them. Not an awkward silence, but rather a comfortable, calm silence. The sunlight glinted through his cascade of hair, making its blackness dance the deepest blue. She felt a sense of complete serenity.

"I can help," he said.

The old lady thought for a few moments, all the while looking at the same man, she had seen a lifetime ago. Realisation dawned in her intelligent chestnut eyes. She looked him up and down for a few moments before nodding. "I *think* I understand."

She averted her gaze from this impossible vision and watched the birds and their frantic scramble to steal the nearest available nut or seed. She thought for a time. "I am old because I have lived a lifetime. My lifetime. I have lost a husband and a son, both of whom I very much look forward to seeing again. I have no need of living another life."

The Dandy nodded. "Loss is the greatest ordeal our God inflicts upon us. That is why he gifted each of us with a heart."

She returned her eyes to meet his and smiled at his wisdom. A robin landed next to her on the arm of the bench, pecking at a small pile of seed she had placed there. The little bird cocked its head at her and the Dandy between picking at the seed. "He comes every single day," explained the old lady. "Dancing his dance, as bold as brass he is." Another pleasant contented silence sat between the two as they each observed the little bird.

"I used to love dancing," she sighed eventually, looking lamentedly at her swollen ankles. "Arthur and I would go every Wednesday and Saturday to the ballroom down Camberwell High Street. I loved the Viennese waltz best of all. All that spinning and twirling. So elegant it was. Arthur preferred the quickstep, but I always found it hard to keep up. Arthur was so fit you see. He used to sprint for the Harriers he did." She stopped to think, a tear clouding her eye. The Dandy put his arm around her shoulder. She hesitated, catching her breath. "I never did get to dance with my son. He was taken from us too early. How I would have loved to have danced with him at his wedding." Her voice cracked as hot tears filled her eyes.

The Dandy held her more closely." Close your eyes, my dear, you must rest now." She closed her eyes and watched the light dance and shimmer across her inner eyelids. She could feel the heat of the sun as a blend of shapes and colours shifted and swirled before her and she began to drift away. She could feel the Dandy's hands gently squeeze hers and she could suddenly feel her feet glide across the dance floor as she spun and whirled, her head thrown back, lights from chandeliers spinning overhead. A firm hand grasped her waist, and another held her hand in a firm but gentle grip. Her hand rested on a hard, masculine shoulder. Spinning like a top she looked into the eyes of her dancing partner. The unmistakeable eyes of the Dandy. He smiled as he led her rapidly across the floor, their feet seemingly floating in air, so smooth was their movement. The face of the Dandy spun faster and faster until it became indistinct, merging into that of her Arthur. Her heart stuttered. "Hello, my Love," he mouthed silently. She had never felt more joyous as in this instant. She danced with her husband for what seemed an age. She felt as though they were flying. Her husband smiled, and his smile became that of her son. She wept. Her joy turned to euphoria as she spun and spun and spun into the darkness.

Van Hoon kissed the tears from her now still face, He took a bright pink dahlia head from his buttonhole and gently interwove it in her hair. "Sleep well, Gemma. The most beautiful of flowers for the most beautiful girl," whispered Van Hoon as he leant forward and delicately kissed her forehead for the last time.

"Art in the blood is liable to take the strangest forms."

Sherlock Holmes - The Adventures of Sherlock Holmes

Bibliography

Researching books is always a labour of love and has once again brought to life the people and events of Edwardian London. Today, as researchers, we are spoiled with a limitless amount of data, as Wiggins would state, literally at our fingertips. It would be impossible for us to include every single reference point, and far easier just to cite Wikipedia, but we have tried to include the most used and most accurate and effective sources.

1) Baring-Gold, WS (1995) Sherlock Holmes of Baker Street: A life of the World's first consulting detective. Wings Books. ISBN13:9780517038178.
2) Conan Doyle, A. (1986) The complete illustrated Sherlock Holmes. Omega Books. ISBN:1850070555.
3) Sandford, C. (2017) The Man Who Would Be Sherlock: the real-life adventures of Arthur Conan Doyle. The History Press.ISBN:9780750965 927.
4) Stoker, B. (2015) Dracula. Sterling Publishing. ISBN:9781435159570.
5) Farson, D. (1975) The Man Who Wrote Dracula: a biography of Bram Stoker. Michael Joseph, London. ISBN:0718110986.
6) McNally, RT & Florescu, R. (1994) In Search of Dracula: the enthralling history of Dracula and Vampires. Robson Books. ISBN:1861050860.
7) Shelley, M. (2003) Frankenstein: or, the Modern Prometheus. Penguin Classics; Rev Ed edition. ISBN10:0141439475.
8) Florescu, R. (1988) In Search of Frankenstein: exploring the myths behind Mary Shelley's monster. Robson Books. ISBN:186105033X.
9) Lewis, RWB. (2002) Dante: A Life. Pheonix. ISBN13:9780753813195.
10) Sharma, M. (2018) The Development of Serial Killers: a grounded theory study, Master's Thesis, University of Illinois.
11) St Paul's Cathedral, London (Communications Manager).
12) Shpayer-Makov, H. A Work-Life History of Policemen in Victorian and Edwardian England. https://www2.clarku.edu/faculty/jbrown/papers/shpayer. pdf.
13) https://bakerstreet.fandom.com/. Online encyclopaedia of all things associated with Sherlock Holmes.
14) https://www.tate.org.uk/art/art-terms/b/bloomsbury/art-bloomsbury. Background on the Bloomsbury Group and Roger Fry.
15) https://www.culture24.org.uk/history-and-heritage/tra43336. All about the Chinese community in the Limehouse region of London at the turn of the 20th Century.

16) https://www.geographicus.com/P/AntiqueMap/London-smith-1892/. Antique map of London.
17) https://christianhistoryinstitute.org/magazine/article/dante-divine-comedy-recommended-resources /. Dante Alighieri and the Divine Comedy resources.
18) https://www.british-history.ac.uk/old-new-london/vol3/pp329-337/. Scotland Yard and the history of the London Police.
19) http://www.nationalarchives.gov.uk/suffrage-100/. The history of the Suffrage movement in Britain.
20) https://www.historicalemporium.com/mens-edwardian-clothing.php/. Everything you need to know about Edwardian era clothing.
21) https://londonist.com/pubs/pubs/wapping/. Public Houses in and around Wapping and Limehouse.
22) https://www.britishbattles.com/great-boer-war/siege-of-kimberley/. The siege of Kimberley during the second Boer War.
23) https://www.historic-uk.com/HistoryUK/HistoryofBritain/Opium-in-Victorian-Britain/. Opium dens in Victorian and Edwardian Britain.
24) https://theodora.com/encyclopedia/s2/slaughterhouse.html/. Background information regarding slaughterhouses and slaughtering techniques.
25) http://atkinson-swords.com/collection-by-region/south-east-asia/burma-myanmar/. Burmese knives and weaponry.
26) https://www.jack-the-ripper.org/. Information on all things Jack the Ripper.
27) http://www.edwardianpromenade.com/resources/a-glossary-of-slang/. Dictionary of slang terms used in Victorian and Edwardian eras.
28) https://www.ucl.ac.uk/wolfson-institute-biomedical-research/cruciform-building/. Information on the Cruciform Building, London.

Coming Soon from Ian C. Grant

The Hand of Darkness: A DCI Wiggins Adventure, excerpt.

Chapter 1 - The Toymaker

"That is not danger. It is inevitable destruction."

Professor Moriarty - The Final Problem

For such large hands they displayed a delicacy of touch that would have surprised any onlooker. The squat, sausage-like fingers moved with grace and precision as they dexterously carved the body of the little wooden puppet. His chisel gouged at the softwood with an accuracy and finesse built of long hours of experience. This was to be part of his masterpiece, a collection depicting Tchaikovsky's Nutcracker. He subconsciously whistled the refrain from the ballet's second movement, a barely audible whistle in the quiet void of the room. His hands carefully sanded the little figurine, taking time to smooth the most awkward recesses and hollows. The little soldier was nearly complete, nearly ready for his proudly worn attire of intricate paintwork. Once finished he would be placed alongside his fellow characters in the carefully prepared tableau that awaited his arrival.

He removed his flimsy wire-framed spectacles and rubbed his eyes, irritated and inflamed as they were by want of sleep, and placed the figurine on the workbench at which he sat.

Tomorrow. He would finish it tomorrow.

The four little, lifelike dolls would stand alongside an army of soldiers and mice. The Fairy and her Cavalier would look on at the Polichinelles, and there, completing the scene, the Nutcracker himself.

His naked form rose from the rustic wooden stool, his skin peeling free from the white deal as he did so. Meaty feet padded across to the free-standing, claw-footed copper bath that dominated the centre of the room. He tested the water he had drawn an hour previously and found it sufficiently cooled as to his liking. He stepped over the curled copper lip and lowered himself slowly into the cold water, its blackness lapping at the metal sides, its iciness causing his skin to goose pimple. He gasped slightly as the more tender parts of his anatomy were submerged in the frigid water. A feeling of relief swam over him. He was broad of shoulder and his back showed multiple fearsome welts that ran diagonally from his right scapula to left hip. The hardened scar tissue was bright pink against his pale, strongly muscled back. He reached to his side and his fat fingers fumbled for the hypodermic needle that lay waiting on a neatly folded crimson handkerchief atop a rudimentary three-legged milking stool. The needle entered his pumped vein and he depressed the plunger. He gasped in ecstasy as he felt the morphine solution race through his veins. Satisfied, he lifted a small glass of clear colourless liquid from the same stool and swallowed its contents.

He lay back and sighed in perverse contentment. Yes, tomorrow. His real work would begin.

About the Author

Ian C. Grant is, in fact, two people, namely brothers Grant and Ian Christie.

Grant Andrew Christie was born in Dundee and lives in London. He is married with two children. He has spent his working life as a Manager within the Building industry. He is a talented artist who has work displayed and purchased internationally. This novel stemmed from his wondering how minor fictional characters are affected by the roles they played in major events. As an ardent Sherlock Holmes reader, he turned to Wiggins, lead Baker Street Irregular, and the only one of the Irregulars to be mentioned by name.

Ian Stuart Christie was born in Dundee and is married. After initially working as a greeting card artist, he has now been employed by the University of Dundee University as an Academic Skills Tutor since 1990. Ian also provides high-quality electronic illustrations for research, education and publication purposes. He designed the official Glastonbury Festival t-shirts of 2002 and 2004 and has done cover illustrations for three children's books and recently redesigned the cover of The Foot Journal.

Praise for **"The Reign of the Beast: a DI Wiggins Adventure"** © 2020. ISBN-13: 979-8666985601 - All reviews are from verified purchases on Amazon.com

"This is most definitely a great read! Would recommend this book to all. Once started I didn't want to put the book down. Gripping storyline with fascinating characters and relentless action throughout. Author's attention to detail in his description of life in period London is impeccable."

"Ripper Street meets the League of Extraordinary Gentlemen in this great read. Lots of strong characters, fantastic descriptions of old London and a great plot. A great debut."

"A heart racing tale that takes you winding through London's criminal underworld. Fascinatingly mysterious characters aid Police on the trail of the vicious and monstrous, Beast. A thoroughly enjoyable and captivating read. From first page until the last, this fast-paced adventure will keep you on the edge of your seat. Highly recommended."

"A new spin on the classical tones of Sherlock Holmes with this new turn of the century fiction with a slightly steam-punk feel. Read this if you love the original and have a fetish for top hats, monsters, and detective work."

If you enjoyed this novel and its predecessor, "The Reign of the Beast: a DI Wiggins Adventure" please feel free to post a review on Amazon.com whenever you can. We appreciate your continual support. Thanks.

Printed in Great Britain
by Amazon